I Shall Return

A Paranormal Gothic Romance

&

Kristina Schram

*Mischief*Maker*Media*

Published by Mischief Maker Media (USA)
First printing: May, 2014
Copyright © 2014 by Kristina Schram

Cover Design, Interior, and Technical Expertise: GorKee

ISBN: 978-1-939397-09-6

Visit Kristina Schram on the World Wide Web at:
www.KristinaSchram.com

Acknowledgements

Thank you, my intrepid readers, Heather Duane, Elizabeth Schram, Kendra DeCota, Gordon Unzen, and Ian More. I can't believe you keep reading my books and coming back for more. Thanks for being my rocks!

A special, extra big thanks goes out to Ian More, my Scottish friend, who attempted to point out the error of my ways as I wrote about the Scottish culture. I still probably messed up some of the dinnas and didnas and misused a numpty or a bampot, but that's on me. Thanks, Ian!

The title for this book, *I Shall Return*, comes from Dido's song, *Christmas Day*. I've always found the lyrics haunting, and wondered what they really meant. According to the story, a gentleman stops by a young woman's home, stays for a drink, falls in love with her, and upon leaving, says to her, "I shall return, for you, my love, on Christmas day." And in the chorus, she sings, "Those were the last words I ever heard him say." This story is a tribute 'of sorts' to that song. Furthermore, watching *Monarch of the Glen* (more times than is probably healthy) inspired me to use Scotland as a setting for my story. What a beautiful country!

Thank you, fans, for continuing to read my works. I grew up on gothics and could never seem to get enough of them. I still can't. I don't find many out there these days, so hopefully, fellow gothic lovers, this book will fill a bit of this void. I certainly enjoyed writing *I Shall Return* and hope you enjoy reading it. Cheers!

To all those who believe there's more to this world than
what we can see…

Chapter One

❧

My arms and legs quivered from exhaustion as I scanned the road from left to right. Dark, massive tree trunks lined the narrow dirt lane like prison bars, and above me, leafless trees spun a spider web of black limbs, blocking out broad stretches of sky and sun.

What is going on?

My scratched and dented, red mountain bike picked up speed as I coasted down yet another hill on this road heading seemingly nowhere.

This has to end, doesn't it?

The downward slope made its way back up again and I pedaled furiously, making my calf muscles burn. Rushing wind, spinning chain, and my panting breath blocked out all other sounds—which is why I didn't hear it coming until the last second.

Something. Behind me. Moving fast.

I glanced back. A large black object raced toward me, its shiny chrome bumper grinning evilly, and I pedaled harder, heart in my throat.

Run! Don't look back, just run!

You must get away.

A horn blared, echoing through the tunnel of trees like a call to arms, and I swerved to my left, into the ditch. My front tire caught a raised root and suddenly I was flying through the air in a dizzying rush. Seconds later the right side of my body smashed into the ground, followed by my chin, and for several frightening seconds I couldn't breathe. My eyes flitted about for salvation as my lungs fought to pull in air. In the distance, I heard a door slam, then running footsteps.

At last my breath returned in one great rush and I gratefully sucked inward. I lay there dazed as I breathed in the scent of dirt and crushed plants. Only then did I register the sharp pain in my right arm, shooting upward from my wrist like a sadistic messenger from hell.

Overhead a shadow blotted out what little light there was. My eyes rolled to the left and took in rich moss, lonely stones, dead leaves, then, with a flick upwards, a tall figure standing over me. The form stooped down, kneeling close. A pale face, youthful despite graying temples shoring up short, black hair, appeared before me. Eyes so dark you thought of light reversed searched my face.

"You've come back to me," I thought I heard him whisper. Then, "Are you all right?" He had a Scottish accent, but it was vague and muffled, as though buried beneath layers.

"I, uh, yes, I think so. Still breathing anyway."

His hand reached toward me and I flinched without knowing why—other than that he was a stranger and I was alone with him in these dark and menacing woods. Injured and alone, in a foreign country. My reaction didn't stop him—his hand pushed back the sheath of strawberry blond hair hanging across my face like a curtain. My hair's fineness annoyed me with its unwillingness to do much of anything and so I wore it straight and all one length, typically pulled back in a ponytail. But today I'd broken my barrette while trying to fasten it. I'd been in a hurry and unable to find another in any of my bags, so I'd left my hair down.

"You're bleeding," he said. His voice seemed to come from far away, and there was an echo to it, as though he was repeating himself in swift progression.

My left hand flew to my chin, encountering a slippery trail. "Oh…" I didn't like seeing blood, especially my own, especially after what my mother had done.

A white handkerchief flew into the air like a dove and swooped down to land on my chin. I felt gentle pressure and the throbbing faded a bit. "How did you get here?" the man asked, his tone almost urgent as he pressed the cloth to my wound. "No one comes to this place."

"I-I'm looking for Dundeid Castle. Isn't this the road? And why were you driving so fast?" I nearly shouted this last part, growing angry. "You ran me off the road!"

He pulled back, and his body devolved into a fuzzy blob. "Why would you want to go there?"

His question threw me right out of my anger. "I'm…" I wasn't sure how much to tell him—a total stranger. "I'm staying there," I finished uncertainly, as though I'd forgotten my plan.

"Why?"

"Why do you care?" I demanded, reviving a bit. He was getting too close, too personal. I didn't like too close and too personal.

"Don't go to that place."

"They're expecting me," I explained, though why that would matter I didn't know.

"You can't go there. I forbid you."

I rolled over and struggled to sit up, one arm cradling the other like a sling. "Are you serious? You don't even know me, and I certainly don't know you."

He looked taken aback, his dark eyes hurt. "How could you not know me?"

Ahhh…now things made sense. This guy was crazy, and he had me at his mercy. My eyes searched for my rental bike, hoping to find it wasn't damaged beyond repair. I wasn't sure how I was going to bike with an injured wrist, but I'd find a way. I might look like my mother—my heart-shaped face a frame for a peaches and cream complexion, freckles coloring the bridge of my slightly upturned nose like dust motes, and light green eyes that showed everything despite my willing them not to—but I had my dad's stubbornness and desperation to survive despite all odds.

Taking a deep breath, I pushed myself to my feet with my good hand and backed away. The stranger rose with me, his hands held out as though to calm me, though one hand still clutched the bloody handkerchief. I took in dark clothes, white shirt, nothing more. "I didn't mean to frighten you, Lilia."

Oh, Lord. He knows my name. I typically went by Lily, but my full name was Lilia. Lilia MacKenzie. How had he known? Who was this guy?

"Well, you *did* frighten me," I whispered. "I'm leaving now. If you could just point me in the right direction…" *before I start screaming.*

"You can't ride your bike like that." He indicated my cradled arm.

"I'll push it."

"I'll give you a ride. It's quite some distance from here. The Derings own a lot of property." I thought I heard a note of derision in his voice. His dark eyes surveyed me, waiting for my reaction.

"I'll be fine. I'll—"

"Don't be foolish. You're hurt. I'm taking you—"

"Listen, mister," I pointed at him with my good hand. "Don't you tell me what to do. Just get lost, okay?" As I turned to go my head did a full spin and I sank to my knees. The sky dimmed, then darkened, and I was gone.

~

I awoke to the sound of a car horn, three sharp beeps, then one long one. Slowly, gingerly, I sat up. I was lying on my side in the back of a car—his car—minus my helmet and backpack. The interior was expensive and manly, nearly to the point of being overdone, the combination of leather and earthy cologne dizzying.

I sat up, my head spinning with the effort. He had taken me despite my wishes. *Damnit!* But he had brought me where I wanted to go. I wasn't sure if that made him trustworthy, but it helped me take a slightly better view of his highhandedness.

"We're here." He sounded angry, but resigned.

I scooted over to the window and looked up, surprised at how dark it had grown. The darkness, I soon realized, came from the looming walls of a castle, not the sun setting. Dundeid Castle. Despite feeling sick to my stomach, my fingers ached to pull my camera from my backpack and start snapping pictures of the massive gray towers and the undulating crenellations. The castle resembled something you might see at a Disney amusement park, only this building would be Disney's dark, mysterious cousin. The Richard the Third of castles.

A shiver spread through my body. I was going to be staying here for two weeks. The idea both intrigued and frightened me. What would I find? What would I pick up? Something newsworthy, I hoped. My job counted on it. I had pitched this idea, and now I had to follow through and make a success of it or Father would pounce on my failure like a mountain lion on a fleeing rabbit. Not to mention the fact that if I failed, my boss, Mr. Willeton, would probably fire me. I was a bit of a pet to him, but he was also a businessman and loathed throwing away good money.

But it wasn't just pride or my job that had brought me here. The real reason was darker, harder to fathom, and one I wasn't about to share with anyone.

"Ah, here's someone," the stranger spoke.

The 'someone' was a slight, dark-haired woman, probably several inches shorter than my own five-foot-eight. Her diminutive size would make me look like an Amazon, I realized, and this made me feel better. Her face appeared at the window, small and oval, verging on gaunt, with jarring cherry red lips that put my pale ones to shame. She could be anywhere between thirty and forty, I thought.

She yanked open the door and I slid out, banging my arm. My other arm caught against the car door and I steadied myself against it. I didn't want to show weakness in front of this woman, though I had no idea why. Size-wise I could easily take her. Brains-wise, maybe not. There was a strange cunning in her bold, blue eyes.

And then, just as soon as I thought this, things shifted and all I could see was her concerned expression. "You're hurt!" she exclaimed, reaching out to grab my elbow. I smelled jasmine and lemon and rubbing alcohol. "Come, let me help you."

"I'm all right." I straightened up, wanting to pull away from her touch. "Just a little woozy."

"She blacked out," my driver spoke up, coming around the back of the car. Her red lips pursed as she watched him. "I should carry her, Vivian."

"You'll do no such thing," she snapped, then gave a tight smile. "That's what Brian is for. Fetching." Her head swung toward the house. "Brian!"

Fetching? What was I? A doggie bone?

The main door to the building, smaller than I would have expected for such a grand and imposing structure, opened, and a tall figure strode out. In the gray shadow of the castle, he seemed to glow. My heart skipped a beat. If this were Brian, then perhaps I wouldn't mind being fetched, after all.

"What is it, Viv?" the god spoke. My dazzled eyes took in reddish blond hair, with soft curls and wings, like zealous angels flying about in all directions. The pale lines that come from squinting in the sun framed purple-blue eyes noticeable even in the dim light. The rest of his skin was a honey hue that spoke of life and fresh air and general good health.

"I believe our guest has arrived, Andrew." I stared at her and she shrugged, the right corner of her mouth lifting slightly, pulling a small, nearby mole along with it. "We aren't expecting anyone else, except you…today, anyway," she added swiftly, as if to cover the fact that maybe they weren't expecting anyone else for some time. "Anyway, I was looking for Brian. She might need a bit of help walking. An accident?" Her eyes were speculative.

I glanced at my driver. He was staring at me and I realized he was purposely avoiding having anything to do with the god, Andrew. He had not looked his way once.

"What happened?" Andrew demanded.

"I fell off my bike," I said. "Mr…" I paused. I didn't know my driver's name.

"Mr. Huntington," Andrew provided. "How are things out your way, Greg?" The question was polite, the tone, not so much. His accent grew thicker as he spoke, as though he were purposely trying to sound more Scottish to prove a point.

"Fine," Greg ground out. I was glad to have a name for him. I liked labels. They gave me a sense of order, and with my past, I needed all the order I could get.

"We won't keep you. I imagine you have things to do, money to count."

A small smile on Vivian's face, which seemed no bigger than a monkey's, told me she was enjoying the exchange.

"Och, I've already counted my money," Greg replied, and I suppressed an urge to laugh. "Right after I woke up. It was bloody good fun. Too bad you don't have any of your own."

"All in good time," Andrew replied, and it sounded like a warning.

"It will never happen," Greg countered. "I'll see that it doesn't."

For a brief moment, my mind whirled and I saw them from a distance, looking about to face off in a deadly duel. "Um," I said faintly, feeling embarrassed. "I think I need to sit down."

Vivian and Andrew sprang into action. Vivian guided Greg away, her arm hooked firmly through his, looking up at him the entire time, murmuring words I couldn't hear. Yet his dark, intense eyes never left my face and I shivered with foreboding. At the same moment, Andrew told me he was going to carry me inside. He didn't ask for my permission; simply swept me off my feet. I thought maybe I giggled and felt severely disappointed in myself. I ought to have told him off good, acting like some sort of Neanderthal thug.

We entered the castle and my will to fight against him slipped away. Exhausted and disoriented, I barely took in the splendor, the medieval atmosphere, the dark stone walls, the tapestries and roaring fireplaces, as Andrew turned to his left and carried me up a spiraling set of stairs. We were in the staircase of a tower, I noted distantly. Ah, yes. I had requested the tower room after seeing its photos on Dundeid's website. Not only had I loved the spacious and dark beauty of the room, I sensed a familiarity in it that comforted me.

A door opened and we were standing in a large, cave-like space. A grand four-poster bed dominated a corner of the room. Several small windows high up, and one larger one, let in pale light from a setting sun. It was November in the Highlands of Scotland, though it was an unusually warm one with temperatures in the sixties and seventies, but a late season warm front did not keep the night at bay.

Andrew lay me down on the high bed and I sunk into velvety softness, my eyelids fluttering like moths. "I'll call the doctor. You look gey dreicht to me." Gey dreicht. Scottish for pretty miserable. In the weeks before my trip I'd done my research, gobbling up Scottish words and phrases like chocolate. He moved away, then stopped, and his next words were faint. "It's so good to have you here, Lilia. I've missed you more than I thought possible." And then, louder. "Rest now. The doctor will arrive soon."

Rain began to slash against the windows and I slept, his muted words fading from memory.

Chapter Two

❧

I awoke to a bright light shining in my pried open eyeball. I jerked away, my pupil dilating painfully. "There now, I'm not going to hurt you," a calm, fatherly voice soothed. "You've had enough of that already today, I see."

The doctor had arrived. He was a man in his mid-fifties, give or take a few years, round and cheerful. I guessed that he was the type who liked nothing more than sitting in front of a fire and reading murder mysteries with a glass of good Scotch firmly in hand. He liked a bit of real-life drama once in a while, but not too much—comfort always came first. But I could be wrong. A minor in Psychology didn't exactly make me an expert in the field, though that fact has yet to stop me from coming up with in-depth profiles on everyone I meet.

"That's an awfully bright light you're shining in my eye."

"Ah, you're coherent, too. A good sign."

"And you're English," I said, rubbing my eye.

He beamed. "Right you are. Married a bonny Scottish lass thirty-five years ago and haven't regretted it a moment. How's the head?"

"Fine," I said automatically. He gave me a skeptical look. "I feel a little woozy," I admitted. "I think I passed out on the way here, then fell asleep waiting for you."

"Hm. When's the last time you had a decent meal in you?"

I flinched, annoyed at being caught out. "Early this morning. I meant to eat lunch, but I wanted to beat the rain." I'd arrived in Scotland yesterday, late afternoon, rode ScotRail to a nearby village, checked into a worn-down B & B, showered, then slept until morning. Not wanting to take further advantage of Mr. Willeton's oftentimes patronizing generosity, I rented a bike with helmet and luggage rack for my bags, for the remainder of the trip. For most of my life, I've been an avid biker. There's something about flying along on your own impetus that makes a person feel alive. A fear of being out of shape—too weak and helpless to escape—was an even stronger motivation to bike whenever I could.

In hindsight, it had been stupid to skip a meal, especially when I was still feeling jetlagged, despite sleeping fourteen hours straight. But I knew rain was in the forecast, and I was in a hurry, and time was ticking. I had only two weeks, after all, to do what needed to be done.

"You'll spend a lot of time trying to beat the rain round here. The name's Weatherby," he added. I'd expected him to take me to task for not eating, but he didn't, and I was surprised and grateful. I already had one overprotective father. I didn't need another. "You're Miss MacKenzie, or so I've been told. Come to do an article on genealogy, is that right?"

I nodded. That was the official version. "My boss runs a local paper in my home town."

The doctor nodded as he gently pressed my injured arm, turning it over, this way and that. I tried not to wince. "And where might that be?" he calmly asked. I knew he was trying to distract me from the pain with his questions, but he was also curious. His sparkling, inquisitive brown eyes gave him away.

"Willeton, New Hampshire," I replied through gritted teeth, wishing I could reclaim my arm. "The town was actually named after my boss's ancestors."

"He must have money." The doctor was shrewder than he looked. He set my arm down on the bed with a pat.

"Money to burn," I agreed, giving him a smile. "He wanted a story on genealogy, suggested I look into my own background, and here I am." Within two weeks of suggesting the idea as a story, I was on a plane to the Scottish Highlands. Of course, I had to make it look like my idea had been Mr. Willeton's. He was, after all, a man who liked to give the illusion he was in charge. Exactly like my father. I knew how to handle his type, though I'd just as soon not have to resort to subterfuge to get my way. I'd rather lay all my cards on the table. In this case, however, I was going to have to hide more than I liked.

"A grand adventure!" he deduced. "How I envy you."

"I'm not off to the best start," I muttered, gazing down at my throbbing arm.

He chuckled. "Well, you have that cut on your chin, which I put a patch on, a sprained wrist, and most likely low blood sugar from not eating. I took the liberty of removing your shoes and found nothing amiss on that end. I suggest you take it slow the next couple of days and eat something, my dear girl. The young these days are either too skinny or dreadfully overweight." He began to bind my wrist with an Ace bandage. "I'll tell Miss Dering to bring up an ice pack and something for the pain," he muttered, as though dictating notes to himself. "And a large meal, let's not forget that."

"Is my head all right? I was wearing a helmet, but I think I must have hit my head, too. I kind of passed out. Do you think I have a concussion?" It would explain why I felt so weird, imagining voices, hearing echoes. "I've had one before." I couldn't tell him how I got it, though. That would give away too much. "I shouldn't go to sleep, right?" I wouldn't mind not being allowed to close my eyes. My dreams, always disturbing, had been growing more so these last several months.

"Nonsense. Old wives tale. You can sleep all you want, concussion or not, though I don't think you have one. In fact, from the looks of you, I'd recommend a good, long sleep." Finished wrapping my wrist, he stood to go, his old-fashioned black leather doctor's bag clicking shut with a snap. I sat up straighter. "Enjoy your stay, Miss MacKenzie. And if you need anything, just have Miss Dering give me a call. Though Vivian, being a nurse, should be able to attend to you quite nicely."

A nurse? I couldn't imagine her being a nurse, unless we were talking Nurse Ratched of *One Flew Over the Cuckoo's Nest* fame. Though maybe I was being too hasty. She had truly seemed concerned about my injuries. Best to give her a second chance. I certainly didn't want to make any enemies—not this soon.

I waved to the doctor and he gave me a smiling salute before disappearing out the door—no doubt hurrying home to his hot fire and warm supper. Looking around the room, I thought how quaint it seemed to have a doctor actually make a house call. I was of the impression that the practice had gone out of style decades ago. But I was in Scotland now—a land of people self-assured enough to do as they pleased.

Three raps on the heavy wood door startled me, and it swung open before I could say come in. Vivian strode in carrying my backpack and two small bags in one hand and a folding tray stand in the other. Behind her a stooped man bearing a silver tray backed into the room. Vivian lifted the bags as though asking me what she should do with them and I, feeling a bit like royalty and liking it probably more than was good for me, pointed to a nearby rose velvet armchair that faced a fireplace. She set the bags down, then placed the tray stand by my bed.

Without once looking at me, she stepped aside and the old man set the tray down with a slight crash. Hands shaking, he straightened as best he could and stared at me with hooded gray eyes. His weathered brown face was so wrinkled it made me think of a grape metamorphosing to raisinhood. He wore a tweed cap, mended in several spots with mismatched threads of green and blue and red. His gnarled, heavily veined hands and fingers spoke of arthritis and hard labor.

"You can go now, Brian," Vivian said, tapping her foot impatiently. He nodded deferentially, tipped his cap to me (and was that a wink he threw?—a conspiratorial one?), then shuffled out the door. This was Brian? I wasn't sure how Vivian could have expected him to help me up the stairs, much less carry me as Andrew had. As small as she was, Vivian probably could have carried me more easily than this guy.

"Feeling better?" Her voice was clipped and professional. Now that I thought about it, she did look a bit like a nurse in her long-sleeved, buttoned to the top, gray dress. It fit snugly at the waist like all good uniforms, with a wide black belt helping to relieve a bit of the monochrome palette. I supposed it was good business to keep a health care professional on staff at all times. The Castle not only served for lodging, it offered hunting and fishing packages, walking tours, and whisky tasting parties. People out and about—especially those not prepared for the brutal and unpredictable weather of the Scottish Highlands—might easily run into trouble. Especially those who had attended the whisky tasting first.

"Yes, a bit. Thank you."

"Well, there's loads to eat, some pain tablets in the little paper cup, and an ice pack for your wrist. Tablets first?" She asked it as a question, but I thought it was more of a command. Still, it was a sensible one and I nodded. I tossed back the pills, took the glass of water that her slender, child-like fingers offered, and swallowed. I hoped the medicine would kick in soon. Both my head and wrist ached now.

Vivian crossed over to a walnut-colored wardrobe, pulled out two fat pillows encased in delicately embroidered, rose-colored pillowcases, and tucked them under my wrist. The ice pack was laid across my arm, gently, for all her sharp, crisp movements.

"Can you eat one handed? The pie's easy enough to cut with a fork."

"Yes, I'll manage." I'd manage if I had to stick my face in the food and suck it up. Only now did I realize how hungry I was.

"Excellent. I'll check on you in half an hour, clear things away. Try to keep that pack on during that time." She walked to the door, then turned back. "Oh, and Miss MacKenzie? I'm sorry your first visit to Dundeid Castle has started off so poorly. We didn't make a very good impression, did we?"

"I think you've made a great one," I replied. And by great, I meant spectacular and interesting, especially when it came to Andrew, the god. "It's not your fault I wiped out on my bike."

"Yes, Mr. Huntington was very careless. He drives way too fast." She didn't sound entirely disapproving about this last bit; her red lips curved upward into a small smile. "Your bike has a bent tire rim, but Brian should be able to fix that. If not, you might want to look into purchasing a new tire. Now eat up and I'll check on you in a bit."

"Thank you," I called after her disappearing form, then dug into the hot meal—Scotch broth, Shepherd's pie, and a buttery bread pudding dessert, washed down with thick, creamy milk that clung to my top lip like those milk ads, which I found rather revolting. I used a snowy white napkin to wipe away the residue and took a moment to look about me. The room was painted a lovely old world color, and its walls were covered with dark, luscious landscapes, dotted with an occasional portrait of a stranger who'd lived in a time long gone. In the middle of the room, a pillar rose up to meet the ceiling, which sloped downward in several spots. Ornate designs decorated the ceiling and arches like a painter's canvas. The bed was tucked into the far corner of the room; at its foot was an archway created between the wall and the pillar. The bed faced the larger window, which likely looked out over the long, tree-lined drive of Dundeid Castle. A room with a view. Perfect.

Satisfied by my big meal and my delightful room, I laid my napkin across the tray, at which time, I heard a knock. Vivian was early. "Come in," I called.

The door opened by degrees and I wondered if Andrew was coming to check on me. My breath caught a little at the possibility. I straightened up, pushed back several rebellious tresses with my good hand, and waited. The door opened wider. My eyes registered reddish hair and I nearly choked. It *was* him.

And then, just as quickly, I realized that it wasn't. A young woman, perhaps eighteen or nineteen, possessing a stunning and fragile beauty that made me think of Tennyson's *Lady of Shalott*, shyly entered the room. John William Waterhouse, who'd painted his own version of the lady, must have once met the doppelganger of this girl now staring at me in pale wonderment. I returned the stare, taking in hair the color of tiger lilies and honey, and wide, spring sky eyes. If I was peaches and cream, she was milk and English roses, or Scottish roses, as it were.

"You're finally here," she breathed. Her slender chest, draped in a lavender silk blouse, rose and fell like leaves in the wind. "I feel like I've been waiting forever!"

I blinked. "But I made my reservation two weeks ago—"

"And I've been waiting ever since. My cousin says you're from America and you're a writer and a photographer. That's dead exciting!"

I hid a smile. The poor girl must not get out much. No one else in my life had ever been this impressed by what I did, though there weren't many people in my life to pass judgment. I had no close friends, but I maintained pleasant enough acquaintanceships with my co-workers at the newspaper. The relationship never went any farther than that—my own fault. They'd learned long ago to stop asking me to join them for lunch, as I invariably said no. I couldn't take the risk.

"Not really all that exciting," I said. "I mean, I enjoy what I do, but it's not like I'm covering the wars in the Middle East." I'm not sure I would anyway. I had my own war to deal with—visions of it came to me in my dreams every night, starting thirteen years ago when I was ten, right after my mother had done the unspeakable. "I could do better, is what I mean," I finished.

Her blue eyes were disbelieving. "What's better than traveling on your own, doing a job you like?"

I promptly smothered the pleased feeling that rose inside me. My father treated what I did with barely concealed contempt, only marginally less so when I was promoted my junior year of college to general assignment reporter (he was at his worst when I worked for several years in high school as a copy kid and general dogsbody). So to hear someone approve of my job, be almost envious of it, was like a drug. I quickly stifled the seductive sensation. I couldn't afford to get a big head. Mr. Willeton had taught me, often by giving me the worst assignments any time I got a little too full of myself, that arrogance made for bad journalism. I kid you not—he once made me interview a pig.

"But you're doing something with your life," she insisted, slowly making her way into the room, her long, lilac skirt swishing hypnotically. "I wish I could do something with mine."

"You're still young," I assured her. "You've got lots of time."

"I'm twenty-five," she said, wringing her hands as she crept closer to the bed. "Not so young as that." I stared at her in surprise. She was older than me by two years. It didn't seem possible.

She gave me a grim smile. "I know. My Auntie Viv says it's because I haven't really lived life yet. She thinks I'm too coddled. But that's what happens, I guess, when your parents die when you're only six. Andrew is very protective." She released a soft sigh.

"I'm sorry," I said quietly. I knew what it was like to lose a parent. I also knew what it was like to be, if not coddled, then watched over very closely. "Is…is Andrew your brother, then?" My voice sounded more hopeful than I liked.

She laughed. "He's my cousin—a distant one."

"And Vivian is your aunt…"

"In a roundabout way. She was actually my mother's aunt, but she was younger than Mother, if that makes sense. Mother was the oldest in her family and Viv the youngest—a surprise to her parents, you see. Our family is rather messed up and strewn about, but I think of her as an aunt. She's far too young to be called great aunt, anyway." And she wouldn't like it, either, I thought. "Do you plan to write about us?"

"Well, I'm not sure. It depends on what I find. I'm here to write about my roots. My ancestors on my father's side left Scotland to sail to America back in the nineteenth century. We've lost touch with our relatives here so I thought it would be fun to track them down." While not entirely false, my story wasn't entirely true, either. "From what I could gather, they might have once lived in Inverkinn, which is close by."

"Your work sounds so fun. I could never do anything that exciting."

"Being twenty-five is still quite young, and you're very beautiful. There must be lots for you to do."

Her lips curled into a pretty pout. "That's what cousin Andrew says to me. He says it to mollify me, to *appease* me."

What a strange choice of words. Why would he need to do that?

She saw the expression on my face. "It's because I have an illness."

"Oh, I'm sorry."

"Some days are better," she explained. "It makes it hard to live like you do—free and independent." She bit her lip, then gave me a mischievous smile. "But if I have to be bound by this stupid problem, then I wouldn't mind if the binding were being done by the gorgeous Greg Huntington." She leaned forward eagerly. "You met him, right? He nearly ran you over trying to escape his demons, at least that's how Auntie Viv put it. Rather romantic, hm? What do you think of him?"

"I'm not sure," I hedged, which was true. I had no idea what to think of him. Especially after hearing that Vivian believed he was trying to escape his demons. I wondered what they might be.

Her frown was one of bafflement. "You must have formed some impression of him! I think he's amazing—so dark and brooding. Like a movie star."

Or the undead. The thought was both unkind and inaccurate. If he were undead, his touch wouldn't have felt so warm on my skin and he probably wouldn't be driving, either. The undead merely shuffled about; they didn't race around in cars. Did they? Not likely. Still, this Mr. Huntington bothered me. There was something not quite right about him.

A yawn sneaked up on me. "So can I?" I heard the girl asking.

"Can you what?" I yawned again.

"Follow you about?"

My muscles tensed. "I prefer to work alone," I told her quickly, "but maybe you can help me out once in a while." Her eyes tried to blink back her obvious disappointment. "I would love to take some pictures of you," I added, and she brightened. She *would* make a great subject, I told myself. If the opportunity presented itself I might even arrange her in a Waterhouse pose.

"That would be lovely!" My eyelids fluttered and she took a step away from me. "I'll let you sleep now." She floated over to the door. "My name is Ophelia, by the way."

Of course it is, I thought vaguely, remembering that Waterhouse had painted a portrait starring Ophelia.

"I'm Lily," I offered, even though I was quite aware she already knew that.

She smiled. "Tomorrow, then. I can't wait!" And then she was gone, leaving behind a faint scent of gardenias and lilac.

I began to drift off, wondering vaguely just how strong the pain medication Vivian had given me was. Through the haze in my mind, a sound penetrated—a click, followed by a faint rush of air. Nurse Vivian must be returning. My muscles felt so lethargic that I couldn't react, couldn't say a word in greeting.

The sound of footsteps, slow and sure, echoed across the hardwood floor, and then a solid presence stood over the bed looking down at me. Very tall and very male, I sensed through fluttering eyelids. For what seemed like hours, the man stood staring down at me, and my heartbeat thudded in time to his measured breathing.

"She has come at last," he spoke quietly, and I realized that someone had joined him. "Just like you said. How did you know?"

"I see things. I've always seen things." The voice was low and I couldn't make out who it was. Ophelia? Vivian?

"But you do not see everything."

"No. It doesn't work that way. But I see enough."

"We need her."

"We do."

"This time we can't fail."

"We won't."

There was a sigh from the man, sounding both relieved and resigned.

I could no longer fight the call of sleep, slipping into a dark abyss that kept my dreams at bay, the conversation blotted out like ink over white paper. I wouldn't remember it in the morning.

Chapter Three

✣

I awoke to bright sunshine filtering through the windows spread around my room. My headache had faded, only to be replaced by an overwhelming feeling of mortification. Everyone here must think I was an absolute idiot, crashing my bike and necessitating a call to the doctor. I'd been nothing but trouble.

And to be saved by, not one man, but two. I groaned. One would think I was a Victorian woman, totally dependent on a man to keep her safe. The idea made me want to gag. I yanked back the covers and swung my legs about. Pushing myself to my feet, I was surprised and pleased to find that I hadn't suffered too many bruises. I felt strong and healthy—like my regular self. Even my wrist had ceased to ache. Sticking out from the wrap like pale sausages, my fingers curled and uncurled a few times, testing for pain. There was very little. Good. I'd be able to work today. The camera I used was a bit on the heavy side and I needed both hands to keep it stable.

Excited to start the day, I rushed over to my backpack and pulled out my camera case, surprised I had taken this long to check on my precious possession. After thoroughly examining the camera, then taking a few photographs of myself making faces in the cheval mirror, I felt satisfied my baby had survived the crash intact.

I pulled out my laptop, which I had packed in a foam case, and turned it on, praying it would work. I used it to store photographs and do photo editing, and for writing my columns and checking my e-mail. In other words, this computer was my life, so I was delighted to find everything in working order.

After tucking my tools of the trade away, I realized my bladder was about to burst. A quick scan of the room showed no bathroom, so I ventured down a shadowy, spiral staircase to a narrow hallway, my stocking feet silent on the wood floor. Two doors down I found it, its door standing wide open. While doing my duty I noticed there was a tub, and afterward I hurried back to my room to fetch fresh clothes and soap.

The water was lukewarm, at best, so my bathing experience turned into more of a splash and dash. I didn't really like baths anyway and preferred showers. But here, I'd have to make do. Clean and *much* refreshed—cold water is so bracing—I dressed in jeans, a striped oxford, and a heather gray, wool cardigan, its left cuff unraveling, then pulled on matching wool socks, right big toe delicately darned, followed by my worn biker boots. After some fiddling, I managed to remove the bandage on my chin. The scrape looked raw and there was some bruising, but all in all it didn't look too bad. I decided to leave it uncovered, hoping that the fresh air would help it heal faster. Being a bit of a wimp, I'd left my hair unwashed, which meant it was hopeless, so I pulled it into a limp ponytail and headed back to my room, hoping for the best.

Carrying my dirty clothes, whose knees and elbows were colored brown from dirt, I wondered how I was going to get those stains out, then remembered reading that the castle offered laundry services. While it seemed the ideal solution to my problem, the idea of having someone else clean my clothes grated on me—I didn't like people touching my stuff or doing what I thought should be *my* work. Plus, I didn't want anyone reporting on the state of my clothes—cheap and worn. Being a newspaper reporter didn't exactly pay the big bucks.

There was a knock on the door and I took a minute to compose myself before answering. Standing with my back straight and spine stiff as a soldier ready for battle, I waited by my bed for my visitor to reveal himself.

"Good morning, Miss!" a voice greeted in an accent so strong, it took me a moment to interpret what I'd just heard. A red-haired teen of about sixteen or seventeen peered around the door. Spotting me, her bottom lip dropped in surprise, revealing a pink tongue. "Ye're oot of bed. But I've coom to ask what ye'd like for breakfast. I'm meant to bring it to ye—"

"Oh, you don't need to bring it up," I interrupted as she slid the rest of her plump figure into the room. "I'll come down."

She blushed, freezing where she was. "But me orders were to fetch ye a tray."

"No, no! I'm not an invalid, and I won't cause more trouble than I already have. I'll come down. If you could show me the way..."

Her rosy cheeks brightened painfully and her red curls darkened against the blush. "The Laird doesnae want ye doing anything today. Ye're supposed to relax and..." Seeing my stubborn expression she let the sentence trail away.

My fingers gripped the bedpost. "I don't want to relax. I have work to do."

"But I was told—"

"You were told wrong." My words were cool. I wasn't some helpless young thing and damned if I would let myself be treated like one. All those years—I would never forget how horrible those had been. Never again. "Now I want to go downstairs, so you can either show me the way, or I can wander around for a good hour before I figure it out."

She bobbed a curtsy. "I'll take ye right away."

I relaxed and smiled at her, full of good will now. "Thank you, um…"

"Gertie," she supplied.

"Thank you, Gertie. I'm Lily MacKenzie."

Her heavy-lidded, bland blue eyes, one of which had a tendency to wander a bit toward her nose, dropped to the floor. "I ken who ye are, Miss MacKenzie. We all do. The Laird told us tae make sure yer stay is a good one."

"The Laird?"

"Mr. Dering, that is."

Oh. Andrew. The god. The brochure hadn't mentioned his name and I wondered why not. Surely a bona fide laird would bring in the tourists hand over fist? Americans loved that sort of thing. Plus it would have been nice to know about his status before letting him carry me up all those stairs.

"Well, it's nice to meet you, Gertie."

She bobbed a little curtsy, her dimpled hands grasping hold of a crisp white apron draped over a long period dress the color of reflected sky. "It's sort of a costume," she explained, seeing my assessing study. "I dinna dress this way on me days off."

"I should hope not," I laughed. "They don't make you wear a corset, do they?" She bit her lip, her broad pale brow, dotted with two pimples, furrowed in deep thought, then she shook her head. "Good. I wrote an article on corsets a couple years ago—when they were starting to come back into fashion. Those things are killers. They actually squish your internal organs and can cause permanent damage. A hundred years ago, women even wore them when they were pregnant. Can you believe that?"

Gertie's eyes flitted around the room, as though unsure how to respond, finally settling on my pile of dirty clothes. "I dinna ken much aboot that, but I do ken laundry," she said proudly, and with more than a touch of relief. "Me mum says I'm a whiz at getting oot stains." She gave a big smile, her open mouth revealing a mouthful of strong, healthy teeth.

"Oh. Um…" Her hands clasped in front of her, willing me to say yes. Did laundry really mean that much to her? It couldn't. It was just laundry. "I'd really rather do it myself."

"Of course, Miss." Her round face dropped. "Well, then, if ye'd follow me."

I felt a brief tinge of regret, then pushed it away. There was no need for her to pick up after me. Surely she had better things to do than my laundry. On the way out I grabbed my camera bag, slinging the wide black strap over one shoulder so that the bag rested on the opposite hip, and followed her down the winding, stone steps, slick as marble after centuries of wear.

Gertie stopped every few seconds and waited for me to catch up. I couldn't help myself—I'd never been in a real castle before. I'd always meant to visit Hammond Castle in Massachusetts, but had never made it. Father never let me have the car and when I finally got one with my first job, I was too busy trying to make ends meet (and thereby prove him wrong) to find time to go.

But now, here I was, staying in a six hundred-year-old castle, with some parts dating even further back. The presence of those who'd lived here, died here, danced and grieved here, was so thick it filled my throat and lungs like smoke, and I had to swallow several times just to keep breathing.

We arrived at the Great Hall, a high-ceilinged, wide-open space graced by a flagstone floor and six or seven closed doors spread around the room. Faded tapestries, thirty feet in length, hung on the walls and a large, empty fireplace, unusually situated in a corner, brooded over its lack of use. The room, once the mainstay of the castle, seemed oddly abandoned, at most a way station for the castle's inhabitants. Our footsteps echoed off the walls and ceiling like knocking knuckles as we crossed the broad expanse of floor.

We stopped outside a pair of dark wooden doors, each displaying a series of carvings. The pictures stood out in bas-relief: strange, dragon-like birds in various poses—wings folded in, wings spread, mouth open to emit what would surely be a loud shriek if it could be heard. My fingers itched to pull out my camera and start snapping, but I didn't think that would be proper etiquette. Besides, Gertie was already pulling the doors open. Miss Manners had won this round, though given another thirty seconds I'd have pushed her to the floor and danced around her, clicking away.

The dining area was surprisingly intimate, the small room nearly filled by a long, shiny table. Twenty high-back chairs, each boasting a red strip of velvet to cushion one's back, encircled it. Straight ahead, five floor to ceiling windows curved to form a little nook, which looked out over a smooth lake. This must be Loch Wyrd, which I'd read about on-line. I gazed at it longingly, wishing I were outside to photograph it and the mountains behind it.

A movement from the table caught my attention. "Miss MacKenzie!" Andrew cried. "What are you doing down here? Gertie, can you explain this?" I glanced over at the young maid, whose face wore a combination of fear and worshipful devotion. I didn't know which was worse.

"It's not her fault," I rushed to say. "I told her to bring me down. I didn't want to cause any more trouble for your family or your staff."

He stood and came over to guide me to the table, taking my good arm like a boy scout helping a little old lady cross the street. I glanced back and gave Gertie a look that said, *get out while you can.* She took the hint and scurried away. There was hope for her yet.

"Gertie was supposed to bring you something to eat," he scolded, steering me into a chair next to his own. "I'll have to talk to her..."

I immediately stood back up, startling him. He pulled back, his indigo eyes wide. "If you say one harsh word to her, I'll pack my bags and leave this place." Damn him and his arrogance. I knew he was too good to be true.

"Hold on now!" He pushed me back into the chair. Off-balance I had no choice but to sit. "Doctor Weatherby told me you were to stay in bed. I made sure Gertie understood this. I cannot run a business if my staff doesn't listen to me." He glanced around. "Who, I see, has run off." He shook his beautiful blond head. "So are you going to stay seated without me holding you down?"

I crossed my arms, careful not to jar my wrist. "For the moment. But haven't you heard the saying, 'The customer is always right'?"

He went and sat down in his chair, picking up a linen napkin and placing it in his lap. He was wearing a lilac oxford under a navy blue blazer. A touch of casual mixed with business. "Of course." His eyes fastened on my battered chin. "But sometimes the customer doesn't always know what's best for them."

I let this go. "I meant what I said...I'll leave. Gertie was going to bring me breakfast but I...well, I insisted that she bring me down here."

Instead of arguing, he laughed, surprising me. "Poor Gertie. Stuck between two bull-headed people."

I smiled and unfolded my arms. "So she won't get in trouble?"

"I suppose not, at least not for this infraction. You do look well today." He examined me, more closely than was necessary, and possibly close enough to count every pore on my nose. "Extremely well," he added.

I glanced down at the table, all my bravado snuffed out. It wasn't that I was afraid of men—I'd dated in high school and college. Three short-term relationships (lasting less than four months) and one long-term relationship that survived my junior and senior year of college, ending right after graduation when I discovered that my boyfriend was cheating on me with one of my roommates. So I had experience with the opposite sex. But none of my boyfriends had ever been like this man seated two feet away from me, and who seemed to be a solar system unto himself, or at least the sun in the middle of it. He radiated heat and energy and something else, something as indefinable as the mysteries of space.

I found myself getting pulled in.

"I'd still like Viv to look you over when she returns from the village."

"That won't be necessary. Can I have some eggs?" I asked, feeling the sudden need for protein and a change of subject. "And some orange juice."

I thought I detected a glimmer of satisfaction in those peculiar colored eyes of his, but he only nodded and picked up a silver bell, which resembled the gaping mouth of a wolf. The alto clang brought Gertie running, looking dangerously close to throwing up.

"Yes, Mr. Dering?" She bobbed up and down in a strange sort of off-kilter curtsy.

"Eggs and toast and orange juice for our guest."

The curtsying stopped. "Yes, yer Lairdship!"

He winced. "No need for formalities here, remember, Gertie?"

"Of course, Mr. Dering. Sorry, Mr. Dering."

"Fine, Gertie. Run along now."

She bobbed several more curtsies on her way out of the dining room, disappearing into the shadows from whence she came.

"So you're a laird?" I watched him closely as his fork poked holes in a dry piece of toast. I hoped I would get butter on mine. Lots of it. I suppose that's another reason why I tried to bike everywhere—to offset my carnal desires.

"I am." His response was cool.

"You should post that on your website. It would bring in more visitors. Americans like the idea of gentry, even if we don't follow the practice ourselves, not officially, anyway."

His smile was polite. The heat I had felt emanating from him slipped away, leaving only ice. "Including yourself?"

"Oh, sure. I envy that you can trace your roots back so many centuries. I wish we had more of that in my country…a sense of history, of place."

"Would you like me if I weren't a laird?"

I stiffened. "Whether or not I decide to like you, Mr. Dering, will have nothing to do with you being a laird."

The frost melted. "Fair enough," he laughed.

A moment later Gertie came in with my breakfast. Without looking me in the eye once, she placed a delicate plate and a crystal glass of orange juice in front of me, bobbed a brief curtsy, wide hip knocking against my chair in the process, then scurried away. Watching her go, I wondered if she had already deemed me a troublemaker to be avoided at all cost.

"Thank you, Gertie," I called after her, hoping to get back on her good side. I didn't like not being liked, and besides, a good reporter never puts off a potential contact.

I didn't hesitate to tuck into my breakfast. I thought maybe Andrew was watching as I ate, which was annoying, but I decided not to care. I was hungry, and I had work to do. Two weeks might seem like a lot of time, but I'd learned that uncovering a story could take a while and always longer than anticipated.

"It's hard to believe I had to carry you up to your room last night," Andrew commented, his expression amused.

I flinched. I'd been wondering when—while hoping *not ever*—he would bring that up. "Sorry about that. I must have looked like an idiot. I hadn't eaten, and I hit my head when my bike crashed. I promise it won't happen again."

"Pity," he murmured. I stared at him, but he was gazing out at the loch. "But I'm glad to see you so quickly recovered."

Did he think I had faked my injuries? Oh, dear Lord, that was worse than anything. "I'm a fast healer." I wiped my mouth with my napkin, then laid it down next to my nearly spotless plate. "Always have been."

"Then you'll be able to do your work? I can assist if you need my help."

Help, as in, *personally*? Or would he assign me one of his lackeys?

Either way, the idea was disturbing, but for different reasons. "I'll be fine. I'm used to working alone." His long fingers tapped the table like pecking birds. "But I might need to ask you some questions at some point," I felt compelled to add.

The fingers stopped tapping. "I am at your service, Miss MacKenzie."

I met his eyes and suddenly found it difficult to swallow. "Thank you," I managed to respond. "I'll...I'll let you know when."

"Soon, I hope. I'm quite interested to learn what you find out. What a delight it would be if you confirmed that your father's family really did come from our little corner of the world. You would be one of us, then."

I studied his expression, searching for what he knew, to see if he had figured out my real reason for coming here. But I found nothing in his compelling eyes to signal caution on my part. It didn't mean I wouldn't be careful, though.

"I think it would take more than that to be one of you, don't you?"

He laughed, a low echo of mirth that somehow managed to be alluring. "Perhaps. Which reminds me... If I were you I'd stay away from Greg Huntington."

"Why?" My reporter instincts kicked in and I leaned forward.

"Because I don't trust him." He stood up, pushing back his chair as he rose. "You may go wherever you please in Dundeid Castle. My home is yours."

I nodded, working hard to control my surprise and joy at his having just made my life easier. "Thank you."

He was halfway out the door, when he turned back. "Do you believe in fate, Lily?"

I hesitated. "I believe we make our own fates."

"So you don't think that your every step, every word from your mouth, every choice that you make has already been decided?"

"Absolutely not!" My fist pounded the table in emphasis and I wondered at my sudden ferocity.

"Then you believe in chaos theory?"

"Not complete chaos, no," I conceded. "Perhaps there's a map, but we get to choose the path we wish to take." It was my only hope—this belief.

"But how would you ever know that you were the one making that choice?"

"I'd feel it," I said, pressing my fist to my heart. "I'll know."

"And what if you made the wrong choice?" I caught a hint of suffering in his eyes. Had he made the wrong choice?

"Then I would hope that I'd get another chance."

"If there were no second chance?" he pushed.

I sighed, a sound that seemed to come from miles away, traveling across hills and moors to pass through my lips. "There has to be."

He gave a quick nod and left. *What's his story?* I wondered. What had happened to cause the sorrow I'd seen in his eyes? It seemed like an old wound, but fresh enough to still cause him anguish.

He had left his plate on the table and I wondered if I should do the same. A creak came from the direction of the kitchen and I realized I was being watched—Gertie, waiting for me to leave so she could clear the table. I sighed again, this time just a regular one. I'd have to fight this battle with Gertie another time. If she wanted to be someone's servant for the rest of her life, so be it. I had a different path to take.

"I'm going now, Gertie," I called, pushing back my chair and standing up. "And I'll try not to get you into trouble anymore. Okay?" No answer. "I can't guarantee that, though, being a born troublemaker." I thought I heard a brief giggle, abruptly cut off as though she'd clapped her hand over her mouth. "See you at lunch."

I left the dining room, then stopped in the Great Hall, pondering where to start my search, and wishing I hadn't dismissed Andrew's offer so quickly. The information I needed was here, but where? This place was huge and I'd rather not wander into someone's private quarters. Sometimes my obsession with self-sufficiency wound up biting me in the butt.

"There you are!" Ophelia, wearing a short-sleeved, white blouse and pale blue skirt, advanced across the Hall like a ballerina on stage. Despite her grace of movement, her pale face was drawn and dark smudges haunted the small fields beneath her azure eyes.

She noticed me studying her and frowned prettily. "I suppose you wouldn't want to take pictures of me today. I look awful. Couldn't sleep," she added hastily, as though to prevent any judgment on my part.

Because of her illness? I mused. "You do look the part of the suffering romantic heroine."

Her lips curved upward, satisfied, and I wondered if maybe I shouldn't have turned her insomnia into something desirable. "You should take a nap later, though."

She laughed. "Oh, don't worry about me. I'll sleep when I'm dead." Her smile faded as the last word passed her blue-tinged lips. Was she simply cold, or fading fast? I swallowed hard, not liking the thought of someone so young dying. "Where are you going?"

I held up my camera case. "To work. I was just wondering where to start when you arrived."

She held out a thin white arm. "Then I'm just in time."

I went to her and slipped my uninjured arm through the triangular space she'd made with hers. "Don't you want to eat?"

"There's plenty of time to eat. All day. Right now I want to spend time with you. When do I ever get to meet people my own age?"

I didn't know the answer to that. "I read that you're keeping the Catholic parish's records here at Dundeid while they restore the church."

She nodded and her eyes twinkled. "We keep all that down in the dastardly dungeon."

Dungeon. My hands began to tremble. I knew I'd be staying in a castle, knew castles had dungeons, yet I wasn't prepared to have anything to do with them. I didn't like dungeons. But after all my dreams, I had good reason not to.

Chapter Four

※

"We keep them up on tables, of course, so they don't get damp," Ophelia went on, oblivious to my sudden terror.

My steps slowed until I had pulled us to a stop. "I-I'm not sure I need to look at the records right now."

"No time like the present! Come on." Ophelia dragged me forward and opened one of the doors in the Great Hall. Together we entered a hallway, not a room as I'd expected. We passed through two dark halls and down three short stairways, until at last we reached a wooden door, rounded at the top, with black metal bands crisscrossing it like a cage. A skeleton key protruded from the lock and Ophelia let go of my arm—only then did I realize she'd been gripping me tightly enough to cause marks. Kept well-oiled, the key turned smoothly and there was a sharp click. Ophelia grinned at me, key now firmly in hand. "I never leave the key in the lock when I go down. I'm being terribly superstitious I suppose, but one can never be too careful." I wondered if she was simply being dramatic or if she had reason to be cautious. "*And* I take this." She reached down, picked up a solid flashlight on the floor next to the door, and snapped it on.

I shivered and my cold fingers curled around the camera case strap, as though for comfort. I did *not* want to go through that door.

But it was too late. Ophelia had grabbed hold of my sweater sleeve and was pulling me along. My mind whirled and I heard voices echoing about me as we scurried down the dark narrow stairwell like mice.

Or rats.

I strained to hear what the voices were saying, thinking vaguely that I didn't want to know. That knowing would be harmful.

Fàilte …

He's mine!

I cannot believe he could ever love another.

Let me out of this hellhole!

Help me…

Oh, dear Lord…

The damp walls closed in on me, and the low, rounded ceiling seemed to lower itself over my head like a clamp. I felt on the verge of screaming when at last the walls opened up into a large space. In the middle of the room were several tables bearing cardboard boxes. Encircling us, ten rusty cell doors waited to admit new occupants. Each cell contained a tiny window, allowing in a faint stream of dusty light. I wasn't sure the windows helped much to alleviate the heavy darkness of the dungeon. In fact, I thought maybe their light only accentuated the shadows, further concealing what might lurk within them.

Ophelia let me go and set the flashlight down on a table. She found a kerosene lantern hanging on a hook by the entrance and lit it with a match from a nearby box of matches. The light reflected off the moist stones and for a brief moment I could actually feel the agony suffered here. Perhaps I was being dramatic, but I had the unpleasant feeling I wasn't exaggerating in the least.

"Well, here they are." Ophelia flung a hand at the boxes, a little frown marring her face. "There are a lot of them, aren't there?"

I nodded numbly. "I don't suppose any of this would be on a computer…"

She laughed and the sound echoed off the walls, sounding more like shouts bouncing back. "I'm not sure Father Chisholm would even know what a computer is. He's as old as the hills and more craggy." She wrinkled up her face to demonstrate his cragginess.

I smiled appreciatively. "You should go on stage."

The wrinkled face smoothed out and her shoulders slumped. "I'd like that, but…"

Crap. I'd forgotten her illness. She seemed so vivacious, like a little girl showing off. "Maybe someday," I offered.

"Yes, someday I'll get to do what I want. But today I'm helping you." She looked at the boxes again. "Where do we start?"

I'd been wondering the same thing. "With one box at a time, I guess."

Ophelia sighed, running her finger along the top of one of the boxes. "I'm not much for reading. It makes my head hurt." She gave me an apologetic smile.

"You should go eat," I told her. I didn't want her to go, leaving me in this dark, musty room all alone, but she was sick, after all, and she needed sustenance.

"Maybe I will. Don't go away." She gave me a pleading look. "I'll come back when I'm done."

Before I could say, "I'll be waiting for you," she was gone.

Along with the flashlight and the key, I realized seconds later. I ran to the entryway and called down the dark corridor, but there was no reply. She had flown from the dungeon like an escaping bird. *But she'll be back*, I told myself, though my inner voice wasn't quite as strong as I'd have liked it to be. I'd just have to keep myself busy until her return.

I rubbed my arms to ward off the chill settling over me like a poisonous mist. My darting eyes lit on a box sitting precariously on the edge of the nearest table. I went over and pushed the soft cardboard back into a safer position, then opened it up. Inside was a leather-bound register. I unzipped a pocket on my camera bag and plucked out a pair of rubber gloves, a necessity for any good researcher. Once on, I reached in and pulled out the register. The binding was ragged and torn and I worried about opening the book, possibly ruining it, as it was my only hope right now.

Before coming to Scotland I'd done a fair amount of research on the Internet. Scotland prides itself on its recordkeeping, with well-earned claims of comprehensiveness and an accessibility to records that exceeds other British countries. The Scotlands People website, a government-run site that stores records of births, deaths, marriages, and divorces, should have been the place to track down what I wanted to know. Statutory recordkeeping in Scotland began in 1855. My father's family didn't emigrate until 1870 so I should have been able to find something about them. Unfortunately, I soon discovered that the website only contained Old Parish Registers (OPRs) for the Church of Scotland, which is Protestant, and my father's family had been staunchly Roman Catholic. As of my last login I'd learned that the site had begun acquiring Catholic OPRs, but I still couldn't find what I was looking for. If I wanted the information I needed, and soon, I would have to go to the source—where my ancestors had once lived. So that's what I had done.

My father hadn't wanted me to come to Scotland. "The past is the past, Lily," he'd said as he ate his bran flakes at the kitchen table, one flake caught in his neatly trimmed graying beard. "Just let it go." He was an expert at letting it go, peeling off pieces of his own history like an old coat. Once Catholic, he'd renounced religion altogether thirteen years ago, when I was ten. He now called himself a recovering Catholic, if anyone ever asked—anyone that didn't know our family's past, that is.

More accurately, he hadn't wanted me to leave *him*. I wasn't his only child, just his youngest, and the only one still under his control. He had two other children, my half-brother, Jake, who was thirty-five, and my half-sister, Alice, two years younger. My father had divorced their mother to marry mine and thereafter lost any chance at watching his other two children grow up. In a rage, Sadie, his first wife, had packed up and moved to California.

He had paid for his infidelity in other ways, losing my mother ten years after they'd run off to be together. After that, I'd become his whole life. Maybe because I looked like her and sounded like her. I even dreamed like her, though he wasn't aware of this last bit.

I found out about the dreaming part when I was ten, the same time my mother stopped having her dreams and I started having them. The reason I never told my father about my dreams was because I needed to keep something of myself separate from him. There were times, however, when I wished I could confide in him, or in *someone*. Like my father's endless hovering and constant needs, my dreams were drowning me.

As practical and rational as my father could be, he was terrible with reality. Lucky for him, he'd inherited family money—lots of it. My Grandpa MacKenzie, a math whiz, had invested in all the right things at all the right times. When he died in a car accident—coming home from his mistress's house—his money went to his only living child (dad's younger brother, a police officer, had died three years earlier in a drug raid gone bad). My grandmother died of a heart attack soon after the accident. She hadn't known about the mistress until a 'dear' friend pointed her out at Grandpa's funeral. My mother's parents were a mystery to me. I hadn't ever met them, or for that matter, heard anything about them. Which is strange considering my mother couldn't ever seem to let go of the past, evidenced by the numerous historical books she'd once kept gathered around her like chicks.

My father remains a problem. He has fought to control every aspect of my life, except those areas that bore him. Participating in school activities, the buying of clothes, the preparation of food—all these mundane necessities irritated him. I'd had a nanny of sorts who took care of all that. She was kind enough, but she had her own life, her own large family to love. She didn't have enough energy to mother me, which was fine. I didn't want to be mothered.

That's why I got a job when I was fourteen. That's why I never let my father pay for anything. I tried not to, anyway. He was very good at manipulating me, and I was very good at not figuring it out until too late. Like the time he convinced me to continue living at home. "Save money for a down payment on a house," he'd said, which sounded like a good idea at the time, better than just taking the money from him (though, come to think of it, he never offered). I insisted on paying rent, but then I kept finding all this extra cash in my wallet. When I confronted him, he pleaded ignorance, then went on to say how I had saved his life since "that time" and it was so good to have me here by his side, keeping the loneliness and depression at bay. How could I fight that?

I should be grateful, and I was—for not having to live in poverty—but there came a time when I had to make it on my own. I felt stifled and trapped, as though my father had created a long list of IOUs and when the time came—when I decided to break free—he was going to call in his debts.

Luckily, at the same time I started to do the research that preceded this trip, one of my co-workers, Jamie Flynn, began to show an interest in me. Like most fathers, mine didn't think Jamie was good enough for me. Unlike most fathers, he actively worked to keep us apart. So when I eventually figured out that a trip to Scotland was vital, he practically threw me on the plane, waving and dabbing at his eyes as I headed toward the security checkpoint.

"If you love someone," he'd said in the car ride to Logan Airport, tapping his fingers on the steering wheel to the beat of an 80s pop song and grinning widely, "you must let them go free."

That man was absolutely full of it.

But that was okay, because he didn't know my real reason for going to Scotland. No one did. Not my co-workers, not my boss, Mr. Willeton, not the people here at Dundeid Castle. I intended to keep it that way. I had a feeling that if I didn't, if I let my guard down, then I wouldn't be able to end this. And believe me, I needed to end this.

I returned my attention to the parish records, slowly lifting the cover and peering down at the first page. The script was elaborate, delicate and graceful as a Japanese painting, and nearly impossible to read in the dim light. The mold spots and faded ink didn't help, but I didn't let any of that deter me. I was looking for two things: a name and a date.

Time passed as I crept through page after page, searching. Noises—water dripping, distant clanging, voices—continuously interrupted my pursuit, but I kept going. My tired eyes were beginning to itch when I heard a noise coming from down the hall.

I shall return…

It was barely more than an echo of a whisper, but I heard it as clearly as though it was in my head. "Who's there?" I called.

No answer.

I shall return…

My fingers, already cold, froze into frightened curves. Someone was coming. "Hello?" I forced out. "Is someone there?" I heard a panting sound and footsteps, like something was racing toward me. "It's me, Lily…" my voice quivered, "just doing some work."

"Of course it is, silly!" Ophelia bounced into the room, out of breath, her lovely cheeks flushed. "Hey, that rhymes! I suppose you got that a lot growing up. Anyway, sorry it took me so long. Auntie Viv caught me and made me take my medicine, then she wanted me to rest. Next time, I've half a mind to spit that horrid stuff out. I hate how it makes me feel! Like a damn zombie."

"I didn't notice the time," which wasn't true, but one of those diplomatic white lies. "I've been too busy looking at this." I nodded at the register.

She came up beside me, her slim body shaking slightly with the cold, and I felt positively gargantuan and blooming with health next to her. Protective, as well. She was so fragile. She squinted at the page. "You're going to need some specs after this."

"It's giving me a headache, all right, and I'm starting to suspect these records don't have what I want. The dates are all wrong—too early."

She frowned, the delicate skin between her eyes puckering slightly. "What date do you need to find?"

"This register only runs to the 1850s. I need a slightly later date. I imagine it's in one of the other boxes."

"No, it's not." I glanced over at Ophelia, surprised to hear how excited she sounded when to me this was *not good news.*

"Greg Huntington has been doing his own genealogical research. He took half of the boxes, dating from about 1855 onward."

"You don't say," I replied softly, feeling something tug at my mind.

"This is the perfect excuse for us to go over there!" she continued happily.

Us? "Are you sure you're well enough? You look a little drained," I added for good measure.

She laughed. "I've never felt better. We'll go after dinner."

I glanced at my gold Cartier wristwatch, an expensive gift from my father that I only wore to shut him up about how much it cost. I would have preferred a Timex. "We still have an hour until then. Maybe I should keep looking—"

"You can take my picture instead. I've always wanted to be a model." She struck a dramatic pose, the back of her hand draped across her brow, head thrown back. Then she laughed out loud, ruining the effect.

"The lighting's not the best… "

"Oh, give it a try. Please."

I just want to get out of here.

But she looked so eager and happy that I relented. "Okay, I'll take a few. Stand by the lantern." I didn't have my portrait kit with me, which I used to light scenes when necessary, so I moved the flashlight on the table to shine on Ophelia's face. Both it and the lantern provided a nice sphere of light around her. After peeling off my gloves and returning them to the bag, I fiddled with my camera and hoped I made the right corrections. Some photographers took amazing pictures in low light settings; in that respect I was still a work in progress.

For the next half hour, Ophelia enjoyed posing as I directed her to various spots, adjusting the lighting and my camera. I, too, was having fun, briefly forgetting that I hated it down here.

Finally, I lowered the camera. "I think we have enough."

Ophelia's eyes glittered excitedly. "I really liked that. Maybe I should be a model. Everyone says so, but I'm not so sure I've the looks for it."

"Don't start calling agencies yet," I warned her. "Let's see how your photos turn out. False hope is worse than no hope at all." I'd learned that lesson well.

She shrugged. "But without hope, you might as well be dead." Her flat voice sounded as though she had learned her own lessons on that count.

I pressed the review button and peeked at the first photo. It looked good. "Take a look, diva girl."

She hurried over to peer into the viewer. "I do look good," she breathed. "Go to the next one." Photo after photo showed that Ophelia did indeed have the modeling touch. Most people think modeling is easy, but not everyone can pull it off. There's an element of acting that goes into the effort.

We had neared the end of the photos, to where Ophelia had posed inside one of the cells. I hadn't wanted her to, but she'd insisted. At the very last photo, after Ophelia pulled back from the camera, flushed and pleased with the experience, I leaned in closer. What I saw made me want to scream.

There was someone with her in the cell.

Chapter Five

❦

I managed to convince Ophelia to put off another viewing of the photos until I could download them onto my computer. "When you see them on screen, you'll get a better sense of how they look," I explained, surreptitiously checking the prison cell to be sure no one was hiding in it. What I didn't tell her is that sometimes what looks good in the viewer doesn't translate well into an actual photograph. More importantly, I had to move that strange photo somewhere else so she wouldn't see it, and where I could study it further and prove to myself that the image was only a trick of the light.

I hurriedly packed away my camera. "Let's get out of here," I begged, wishing I'd told Ophelia more about what I was looking for in the first place. Then I wouldn't have wasted an entire morning, wouldn't have had to visit this place, wouldn't have seen that face.

She chattered away at me as we climbed the stairs, and I barely registered what she said, nodding and uh-huhing when it seemed appropriate. In the Great Hall I tried to make a break for my room, but she steered me toward the dining room with a firmness that belied her illness.

"I can't wait to tell Auntie Viv what I've been doing."

"Will she approve of you being down in the dungeon?"

She lifted her chin defiantly. "I don't give a fig. She acts like she's my mother and I'm tired of it. If I want to pose for you, I will."

"Fine. But leave me out of it, okay? I have a job to do." *And getting involved with the people here wasn't a part of the plan.* I was going to have to watch myself. A reporter must remain objective at all times, and here I was, feeling sorry for a sick girl and potentially getting myself into trouble for doing things to jeopardize her health.

I managed to stifle a frustrated sigh as we headed into the dining room, which was empty. Good. No confrontations for the moment. Ophelia directed me to a chair, then sat opposite me. "I can't wait to tell Greg about my modeling. He still thinks of me as little Phe, seven years old and dull as dirt, even though he's only five years older than me." Which put him at thirty, I quickly calculated. "But he acts like decades stand between us, centuries even. I *have* to make him see me as a woman." Her fists clenched emphatically and her lips thinned to two sickly white lines.

"You think modeling will do that?"

"It couldn't hurt." She fiddled with a heavy butter knife and it clunked against the silky white tablecloth. "Nothing else has worked."

Which told me that probably nothing ever would. Still, I was curious and my reporter instincts kicked in. "Tell me about him." I leaned forward, put on my best empathic expression that conveyed, "I've been there," and invited her confidence.

She glanced at the doors to the kitchen and the Great Hall, then, satisfied no one was coming, bent her head toward mine. "He's been away for some time. Only just returned a month ago, actually. He was living in Edinburgh running the family business, which has to do with real estate or construction or something like that. Auntie Viv says he could do his work from his place, with computers and cell phones and all that, but he chooses to work in Edinburgh." She waved an airy hand. "I don't understand what he does, but then," she smiled sweetly, "luckily for me, men don't expect women to be interested in business."

A part of me wanted to argue that not all men were that way. Besides, a lot of women could talk business just as well as, if not better, than any man. But I kept my mouth shut. Reporters don't have opinions. They don't share them, anyway. Certainly not with the person they're interviewing.

"Why did he go away?"

She shrugged, the bones in her shoulders making dents in her thin blouse. "No one tells me anything round here. At thirteen, he was sent off to boarding school in England," which explained his watered down accent, "but he always came back for holidays and summers, thank goodness. And then, when he was eighteen, his mother remarried—his father died when Greg was eleven, from leukemia, I believe—leaving him Mochrie Manor, which is absolutely gorgeous, by the way, along with a boatload of debts from his gambling and his illness. Mrs. Huntington—she's a bit of a flake—wasn't very good with money, either, so even though Greg planned on attending university, he went to Edinburgh instead and took over the business, which was failing at the time."

"And he never came back?"

"If he did, he did it in secret, like a spy." The idea, just now occurring to her, obviously rankled, and her delicate nose wrinkled in annoyance.

"Why doesn't Andrew like him?"

She sighed prettily. "Oh, he's jealous, I suppose. They used to be best friends. We all played together. Andrew, Greg, Auntie Viv, and I." If that was the case, then Vivian was probably closer to thirty than forty. *Dang.* "Dundeid Castle has been in debt forever and it's always falling apart and Andrew has had to turn it into a tourist trap and he hates that sort of thing. He hates having to cater to a bunch of dunderheid tourists."

I had the feeling she was quoting someone, likely Andrew himself. The funny thing was, she'd forgotten that I was one of those *dunderheid* tourists.

"What would he rather do?"

She laughed. "I don't especially know, actually. When he's not riding his horse or fishing or walking the estate, and whatever else it is he does outdoors, he holes up in his special room whenever he can. I'm not sure what he does in there, but once, when I was fifteen or sixteen, I peeked inside and caught a glimpse of lots of dusty books and some old glass bottles on a table before he shut the door in my face."

Sounded intriguing. I might have to take a look at Andrew's special room. He had said I could go anywhere in the castle—carte blanche, straight from the horse's mouth. And now that I knew there was a 'special' room, I had to know what was in there. After what had happened to my mom, I had developed an obsession with uncovering the truth. Unlike most people, who only want to forget about what they don't understand or anything that's too psychologically or emotionally overwhelming, I was like a dog digging for a bone. I had to know. I'm not sure, though, what exactly it was that I was looking for, nor what I would do when I found it.

"You never tried to get in there after that?"

"Oh, I lost interest, I guess." She shrugged and I had the feeling few things ever held Ophelia's interest for long. And those things, or people, that did, suffered for it.

"Really? I couldn't stand knowing there was a secret room filled with all sorts of strange and mysterious things and not want to get inside."

Her eyes focused on mine. "What Andrew does," she answered, her voice disapproving, "is none of my concern."

I pulled back, feeling firmly put in my place. "I see. Of course he has a right to privacy. Just as you do."

Her eyes shifted away. Aha. I had found her Achilles heel. Ophelia had a secret and chances were, it had something to do with Andrew. Immediately, I had to know what it was. As I've said, always having to know is *my* Achilles heel.

The subject of our discussion entered the room at that moment, prompting Ophelia to pull away from me, cheeks flushed. I realized this was the first time I had seen the two of them together. "Hello, Andrew," she greeted airily. "We were just talking about you."

It was my turn to blush. She wouldn't tell him about what, would she?

"All good, I hope?" He paused, considering his words. "Actually, who wants to be all good? Right, Lily?" He turned to face me and once again I was struck by his vitality and good looks.

"Depends on who's doing the judging," I replied.

He laughed. "Good answer." He pulled out his chair at the head of the table and sat down. "Is Viv coming, Phe?"

"I don't know. She didn't say."

He frowned. "Weren't you with her? I thought she was doing some...tests with you today." He glanced sideways at me. I pretended not to notice, fiddling with the napkin in my lap.

"She did. Then I took a nap. Then I joined Lily—down in the dungeon."

He jerked back in his chair. "The dungeon? Hideous place. Why would you want to go down there?"

"Because that's where the parish records are stored, remember?"

"What? Where was I when this happened?"

"You were tending to Nightmare's foaling."

"You have a horse named Nightmare?" I interjected.

He grinned. "She's black as night and she's a mare. I couldn't resist." He turned back to Ophelia. "Who gave old Chissie permission to do that?"

"Auntie Viv. She didn't think it would matter one way or the other. Father Chisholm was quite distraught. It was the least she could do."

"I still don't see how Father Chisolm had visited our home and I wasn't told."

"He didn't come himself. It was that assistant of his...Harry something or other."

"Yes, well, next time I'd like to be asked. I am the...I am responsible, after all."

"Well, not for all the records," I said, spotting a perfect opening. "Apparently Greg Huntington has a number of them. I thought I'd bike to his house after lunch and ask permission to go through the records. The date I'm looking for isn't in the ones here."

"What?" Andrew stared at me as though I'd asked when the next flight to Mars was.

"I thought I'd take her there," Ophelia jumped in, trying unsuccessfully to keep the excitement and yearning out of her voice. "She doesn't know the way."

The look he turned on her could have broken rocks. "Absolutely not, Ophelia. You're busy this afternoon."

"Who's busy?" Vivian asked as she entered the dining room in a navy blue dress uniform similar to the style she wore yesterday. She was slightly winded, as though she'd been running.

"You're late," Andrew informed her. "Where were you?" There seemed to be more to the question, to the accusation, than just a reprimand or a request for information.

She sat down. "I'm quite aware of the time, Andrew. One of our tenants has pneumonia—Mrs. Brodie. I just bundled her off to hospital. I think she'll be all right, but I didn't want to take chances."

"Dr. Weatherby couldn't handle it?"

"He was attending to his patients. I sometimes think you forget he's not our private physician, Andrew."

He leaned back in his chair. "After dinner, Ophelia wants to escort our guest to Huntington's place." Realizing he had lost whatever argument he'd been trying to make, Andrew changed tactics. He seemed to want to be angry with Vivian.

"I can't imagine you'd be up to that, Phe." Vivian's face, except for a slight pucker in her lower lip, was devoid of emotion. "When starting a new medication, one wants to be careful."

Unlike Andrew, Vivian felt no need to hide Ophelia's medical condition. I avoided meeting Andrew's eyes, which I'm sure were assessing my response.

Ophelia looked ready to cry, her eyes welling with misery. "I'm only trying to be helpful. Lily wants to go and doesn't know how to get there so I volunteered to take her. What's wrong with that?"

Was she truly throwing me under the bus, or had she forgotten how much she wanted to go herself? Maybe she couldn't admit the real reason to them, or she'd be banned for certain from going. Though, really, she was an adult. Why couldn't she come and go as she pleased?

"If you give me directions, I'll walk there myself. I really don't want to cause trouble."

"Why do you need to go to Huntington's?" Vivian's attention was on me and again I felt that threat—of attack, of warning, of something. I wasn't sure what exactly was going on, but I was determined to find out why a woman who'd never met me found me threatening.

"I need to do research for my article. Apparently he has some of the parish records."

"I'll send Brian round to fetch them," she told me crisply. "No need for you to go all that way. In fact, I advise against it. You're only just recovering yourself."

"I feel fine. Yesterday was just a matter of jet lag and not eating. Even my wrist feels better." I determined to take the wrap off at my first opportunity so she could no longer use it as an excuse against me.

"He lives a few kilometers away, Lily," Andrew told me, soundly faintly amused. "Quite a ways to walk, I'd say. I'd drive you myself, but I have a previous engagement. Perhaps you'd like to come along? Ask me questions about the locals? Wouldn't that help with your research?"

What would help is if you both would stop trying to keep me from seeing Greg Huntington. Still, I didn't want to make too many waves. Not yet. I avoided Ophelia's eyes. "All right. I guess I could pick your mind."

"Splendid." Ophelia glared at him, then twisted away to stare out the window, her stiff back and set jaw sending out waves of discontent. Could her secret be that she hated her own cousin?

"I'll send Brian to fetch the parish register," Vivian suggested. "Just the register, right?"

"Um, yes. That should do it." I didn't say that if the register provided the information I wanted, then I'd need to see all the other paperwork the parish might have in their possession. Which would still mean a visit to Mr. Huntington, even if I had to sneak over there to do it. I needed to track down Brian and ask him about the state of my bike. I had some spending money courtesy of Mr. Willeton and my own meager bank account. If he had to buy a new tire, so be it. I needed that bike. Renting a car, I realized too late, would have been a better idea. But I hadn't, so I could only curse my own stubbornness and lack of foresight, and hope for the good weather to hold. It was nearly a useless hope. It was November in the Scottish Highlands, after all, and snow was not out of the question. Still, I'd biked in the snow more than once during an unexpected Nor'easter. I would do it again, if need be.

Gertie pushed a silver cart bearing a tureen of hot soup into the room, followed later by platters of roast beef, thick bread, hunks of cheese, and a bottle of wine. Because of my mother, I rarely drank, but when in Rome…well, it seemed like the thing to do. So, after Andrew had given the bottle his approval, I didn't stop Gertie from pouring the rich, red liquid into my crystal wine glass.

"I hope you enjoy this little gem," he said, raising his glass to me. "Slainte."

"Slainte," I replied, tilting my glass toward him, then to a morose Ophelia who had only water in her glass, then to a thoughtful Vivian, before lowering it to inhale its earthy bouquet. I placed the cool glass to my lips and took a sip. The wine passed over my tongue, swirled around my mouth, and ended as a warm, spicy river flowing down my throat. Lowering the glass, I smiled at Andrew who was waiting for my reaction. "Excellent," I declared. I had once written an article on wine tasting, attending a one-week class at a local winery. I wasn't a sommelier by any means, but my taste buds had been schooled enough to appreciate a good wine.

"It's one of Dundeid's own. From 1870."

I gasped, nearly choking. So old, and undoubtedly extremely rare. And also, coincidentally, the year my father's family left Scotland to sail to America. "I'm honored, Andrew."

I drank again, feeling as though I was taking sips of the past. I detected a familiar woodsy flavor, like renewing an old acquaintance, and shivered with delight. At that moment, I became aware of Vivian's gaze. I glanced over and found her blue eyes regarding me shrewdly. A smile followed, though the expression in her eyes never changed.

Her cool assessment unnerved me. "Before coming here," I pushed out, "I read somewhere that Scottish people, like New Englanders, take some time to welcome newcomers. I see that the occupants of Dundeid are an exception." I said this with a smile, though underneath I was wondering why such a hearty welcome, and for someone they'd never met.

It's so good to have you here, Lilia. I've missed you more than I thought possible.

The words slid into my head and when I realized who'd spoken them, I promptly bit down on my tongue. *Andrew. Wasn't it?* I couldn't quite remember.

"But we're welcoming one of our own," Andrew claimed. "Once a Highlander, always a Highlander."

I peeked at Ophelia who was staring at her cousin in an odd way, as though trying to figure out what he was up to. Vivian was calmly eating her soup.

"But that remains to be seen."

"I know what you are, Lily," Andrew said. "I know *who* you are. And I welcome you."

My lips smiled, my head quickly ducked low to hide my eyes, which, like Vivian's, were not smiling at all. What did Andrew know about me? What did he think he knew?

"Thank you," I said softly, strangely demur. "I'm glad to be here."

When my eyes lifted, I found Ophelia now had me in her scopes, regarding me carefully—a specimen in a jar. Then she winked and I knew I was forgiven for mucking up her plans this afternoon. She understood what I was up against. She lived with these people. All of them were intractable and immovable as the mountains surrounding the castle.

"So what was I needed to do today?" she asked Andrew, turning to look at him.

"You're helping me make calls for the Gala event," Vivian answered for him. "We need to confirm several vendors. Remember?"

Ophelia shook her head. "You never said…"

"I did say. Really, Ophelia. This forgetfulness of yours is why we're changing your medication." Vivian turned to me. "Ophelia told you about her illness?"

"She mentioned it, yes."

"Then you would agree that it's important we don't do anything to overexcite her."

I glanced at Ophelia. Her lips were pale, quivering with repressed anger at being treated like a child in front of a stranger. I didn't blame her, and could also understand why at times she tended to *act* like a child. "On the other hand, you can't let her get too bored," I said. "Boredom can be just as unhealthy as overdoing it, especially for young people."

Vivian's dark eyebrows rose, either in response to my arguing with her or to my apparent exclusion of myself from the 'young people' group. "Of course. Which is why we keep her busy. Ophelia is never bored. Right, Ophelia?"

But Ophelia was once more staring out the window at the loch, arms crossed tightly over her chest. Vivian shrugged as if to say, "See?"

Poor Ophelia.

We finished our meal with desultory conversation, Vivian asking surprisingly knowledgeable questions about New Hampshire. What was the climate like? What did the tourists like to see? Did New Hampshirites really believe in our motto, "Live Free or Die?"

"Absolutely."

Andrew listened intently to my answers, seemingly content with his passive role in the conversation. At my last answer, though, he perked up. "Would you really be willing to die for your freedom?"

"Of course I would. Without freedom, life isn't worth living."

"If you were imprisoned, you'd want to die," he interpreted.

"Oh, I doubt I'd take it that far," I laughed. "It's more about the principle of freedom. The freedom to choose, to think and say what I like, to be self-sufficient."

"I'm of the opinion," Vivian intruded, "that there are certain people who need to be told what to think and what to say." She held up her hands to stay my protest, at the same time studiously keeping her eyes off Ophelia. "I'm not being hardhearted, I'm being practical. What do you say about the numerous voters in your country who vote for a candidate they don't know anything about? Wasn't a monkey once voted into office?" I shrugged, feigning ignorance, because most likely one had. She went on, unimpeded. "Too many people in this world are uninformed and uneducated and often make choices that will harm them."

I leaned back in my chair, pretending to consider her logic. "Hm. Yes. That sounds quite rational, Vivian. It also sounds exactly like what men used to think about *women*. Some still do." I glanced at Andrew, wanting to catch his reaction. His expression, though, was bland, giving nothing away.

Vivian was not impressed. "Women can be very silly. I've met more than my fair share."

"I've met more than my fair share of silly men," I countered. "That doesn't mean I condemn them to living out their lives as mirrors, reflecting only what they see!"

"Well," Vivian huffed, her nostrils flaring as she threw her napkin on the table. "I see you're quite the modern woman, Lily. Good for you." She rose from the table, banging her chair against it as she pushed it in. "If you'll excuse me, I have loads of work to do. I'll ask Brian to fetch your records. Ophelia, come." She held out her hand, the look in her eye brooking no argument. Ophelia glanced at me, then over at Andrew.

"Go along now," he told her. "We want you well, don't we? And part of that is taking on your share of responsibility."

"I thought you were on my side, Andrew." Her fingers were curled into tight cauliflowers. Not hate for him, then, but something else?

"I *am* on your side, Phe. Someday you'll see that."

She looked doubtful. "I think you believe that now, cousin. But in the end, I believe you'll sacrifice me for the greater good."

I stared at her. Sometimes she said the most cryptic things, as though it wasn't really her, but an older and wiser version speaking.

On her way out she didn't once look at me. My eyes fell on her plate, noting she had eaten very little, the various foods built up into strange shapes—a cheese pyramid, a road of beef, balls of bread dribbled with soup. No doubt she would sneak into the kitchen later on to eat. I hoped.

Andrew tapped the table with the end of his butter knife. "So it's just you and me, Lily."

I've missed you more than I thought possible.

Had he really said that earlier? Or had I imagined the words? All at once I remembered when he'd spoken them—right as I was drifting off to sleep the previous night. A deceptive time, when the mind is straining to be released from the chains of consciousness. Anything could happen then, including creating what isn't really there. I didn't want those words to be a product of my imagination, though. I wanted them to be real.

"What are we up to, then?" I asked, drinking the last of my wine, then checking for any dregs. I had never tasted anything so lovely in my life.

"I'm heading to one of the estate's crofts to check its roof."

"Do you mind if I download the photos I took in the dungeon first? My card's full."

"I can't see why you'd want to be reminded of that dreary hole in the ground. Viv always wanted to play down there when we were bairns. Not me. Too dark and too many ghosts. Fresh air and sun, that's all I've ever wanted. Viv especially liked locking other people up. She always let them out, of course."

I shivered. "I wasn't exactly thrilled with the place myself. Did you really see ghosts down there?"

He laughed, then stood up. "Of course not. But I'm sure they were there. What's a dungeon without ghosts?" I pushed back my chair, wondering if he was telling the truth. "I'll meet you outside in twenty minutes?"

"Sounds good."

It took me ten minutes to find a plug-in in my room, hidden behind the wardrobe and coated in dust. Someone was neglecting her duties.

Gertie, perhaps? I smiled to myself. It might make good blackmailing material if I needed to grill her at a later date. Not as advantageous as a criminal offense, but maybe just as bad in a house that survived on keeping guests happy. I'd never tell on her, of course, but she didn't know that.

Turning the computer on and importing the photos took another five minutes. Once the pictures were downloaded, I scrolled through to the very last photo in the group. Double clicking it enlarged the photo and I leaned in for a closer look. I blinked twice, then looked again.

I had captured a ghost on film.

Chapter Six

❈

I glanced at my watch, feeling shaky, but there was nothing I could do for the moment. Andrew would be waiting for me. I closed the program, then the lid, not bothering to shut down. As soon as I returned, I would enlarge the image and sharpen the details. Then I'd be able to see who this 'ghost' was. One of Andrew's ancestors? Or maybe an ancient enemy. More likely a trick of the eye or a dust mote. I found it amazing how often, upon closer inspection, what looked like one thing turned out to be something entirely different. I could only hope that this was one of those times.

Camera case in place, I bounded down the stairs, two at a time. My feet seemed awfully eager to rush to Andrew's side. My mind forced them to slow—no need to look desperate. Moving at a more sedate pace, I left the castle. A warm breeze out of the west caressed my forehead as I waited in the courtyard. A moment later a battered black Jeep appeared from around the castle and skidded to a stop five feet from where I stood. The door swung open and I climbed in.

"Your chariot has arrived." Andrew grinned as he shifted into gear and sped off down the tree-lined, dirt drive. About a hundred yards along, the road split in two. We took the track to the left, passing through a section of thick woods, which soon opened up to reveal glorious hills, undulating across the landscape like massive burial mounds.

"Phe likes Huntington, doesn't she?" Andrew asked, shifting as the Jeep climbed upward.

Talk about sticking someone between a rock and a hard place. "Um, well…"

He laughed, glancing over at me. "Don't worry. I've already guessed it. She's not very subtle, our Phe. She's also got extremely bad luck when it comes to the opposite sex, doomed always to fall in love with the wrong man. Huntington isn't the first, you see."

"Poor girl."

"Girl? She's hardly that any more, though I do see what you mean. I suppose we're to blame—Viv and myself. We watch her very closely. But everyone needs someone to look after them, don't you agree?"

I wasn't sure that I did. "My Great Aunt Minnie never married and as far as I know, never lived with anyone."

"Ah, but was she happy?"

I took a moment to consider his question. I hadn't seen her since I was nine and my memories of her were through a child's eyes—distorted, faded, distant. "I believe she was. She lived in a small cottage and wrote a column for the newspaper and read lots of books and had a garden. She might have had a close friend or two. I think I remember them being mentioned in the postcards she occasionally sent. She lived on an island off the coast of Maine. Very isolated, but I got the impression that she wanted it that way. I think I wouldn't mind that life so much myself. Not having to answer to anyone, not being tied down."

"That would be a waste, Lily. You, alone, and not sharing your life with someone you loved. A real shame, that."

I thought of living with my father—how stifling he could be, how responsible I felt for him. I never wanted to go through that with anyone again. If I had to remain single to stay free, so be it. "I think the world will survive without *me* getting married," I said with a laugh, though I was perfectly serious.

He didn't share my mirth. "Your parents approve of this?"

"It's partly because of them that I'm choosing to live differently."

He looked thoughtful. "My mother's biggest hope for me is that I marry."

"That's so sad."

He roared, slapping his palm on the steering wheel. Twice we almost went off the road. "Please! I don't want your sympathy."

"All right. I won't give it. But I will wish you good luck. Hopefully whatever you choose to do will make both of you happy."

He rubbed his face and I noticed the scars that whitened two of his knuckles. "I wish I did have a choice."

I was about to protest that one always has a choice, but something about the set of his jaw stifled my words. "So what can you tell me about the people of this area?" I asked instead.

"Your people, you mean?" His eyes sparkled teasingly.

"That remains to be seen."

"We Scots are a stubborn folk, as full of pride as a bucket after a rainstorm, and we like to think of ourselves as great warriors. We're independent and maybe a bit moody, but always entertaining."

"You made up that last bit, didn't you?"

"I wouldna do that," he spoke with a sharpened Scottish burr, "tae such a bonny lass as yersel."

"You just did."

"Did I mention that we like to fight?"

I smiled. "So are there any MacKenzies around here?"

"We're visiting one today."

"Really?" My heart jolted in my chest. "Is that why you wanted me to come with you today?" So his motives in putting off my visit to Greg Huntington weren't entirely impure. I was sure, however, that Vivian's were.

He nodded. "His name's Ian MacKenzie. He looks after the estate's sheep and in return gets a small wage and stays in the croft free of rent. Sheep are hardier nowadays and don't need as much looking after, but he does the sheering and the lambing and when needed, the slaughtering. He's a throwback to another time. He even milks the sheep and makes cheese. We sell it at the castle gift shop—you haven't seen that yet, have you?" I shook my head. I wasn't interested in trinkets; I sought a different sort of souvenir. "He's a bit of a recluse, like what you claim you want to be. He might be a good lesson to you on the dangers of isolation."

"I can't wait to meet him."

"Well, that's the difference between you. He *can* wait to meet you. In fact, he'd be happier left alone. He's a bit of a curmudgeon."

"Surely he'll answer a few of my questions?"

Andrew shrugged. "That remains to be seen."

The car dipped and righted, knocking us back and forth. The road was growing rough and I kept quiet, allowing Andrew to concentrate on his driving. Despite the poor terrain, he kept the pedal to the metal. Soon enough, the seatbelt I'd forgotten to buckle was grabbed and clicked into place. Afterwards, I held on for dear life as best I could with my one good arm. Whenever I could, though, I snapped photos of the starkly beautiful landscape. I doubted they'd turn out, but I couldn't help myself.

A small grassy track veered off to the right, which Andrew took without pause. We climbed the track for ten minutes, then descended into a rocky valley spotted with sheep. As we rounded a sharp corner, a small stone cottage with a thatched roof and a chimney burping smoke came into view. A mangy dog, spotted black and white and brown, lifted its chin, barked lazily, then glanced back at the cottage expectantly. A few moments later the door opened and a tall man emerged, holding a shotgun. His hair was as steely gray as the sky overhead, his eyes green like my own.

Andrew stopped the Jeep and rolled down his window. "What business have ye here?" the man demanded, waving the weapon at us.

Andrew leaned out the window. "Relax, Ian. I've come to check on the roof and I brought you a visitor."

"The roof's fine. I told ye I'd take care of it."

"Using what?" Andrew said calmly. "Looks to me," he said, squinting up at the roof, "that you're going to need some wood and new thatch. The birds are taking it all."

"Stop yer haverin', boy! I've been seein' tae this roof for decades. I'll see it through a few more, I reckon."

Andrew laughed. "You let it go like this, Ian, and I'll be dragging your cold, dead body out that door within the year."

Ian scowled. "I dinna like visitors." He nodded at me.

"Even one of your own?"

The scowl deepened. "Especially one of me own."

I couldn't help myself. I laughed. For that slip, I earned all of Mr. MacKenzie's attention focused solely on me. "I've got a MacKenzie that I'd just as soon not have around myself," I hastened to explain. "At least not as often."

The eyes narrowed, then Mr. MacKenzie came to a decision. "Coom inside. Ye," he glared at Andrew, "can wait in that contraption. And next time ye get it in yer fool heid to 'help' me, feel free tae jump in the loch tae rid yersel of the notion."

Andrew's jaw tightened. "Now see here, MacKenzie…" But Ian had turned and entered the little hut.

I glanced at Andrew, shrugged, then followed after the man. Inside, the hut was surprisingly warm, despite Andrew's warnings about imminent death. The décor was a bit bare for my tastes, but homey enough. A book lay open on a simple wood table. A cast iron pot hung on a long hook, which swung out from the wall to extend over the fire. I smelled stew, most likely mutton. A wheel of pale, creamy cheese rested on a thick blue plate. Next to it sat a silver pitcher. The shotgun seemed to have disappeared.

Ian grabbed a mug from a shelf near the table and filled it from the pitcher. He sliced off a hunk of cheese and handed it and the mug to me. After indicating a chair in front of the fire, he poured a mug and sliced a generous hunk of cheese for himself.

"I'd offer ye some stew, but it's not done yet."

"Oh, thank you. This will be great." I took a delicate bite of the soft cheese, which reminded me of Camembert. The flavor was earthy and rich and I took another, larger, bite. Lifting the mug to my mouth, I smelled honey and strong alcohol before taking a sip. It was mead.

Again, my wine classes were coming in handy. Mead, I'd learned, was honey wine and rarely made today. The drink was delicious, sweet, and very strong.

We sat and ate in companionable silence, for the moment neither of us feeling the need to speak. I knew Ian wanted to say something, but I let him get to it in his own time. Some people would not, *could not*, be rushed. Interviewing a reluctant subject requires patience. Sometimes you simply have to wait. Eventually they'll talk. They all do. Everyone has something to say. Everyone wants to be heard.

Even Ian, a man who, according to Andrew, spoke little, if at all, to anyone. Normally I would be burning with curiosity. But today I enjoyed what I was doing here and now—eating cheese and drinking honey wine and toasting my toes in front of a blazing fire.

"I'm guessin'," Ian finally spoke into the warm silence, "that yer descendant left Dundeid tae travel tae America." He cleared his throat, already growing raspy from use. "How did ye find oot aboot us MacKenzies back here in Scotland?"

"Well, I wasn't sure if any of you were still around. But I found a letter, dated 1870, posted from Dundeid. I believe it was your ancestor who wrote to his brother, Robert—my ancestor—pretty much damning him."

Ian looked surprised. "For what?"

"He didn't say. I thought you could tell me. You see," I paused, wondering if I could trust him. Then I remembered who he was. Ian, the recluse. Who would he tell? Besides, he seemed trustworthy. "You see, Mr. MacKenzie, I keep having these dreams. They've been haunting me for years, actually. I thought that if I came here, I could find out a few things, and then my dreams would stop running my life."

Okay, so much for my trusting him. I hadn't really told him anything. Years of always asking, but never telling, was a hard habit to break. But Ian didn't seem to mind as he lit up a pipe. The pungent smell of tobacco filled the air, blending with the crisp smell of wood smoke. "If ye want tae ken yersel, sometimes ye got tae look tae yer past."

I leaned forward. "What are you saying?"

"Everyone these days, they're tryin' tae find who they are. But yer quest's a bit different." Smoke curled upward, obscuring his Celtic eyes.

I bit my lip, my hands wrapping more tightly around my half-empty mug. "If you know something, please tell me."

"We've both been through this before."

"What do you mean?"

"This goin' in circles. Round and round. I'm growin' weary. I want this tae end."

"Want *what* to end?" I breathed, my voice barely a whisper. "What are you talking about, Mr. MacKenzie?"

"Time'll tell. The only thing I have of worth tae pass along tae ye is tae be sure ye dinna trust the wrong one. Trust yer instincts. Dinna heed words—they come cheap. Heed only what yer heart tells ye."

I stared at him. "My heart is what gets me into trouble, Mr. MacKenzie. Every time I give in—because my heart tells me it's the right thing to do—I end up paying a price for it. I'm tapped, Mr. MacKenzie. I have nothing left to give. From here on out, I have to listen to my head. You must see what I mean." I realized my hands, my entire body, were entreating him to say, "Yes, lassie, I understand exactly." But he didn't, and I quickly pulled back.

He stared into the fire, softly puffing on his pipe. There was a quiet *hiss, hiss* as he pulled the smoke into his lungs. Seconds later it crept back out around the stem of his pipe. "Noo ye understand why I live alone."

There was silence after that. I finished my drink, then stood up, a little wobbly. Ian didn't move, mesmerized by the fire, perhaps, or simply too tired to stand again. I thought he must be in his seventies at least. I set the mug on the table and headed quietly for the door. Opening it, I turned back. "Thank you for the cheese and wine, Mr. MacKenzie. For listening."

"I'll be here, Lilia," he roused himself to speak, though he didn't turn his head. "If ye need me, I'll be here."

"I'll remember that."

It was only when I climbed into the car to sit next to an obviously irate Andrew that I realized that Ian had known my name. And like Greg and Andrew he had called me Lilia. That could only mean one thing. I had come to the right place.

Chapter Seven

※

Andrew had the grace to wait sixty whole seconds before exploding. "What the hell took you so long in there?" We were already halfway down the drive by that point. Those seconds seemed rather like what I would imagine suffocating to death would feel like. His ire sucked all the oxygen out of the car. At one point, I cracked the window and pulled in fresh air.

"He's not exactly a fast talker," I snapped, the effects of the strong alcohol emboldening me. "And besides, why did you bring me with you, if not to help me?"

"You were in there for half an hour while I sat outside freezing my arse off!"

"Oh please, Andrew," I retorted, not backing down. "It couldn't have been more than fifteen minutes, tops. Besides, you wanted me to talk to Mr. MacKenzie and I did. Don't you want to know what he said?"

"You're going to tell me?" He sounded disbelieving.

The Jeep rocked from side to side and my elbow banged against the door. "Why wouldn't I?"

"You don't strike me as the type of person who shares her secrets easily."

"This isn't exactly a secret. Anyone could find it out."

His long fingers tapped the steering wheel. "Save me the effort, then?"

"When I'm good and ready." I crossed my arms.

"All right, all right! I know when I've been beaten. I'm an absolute blackguard, Miss MacKenzie, and I'm sorry I bit your head off." "You'd better be sorry, and apology accepted. Mr. MacKenzie confirmed that my father's family came from this area. Ian is, in fact, a relative of mine. And he makes very good cheese."

Andrew's laughter was more like a celebratory shout. "I knew it! You're one of us! I told you!"

"So did you tell him my whole name?"

"Oh, sorry. I forgot to introduce you, didn't I? Bad manners on my part, I'm afraid."

I fiddled with a stray thread on my camera strap. "No problem. I just thought maybe he'd heard it through the grapevine." But that wouldn't have happened—Ian avoided people. Andrew didn't pick up on my line of thought, however, which was that Ian MacKenzie had no way of knowing my first name and yet he did. "We'll have to celebrate your discovery. Maybe this will be what finally convinces Ian to grace our annual Dundeid Castle Gala."

"I doubt that, but it sounds interesting."

"As part of our kick-off for the holidays, we hold a fair," he explained, looking rather proud. "Later in the evening we host the Dundeid Gala Ball—you've yet to see the ballroom, I'll warrant. Local businesses donate the food and drink and we let them advertise on our website for the year. Viv came up with the idea. She's got an amazing mind for business. Not sure why she went into nursing."

"To help people?" I ventured.

"Oh, yes. That, of course. But still…to waste such a mind." He sighed. I had a feeling he'd just as soon hand over all of the castle management to her. "Anyway, that will be on Saturday." He grimaced. "Less than a week away. We prepare all year, but still, the last couple days are hellish."

"If you need any help…"

He waved his hand. "Thanks, but we've got it covered. That's what Phe and Viv are doing now, in fact. I imagine I should join them."

"Well, let me know if anything comes up. I don't mind helping."

"You're our guest, Lily. But I appreciate the offer. You'd fit in quite well at Dundeid." He glanced over at me, his eyes appraising. "What else did MacKenzie tell you?"

"Um, well, not much. We mostly sat and ate cheese and drank mead."

"He shared his mead with you? Well, now. I'm impressed. How'd you manage that?"

I shrugged. "Must just be my natural way with people."

Andrew grinned. "Must be. That man wouldn't share a secret with God, and certainly not his mead." I had a feeling that Ian's ancestor had been the same way and had not shared the story about his brother with his family or anyone else. Perhaps he'd even led people astray, with a word here or there, about what had really happened. The MacKenzie pride wouldn't let him do anything else.

"Well, it was very good. I'm sorry you're not worthy."

"Me, too." This time the look he aimed at me lasted longer, but I didn't meet it, turning to gaze out the window at the incredible scenery, pretending to be focused on it, but instead thinking furiously. What role did Andrew play in all this? My dreams were nightmares for good reason—someone in them wanted me dead. Was it him? I hoped not. I was starting to like him quite a bit. He was incredibly good looking, which didn't hurt his cause, and he was easy to talk to. He also acted like a mature adult (other than getting mad about being left out in the cold at Ian's croft), which was something I didn't see enough of back home.

"We're home," he announced, startling me. I had become so involved in my thoughts that the scenery had failed to register. He turned off the Jeep. "You'll be all right on your own?"

I nodded. "I might take some photos of the castle, if you don't mind."

"Not at all. Go anywhere you want. I hope that you grow to love the place as I do."

"That won't be hard to do."

He smiled, pleased. "You see? You really are one of us."

We both climbed out of the car and with a half salute, Andrew disappeared into the castle, taking his radiance with him. The day grew suddenly dreary, the castle looming, and I found I didn't want to go inside just yet. Instead, I wandered around back to the loch, passing a series of small buildings with dusty windows—a warm light spilling from one—after which came an extensive flower garden.

The loch was immense, even though half of it was hidden around a bend. Dark as a mirror at night, it made for great photos. Standing on the sandy beach, I snapped the mountains reflected in the water, zoomed in on a bird skimming the loch's surface, then focused on the dark clouds scudding across the sky. When it started to rain, I shoved my camera into its case before the downpour began and raced back to the castle. Breathing hard, I scurried inside, just as the deluge broke, and headed up to my room. Once there, I discovered the door slightly ajar. Had Ophelia come up to see me? If so, I was going to have to set some boundaries with her—no entering my room without permission.

Full of indignation, I pushed open the door and strode in. But it wasn't Ophelia I found. It was Greg Huntington, and he was sitting on the edge of my bed as though he had a right to be there. "You!"

He was holding a large book in his hands, opened halfway through. At the sound of my voice, his head swung up, and his expression transformed from fervent study to cautious delight. "Hello, Lily."

"What are you doing in my room?"

"I wanted to see how you were faring."

My brow furrowed. "Oh. Well, I'm fine. As you can see. Your telephone's not working?"

He held up the book. "I brought you this."

I stared at it suspiciously. "What is it?"

"The parish register. Brian came to fetch it, but I thought I'd bring it myself." When I made no attempt to take the register from him, he set it down on the bed.

"I was under the impression that you weren't exactly welcome here."

"No, I'm not exactly welcome here, but I try not to let trivial matters deter me."

"So what did you do to get banished?"

"What did *I* do?" He pressed an offended hand to his chest. I took note of the dark hairs that skirted the edge of his hand and rode up his arm, disappearing beneath a white cuff. "Why would you assume that I'm the villain? You aren't playing to the stereotype, are you? Golden boy versus the dark, swarthy bad guy?"

I studied him. Was he putting on an act? Though he could be right. Where Andrew radiated brightness, Greg Huntington seemed to repel it. If Andrew was the sun, Greg was a black hole. "All right. If Andrew started it, then why?"

"How should I know?" He pushed away from the bed and meandered around the room, restless. I stared at his broad shoulders hunched slightly, hands clasped behind him, as he peered out the window.

"Ophelia thinks that Andrew is jealous of you because you have money and don't have to open up your home to tourists."

Greg spun around, his expression fierce. "This started before I made money. We used to be best friends. I just don't get it and it kills me that he hates me now." His eyes begged for understanding, pulling me in as though an invisible thread linked us together. Then he blinked, and just like that, I was shut out again.

"Ophelia said you all played together as children."

"That's true."

"So what happened?"

"I told you. I don't know." He rubbed at his forehead. "I wish I did."

"Are you jealous of Andrew?"

For a moment, Greg's features seemed almost demonic. Then he smiled, though there was no humor in it. "Isn't everyone?" His right hand spun a thick, silver bracelet shaped like a snake biting its own tail around and around his left hand.

"It's different for you. I can tell."

"So you're a psychiatrist now?"

"Let's just say I've had to learn a lot about human nature, in order…" I stopped, not wanting to give too much away.

"Go on. Finish the sentence." His eyes, those other worlds, were merciless. I couldn't escape. My hands started to tremble.

"In order to survive," I finished quietly.

"Ah, yes. It hasn't been easy for you, has it?"

My wits sharpened and I jerked back from the abyss. "What do you mean?"

"I know about what happened to your mother."

"What? How?" I couldn't breathe. I'd told no one about her. Ever.

"You're not the only one here who can investigate. The Internet is a great tool, isn't it?"

"You can't… You don't know *everything*." Lord, it was hard to even swallow.

"I know enough."

This subject had to change…*now*. I was not going to travel down that dead-end road. Not here, not in this place, not ever, if I could help it. "Why did you call me Lilia?" I gasped, desperate.

His confidence wavered. "When?"

"On the road. When I fell off my bike. You called me Lilia."

He shook his head. "I didn't know your name until I heard Vivian speak it. And she said Lily. Not Lilia."

"No, I heard you say it." Andrew and Ian MacKenzie had called me Lilia, too.

"Why would I have called you by name when I didn't know who you were or even that you were coming?"

I stared hard at him, daring him to fess up. "All right," I conceded. "Maybe I heard you wrong. But you *did* forbid me to go to Dundeid Castle."

His expression was surprised and I caught a hint of vulnerability in his sharp features. "I did no such thing. I'm not the kind of man who goes round telling people I've never met what to do." He paused. "However, if I were that sort of man, I certainly would've told you to stay away from this place."

"Why?"

"Because of Andrew, of course. He doesn't need to have yet another female mooning after him like a love-struck teenager."

My eyes widened in indignation and I very nearly stomped my foot. "I'm not mooning after him!"

"You will be." I kept waiting for him to laugh, but he didn't crack a smile.

"Even if I did *moon* after him, it would be *my* business and certainly none of yours."

Suddenly the air in the room grew close and hot. I felt stifled, suffocated. My chest rose and fell like ocean waves. "You can't possibly mean to stay here," Greg spoke from a distance. "Not after all that has happened to you."

"I am a guest here, Mr. Huntington." My voice sounded strange, and everything around me seemed like a dream, hazy and incomplete. "I shall stay."

"You don't understand. I have reasons for warning you off."

"And what might those be?" My words echoed in my ears and I grew warmer.

"I don't even understand them myself. It's just a feeling. I get them sometimes."

"Mr. Huntington—"

"Please call me Gregor."

"Gregor, then," I pushed out, feeling faint. "I cannot just leave. I am here to—"

A cool breeze wafted past me, blowing away the heat, which threatened to engulf my senses. My eyes met his. He looked distant as though miles and years away.

"Did you just call me Gregor?" he demanded.

I shook my head. "No," I lied. "Of course not." But I had. He'd asked me to, hadn't he?

He reached out to me, possibly testing to see if I was real, or a ghost. When his hand touched my arm, I shivered as though someone had trod upon my grave, but I let it stay where it was. "You can, you know. I'll call you Lilia. It'll be our secret."

I yanked my arm away. "I'm tired of secrets! Don't you know that's what I'm here to do?"

His eyebrows drew together, not understanding. "What do you mean?"

"I'm here to learn secrets, Gregor. Root them out if need be."

"And what is it that you think you're going to find?"

"I'll know it when I find it." I turned my back on him, headed to my laptop, and opened it. "Now, I have work to do. If you'd show yourself out, I'd appreciate it."

"This conversation isn't over." His voice was low, almost threatening.

My hackles rose and I fought to remain calm. "It is for now. When I need to speak to you again, I'll find you. Until then, leave me be. I won't be hassled."

"Is that what you think I'm doing?" I shrugged, sensing his presence close by. The photo program opened and I quickly searched for the Dungeon Folder I'd created.

Odd. I couldn't find it. Something must have gone wrong with the file. Well, it didn't matter. The photo program always stored the original downloads in the last import folder. I clicked on it and scanned through all the photos I'd taken on my trip so far. There were several from Edinburgh and quite a few I took on my bike trip—I especially liked the massive Victorian building I'd captured about ten miles back. But there were no dungeon photos.

Frantic, I ran a search for dungeon, for the year, for the month. Nothing came up. I smacked the table with my hand, furious.

"Is something wrong?" Gregor had come to stand behind me, peering over my shoulder at the computer screen.

I rounded on him. "What did you do?"

His eyes widened and he held up his hands. "Listen, spitfire, I didn't do anything. So you can just stop aiming those lasers at me."

"Someone deleted my pictures!"

He frowned. "All of them?"

"Don't play innocent! You were the only one in here!"

"I was in your room for all of five minutes before you came, and I didn't touch your computer."

"Someone did." Five minutes was enough time...he could have done it.

"Well, it wasn't me. Are you sure you didn't just put them somewhere else?"

"I'm sure." I felt sick. The ghost photo was gone and now I'd never know who or what it was. Someone had come into my room and not only violated my privacy, but destroyed my property.

But who?

"You'd better go," I said, my voice thick with disappointment, and something else—fear.

"I'll be back, uninvited or not, Lilia. Know this. You said you came here to uncover secrets, but I think you're hiding one of your own."

I swallowed hard. He'd said he knew about my mother. But did he know everything?

"Just go."

"I will. But I'll be back. You can't stop me. Until we meet again, Lilia." The last words were soft, distant.

They echoed in my mind long after Gregor left.

Chapter Eight

❀

I spent the next twenty minutes searching my computer for the photos. In the end, they were nowhere to be found, not even in the computer's trash. If only I'd saved them on my USB-stick! Frustrated, I imported pictures of the loch and the croft onto my computer, carefully checking each for ghostly faces. There were none.

To be on the safe side, I copied all the photos I'd taken so far onto my USB-drive. I had a feeling no one would touch them on my computer, though—my earlier photos had been left alone. Whoever had deleted the photos of Ophelia in the dungeon hadn't wanted me to see something. And the only something I could think of that made sense was the face.

The question was, who knew about the photos? Ophelia, of course. Andrew, too. Perhaps Vivian, if Ophelia told her about them as she said she would. Would Gertie or that old man, Brian, know how to work a computer? Was I being terribly stereotypical for asking? Probably. Still, the chances weren't high that either one of them had messed with my computer. And then Gregor—I had to stop calling him that—*Greg* had been in my room. He claimed he'd been here five minutes at the most, but he could also be lying.

If so, why?

This time I shut down my computer—a password was needed to access my desktop—and hoped no one here was savvy enough to crack it. I shoved the laptop into my bag and pushed the bag under my pillow, flattening the area as best I could. Then I hid my USB-stick in the wardrobe. Feeling a little more secure, I grabbed my camera and headed out the door, determined to find out who had dared touch my computer.

Full of righteous indignation, I didn't especially pay attention to where I was going as I searched the rooms throughout the main part of the castle—knocking first, then swiftly opening doors with a bang. The thought occurred to me that I might find Andrew's secret room, but I never came across a locked room or one filled with bottles.

After about twenty minutes I found a spiral staircase, like the one leading up to my tower. But was this my tower, or another one in the castle? I supposed that if I kept going I would find out soon enough.

What little light there was shone dimly, casting dull shadows at me as I trudged up the steps. My determination to find out who had deleted my photos had faded with the passing minutes, until finally I decided that maybe it was best to keep that information to myself. No need to tip off the offender that I knew what he or she had done. Having the element of surprise on my side might work to my advantage. Or it might bite me in the butt.

The door above me stood slightly ajar, revealing a sliver of light and nothing else. I climbed to the top step, took a deep breath to stifle the wave of apprehension coursing through me, then knocked. The door moved beneath my touch.

"Hello?" I called loudly, pushing lightly on the dark wood.

"Who's there?" a shaky voice called.

"It's me…Lily MacKenzie. I'm staying here at the castle. The Laird said I could look around. I hope I'm not imposing."

I stepped through the open space into a tiny, round room that couldn't have measured more than ten by ten. The walls were stone, the rectangular windows small and dusty. It was a tower, all right, but not like my tower room in the least. The furniture was sparse—a bed covered with a rough blanket the color of dead grass, a plain bedside table of pale pine was next to it. There was a three-drawer chest, and a black wooden chair that sat next to one of the windows, which also was the only bit of glass in the room that was clean. Nearing it, I realized it looked down over the gardens. In the chair, a bent over figure, thin, almost emaciated, stared at me with shocked eyes. She wore a long, plain gray dress.

"Lilia? Is that you?"

"Um, yes. I'm Lily. And you are…?"

Her eyes, dull blue, grew troubled. "Why has it taken so long for you to come see me, Lilia? There's so much to do!" Her voice was raspy from disuse or overuse, I wasn't sure which, though I thought the former made more sense, as isolated as it was up here. She reminded me of Ian, the resident sheepherder. Both of them lived life cut off from others, but was it by choice for this woman?

"I've only just come. I'm staying in one of the rooms here at the castle." I wrapped my arms around my body and shivered. With no apparent heat source, the room was very cold. But that wasn't the only thing that pulled the warmth from my body. She, too, had called me Lilia.

Her hands, heavily veined, rose to her bird nest of hair, white and tangled as though worked at by anxious fingers. "Why did you go away?"

My adult eyes pitied her, saw her as someone caught in the grip of mental illness. My ten-year-old eyes saw something different. They saw a harbinger of death in the guise of an old woman. No—more than a harbinger. She was the instrument. She was going to kill me. I backed away, and her hands, those wretched claws of desperation, followed me as though attached by strings.

"Please don't," I whispered. "Please don't do this."

"Don't go!" she begged.

"Whatever I did, I'm sorry. I'll fix it. Just don't do this!"

Her hands retreated. "I only wanted to help you plan your wedding, Lilia. You've become like a daughter to me. Won't you let me help you?" She sounded nearly rational at that moment and my deceived mind slowly revived, returning from the hell into which I was descending.

"I'm not getting married," I told her in as loud a voice as I could muster. I felt strangely disconnected, not quite here in this room, yet rooted to the floor.

"Soon you will," she declared. Her bent body, like a vessel filling with air, straightened up. Her eyes grew sharp and her hair seemed to wrap itself into a neat bun. I blinked. "What are your plans for a honeymoon, dear? The continent, perhaps." Her eyes twinkled. "Paris? Rome? I know!" She clapped her hands like a child. "Both! Oh, this is so romantic," she purred, looking wistful. "Won't it be wonderful?"

"I think you've mistaken me for someone else," I replied in a shaky voice. "I'm just a visitor. You and I have never met."

"How can you say that, Lilia? You're my reason for living. You've revived us all—your coming here is fate. This was meant to be!"

My teeth bit into my lip, pressing hard, just avoiding drawing blood. "I'm going to go now. I'm sorry I disturbed you."

She was out of her chair and gripping my arm before I could draw my next breath. I hadn't realized she could walk—she and the chair seemed bound together—much less move so fast. This close I could see the remnants of the color her hair had once been—red strands nearly hidden amongst hundreds of white snakes. My eyes focused on those hairs; they were my only connection to something sane, or so my confused mind believed.

"You don't understand. I've given my life to this. It has to happen!"

With great effort, I pulled my arm from her grasp. "You never told me your name," I said, working hard to salvage any semblance of rationality in this bizarre exchange.

She pulled back, affronted. "Why, you silly girl. I'm Victoria!"

"It's nice to meet you, Victoria. Now if you don't mind…" I took a step backward.

Her blue eyes blinked at me, hurt. "You really don't know me?"

I shook my head. "No."

"I'm Andrew's mother!"

The hamster wheel finally kicked into gear. Andrew had told me his mother's greatest desire was to see him married, though he'd never mentioned that she was insane. I imagined that the door to this room was typically kept locked. If so, what a cruel place to keep her! I couldn't see Andrew making the decision to do so, but Nurse Vivian on the other hand… I wouldn't put it past her to make the order. Still, Andrew should have stood up for his mother.

"I'm sorry. I didn't know. Is there something I can get for you, Mrs. Dering? I didn't mean to disturb you."

My words, intended to soothe, had the opposite effect. Her features reverted back to my first impression of her—wild, vacant—and then suddenly she was back sitting in her black chair, as though she'd never moved. Even so her next words came clear and rational as any sane person's. "When you're ready, Lilia, you'll come back."

I shivered and backed away toward the door. "Goodbye, Mrs. Dering. It was nice to meet you."

There was no response. She was staring out the window, lost again in another world. I turned and fled back down the stairs, careless of the noise I was making. Eventually I found myself heading toward my room, as though my feet knew where to go, even if my mind did not.

Slamming my bedroom door behind me, I turned the night latch beneath the brass door handle, then dumped my camera case on the bed and plopped down next to it. What was wrong with me? I was supposed to be a reporter—nerves of steel, relentless, a ferreter of information. Instead, I'd acted more like a frightened jellyfish. She was only an old woman with dementia, not some serial killer intent on using me for her bizarre rituals. She wanted her son married and had seen me as a prospective bride. Harmless, right?

So why did she call you Lilia?

I fought the chills threatening to shake my body apart. It was a mistake. Perhaps in Scotland if your name is Lily, they call you Lilia. In South American countries an Edward would be Eduardo, in Italy, Robert would be Roberto. No mystery here, simply a cultural linguistic habit.

My tense shoulders slumped a little and I lay back on the bed. For now, I would accept this rationale, but only because I wanted to, *needed* to. I wouldn't let the issue of leaving an old woman up in a tower slide, though. She might be the epitome of the Scottish word fey—eccentric, slightly mad, a seer of calamity—but that didn't mean she didn't need help. If nobody would be her advocate, I would.

Feeling better, I threw out my arms and my hand hit something hard. The register. I rolled over and grasped the large book with both hands. I'd forgotten all about it. I wondered why Greg hadn't asked me why I wanted it. I decided that after I looked through it, I'd hunt Brian down and see if he had fixed my bike. Tomorrow, fixed bike or not, I would visit Mr. Huntington and find out what his story was—why he had wanted the register, what his interest was in me. He also might have information about my father's ancestors.

The register resembled the other one I'd studied in the dungeon— old, crumbly, and hard to read. I dug my gloves out of my camera case and pulled them on. In moments, my finger was flying over the words. Two hours later, after acquiring a sore neck, strained eyes, and a painfully bent spine, I found it. The name. *Lilia.* And a date. *1880.*

I frowned. That couldn't be right. 1880 was too late. My father's family had left the area in 1870. I sighed and rubbed my aching forehead. Had I come all this way for nothing? My mind drifted back to the day I'd told my father my plans and his reaction to them. "Even your mother, as crazy as she was, wouldn't approve of you doing something so foolish, may she rest in peace."

"Would you stop saying that?"

"I thought you'd like it if I sounded more positive about her."

"She's still alive!"

"Like I could forget," he grumbled.

Still alive... Thirteen years ago my mother attempted suicide by cutting her wrists. Like with most things in her life up to that point, she wasn't successful in her endeavor. She lives in Paris now, in a tiny apartment overlooking the busy hub of the city, painting to her heart's content. She's very much alive, though to me she might as well be dead. I never see her. It's a condition of my father's. He gets me; she gets to stay out of jail.

It's not illegal to attempt suicide, of course. Murder, on the other hand, *is* against the law. When I was only ten years old, my mother tried to kill me.

Chapter Nine

❦

Tired of reliving this memory, I forced my mind back to the topic that had triggered my reminiscence in the first place. I'd found the name, Lilia, only to learn that the date was all wrong. It couldn't be a coincidence, could it? If so, it was an odd one. I hadn't once come across another Lilia.

I spent the next hour paging through the rest of the parish register. Lilia did not show herself again. My fingers returned to the page I'd marked with a piece of scrap paper for the 1880 Lilia. From what I could make out, her last name was O'Keefe, but that's all I learned. I couldn't determine what the 1880 date meant—baptism, marriage, death? The last name, O'Keefe, hinted at Irish roots, which really told me very little other than that her father was probably Irish, or his ancestors had been.

I was about to give up when I spotted two words scribbled off to the right in faded, ornate letters, unreadable to the naked eye. I ran to my backpack and pulled out my 'detective' kit, containing tools useful in research, one of which was a magnifying glass. Grabbing the book once more, I peered through the thick glass at the miniscule script. Even then, I had trouble reading the words.

Finally, I had it, figuring out that the 's' was actually an 'f.' *A new life.* The date was for a birth, then. Lilia O'Keefe had been born in 1880, far too late to have come over with my father's ancestors. I groaned in frustration. So who was *this* Lilia? Maybe I was barking up the wrong family tree. Then again, according to my mother, I still had good reason for pursuing a Lilia in Scotland.

"You want to know why I named you Lilia?" Mother slurred. She was a bit on the tipsy side when I asked her one snowy afternoon. For once it seemed I had gauged her mood reasonably well. After two drinks, she was rather chatty, and even, one might say, happy. Plus she was willing to talk to me.

I simply nodded in response, afraid to speak and ruin things. Sometimes she forgot I was only ten. A part of me enjoyed this oversight— what kid wouldn't like being treated as an adult? The sane part of me knew that sometimes this was wrong, and I reacted accordingly— warily and with a strange feeling in the pit of my stomach.

"It was the only way to appease them," she answered.

When she didn't go on, merely took another sip of her Merlot and gazed out the living room window at the falling snow, I gently prodded, "Them?"

"The dreams. When I was pregnant with you, that's when they started. I wanted to name you Beth, but the voices got so bad, so insistent, I couldn't even sleep."

"What did they say?" I whispered, feeling suddenly as though I didn't want to know, that to know would start something I wouldn't be able to stop.

"'Her name shall be Lilia' they told me. Those voices—those damn Scottish accents, so brutal when they want to be." Her face curdled like old milk. "They didn't stop until I promised."

"That doesn't sound too bad," I ventured. "Lilia is a nice name." Better than Beth, I thought. More exotic, anyway.

She tipped her glass at me like an accusing finger. "You have no idea, Lily! They showed me things. They made me do it. I didn't want to name you Lilia! What a name to live up to. It means purity and innocence, you know."

"Wow, talk about getting it wrong," I joked, feebly.

"Oh, don't say that." She reached out to stroke my cheek with her speckled hand, never quite free of oil paint. "You're perfect as you are. I wouldn't do anything to change you. Well, except your name." I laughed, but she didn't join me. She had slipped away to another, far away world.

I stared at the name Lilia, willing it to tell me more. Willing it to connect itself to my dreams and make sense of everything. But I was at a loss, now more than ever.

There was a knock on the door and I quickly slid the register under my pillow, an automatic reaction. My father had a habit of "checking up" on me. Really they were just surprise inspections designed to keep me pure and innocent. Ah, the irony.

I peeled off my gloves and shoved them into my camera case. "Come in," I called, forgetting I had locked the door.

But the door swung open anyway, making me wonder if the lock was just for show. I shivered a little and reminded myself to push something in front of the door at night. Ophelia quickly slipped inside, shut the door behind her, and leaned against it, breathing hard. "I got away!"

I couldn't help laughing at her dramatics. "You're on the lam?"

She nodded. "And now you're an accomplice because I won't let you kick me out."

"Don't you think Andrew would get mad that you're bothering the guests?"

She waved that away, then pressed her ear against the door. "Nobody's coming." She smiled, then joined me on the bed, plopping down and bouncing a few times. "I'm so sick of planning for this stupid ball! Who cares about how many plates we need or who's coming with what to sell? I'm more worried about what to wear. This might be my last chance to impress Greg. I heard he's returning to Edinburgh next week."

The news was surprisingly unwelcome. "Permanently?"

She lifted one shoulder. "I'm not sure, but I'm not taking any chances."

"Where did you hear this?"

Her nose wrinkled. "I overheard Auntie Viv talking to him on the phone. She was probably only confirming his attendance for the ball," she added, as though trying to convince herself.

"And is he coming?" She glanced sharply at me, but relaxed when she saw my face registering only polite interest. I was glad she didn't know me very well, as I was only too interested in hearing her reply.

"He is!" Her face shone. "You're coming, too, of course. What are you wearing?"

"Me? I don't know. I didn't pack my ball gown for fear it would get crushed."

She smacked me on the arm. "Very funny. I know! We'll look in the attic. There are lots of clothes up there. We'll just need to find something that doesn't look too shabby or moth-eaten. I know just where to look, too."

I suddenly felt excited. "Sure. Why not?" It would be fun to do something lighthearted for once. I wasn't one to hang out with my girlfriends and do girly things—not after what Mother had done to me, and I felt a small regret at missing out. Besides, I wanted to go to the ball, for many reasons, beyond the desire to dance, though I knew how to do so reasonably well. Father's idea of raising a girl involved sending me to finishing school during the summer. For five tedious years, I attended Mademoiselle Lefit's Charm School. There I painted and played the harp (of all things), learned the proper way to walk and talk, and took dance lessons. I could dance a quadrille, the waltz, and even a

Scottish reel (Father insisted, and Mademoiselle Lefit was awarded accordingly). I was officially a very charming young woman.

But business must always come before pleasure and I made myself ask, "Ophelia, you know all those photos I took of you in the dungeon?"

"Oh, yes!" She looked at me expectantly. "Can I see them now?"

"Actually, no," I replied, watching her face carefully. "Someone deleted them. You didn't come in and look at them while I was out, did you? Maybe press the wrong button?" I added hopefully.

Her disappointed expression answered my question. "You think *I* did it?" There was more than disappointment there, I realized. She was offended. Or maybe wounded was a better way to describe her crumpled features.

"Accidentally," I hastened to qualify. "I came back to look at them and they were all gone. I just want to know who did it."

"Me, too!" The hurt disappeared, replaced by anger. I felt it radiating through her fine skin like steam off tar. "I've been waiting to see them all afternoon!"

"Maybe we can take some more another time—when you're wearing your ball gown," I added, inspired.

She nodded, slightly appeased. "When?"

I saw she wasn't one to procrastinate and admired her for it, except for the inconvenience it would cause me. "I don't know. Not today." I'd experienced too much today. I felt as though I had packed in a week's worth of activities into twelve hours.

She sighed. "Fine. We'll just find our gowns today."

"I think I can manage that."

She jumped off the bed. "Follow me."

We passed through long, dark halls, a gallery filled with ancient portraits, and up and down stairwells more than a couple times. At last we found ourselves in the attic, a surprisingly small room overlooking the loch. A fine coat of moisture covered the windowpane of a tiny window—the only light source. It reminded me of the old woman, and I thought of asking Ophelia about her. But I held back. I didn't want her knowing I'd been snooping around the house.

"I keep a torch up here." She reached down and grabbed a heavy, silver flashlight, switching it on and flashing it around the room, highlighting cobwebs and dust. "I come to the attic when I want some privacy. Auntie Viv just doesn't know when to give it a rest sometimes. Always going on about how I need to improve myself and get more involved in running the castle. Really, I love Dundeid, but I'm sick to death of hearing about how much more I should." She headed for a couple of wardrobes pushed up against the far wall. "Come on. There're a lot of old dresses here. Won't Auntie Viv be surprised when she sees us all dressed up? She'll think I'm taking the initiative— showing Dundeid off in its best light, when really I'm just trying to show myself off in *my* best light." She grinned at me over her shoulder.

The wardrobe doors opened with a whoosh, carrying a strong smell of lavender and lemon toward me. I sneezed, then again, and again.

"Bless you," Ophelia said, each time.

"Thank you," I muttered, pulling a white, folded handkerchief out of my pocket and wiping my nose.

"Wouldn't want the devil claiming your soul, now would we?" She laughed.

"I thought the blessing was to keep evil spirits from getting in," I replied stuffily, tucking my hanky back into my pocket.

"Do you want to do that?"

"Keep the evil spirits out?" She nodded. "Um, *yeah*. Wouldn't you?"

"I might welcome a little demon taking up residence, maybe push me to be more adventurous, more *daring*. Life here can be dead boring!" She plunged her hand into the shadows and pulled out a gorgeous, sky blue velvet gown with a plunging neckline and capped sleeves. The tiny waist was more suited to a child than a full-grown woman. The long, slim skirt had Pannier drapes, which created fullness at the hips and accentuated the smallness of the waist. Most of the dress was covered with a variety of ruffles, bows, and ribbons. It was beautiful, but a bit fussy for my taste. "This is my favorite!" Ophelia gushed. "I've been waiting for the perfect moment to wear it." She held the dress up against her body, one hand lovingly stroking the soft material.

"It's in really good shape," I commented, looking it over. No holes, no musty smell, the color as bright as the day it had first been worn.

"I keep an eye on the clothes up here since no one else seems to care about them. The wardrobe, which I used my own money to buy, is lined with cedar and I make lavender, rosemary, and lemon peel sachets to keep the moths away. Much better than those stinky mothballs everyone thinks they should use."

"Mothballs are poisonous, aren't they?"

Ophelia laid her dress across the back of a chair with a broken seat, then returned to the wardrobe. "All I know is that they stink."

"Here's one for you." She pulled out a simple, but beautifully cut, peach silk gown that matched the style of the other dress, but with less embellishment, which I preferred. Delicate roses sewn along the daring neckline, increasing in size around the cuff of the capped sleeves, were the only accoutrements. "There are even shoes." She reached down and pulled out kid slippers that matched the dresses.

"They look barely worn."

She smiled. "Let's try everything on."

"Here?"

"No one ever comes to the attic." She pulled off her shirt, then slipped out of her pants. She wore a lavender bra and underwear set and her skin, pale and mottled purple from the cold, nearly matched her undergarments. "Come on!" she urged.

"Oh, fine." Moving quickly—it was quite frigid up here—I stripped down to my plain white skivvies and attempted to pull on the dress. The fit was tight, but finally I managed to squeeze myself in, though a shoehorn might have sped up the process. The laces in back would have to stay very loose, I decided, if I were to survive.

Ophelia, her gown on, turned about and gasped, her hand flying to her mouth. "Oh. You look really good."

"You don't have to sound so shocked." I wasn't entirely joking. Did I look that bad in my regular clothes? "I'm not nearly as stunning as you, I'm afraid. I'm more like a fluffy cloud and you're the radiant sun." I was being dramatic, but for a good cause. In some ways, Ophelia seemed almost arrogant, but more often I sensed an underlying fragile self-esteem, which dictated her life, or lack thereof, as she claimed.

Her face cleared. "I do look good, don't I?" She laughed with wicked delight. "Do the slippers fit?"

I pulled them on. They did…perfectly, which was odd considering I wore a size eight and back then, women were much smaller than to-day's bonny lasses, especially us rudely healthy American girls. The dress also fit surprisingly well, even without a corset, which had been a common item of underclothing. The length was perfect and the curves of the dress hit exactly where my body curved, though there wasn't much natural curving so I was rather pleased with the effect.

What I saw in the dusty cheval mirror was almost stunning. I looked feminine, a mode I typically avoided affecting simply because it wasn't very practical. Long nails and photography, dresses and biking—they don't exactly go together. But this…it was a miracle. I was a woman!

Hear me roar.

Thank goodness Father wasn't here to see my metamorphosis. He'd
bust a blood vessel, especially knowing that I was about to attend a ball
with two very attractive men in attendance. I shook my head. He was
so old-fashioned sometimes. And all those years I'd spent appeasing
him, dressing like a boy. Not that I was about to start dressing like this
every day, but apparently I wasn't as hopeless a case as I thought I was.

Ophelia watched me stare at myself in wonder. "You're a regular
Cinderella."

I snorted, blowing the effect. "Yeah, right… More like the ugly step-
sister, compared to you."

"A cloud can cover up the sun, you know."

"Please. Like I could compete with you, Ophelia." While the words
were honest, I thought I detected a bit of obsequiousness in them. I
seemed to want to get on Ophelia's good side.

"Are you competing with me, Lily?"

I glanced over at her. It was a strange question. "Why would I do
that, you dork? Now knock off the drama and get over here." I pulled
her in front of the mirror, standing behind her. "You should wear your
hair up." I reached out, tentatively, and pulled her hair off her neck.
"Like this." I wrapped the thick, opulent strands in a coil, like a sleeping snake.

Her eyes lit up, pleased. "You're right. I look older."

"You should wear your hair like this more often. The style shows off
your long neck. You look like a swan."

Ophelia's hands took over and tried different styles. She sunk into a
reverie of admiration. I watched her for a bit, then wandered over to
the dusty window. I used my fist to wipe away a small circle. Peering
out, I spotted Andrew striding across the lawn, purposeful and a wonder to watch. My lids lowered and lifted slowly, as though on the verge
of sleep, and the spaces inside my mind grew soft and hazy as a warm
summer day. After he disappeared around the other side of the castle,
my eyes closed at last and words, from faraway, spun into my mind.

We could make each other so happy, Lilia.

But we hardly know each other.

Don't you feel it? Like we've known each other forever?

I feel so confused—I don't know what to think, what to do. I need more time.

*Time isn't what you think it is, Lilia. There's so little of it, and yet it's endless,
like the heavens. Say yes now. Say yes, Lilia!*

My eyes flew open and I spun around. Ophelia was still posing in
front of the mirror, trying out various flirtatious pouts. She looked so

normal, so real, she calmed my breathing and rooted me to the here and now.

Where had those words come from? Who had spoken them? *Say yes, Lilia.* To what?

And to whom?

Chapter Ten

✤

We decided to take our dresses to our bedrooms to air out. Supper was in half an hour and we parted ways to freshen up, Ophelia laughing and twirling her way down the hall. I hung my dress on a small nail close to my bed and went over to look in the mirror. Tired, green eyes peered back at me. It had been a long day and the overwhelming desire to take my meal in my room and then go to bed nearly overwhelmed me.

But solitude wasn't an option. I had limited time here and although I'd learned some things, I was still as clueless and confused as ever. I'd determined that my ancestors had come from this area. I'd found a Lilia, but the fact of her existence led me nowhere. And while I was where I wanted to be—staying here in Dundeid Castle, surrounded by history—it was nonetheless a wild, swirling mess that refused to coagulate into any kind of coherence.

With a sigh, I proceeded to brush out my hair. Looking decidedly limp and oily, I tried a trick I'd picked up from a fashion article I'd been forced into writing (one of my punishments for getting above myself, as Mr. Willeton put it). A little baby powder rubbed in at the roots and—voila!—instant makeover. I wasn't entirely convinced while writing the article that it would work, but when I tried the powder I found the result wasn't too bad. I finished my effort by twisting my hair into a chignon of sorts.

Seeing my reflection in the dark mirror was a little startling. I'd never worn my hair in a bun, considering it a bit matronly for someone in her twenties, but the outcome surprised me. Like Ophelia had with her hair up, I looked beyond my years, but in a good way. Inspired by my success, I changed into a pair of ballet flats, close-fitting, navy blue slacks, and a sea green blouse that had once been my mother's. The overall effect wasn't bad. At any rate, the outfit would have to do, being the extent of my dress-up clothes. My wrist, upon inspection, looked worse than it felt—all puffy and bruised—so I decided to wear the bandage for another day or two, if only for vanity's sake.

I found my way to the dining room, arriving before anyone else. Rather than sitting down right away, I crossed over to the windows to look out at the loch. The sun had already disappeared behind the mountains, which cast their giant shadows across the water like lurking beasts.

"Beautiful, isn't it?"

I swung around. Andrew had arrived, dressed for dinner in an un-outdoorsman-like navy blue jacket and pale gray turtleneck paired with heather gray slacks.

"Stunning," I replied as he walked toward me, though I wasn't talking about the loch.

"I'll bet you don't have views like that in New Hampshire."

I shook my head, still staring at him. *No, indeed.* "Oh, we hold our own. We have mountains and lakes, and the ocean, too."

He came to stand by me, his arm brushing against mine as we turned together to gaze upon the loch. Daylight had nearly disappeared and I could see our reflections in the window more clearly than the loch as it faded into the darkness. "Would you miss it? If you never went back?" He watched me closely, as though his life depended on my answer.

"Yes, I would." I'd never thought about it before, but what I said was true. I would miss New Hampshire. Being a reporter, I had traveled all over the state, getting to know the people, the landscape, the history. I was very proud of my birthplace, especially now that I was considered a true native myself (meaning, five plus generations in the ground).

He looked disappointed, then rallied. "Well, I guess I'll give you a few more days to fall in love…"

I laughed. "Dundeid is very beautiful. But I don't think it's the place for me."

"I'm not doing my job then."

"On the contrary. I feel well taken care of here. I plan to give you a glowing review. There's one thing I wondered about, though…"

"Go on," he encouraged.

"I met a woman this afternoon, up in a tower. She seemed very unhappy and that room…"

His expression in the dark glass didn't change as he listened, though I could feel his body grow tense. "Yes?"

He wasn't making this easy, but I wouldn't be deterred. "Well, I was wondering who she was. I didn't mean to pry, but I was exploring the castle—" well, I had been, sort of, "—and I took a wrong turn. She didn't seem well to me. I'm not sure that tower is the best place for her."

"You're thinking there's some terrible secret, aren't you? A mystery to root out and report about?" His tone was joking, but I had a feeling he wasn't joking, not in the least.

"I'm not a character out of *Northanger Abbey*, Andrew, seeing dark mysteries everywhere. I just want to know if she's okay. It was awfully cold up there, and she seemed very lonely to me. She thought you and I..." I waved my hands in the air, a lame attempt to cross out what I'd just said. "Oh, nothing."

"Don't stop now. She thought you and I...*what?*"

I swallowed hard, lacing my hands together. My palms were sweaty and itchy—my emotional thermometer. I decided to change tactics, adopting my most authoritative voice. "She shouldn't be up there. It's not healthy."

"Andrew's mother prefers to stay in the tower, Lily."

Startled, Andrew and I spun about in unison, meeting arm to arm as we turned about. Vivian had entered the room, and she looked amazing. Gone was the bland nurse's uniform, replaced by a long-sleeved, rose gown. Her dark hair was piled up on her head like a Greek goddess and her red lips were even redder than usual. She wore mascara and eye shadow, even diamond stud earrings with a matching necklace.

I suddenly felt terribly underdressed, and that made me petty. "She thinks Andrew and I are getting married," I announced triumphantly. *Beat that, Missy!*

But instead of looking shocked, Vivian smiled, a dark eyebrow rising knowingly. "She's quite a character, Mother Dering. She keeps us on our toes with all her doings."

I had a hard time believing that. "We can't be talking about the same woman. She seemed more sad and lonely than mischievous."

"Mother is harmless," Andrew put in. He grasped my hand and I had to bite my lip to keep from gasping. "To others, anyway. She's not as kind to herself."

"What Andrew means," Vivian asserted in a cold tone, and Andrew dropped my hand as if it were a hot potato, "is that Mother Dering has a martyr complex. She feels she should suffer."

"That's awful! Why would she feel that?"

She shrugged. "Who knows? She's had a good life, but in this last year she's grown increasingly agitated, her behavior worsening almost on a daily basis. Four or five months ago, she wanted her room moved to the tower and refused to speak to anyone until she got her way. She won't eat more than two small meals a day. She doesn't bathe or change her clothes. In my professional opinion, we should put her in a home—there's one not far away that's set up for people like her. But Andrew refuses to do that." She gave him a look that was both stern and fond.

"I'm sorry, Lily." Andrew turned to face me, his hands outstretched, and of their own volition, mine reached out to his. He grabbed them and squeezed lightly, smiling into my eyes. "To subject a guest to that sort of scene is unforgivable. Usually we keep the door locked—on Mother's request," he hastened to add when my eyes registered alarm. "She sees visitors as a treat she doesn't deserve. You see, my father died when I was three and she took it hard, almost as though she was responsible." He looked sad. "So, what can I do to make it up to you?"

"Nonsense, Andrew. I'm fine. We Americans are a hearty stock—not so easily frightened."

"But I'd like to do something!" His eyes bored into mine and I allowed myself to travel along those violet-blue corridors into his mind, down to his heart. In the end I found nothing there but my own silly desires.

"I want to see your room," I heard myself saying, sounding very far away. There was a gasp and I felt my head slowly turning toward Vivian. "Ophelia says it's very mysterious, and I love mysteries."

Andrew blinked. "Your wish is my command, my lo—"

"Andrew!"

We both jerked, the connection broken like glass. Andrew was the first to recover, dropping my hands for the second time that evening. "Yes, Viv?" His gaze challenged her to say a word. Her eyes slid away from his, toward mine as she pulled out a chair and sat down.

"Why don't you go see where Ophelia has got off to? She ran off this afternoon and I'm tired of chasing after her." She didn't take her eyes off mine as she spoke.

Andrew sighed. "That girl. She needs to grow up. I'll be right back, Lily."

I nodded. When he was gone, Vivian dropped her gaze, taking the white linen napkin from its silver ring and unfolding it across her lap. I held my position, crossing my arms as though raising a shield, knowing perfectly well an attack was coming.

"Ophelia visited you today—twice, wasn't it, Lily?"

I blinked. This was it? This was the attack? "Yes, she did. She showed me the dungeons this morning, which you already know about. And this afternoon she stopped by to say hello."

"You must send her away when she does that. She can become quite a nuisance and I really don't want her making a habit of such unbecoming behavior with guests."

I studied her pale face. "That puts me in an awkward position, doesn't it?"

Vivian looked up, her expression bland. "Yes, I guess it does."

"I'm not family, you see," I went on, determined to get her to acknowledge my point. "So I have no real power to tell someone where they can and cannot go in their own home. As you pointed out, I'm only a guest here." They didn't treat me like one, though, airing their issues in front of me like so much dirty laundry. I wanted to know why.

Vivian studied me for several aggravating seconds, during which I refused to look away. "I'll speak to her about it."

"No, don't bother. I don't mind her visiting once in a while, and if she does start to visit too often, I'll tell her so myself." *But kindly.*

"Oh, consider it already done, Miss MacKenzie. We're running a business here and Ophelia needs to understand that."

"Vivian, no—" I began, but the doors opened and Ophelia burst into the room.

"Sorry I'm late!" She gave me a surreptitious wink and I suppressed a wince. Somehow I was going to have to get to Ophelia before Vivian did. I didn't want her to think I was behind this 'lesson' Vivian was intent on administering. "I was doing something very important."

"For the castle, I hope." Andrew followed her in, pulling out her chair for her.

She smiled up at him as she sat down. "Of course, Andrew. The castle is my life." She sneaked a knowing glimpse at me. I smiled sickly.

"Ophelia," Vivian began and my stomach sank. She wouldn't... "I'm afraid there's been a complaint about you bothering the guests."

She would.

"Hey, wait a minute—" I began.

"What do you mean?" Ophelia glanced over at me.

Vivian looked stern. "The guests are here to relax, Ophelia, not to entertain you."

"You don't want me around?" Ophelia's eyelids fluttered, on the verge of tears.

"I didn't say any such thing," I protested, looking to Andrew for help. He was examining a bottle of wine Gertie held out to him, her wide eyes averted, cheeks flushed. She was hearing everything and

Vivian didn't seem to care. Andrew was oblivious to the world around him as he indicated his glass. She poured a thumb's width into it.

"You could've just said," Ophelia whispered. "I thought…"

"But I never said anything about you," I begged her to understand. "I never complained. Vivian is making this out to be a big thing when it never was. Not with me."

Vivian turned her guns on me. "Then you're fine with people deleting your photos?"

"How did you know about that?"

"Gregory said something about it. That you lost all your photos."

"You told him I deleted your photos?" Ophelia gasped.

"No! I accused *him* of doing it. He was in my room and—"

"He was in your room?" Ophelia's lower lip trembled and she bit down on it. "I mean, what was he doing *there*?"

Vivian looked quite pleased with herself now. But why? What did she gain from this? Did she like seeing other people suffer? Maybe she was a closet sadist.

"He brought me the other parish register and then he left. He was only in my room for about five minutes."

"Why didn't you tell me?"

"To be honest, I didn't think of it. I was more worried about the photos. I knew you'd be upset if they were gone."

"But you asked me if I'd done something to them. I remember now. This afternoon."

"I thought maybe you got excited to see the photos and accidentally pushed the wrong button. That stuff happens."

"I don't even like computers," she pouted.

"Of course you don't, Phe," Vivian intervened, her voice soothing. "We all know how you don't like machines. They give her headaches," she explained, turning to me, and the look on her face conveyed, "You should know this."

"I can't believe you'd think I might've done something like that, Lily." Ophelia glanced back and forth between Vivian and me, looking for someone to make this better. Vivian's expression, damn her, was sweet and protective and totally understanding. I imagine mine was scowl-ridden.

"I was just trying to figure out how an entire file could be deleted off my computer, that's all."

"Maybe there was a power surge," Andrew offered, finally engaging. "Wine, Lily?"

Feeling hot and anxious and unfairly on trial, I nodded vigorously. Gertie came around the table. "Fill it to the top," I muttered, and she obliged. Both Ophelia and Vivian declined, leaving me to look like a lush. I defiantly took a gulp, only just barely managing to hold back a sputtering cough dying to make its way out, if only to complete the humiliation of this scene.

"So Greg was only in your room for a little bit?" Ophelia tried to look casual as she spoke, as aware of Andrew and Vivian's sudden attention on her as I was. She failed the attempt, her pale face hopeful, her young eyes full of yearning.

"What the hell was Greg Huntington doing in my house?" Andrew roared, and I jumped. He really had tuned out of the conversation.

"Like I just said, he brought over the parish register—the one I told you I needed for my research. He didn't stay long."

"Of course he didn't stay long," Ophelia rushed to point out. "He's a busy man. He was being polite and checking up on you after your accident. Right?"

"Funny applying the word polite to Greg Huntington," Andrew snorted.

"Oh, Andrew!" Ophelia exclaimed. "I don't know what you have against him!"

"Yes, Andrew." Vivian looked like the cat who's eaten all the cream and is searching for more. "What do you have against the poor man?"

"*Poor* man?" Andrew sputtered. "You of all people, Viv! I thought you were smarter than that."

"Dinner is served," Gertie called hesitantly from the doorway to the kitchen. She gripped a giant silver platter.

"Do come in, Gertie," Vivian beckoned. Her expression was cool now, in control. "I imagine our guest is quite hungry. She isn't used to our family rows yet. They can be quite enervating."

I wasn't hungry in the least. Not after the bloodletting I'd just witnessed. Most of it being my own blood, I felt a little woozy. I swallowed some more wine, enjoying the tangy Chardonnay and understanding a little more why people liked to drink away their troubles. Alcohol was so deceptively calming and soothing. It makes you, if not forget, at least more willing to accept what you can't blot out.

Ophelia, on the other hand, seemed to have found the appetite I had lost. She ate with relish, occasionally stopping to stare at me, or Vivian, sometimes at Andrew, then shifting back to me. She seemed to be calculating something in her mind and I wondered, with a little shiver of dread, what it was producing.

The conversation during the remainder of the meal focused on the Gala event, with Andrew and Vivian doing most of the talking. Before dessert was announced I excused myself, barely able to keep my eyes open. Andrew half-stood and I waved him off. "I'll be fine. Just some belated jet lag. Thank you for the lovely meal."

I could feel their eyes on my back as I walked away from the table, even when the doors closed behind me. Then my ears began to burn—figuratively, of course. But I was almost sure they were talking about me. The temptation to turn back and listen at the door was strong, but I resisted. I wasn't sure I wanted to know what they were saying. And I really was tired.

I hated tubs, but I hated feeling grimy even more. I took a quick bath, washed my hair, and soaked away the dirt. After drying off, I wrapped my hair in a towel and pulled on my blue flannel PJs with sheep on them. I'd brought the clothes I'd been wearing when I wiped out on my bike and washed them in the tub. Assuming I was the only one who used this bathroom, I left them in the tub to drip-dry.

Back in my room, I saw that someone—probably Gertie—had started a fire in the fireplace. It crackled cheerily and I added two more logs to keep it going. Feeling better, I tucked under the covers with a photography magazine. After reading it, I tossed it aside, my eyes drawn to my ball gown. In the lamplight I noticed some dark stains on the hem—mud, I thought. Seeing the spots, I smiled. Here was my ticket to redemption with Gertie. I wasn't about to touch the fabric—it had to be at least a hundred years old and very delicate—but Gertie would be thrilled to clean it and I would reap the rewards twice, getting a clean dress and a willing source.

Oh, how devious I was! I let loose a maniacal laugh, just for fun, and it echoed around the room, which made me laugh some more. Boy, I really needed a good sleep. I was getting slaphappy.

Still looking at the dress, I started wondering about when it might have been made. I pulled my computer out from under my pillow and flipped it open. The castle's website claimed they had wireless Internet service, and they did, but it was slower than a snail. As I waited for the Victorian Fashions website to pop up, I thought about all the strange things that had happened to me since arriving.

I wasn't sure what was going on, but I did know a couple things for certain. One, Vivian didn't like me and was doing her best to drive a wedge between Ophelia and me. Two, I was having a hard time being myself here at Dundeid, often dismissing avenues I would normally pursue like a dog after a cat. Either I was getting soft, or something was holding me back from being, as I perceived myself, the Truth Hunter.

Greg Huntington was the exception to this rule. I felt determined to ferret every last ounce of information out of him. Maybe because I didn't believe or trust him. First thing in the morning, I would visit his house for a little interrogation session. He knew things about my mother, and I had to determine exactly how much. He had the power to ruin everything. After assuring myself he was no longer a threat, I would find Andrew's mother and ask the hard questions. Did she really want to stay in the tower? Did she actually believe her son and I were meant to be married? Did she really blame herself for her husband's death?

The site finally loaded and I spent a lot of time scanning and search-ing, until at last I had the answer to my question. The dress design was similar to a ball gown made in 1880. Not 1879, where the dresses still sported a train in the back, and not 1881, when the beginnings of the bustle were returning. At least, that's what I could figure out from the pictures I saw, but I was biased and could be trying to fit the facts to the story. Still, it was an interesting coincidence to find a dress made in 1880, the year the first Lilia was born. I made sure to bookmark the page for later reference, thinking perhaps I could use this information for my article.

After shutting down, I closed the lid and slid the laptop under my pil-low, then turned off my lamp. I was exhausted. Lying down, my eyes fluttered in the moonlight that had broken through the clouds and was now shining through the window. I fell asleep quickly to the sound of popping embers and the smell of wood smoke, and soon slipped into a dream. I've dreamed this dream thousands of times and yet, after each experience, I only remembered one frustrating bit—the very end. After racing through a blurred series of events that I'm sure contained a story, just one I couldn't read, I found myself running down a long road to nowhere.

Feet sore, heart pounding, I flee from an unseen pursuer. "Please don't!" I shout aloud. "I didn't mean for it to happen this way!"

My pursuer doesn't answer. He, or she, is behind me, a dark solid mass racing toward me like death. I stumble and fall and am caught as easily as a pet rabbit. As soon as the hands encircle my arms I know I won't get away. I won't ever escape.

That feeling—that horrible, horrible feeling—of knowing I have no control over what happens next is absolutely the worst thing I've ever felt. Whenever people read or hear about someone who's sick or dying, they typically want to know what happened. What did the victim do to end up that way so I don't do it myself? It sounds heartless, but people need to believe they have control over their own fate. They read in the newspaper that the girl who died in the car accident wasn't wearing a seatbelt. *Oh, well,* they tell themselves, *I always wear a seatbelt so I wouldn't have died.*

I'm one of those people. I conjure up countless fantasies where I always manage to escape from harm, survive the worst, fight off the seemingly inevitable. Temporarily, I'm the master of my life. And then my dream comes at night, when I'm completely helpless, and I wake up, barely stifling a scream, knowing I'm just fooling myself.

Still, I don't stop entertaining the fantasies. They're all I've got—my thin, cold line between madness and sanity.

Yet despite feeling as though I have no control, I still needed to know what happened once my pursuer caught me. That's the reason I came to Scotland. The answer lay here in this ancient country…lurking somewhere in the heart of my enemy. And I needed to take control—I needed to change the outcome of my dream.

Or suffer the consequences.

Chapter Eleven

"Lily!"

I jerked upright, just as the dream hands enclosed my arms, and they vanished. Someone was outside my door. I watched in disbelief as the knob, caught in a band of moonlight, slowly turned. I'd forgotten to push something in front of the door to keep out predators.

"Lily?"

"Who's there?" I called, but I already knew who it was. "Come in," I said more loudly.

The door opened and Andrew stepped inside, still dressed in his dinner clothes, though I noticed his jacket had disappeared. "You were yelling," he said. "Oh, sorry. You're in bed." Funny, he didn't look sorry.

"Bad dream."

"I have bad dreams," he said, surprising me. He looked too healthy to be haunted. "Dreams that I'd gladly give my left arm to get rid of."

"Not your right?"

He smiled wistfully. "I'm right-handed."

"So what are they about? Your dreams?"

He made no move to come closer, lingering in the doorway. "I don't really know, except that I lose everything. That's what I remember."

"I'm sorry."

He nodded. "Come. I said I'd show you my room. I couldn't sleep so I thought I'd make you suffer with me."

Too surprised to laugh, I slid out of bed. As quickly as I could—before he could change his mind—I pulled on a pair of slippers and went to the door, closing it behind me. I didn't want anyone to know I was gone.

It briefly registered that maybe I was doing something stupid. What did I really know about Andrew Dering? He seemed a nice enough person, though he did have a bit of a temper, which I'd witnessed at Ian MacKenzie's croft. What if he decided to turn that anger on me? I shook my head. Ridiculous. If I wasn't careful I'd think everyone living here had a hidden agenda. Then I truly would be like the over-imaginative heroine of *Northanger Abbey*.

We didn't speak as he led the way through the dark corridors. His hand, wrapped around my arm, guiding me, felt big and warm. My breath was coming quickly—this midnight jaunt was highly irregular. I felt both excited and a bit trepidatious. Getting caught wouldn't be... My mind stopped the thought and dissected it. Getting *caught?* I wasn't a child, and I wasn't doing anything wrong. So why was I worried about someone finding out that Andrew and I were heading to his secret room under the cover of darkness?

Of course, put that way, it did sound a bit risqué. Even in this day and age. Still, I was a modern, adult woman. I could do as I pleased and if someone (i.e., my father or Miss Vivian, the Gargoyle) didn't approve, so what? It wasn't as if I planned on sleeping with Andrew, as tantalizing as that might be. I wasn't the type of person to jump into bed with someone I just met.

The trip to his room took longer than I thought, but I didn't mind. There was something exhilarating about sneaking around a spooky, old castle with a gorgeous man, while everyone was sleeping (hopefully). I vowed that if ever the opportunity presented itself again, I'd seize upon it.

"Here we are," Andrew whispered, stopping halfway down a long, carpeted hallway dimly lit by wall sconces. He dropped his hand and pulled out a ring of keys from his jacket pocket. "Ready?" The question was half-serious, half-mocking.

"Ready as I'll ever be."

He flung open the door. As soon as I stepped into the room, he shut the door quietly, almost furtively, as if he didn't want anyone to know we were here. A small part of my mind registered his action, but the rest was taken up with the scene before me. Ophelia's description had not done the place justice. Six small kerosene lanterns hanging on hooks, along with a robust fire in the fireplace, lit the high-ceilinged room. A long table covered by beakers and test tubes, wires and Bunsen burners, piles of rusty horseshoes and bells, old copper pots and aluminum cans, sat in the middle of the shadowy room.

"Fascinating, hm?" He went to stand on the other side of the table, putting it between us.

"So you're *really* a mad scientist?" My voice sounded, even to my ears, incredulous as I moved to join him. The last thing I would have thought this blond god would be was a scientist, though the mad bit might still apply.

He laughed. "This room was like this long before I was born. I've been told that, among other things, my ancestors were interested in manipulating chemical processes to prolong life. They wanted to live forever."

"Did anyone come up with anything?"

He gave a dry laugh. "They're all dead, so I suppose that's your answer."

"So what do *you* do in here?"

"I don't know." He looked away, tapped at a pot. "Nothing useful. I just like coming in here, dabbling a bit in this and that."

"You're looking for something," I guessed.

He shrugged, his fingers rolling a glass tube back and forth. "Maybe."

"An answer to your dreams."

"Yes," he breathed. "And it's in here—I know it is."

"Maybe the answer is in here." I leaned over and tapped at his head. "Carl Jung and a little dream analysis might do you more good than all this." I didn't know why I was making light of his troubles, having them myself, but I felt it necessary.

"Maybe I already have."

"You've seen a psychologist?"

"No. I didn't see a doctor. Viv worked with me."

I frowned. "Correct me if I'm wrong, but isn't that a little unethical? You're related—she can't possibly remain objective."

"You know something about everything, don't you?" I couldn't tell if he was impressed by my font of knowledge or annoyed by it.

"I'm just saying—"

"Viv and I are about as strongly related as you and I are, Lily."

"But she lives here..." I stopped, unsure why I cared. "She doesn't treat Ophelia, does she?"

He smiled a little, as though the idea amused him. "Ophelia has a doctor who specializes in her illness. A Dr. Mills. He's young, and I'm afraid Phe once had a crush on him, though I made certain he understood nothing could happen in that department. He seems to know what he's doing, though. He runs Havensrest, the place Viv mentioned might be good for my mother. Viv merely makes sure Ophelia takes her medication and then watches for side effects." So Ophelia had once had a crush on her doctor, and Andrew had put the kibosh on it. Perhaps Phe's secret wasn't so much about Andrew, but about his rejection of Dr. Mills, likely a commoner, as a suitable spouse for his cousin.

"Is Ophelia..." Certain questions never get easier to ask. "Well, is her illness fatal?"

Andrew looked away. "It can be."

For some reason, I couldn't bring myself to ask what it was she had, probably since no one seemed particularly anxious to share this information with me. "I'm sorry to hear that."

"Viv watches her carefully. She won't let her do anything rash. I trust her absolutely in this. You should, too."

He looked at me, waiting for my reaction. "I'm sure she's quite competent."

He smiled, satisfied. "I want you to like everyone here, Lily. I want you to be comfortable."

"You want me to write a good article about you," I teased.

But his radiant smile didn't come. "My mother sees things," he replied.

"Your mother?" His change of subject threw me. "What kind of things?"

"The future. She sees things that are going to happen. I think that's one reason why she locks herself away—out of guilt at being the bearer of bad news."

A brief memory from my first night—a time that seemed months ago, but was only a little over twenty-four hours—flashed through my mind. Someone had stood by Andrew, told him she saw things, had always seen things. Not Vivian as I'd assumed, but Andrew's mother. Funny how I couldn't associate the woman of that night with the weak, old woman I'd met in the tower. What else had she said then? That she didn't see everything, I remembered, that they needed me, that they couldn't fail this time.

My stomach flipped, recalling that vague bit of memory.

"What do you think of me, Lily?" Andrew asked suddenly.

I was so shocked by the question, I actually stepped away from him. "I hardly know you."

"I'm aware of that," he replied impatiently. "But you're a reporter—you have to sum people up quickly. It's your job. I need to know what people think of me."

"That's the dumbest thing I've ever heard." His eyes widened. "Oh, please. You look like a Greek god, you own a castle, and you don't drool. In my country, your kind is known as a catch or a hottie, even a TDF."

"TDF?"

"To Die For."

"And *you* feel this way about me? That I'm...to die for?" The juvenile phrase sounded odd coming from him.

I snorted, flustered. "You don't believe in holding back, do you? Keeping things close to the chest?"

"I don't have time for that, Lily. Something is about to happen and I plan on being ready for it this time." *This time?*

"And part of being ready is knowing what I think of you?" I was saying whatever I could to avoid answering him.

He moved around to the other side of the table, sliding his finger all along its smooth walnut surface. A moment later he was facing me, hands supported on the table, body bent toward me. "You're an important part of my future. I know that seems crazy to you, Lily, but it's true."

"So you agree with your mother? That we're getting married?" I gave what I'd hoped would sound like a scoffing laugh, but which came out an anxious bleat instead. I coughed nervously.

"I told you...my mother sees things."

"And she sees us getting married?"

"Not exactly..."

I held up my hands. "Listen, Andrew. This is getting weird. I don't know what's going on with your mother or what your dreams are telling you, but I do know this. I'm here to do a job, and I'm going to do it, and then I'm going to leave."

"I know you're here to do more than just a job."

I stared at him, feeling hot and trapped. "Who told you that?"

"Mother did."

"What did she tell you?" I felt angry, and scared, too, which made me even madder.

"She says you're here to complete things. To finally end this façade," he waved his hand around the room. "To begin again."

I blinked, feeling suddenly tired. "You aren't making sense, Andrew. I'm here to write a story on your castle and to research my genealogy. That's it." I was lying through my clenched teeth, but I had to. My survival depended on it.

He regarded me, his own gaze strong and steady, his eyes black in the darkness of the room. "Remember when I asked if you believed in fate?" I nodded, wary. "And you said you believed people make their own fates."

"Yes," I breathed, feeling my lungs deflate, weighted down by that one word.

"Then I need you to pay attention to what's happening here. If you truly believe you can choose your path, then you're our only hope."

"That's ridiculous. If I can choose, so can you."

"I don't make good choices, Lily. Trust me on that."

"What if I don't, either?"

"Then that will be it and we must accept what happens."

I didn't like hearing that. "Listen, you can't just throw out all these vague warnings and then expect me to know what to do. It isn't fair."

He swiped a hand over his face. "If I knew what this was all about I'd handle it myself. But I don't. All I have are my dreams and a mother who's determined to see me married to you."

"Would you *want* to marry me?"

"Why not? You're smart and capable. I can talk to you. You're easy to get along with."

I sighed wistfully. "How could a girl resist such a proposal?"

"It isn't a laughing matter, Lily. There's meant to be something between us. It seems best, don't you think, to just go along with it."

"The only place I'm going is to bed. I'll go alone—I remember the way. I'll see you tomorrow."

He watched me go, but when I turned back at the door to say goodbye, he was staring down at his palms as though willing them to tell him the future. I found myself reluctant to leave. "Good night, Andrew," I whispered to him. "I hope you'll sleep better now."

He didn't answer until I had nearly closed the door behind me. "Do you want to know what I dream about, Lilia?"

I froze, my hand clutching the icy doorknob, my forehead pressing against the doorjamb as I stared sightlessly through the crack.

"I dream about you."

I ran all the way back to my room.

Chapter Twelve

✧

I awoke the next morning, tired and cranky, yet determined to continue my quest. Dressed in my best reporting outfit—slim black slacks and my kick-butt biker boots, a long-sleeved white shirt, a raincoat because it looked threatening outside, and my camera case, small notebook stuffed inside—I set off for the dining room. It was empty when I reached it, though I passed three unknown people, two men and a woman, all hurrying across the Great Hall to destinations unknown. I sat down and a moment later, Gertie came in.

"Where is everyone, Gertie?"

"Making preparations for the ball, Miss."

"Didn't they eat?"

"Miss Ophelia doesnae eat breakfast most mornings, Miss Vivian eats early, and the Laird grabbed something from the kitchen and left agin."

Almost as though he hadn't wanted to run into me, I couldn't help thinking.

"Well, I'm not terribly hungry myself."

"The Laird said tae fix ye a good meal. He doesnae want ye going hungry, see." She peered at me anxiously, obviously worried I was about to get her into trouble...again.

"I'll take eggs, toast, and orange juice. Will that do?"

She nodded, smiling. "I'll be back wi' it soon, Miss."

About to turn away, I grabbed her plump arm. "Just a minute, Gertie." She froze, as though afraid I might beat her. I quickly let go. "I was just wondering if you could clean the gown in my room. There's some mud on the hem. Ophelia and I are dressing up for the ball."

Gertie's normally dull blue eyes gleamed. "Oh, Miss! I'd be honored. That material's a right devil tae clean. I canna wait!"

"You're a strange one, Gertie," I laughed. "But I appreciate whatever you can do. There's no way I'd be brave enough to clean that dress myself. I'd totally ruin it." It was true, and also the right thing to say.

She beamed at me. "Dinna worry, Miss. I'll clean it right up. It'll be absolutely perfect just in time for the ball."

"Thanks, Gertie." She left me, practically dancing on her way out.

While she prepared my breakfast—or did whatever she did in the kitchen—I fiddled with my camera, making sure the lens was clean and the settings were how I liked them. Soon my poached eggs and hot buttered toast arrived and I found I was very hungry and grateful to

Andrew for thinking of me. I couldn't understand, however, why he would bother when he dreamed again and again that I ruined everything for him.

Setting my napkin down, I pushed away from the table feeling frustrated, but full. There was something going on here, lurking under the surface like an enemy's submarine, something slippery and strange that I just couldn't nail down. Why would a gorgeous man want to marry someone he'd only just met? Granted, his mother wanted the marriage to happen (which was odd in itself), but Andrew didn't seem like the type of person to do whatever he was told. Not for the first time I wished I hadn't run away last night, like a frightened child. I should have asked him what he dreamed, gotten the details. Maybe there was a link between his dreams and mine. Maybe he remembered more than I did and together we could figure out what all this meant. I promised myself the next time we were alone together I would interrogate him mercilessly.

But now it was time to track down Mr. Huntington. I headed outdoors in search of Brian and my bike. The first place I tried was the small workshop I'd spotted on my way to the loch to take pictures. Smoke slipped lazily from a chimney shy of a few bricks at the top, like knocked out teeth.

I rapped on a door the color of driftwood and waited. After several seconds, I knocked again, my third rap flying into open air as the door swung open. Brian stared out at me. His gray eyes squinted, and his thin, dry lips pushed together as though trying to keep something out, or in.

"Hi, Brian!"

His veined hand reached up to the rim of his stained woolen cap and tugged it gently. "Miss."

"I was wondering if you fixed my bike?"

His eyes flitted to the left, though I couldn't see what he was looking at, standing as I was outside on the doorstep. "It be broken."

"Still?"

He nodded and started to close the door. I stuck my foot in the crack—an age-old maneuver taught to me by a senior reporter for when someone is being less than forthcoming (he pulled this move on everyone; I saved it for the mean ones, or when I was desperate, like now). "When do you think you'll have it fixed?"

He shook his head, holding tight to the door. There was something inside that he didn't want me to see. I had a strange feeling it was my bike, and that he had fixed the tire and didn't want me to know.

"Well, why don't you let me have it back? I'll find someone who can fix it."

He shook his head, his lower lip trembling like old hands. Brian was afraid. "Almost done wi' it. Coom back tomorrow."

"All right, fine," I relented. For the moment. "Then can you show me a shortcut to Mr. Huntington's house? I need to ask him some questions."

He gave me a relieved grin. It seemed he wanted to help me and this was one way he was allowed. Perhaps I hadn't imagined that conspiratorial wink when we first met. "That I can do." He stepped outside, closing the door firmly behind him. Grabbing my coat sleeve, he guided me to the front of the castle. This close, he smelled of smoke and oil, wood shavings and sweat. After looking about for a good ten seconds, he nodded, as though satisfied no one was watching. "Ye'll be wantin' tae cut across that way tae the moors." A crooked finger pointed toward a small path in the woods. "There be Wolf's Rock standin' atop Stonehaven Hill. Cross the wee burn, and head straight past Devil's Cairn. It canna be more than a couple kilos, goin' that way. But ye watch yersel, bairn. Yer way be hard."

He leaned down and looked me in the eye, his own moist with age and the world's sorrows. I met his gaze and swallowed hard, willing myself to stop being so fanciful. "I will," I promised.

"Ye must get it right." He straightened up and glanced toward the wood.

"I didn't plan on wiping out on my bike, Brian," I said dryly.

He gave me a sideways glance, then shook his head as he gently pushed me toward the path. "Just watch yersel," he called after me. I flipped him a wave over my shoulder as I started jauntily toward the trail. I'd worn sturdy boots, after all. I would be fine.

The wide path made for a nice walk and I felt my spirits rise with each step. With a smile, I realized I was looking forward to dueling with Greg Huntington. I needed to get back to my old self, the girl who refused to desist from getting the scoop even when in danger. Mr. Willeton both admired and admonished this trait in me, scolding me and praising me in the same breath (especially the time I'd witnessed a robbery at a gas station—I was filling up with gas at the time—and followed the robbers to their home, only to get shot at for my troubles.

But I got the story and the photos to go along with it, plus a police commendation, though they scolded me a bit, too. My father nearly blew a gasket).

Anyway, since Greg had called me a spitfire, I thought it only appropriate that I try to live up to his name for me.

After about ten minutes of walking, the woods opened up onto the moors. I stopped for a moment and gazed about in wonder, struck by the beauty of the scene. No cars, no buildings, nothing to mar the landscape. Simply rock and soil and endless sky. Inhaling deeply of fresh Scottish air, I moved on, heading for the massive stone in the distance that, judging by its canine profile, could only be Wolf's Rock.

Unable to resist, I snapped several photos as I neared the rock, then several more when I reached it. Light green and gray lichen covered its surface like a blight—a lupine with skin issues. Still having a way to go, I tucked my camera away and followed the direction the stone's snout pointed.

The threat of rain became reality only minutes after I started marching. Mist came at first, a hazy sheet of moisture that felt rather nice on my bare skin. Then the drops thickened into rain, pelting my head and face with increasing ferocity. It was about this time that I realized I hadn't brought gloves or a hat along. Foolish me. Typically, when on a job, I dressed warmly without a care to my appearance. Today, however, distracted by the task that lay ahead of me, by the fact that I'd dreamed again last night, and fooled by the unusually warm weather, I'd grown careless. My oversight had nothing to do with wanting to look good for Greg Huntington.

I walked faster, slipping on the wet stones. After falling twice and scraping the palm of my good hand, I slowed down. I didn't need another sprained wrist. The sleeves of my coat were long and I managed to wrap my hands in the material, warming them a bit. Even so, my fingertips stung with cold and a chill began to creep under my shirt and into my body. The lovely day had fast turned to misery. Even with the raincoat, the rain managed to find cracks and fissures to seep through, all the way to my goose-pimpled skin.

The burn, when I reached it, was quaint, but I wasn't in the mood for quaint. I crossed the little bridge and hurried on, head low, teeth chattering. The thought of turning back never occurred to me and I stumbled onward, hoping I was heading in the right direction.

Devil's Cairn rose out of the landscape like the devil himself—a great pile of rocks, which split into two separate piles about five feet in the air. Horns, I gathered, as rain ran down my face and dripped off my chin. It shouldn't be long now to Huntington's place.

But then the shivering started. I stumbled, cracked my knee on a rock, and fell forward. Stunned by the pain, I couldn't move, couldn't pick myself up. "Bloody hell!" I cursed under my breath. Suddenly I was shaking so hard that the earth below me trembled. Or was that the devil rising up to take me? The pounding roared in my ears. The whole world was going crazy. A distant part of me knew I was overreacting, but I couldn't help myself.

"Lilia!" The earth suddenly stopped shaking. "Good Lord, what are you doing out here? You'll catch your death. You're bleeding." Hands reached down to me, and this time I didn't flinch—I was too frozen. Greg picked me up and swung me onto his gray horse. Upright and shivering, I grabbed hold of the horse's black mane. Dressed all in black, his usual attire, Greg mounted behind me, reaching around to grab the reins with one hand and encircle me with the other. "Yah!" he shouted and the horse bolted forward.

We pounded across the open moors, down a hill, and with a bit more struggle, up the other side. Our breath came in short pants that created a trail of tiny clouds blowing away behind us like fleeing phantoms. Greg's back was warm and I felt the heat radiating off him, enveloping me like a blanket. At the top of the hill, he slowed and I caught sight of his home. The enormous building looked like something out of a BBC period production and I could only blink in dull surprise as we galloped toward it.

If Andrew and Greg had been competing for my affection, they would be neck and neck. Coming from money, I was used to grandeur. And typically I hated it in every sense. All show and façade and covering up the truth was how I saw my father's mansion, his friends' impressive cars, none under a hundred grand. The women dressed exquisitely and expensively and bought faces and bodies to match. I despised all of that. Not only was it a sad waste of money, it made the rest of the world feel entirely inadequate. Which, come to think of it, was probably the point.

But I had a weak spot for old world glamour, for ancient, sprawling homes and magical balls and beautiful carriages. I wasn't a tomboy through and through, much as I wanted the world to think so. I liked pretty things. But I knew that if I let my father see this weakness, he'd exploit it. And I would cave. I expected the truth from myself, just as much as from others, so I knew my limitations.

The lawn we crossed was flat and green against the dark sky. The mansion itself was pure Gothic architecture and utterly delightful in all its macabre grandiosity. We turned onto a gravel drive flanked by mossy oaks for about a hundred yards before opening up again.

"You like it," Greg spoke as he pulled the horse to a halt. "I knew you would."

"Oh, it's all right," I replied. "A bit on the small side. More like a summer cottage, really."

He slid to the ground, then reached a black-gloved hand up to me. He was smiling. "You like it better than Dundeid." I took his gloved hand, barely feeling the leather against my frozen skin, and slid down the side of the horse.

"Dundeid has a loch," I said when I landed.

"Mochrie Manor has a waterfall."

"Hmm...that I have to see."

"Not now. We must get you inside, get you out of those wet clothes."

"And into what? I don't think you're exactly my size."

"Well, if you insist on wearing clothes, my sister keeps some in her room. You're about the same height."

I gazed at him, surprised. "I didn't know you had a sister."

A dark-haired young man in breeches ran up to us and took the horse, patting him on the nose and speaking gently as he led him away.

"Can you walk?" Greg demanded when the boy was out of sight around the other side of the building.

I straightened up. "I'm not an invalid."

"I never said you were. But I saw you fall. You appeared to have hurt your knee."

Damned if I was going to let myself be carried by yet another man. "I'm fine."

He shrugged, though his eyes lit up with amusement. "Come along, then."

After three steps, I cursed my stubbornness—yet again. But I would not give him the satisfaction of being right. I would *not*. He glanced back, right eyebrow raised. "I'm fine," I ground out, my kneecap throbbing like a drum.

"So you'll let the Laird carry you, but not a lowly commoner like myself?"

"He just *did* it!" I gasped. "I didn't even have a chance to say no." His look was highly skeptical. "I had a concussion!" Well, probably not, but still…I was food deprived.

"So if I were to sweep you up into my arms, you wouldn't protest?"

"I'm saying no such thing. This time I don't have a concussion, and I have a black belt in karate that I'm not afraid to use." I'd taken an 8-week course in self-defense, but same difference, right?

He laughed, moving toward me. "I'll take my chances."

And before I knew it, I was in the air and he was carrying me through the double doors, into a spectacular foyer.

"Put me down!" I cried. I wanted to struggle, but I also wanted *not* to fall on the flagstone floor we were crossing. I had enough injuries—I didn't need any more. Besides, I was more interested in looking around. I loved all things Victorian and all around me were all things Victorian—from the potted ferns to the luxurious wallpaper and heavy blue velvet curtains.

Greg carried me up the stairs, down a long hallway, to a room at the other end. Inside, he set me down on a high bed, which I promptly slid off. "I'm going to get it wet!" I argued when he glared at me. "It's too pretty for that." I ran my hand along the cream coverlet, which was soft cotton, hand-stitched with roses along the edges and a circle of them in the middle. About ten pillows were stacked up against the headboard.

"Water dries, you know."

"Can I just get a towel?"

"I want you to take a hot shower. There's a bathroom," he indicated the door, "and Sophie keeps her clothes in here." Here was a wardrobe near the bed. I must have looked uncomfortable because he added, "I'll put your clothes in the dryer and you can wear them home."

"Fine." I tried to keep from scowling, but I couldn't help it. He was being kind, but I wasn't having it. "Well?" I said after thirty seconds had passed.

"Well, what?"

"You need to leave."

He grinned. "Are you sure you don't need some help with your clothes?"

I grabbed a pillow off the bed and threw it at him. "Get lost, perv."

He easily caught the pillow, considered throwing it back at me, then decided against it, setting it gently on the bed. His move put him within an inch of where I stood, cold and shaking. "You've got twenty minutes," he whispered provocatively.

As soon as he left, I tore off my wet outer clothes and my wrist wrap, then dashed into the bathroom. It was surprisingly modern and light and the water was nice and hot. I heard the bedroom door bang shut and I froze. Had it been twenty minutes already? Turning off the water, I dried off as quickly as I could. Wrapping a pink towel around my hair and one around my body, I peeked into the bedroom. No one was there, but my clothes were gone. Someone had fetched them.

The open wardrobe revealed an assortment of clothes that stunned me. His sister had left these behind? I couldn't fathom it. Who needed so many clothes? I decided I probably wouldn't like Sophie, who had to be a spoiled princess if I ever saw evidence for one. She even had a vanity table covered with makeup and perfumes and jewelry. What did this girl do? Sit around and look at herself all day? Yuck.

Feeling sanctimoniously virtuous for not having nearly so many clothes myself and for using next to no makeup, I pulled out a pink sweater, a white blouse, and a pair of jeans. Everything fit rather well, if a shade on the short side. Luckily my socks had survived the rain reasonably well and I pulled them back on. The boots I left off. Even I know black biker boots don't exactly go with pink cashmere. Then again…why not? I pulled them on, feeling defiant and back in charge.

I was towel drying my hair when the door swung open. "You're quick," Greg announced, looking disappointed. "Let me do that." He held out his hand for the towel.

"I can dry my own hair, thank you very much."

"I never said you couldn't. But I can do it better."

This time he didn't wait, simply took the towel from my reluctant hands. He had a way of backing me into a corner. If I clung to the towel, I'd look like a child. But giving in had the same effect.

Damn his eyes.

My chin lifted in an attempt to maintain some dignity as he applied the fluffy towel to my damp hair. His motions were gentle and smooth and actually felt quite nice, I must admit. His expression when I peeked up at it was a combination of smugness and pleasure.

"Okay, that's good," I said heartily, stepping away.

He handed me the towel. "I can comb it out for you."

"I'm not six."

"You seem to feel the need to assume you know my thoughts. I know quite well you're not six, that you can take care of yourself. But haven't you ever wanted to be taken care of, Lilia, if only once in a while?"

I bit my lip. He'd hit a sore spot. I'd spent a lot of my life proving I was tough, that I was strong, that I was not my mother. But that didn't mean I didn't want someone to share some of my burden sometimes. Just not my dad. Never my dad. He'd hold any weakness I displayed over my head for the rest of my life.

"What do you know about my mother?" I demanded. Going on the offensive was so much more satisfying than being a target.

He wandered over to the dressing table and picked up a silver-backed brush. He held it out to me and I took it from him. As I brushed my hair, he watched every move, every stroke. I shivered. Having once thought I was a more than adequate hair brusher, I now found myself doubting my skill.

"I know enough," he said.

I had to know if he knew everything. I had to know if he knew the truth. I couldn't forget it. In fact, I see that day as clearly as my own face in the mirror. Every lash, every freckle, every blemish and flaw. Memorized. Irrevocably, irretrievably, unavoidably committed to memory. Lord knows I've done everything I could to erase that experience, to no avail.

"Lily!" The voice was the one Mother got when a migraine was coming. Panicked, full of pain. "Lily, come here!"

She was calling from the bathroom. Dashing down the hall, my sneakers made little thudding noises on the wooden floor of our nineteenth century farmhouse. The sooner I reached her and gave her her medication, helped her to her room and drew the blinds, the less likely the migraine would blow up into a two-day event. With luck, there would only be a few hours of suffering—on both our parts.

I pushed on the white door and it banged on the toiletry shelf, which stood against the wall. Cringing at the noise, I hurried inside and around the door. Typically Mother was sitting on the toilet seat, lid down, clutching her head in her hands. Not today. Today she was stretched out in our white, claw foot tub, fully dressed, even though the tub was filled nearly to the top with water. Her eyes stared up at the cloudless sky through the skylight Father had installed over the tub.

"Mother?"

"Come here." She motioned to me, though her eyes stayed focused on the rectangle of blue.

I stepped toward her, one foot stretching slowly forward, as though testing questionable floorboards. I stopped, just out of her reach. Something was wrong, but I couldn't tell what. Did she have a migraine? Or had she had too much to drink? Sometimes that happened, too.

"I'm here, Mother."

"Closer." She beckoned. I took another step. Her wet hand darted out and grabbed my wrist, pulling me toward her. "I don't want to do this, Lily, but it's the only way."

"Do what?" I whispered.

"It's the only way," she continued, not hearing me. "We must stop this now. I can't let them do this to you over and over. It's cruel. And really…" she paused, her teeth working at her bottom lip like tiny white spades. "I can't take it anymore. These dreams…I hate them, Lily. This has to end."

My other hand reached out and patted the one gripping me tightly and cutting off the blood to the rest of my palpating arm. "Let me get you into bed, Mother. Everything will be all right in the morning." I was lying. The situation might improve a bit, but it never really got better. But all I had was now. I'd deal with later, well, later.

"Don't fight me on this, Lily. Fighting will make it so much worse."

I suppressed a sigh. "I'm not fighting you, Mother. I just want to help you into bed."

"Oh, Lily. You're such a good girl. You don't deserve this…"

I agreed with her on that. "Don't worry about me, Mother. I'll be fine. Right now, let's get you out of that tub and into something dry and warm and I'll…Agh!"

The attack came quick as a snake, her free hand flying toward me, sharp, shiny blade flashing. "No!" I jerked away, but not before the blade sliced my arm just below my elbow. Her hold loosened and I flew backward, bashing my head against the toilet seat. Dazed, frightened, and in pain, I pulled myself to my hands and knees and crawled away from her, out into the hallway. There I collapsed, unconscious and bleeding.

My father found us, first me, then Mother. She had lost a fair amount of blood after cutting her wrists, but she recovered quite rapidly. I got a concussion and twenty stitches out of the deal. Father told the emergency room physician that I had passed out from the shock of finding my mother, hit my head, and cut my arm on the radiator when I fell. My father knew the chief of police, so the investigation was professional, but not intended to pursue the truth. They thought they already knew it, believing my father's lie.

Along with my scar, I inherited something even worse—my mother's dreams, the first of which came to me when I was lying on the hallway floor, unconscious. I heard later that when she woke in the hospital, Mother was actually smiling. Father told me this, his incredulity and rage intermingled like sand and water. But I understood. She was free. When Father told her his plan, however, she stopped smiling. I heard about this part, too—about how she looked like her world had exploded. He both relished her pain for what she had done—attempted to do—and wished he could undo it all so we could go back to the way things were.

Personally, although the dreams were bad, I didn't want to go back to the way things were. With Mother out of the house, I could breathe again. I could be ten and a child. Little did I realize, lying in my bed, Father sitting next to me and relating all the sordid details so that I wouldn't ever forget what she had done to "ruin us all," that he would end up being just as bad, if not worse. He let me be a child, all right. Like one who needed someone to wipe her butt and feed her crackers. I've spent the last thirteen years trying to prove to him that I wasn't a child, and so far I've failed miserably.

I snorted angrily, coming back to the present. "That means nothing to me. I want to know how much you know and who you're planning to tell."

Greg's face tightened into a cool mask. "I've no intention of telling anyone anything. And I only know this information because I wanted to learn more about you. I looked up your name on the Internet. From there, it was easy to track your dad. I learned that your mother took ill, then your parents divorced and she moved to Paris."

"That's everything?"

His eyes shifted. "More or less."

"You found out what 'took ill' means, didn't you?"

He shrugged. "I had to know…ever since I saw you I haven't been able to stop thinking about you. So I did what I do best…I researched you. I found out things about you. It took a little digging, but not as much as I thought it would."

I felt sick. "You bastard. You had no right to do that!"

"On the contrary. I had every right."

He stopped there, forcing me, furious and afraid, to push. "Go on! Tell me what gives you the right to pry into my life?"

"Because when I first saw you, I *knew* you." The way he said that word was entirely too intimate.

My heart knocked inside my chest. "You said…"

"I know what I said in your bedroom, and I meant it. I didn't know your name. But I knew *you*."

"How?" I breathed.

"Because I dream about you, Lilia. Every single night…"

Chapter Thirteen

The heat rose from my chest, up into my face. "Damnit, not you, too!"

He blinked at me, obviously not expecting my reaction. "Who else is dreaming about you?"

My fingers tightened around the cool handle of the brush. "What do you dream? I have to know."

"Answer my question, and I'll answer yours."

"Fine. Andrew dreams about me." I walked over to the vanity and set down the brush carefully. My eyes in the mirror were feverish, glassy and wild. I looked away. "He says I keep him up at night."

"What does he…what does he dream about you?"

"He didn't say. I ran when he told me. Earlier he'd said that everything gets ruined in his dreams. I didn't want to face up to what that meant. This is all so strange. And now to find out you're also dreaming about me…"

"You have dreams, too," he guessed.

"Yes," I admitted reluctantly. "Since my mother attempted…to kill herself." He didn't need to know that she'd tried to kill me, too. Nobody needed to know that. I wished I didn't.

He leaned toward me and my skin flushed hot. "I'm so sorry about your mother, Lilia."

"You're really going to keep calling me Lilia?" I had to get off the subject of my mother *now*.

"Why not? I like it better and it suits you."

"You know that Lily means purity and chastity and all that crap."

"Maybe that's why I'd rather call you Lilia." He gave me a devilish smile. I wasn't sure if I wanted to cold cock him for what might be an insult or take his cheek as a compliment.

"So the extra 'a' cancels out the purity and chastity?"

"I simply don't think anyone as feisty as you should be burdened by a name."

"At least you're not calling me Tiger."

"I could."

"Don't."

"Are you hungry?"

"Not really." I shivered. "Got a roaring fire I can sit in front of?"

"I'm sure there's one round here somewhere." He extended his arm to me, and after a moment's hesitation, I took it. My knee was still throbbing and I decided I'd just look ridiculous hobbling after him. No matter what I chose, my pride was going to take a hit—might as well get something out of it.

We limped down the hall, and I used Greg's arm and the railing to get down the stairs. There seemed to be more steps than I remembered. We crossed the foyer, took a left down another hall, and finally entered a small room which, with its high ceiling, was surprisingly cozy, and which did indeed have a roaring fire.

"Sit here." He indicated an overstuffed, floral-print chair with matching ottoman in front of the fire. He bent down and helped me lift my leg up onto the soft footstool, then grabbed a pillow off another chair and tucked it under my knee. I realized he went out of his way to touch me whenever he could, and I also realized that I liked it. "I'm going to get you an ice pack."

"Don't you have a servant to do that?" I asked flippantly, rather enjoying being waited on.

"He's washing my Aston Martin." With that, he was gone, leaving me to contemplate the lovely room. Murky outdoor light filtered through the diamond panes of three recessed windows. Beautiful paintings decorated the walls and built-in bookshelves filled in the rest of the space. Exotic artifacts, likely acquired when traveling abroad was de rigueur, were spread casually around the room. I determined that this would not be the more glamorous formal parlor used for visitors, but a family room. I felt strangely flattered that Greg had welcomed me into his inner sanctum.

He returned ten minutes later with an ice pack, followed by a little, round woman built like a robin, all bosom on top and two skinny legs to support her. She wore a gray skirt and sweater set that might possibly date from the 1940s. A pearl necklace around her short neck was her only adornment. She set a tray down on the table next to my chair and proceeded to pour me a cup of golden-brown tea as Greg settled the ice pack over my knee.

"This is Mrs. Lennox," he introduced, "without whom I'd wither away and die."

"Oh, you!" She swatted at him before turning to me. "Welcome to Mochrie Manor, dear. Here, take these. For the pain."

I took the two pills nestled in her plump palm. "Thank you. I'm Lilia MacKenzie." I stopped. Had I really just introduced myself as Lilia? "I mean, Lily." Greg lifted a wry eyebrow.

"Pleasure to meet you, Miss MacKenzie. You'll be staying at the castle, then?" Her reddish round nose twitched like a rabbit's as she held up a sugar cube trapped in silver tongs. I shook my head and she dropped it back into the pot.

"Yes. I'm doing a story on genealogy."

"Ah, well. I hope you find what you're looking for. Sometimes the past is meant to be left alone, don't you think?" Her inquisitive eyes peered into mine, searching for answers to questions she wouldn't dare speak aloud. "Stirring things up causes trouble, I wager. More than most folk can handle." She shook her head, solemnly. "No, I'd just as soon stay in the present."

"But if we don't study our past and learn from our mistakes," I argued, "then surely we're destined to repeat them."

"Oh, not necessarily! I warrant I've been looking forward to the future my whole life and I've no doubt I'm the better for it." She straightened up. "There now, get some of that tea in you before you catch your death." She glanced at a tiny silver watch trapped in the crease around her wrist. "Dinner is at one o'clock."

"I don't think I'll be here—"

"Thank you, Mrs. Lennox," Greg interrupted. "We'll be there."

She bustled out of the room, looking quite pleased with herself and her lot. Maybe she was right. Maybe it would be better to forget everything and start over. Focus on the here and now.

"I didn't plan on staying for lunch," I told Greg, mostly to erase the smug look on his face. "I didn't even tell anyone at Dundeid that I was leaving." I swallowed the pills and washed them down with a gulp of hot tea that warmed me pleasantly. I took another sip for good measure.

"You're a big girl, as you seem so intent on proving. I'm sure they'll be all right without you."

"That's not the point and you know it." He sat down in the chair opposite me, looking more complacent than he had a right to. He deserved to be taken down a peg or two. "It's just that I had plans…with Andrew…"

He sat up, jerked right out of his superior self-congratulations. "You've plans with Andrew to do what?"

It was my turn to smile. "Calm down, *Tiger*. I had plans to ask him about what he dreamt. Which reminds me. What do you dream?"

"I'll tell you after lunch."

"That's blackmail!"

"It's good business. What do you say?"

I crossed my arms, realized I looked like a child, and uncrossed them. My restless fingers tapped on the arm of my chair. "Fine. But you'd better tell me everything."

"I'll tell you everything I know. I promise." He was being very careful with his words and I had a feeling he was up to something.

"Ophelia says you're returning to Edinburgh soon."

"She did, did she?"

"Yes, she did. And don't answer like that. You're wasting my time."

He laughed. "I won't answer like that if you ask me what it is you really want to know."

"Fine. Is that a permanent move or just a business trip?"

He leaned forward, resting his elbows on his knees. "Why do you care?"

"I don't. But Ophelia does." I bit my tongue, feeling traitorous. "I mean, you know... She remembers you from childhood, and she doesn't get out much with her illness so gossip about her neighbors is akin to gold."

He studied me and I tried to maintain eye contact. It wasn't easy—his gaze was quite intense. "I haven't decided."

"Why would you want to leave this place?"

"There's nothing to keep me here."

"Only family history, childhood memories..."

"My memories of this place..." He hesitated, picked up his teacup, then didn't drink from it. His finger rubbed on the side of it instead, as though trying to remove the delicate paint. "They'll always be tinged with pain, I think."

"Because of your dad? Ophelia mentioned something about him dying from leukemia. I'm sorry."

"Thank you, and his death is a part of it, but I've felt this way since before then. A certain sadness, a longing, as though something were missing. Like I needed to do something, but I couldn't."

I frowned; his feelings echoed my own too closely. "I can relate to that." I sighed and rubbed my forehead. "So what brought you back this time?"

He slumped against his chair, looking at the fire. "A whim."

The dark expression on his face said something different. Greg looked like a man driven by demons. He hadn't come home for a lark. Something, or someone, had forced his hand. I took a sip of tea before saying, "Vivian is quite pretty."

"Yes, she is." Dang. "She seems to have a good opinion of you." I peered over my teacup at his profile. He didn't react.

"And what gave you that idea?" He turned to face me.

I wasn't going into details. "Well, she invited you to the ball knowing that would anger Andrew."

"To neglect to issue me an invitation would be a tactical error on her part. The Gala is the social event of the year and depends on the attendance of the many young, unmarried women whose parents own businesses here in Dundeid. Not to sound arrogant, but my presence is a draw for the young, single lady of elevated birth. I'm rich, I'm unmarried, and I come from a good family, so I must be invited. Vivian knows her duty, as does Andrew. He won't like it, but what can he do? Besides," he grinned, "everyone's invited to come."

"You could've just said that in the first place."

"Then I wouldn't have gotten to see that precious look on your face."

I ignored this. "But Vivian issued you a personal invitation."

"She was simply confirming that I was coming. When I found out that you were going to be there, I said yes."

"Another opportunity to annoy me?"

"Another opportunity to see your beautiful face."

I took another sip—gulp—of tea. "Oh, well. Hm. Um, I'm wearing a ball gown. Ophelia and I found it in the attic."

He didn't respond, merely drank the rest of his tea, then set the empty cup down on the tray. "After the ball, I'd planned to leave for Edinburgh for good. But now…well, we'll have to see."

"I'll tell Ophelia and Vivian your new plans. I'm sure they'll be pleased."

He smiled. "You can tell Andrew, too. Watch the look on his face when you let him know—I'd like to hear about it. Better yet, snap a picture." He stood up. "Come. We'll take a tour."

I glanced at my knee. The throbbing had settled to a dull roar—I thought I could walk without assistance. I stood without help, but Greg quickly took my arm, giving me no choice but to borrow a bit of his strength. Exhaling a deep sigh, I resigned myself to being treated as an invalid. And after the first few steps, I actually began to enjoy myself. The guys I'd dated back home had never been this gallant. At most, they might offer to pay half for our date—except those who knew how much money my dad had. Those losers didn't offer, expecting me to pick up the whole tab. I did it, if only as a matter of pride, but I didn't go out on a second date with the cheapskates.

"As you can see," Greg commented as we strolled down a long, wide passage off the foyer, "although this is a hallway, it's quite big and allows one to walk along it without running into anyone else."

"You could drive two cars down this hall and not run into anyone else. Where does it lead? Heaven?"

He chuckled. "My ancestors wanted visitors to believe that. But, really, only to the formal parlor. There's a shorter way to get to it, but this hall was used if there was a desire to impress the visitor. Then there's the music room, a library, and a gallery in this wing. The dining room and ballroom are on the other side of the building."

"No conservatory?" I joked.

"That's located at the back of the manor. The bedrooms are all upstairs. We could skip all this and head on up. What do you say?"

When I glanced over at him, his expression was bland, as though he really did want to show me the bedrooms purely for ascetic reasons. "Another life, maybe," I replied.

He leaned toward me. "I can't wait that long, Lilia," he whispered. We stopped walking, just outside a doorway, both staring at each other with such intensity that we could have ignited the wallpaper. And then he pulled back and it was over, whatever *it* was. "Here we have the formal parlor." He politely indicated the way and we stepped inside a high-ceilinged room, beautifully decorated, but a bit formal for my taste, with its antique chairs and delicate tables. I did like the small harpsichord. It looked well-used.

"Very nice," I murmured. Then something struck me, a brief vision, a memory of playing the little piano, liking the sound it produced. "You know, this room feels familiar to me."

"Does it?" He sounded oddly hopeful.

"Vaguely." I looked around for another few seconds, then shrugged. "I can't be sure. If you've seen one formal parlor, you've seen them all," I joked.

"Let's try the gallery," he said eagerly.

As though on a mission, he pulled me through a nearly hidden door in the parlor wall. We entered yet another good-sized room, filled with paintings and statues and displays ranging from pottery to ancient metal work. "This is amazing," I breathed, pulling from his grasp and heading toward a David-like statue.

"Is this room familiar?" he demanded.

"It's possible, but either way, your collection is wonderful."

"I'm thinking of donating several pieces to the National Museum of Scotland."

"That's a great idea."

"You think so?"

"My father's a wealthy man, but he never parts with any of his money. Well, he tries with me, but I can't see it as an act of generosity."

His fingers tapped at the base of a statue portraying a naked man and woman thoroughly engrossed in one another. "What do you see it as?"

"I'm pretty sure he's trying to buy my affection. Actually..." I paused, trying to determine exactly what it was he was trying to do. "He's trying to buy *me*," I realized. "Plain and simple. He doesn't like being alone."

"Do many people?"

"Probably not, other than your true hermit, I suppose. But my dad's not a hermit. He has business friends, and occasionally they'll go golfing together. Other than that, he stays home and spends his time sticking his nose into my business." I sounded rather pouty, but living with his neediness day after day was exhausting, and frankly, too much responsibility for any one person to handle. He was my father, not my friend, and I had to constantly fight to maintain boundaries with him.

"What was he like before your mother...left?"

"His life revolved around my mother. But when she went away, I got..."

The words never left my mouth, but Greg understood immediately. "You got stuck with him."

I pulled in a quick breath. I'd never looked at it that way before, but as the British say, he was spot on. "You sound like you've been there."

He smiled enigmatically. "Let's just say I understand taking on a difficult responsibility. He must not have liked you coming here."

"He actually forbid me until he found out that this guy at work, Jamie Flynn, had the hots for me. Jamie is very good-looking and really nice and easy to talk to. He's respectful and has goals. The very idea of him scared the crap out of my dad."

"And you like this Jamie." Greg's tone was flat, but his eyes were fiery.

"Of course I do. There aren't many men out there like him. He even helped me with my dad."

"How?"

I smiled, remembering our little agreement. "I helped him get together with the girl he was really interested in and in return, he pretended—in front of my dad, who has a bad habit of visiting me at work unannounced—that he was in love with me."

"I imagine the girl wasn't too happy about that." Greg, on the other hand, sounded thrilled.

"Oh, Terri knew about it. That was part of the deal." Thinking back, given a little time, I might actually have become friends with Terri and Jamie. We'd had a lot of fun working out the details of my charade, though Terri didn't realize that behind it all was the goal of getting her and Jamie together. She just thought we were playing a joke on my dad, and since being a proofreader was rather boring work, she jumped at the chance to do something fun. At any rate, neither seemed to care that my dad was rich or that Mr. Willeton favored me. Besides, they knew that being one of his favorites wasn't always such a good thing. They were even thrilled I'd gotten this gig in Scotland. In return for their enthusiasm, I made sure to talk them up in front of Mr. Willeton whenever possible.

All in all, my master plan went smoothly. After dad's visit to the office and his subsequent meltdown, I urged Terri and Jamie to go get lunch together, my treat. They did, and have been dating ever since. Jane Austen's Emma would've been green with envy at my matchmaking skills. I was quite wily when I wanted to be.

"You're a devious one, Lilia MacKenzie," Greg commented, echoing my thoughts.

"I can be when necessary." I moved over to gaze up at a magnificent landscape painting of dark, wild moors and gray, windy sky. A tiny figure in white stood off to the right, her back against the racing clouds, the wind blowing her pale locks upward into the sky like flying snakes. "I like this one."

"An ancestor of mine painted it."

"It's very good."

Greg swung away, restless. "Why did you come here, Lilia?"

"To do a story on—"

"That's not really why and you know it."

"It's what I'm getting paid to do," I tried.

"And what have you found so far?"

"I discovered that I'm related to Ian MacKenzie and that there was some sort of argument between his ancestor and mine—they were brothers—before my ancestor sailed to America."

"What else?" He was relentless.

"That's pretty much it. It's been a couple of slow news days."

"I gave you the register. I know you went through it."

I bit my lip. "Yes, I did."

"And you found her name. *Your* name."

"Yes." I didn't look at him, keeping my eyes focused on the tiny figure in front of me.

"So what do you think of that?"

"I thought it was an interesting coincidence, though I didn't find what I was actually looking for."

"Which was?"

"My relatives." I wasn't lying, but I could tell by his angry brow that he didn't believe me. "I'm telling the truth," I insisted.

"You told me you'd come here to find the truth."

"Yes. I'm a reporter. That's what I do."

"When you told me about your quest, your words sounded much more personal." He snapped his fingers and I flinched. "I remember now. You actually said you were here to learn secrets."

I shrugged. "Secrets, truth, it's all the same."

"For someone obsessed with finding the truth, you certainly aren't all that big on telling it."

I swung to face him. "I'm not obsessed! And I haven't lied to you once."

He didn't back down. "But you're not telling me things, either."

"That isn't lying. Besides, I have to protect myself somehow so I can finish this."

"Start by trusting me."

"Why you?"

He rubbed his hand over his face. "I don't know. Because of the dreams?"

"Andrew has them, too."

"Andrew has too many people he has to keep happy."

"And you have no one…"

He frowned. "It's not just me—"

"Not good enough. Nothing personal, but I'm going to stick with trusting myself, and only myself. It's what I've done all my life…I don't see any reason to stop now."

"*All* your life…?"

"Well, yes…" I was tempted to tell him how, from as early as I could remember, my father had clung to and obsessed over my mother and asked me to watch over her when he wasn't around. But I said nothing.

He studied me for several moments. "You know something, Lilia? You and I are a lot alike."

I laughed nervously. "Is that a good thing or a bad thing?"

"That remains to be seen." His dark eyes flitted away. "On to the library?"

"Sounds good," I replied, all the while thinking I wasn't the only one who had secrets. Greg knew something, too, and he was keeping it to himself. But what did he know?

More importantly, how was I going to get it out of him?

Chapter Fourteen

In the library, Greg told me about his sister. "Sophie's the reader in the family," he said after I commented on how loved the worn books seemed. "She'd live in a book if she could."

"Oh?" To say I was surprised was a bit of an understatement. "She *reads*?"

He smiled, quick to grasp my error. "Mother decorated that room for her. It's nothing like Sophie, but doing so made Mother happy and gave her something to occupy her time after Father died."

"So all those clothes...?"

"Another one of Mother's efforts to connect with her "wayward" daughter. Sophie has always typically worn dark colors only, mainly because then she doesn't have to worry about matching...or stains."

"She's like me that way."

"Not at all."

I glanced at him. "What do you mean?"

"You dress like you do as a protest." I actually wanted to protest that, but thought it'd be better not to prove his point. "Sophie dresses like she does because she feels no inclination to worry about what she wears. She's too busy thinking about nuclear physics."

"She's a nuclear physicist?" I was finding that I had to severely revise my snotty opinion of Greg's sister. I was grateful I'd never shared it and hoped fervently I'd learn a lesson from my hasty condemnation.

"That's what she has her Ph.D. in, and what she teaches at University, but I truly think she's a philosopher at heart." He pulled out a translation of Plato's *The Republic* and idly thumbed through it with a reminiscent smile. "She loves arguing."

"She sounds fun."

He laughed. "I don't know if I'd use the word fun to describe Sophie. But she's always interesting."

"Does she ever come home?"

"Not usually. She prefers Edinburgh, where she can meet with her friends and discuss quarks all day long."

"I suppose there isn't much for her here."

"I once thought…" Greg stopped talking, taking a moment to tuck *The Republic* back on the shelf. "Well, that she and Andrew might make a go of it."

"Andrew? And a nuclear physicist? Talk about going against the laws of nature."

"What? You question his intelligence?"

"Not at all," I murmured, remembering his secret room. "Has your sister ever dabbled in chemistry?"

"She dabbled in all the sciences before settling on physics." He paused for a moment, eyes narrowing. "Why do you ask?"

I shrugged. "Just curious."

"Just curious, hm?"

I laugh. "Why don't you show me the conservatory?"

He didn't move for several seconds, regarding me as one would a snake. I gave him my 'mysterious' smile. "I'm going to figure out what you're up to, Lilia."

"By the time you do, I'll be gone." My smile grew wider.

"You wish."

"I wish to see the conservatory."

"Very well. Let's go look at plants."

And that's what we did. Greg remained silent as I oohed and ahhed. The glass room was beautiful, warm and moist and filled with vibrant plants and fountains. "One year Sophie decided she wanted to be an environmentalist, so she converted everything to run on solar power."

"She sounds very enterprising."

"I think you mean energetic."

"That, too. I'm happy when I remember to sort my garbage for recycling. The idea of taking it any further doesn't really cross my mind."

"Mine, either, which is why I'm glad to have Sophie around. She keeps me honest."

"You need someone to do that?"

He grinned, his serious eyes growing younger in a flash. "I have a rebellious streak, I guess you could say."

"Oh, do tell," I said, joining him by the fountain. I leaned over and touched the cool water, making tiny ripples with my finger.

"Let's just say that I like to get my way."

"Funny, I'm the same way. What happens if what you want doesn't coincide with what another person wants?"

"I think you know the answer to that."

"Yes, I guess I do. So I'll apologize now."

"Ha! You don't possibly think you'd defeat *me*?"

"This isn't all-star wrestling. And yes, I do." *I have a feeling everything counts on me defeating you.*

"What do you mean?"

I glanced at him, startled. Had I spoken that last bit out loud? "About what...?" When all else fails, fall back on stupidity.

"You said, 'I have a feeling everything counts on me defeating you.'"

Adrenaline shot through me. "I didn't say that out loud," I replied, choosing my words carefully.

"I'm sure I heard..." His eyes lost focus as he thought hard. "Wait, you said, 'out loud.' What did you mean by *that*?"

Damn, he was sharp. I pulled back from the fountain. "I'm not really sure. Say, do you think lunch is ready?"

"Why are you always so evasive? Do you ever just answer a question?"

I shrugged. For being so hung up on finding the truth, I wasn't doing a very good job of following my own creed. Before this trip, I'd been honest to the point of brutality. But now... Well, it seemed I had too much to lose. I shivered, feeling as though a ghost had stepped inside me, and suddenly I began to doubt myself. Was subterfuge the right way to go? Shouldn't I just tell him the truth?

No, no, no.

"I'm not the only one with secrets here," I said instead.

He had the good sense to look abashed. "But my secrets have nothing to do with you."

"That's a lie."

He pulled away from the fountain and offered his arm. "All right. You got me. We'll go to dinner and we'll talk. I'll tell you all about my dreams and you'll tell me why you're really here."

"All right," I agreed hesitantly.

We left the conservatory, both quiet, lost in our own thoughts. We strolled through several halls until we reached the dining area, a long room with pastoral murals painted on the two longer walls. A gorgeous crystal chandelier hung over a walnut table two or three times the size of a normal table. Greg pulled out an ornate chair facing the windows, which looked out over the moors, and I sat down. He took the carved chair next to me, the one at the head of the table. There was a fireplace behind him and one at the other end of the table. Apparently the Huntingtons did not like being cold while dining. Smart folk.

I silently gave thanks for having attended Mademoiselle Lefit's Charm School. Father might have wanted his daughter to know all the right things, but he himself wasn't one for ceremony. He thought it was a waste of time, and commented accordingly, whenever he could. I rather liked it, though. It seemed a comfort to have a ritual to focus on when in the midst of such grandeur. Call me old-fashioned, but once I mastered the rules I actually felt more at home eating this way.

"Enough spoons and forks for you?"

I picked up an ornate fork and examined it. "I actually like all this, once I get past being left-handed."

"You're left-handed?"

"Why do you sound like I just told you I had a tail?" I held up my wrapped wrist. "That's why this isn't as big a deal as it could've been."

He shook his head, reaching for a silver bell near his plate. The chime was surprisingly loud for such a small object. Immediately, a door behind him swung open. A young woman marched in bearing a silver-serving tray. She stared openly at me, her blue eyes scanning me from head to toe as though taking in as much information about me as she could to bring back to headquarters, which was likely the kitchen. The word 'voluptuous' fit this girl as perfectly as spandex shorts. She wore tight jeans and an even tighter pink blouse with several gold chains slithering down between her full breasts, losing themselves in cleavage I'd never be able to manage even with a push-up bra and wads of tissue. She cracked watermelon-flavored gum as she leaned forward to set a small plate of salad on top of the larger plate already there. Gold dangly earrings swung forward, emerging from the long, curly black hair she wore loose, then back again as she straightened to deliver Greg's plate. She looked young, but there was a toughness in her bold eyes.

"Thank you, Amria," Greg said, his voice level.

"You're most welcome, Mr. Huntington." Her eyes met mine and she winked. It wasn't a mischievous wink and she wasn't flirting, either. It seemed to me that the wink was a promise, or better yet, a threat. When she was satisfied I'd read her message, whether my translation was accurate or not, she turned and flounced away, her fanny swaying back and forth.

"She's one of my sister's projects," Greg answered my unspoken question. "Sophie often picks up strays round the city and finds them work. For some reason she thought I might benefit from Amria's attentions." He sighed and shook his head. "For being so smart, my sister can sometimes be a real bampot."

"Bampot?" I hadn't come across that in my research on Scotland.

"Idiot, or crazy person."

"Oh." I made a mental note to remember that one. "Why?"

"Amria has high expectations in life and one of those include marrying someone with a lot of money."

"You?"

He shrugged. "I'm her best chance, or so she thinks. She's an outcast from her own tribe. Her mother had relations with someone who was not a traveller."

Had relations…what a quaint way to put it, I mused. "People still practice banishment?"

"Some groups do. Travellers, or gypsies, have been treated with contempt and scorn for centuries. Some groups disintegrate as a result. Others grow stronger, building their strength on the belief that their people are special. To remain so involves marrying within the tribe."

"And if they don't, they're banished."

He nodded. "I feel for Amria. She's had a hard life. But I've never felt comfortable round her."

"Too hot-blooded for you?"

"She's in my dreams."

"Oh, well, I can see why. She's very attractive."

"Not that way, Lilia." He picked up his fork. "Eat your meal and then I'll tell you what I dream."

The salad, crisp and fresh, was delicious. While we ate, we talked about the upcoming Gala, and I learned just how important this event was to the local economy. Then I told Greg more about the newspaper and Mr. Willeton. We both pretended for the time being that I truly had come here just to do genealogical research. He gave me some good leads, including suggesting I speak to Father Chisolm in person. He thought printing a quote from a Scottish priest would look good for my article. I agreed. It's hard to get a more reliable source than a man of God.

The food was delicious, the wine excellent, the experience pleasant on the whole, marred only by Amria's growing discontent with each course served or drink refreshed. It occurred to me that she had listened at the door and heard Greg speaking about her. It also occurred to me that Greg meant to be heard.

We had finished dessert—warm custard accompanied by a small glass of sherry—when Amria came in looking triumphant. "You have a visitor, *Mr. Huntington.*" I had to give her credit—just saying his name the way she did was a rebellion in itself. A "you might be my boss, but you don't own me," proclamation.

He placed his napkin on the table. "Who is it?"

One rounded shoulder lifted insolently. "Why don't you go find out?"

A muscle in his cheek began to tic. "Is he in the front parlor?"

"Of course."

"We'll meet him there."

"Whatever you say, *Mr. Huntington.*" Translation: I don't give a crap what you do.

"Shall we see who the intruder is, Lilia?" He offered me his arm, earning me the look of death from Amria as she gathered up our wineglasses. As I stood and took it, the main door banged open, startling us both. Amria smiled, obviously pleased at both our reactions, which were stunned, and then annoyed—on Greg's part, anyway.

"Where've you been?" Andrew thundered. His chest was heaving as though he'd run the whole way. He looked like he wanted to pull me away from Greg, but he stayed where he was, fists clenched, with the long table between us like a moat.

"Is this a trick question?" I countered, working desperately to recover my wits.

"Why didn't you tell anyone where you were going, Lily? You're my responsibility! What if you'd gotten lost on the moors? It's pouring cats and dogs and you'd be soaked. You could have caught your death."

"She's a paying guest, Dering," Greg said dryly, though he was obviously not amused, "not your cousin from County Cork."

"We actually might be cousins, Huntington, and it's not for you to decide how to run my business!"

"Cousins? Where do you get that drivel?" Greg looked at me. I shrugged.

"It's possible," Andrew countered. "I've been doing some of my own research. And there's a connection between us. I can feel it."

"*Feel* it?" Greg scoffed. "Since when have you become the sensitive type?"

Andrew's eyes sparked. "I only mean that I sense a relation. Something I read once, or saw…" He trailed away, trying to remember what it was.

"Miss MacKenzie has the freedom to come and go as she pleases. She's a grown *woman*," here, Greg looked down at me and I suddenly became interested in the fireplace, "who's paying to stay at your establishment. She doesn't need to check in with you."

Andrew looked mutinous. "I was worried. That's not a crime, is it, Lily?" His blue eyes looked vulnerable.

"No, of course not," I said, glad to finally be allowed to speak for myself. "Next time I'll let you know my plans. It's only practical anyway."

"He's not your nanny," Greg mumbled, looking put out.

"I know that, but he's right. I don't know my way around and if I did get hurt..."

"I'll bring you back now," Andrew said quickly, taking advantage of my momentary contrition.

"Not necessary," Greg spoke up. "I'll take her in the motor. We have some...things to discuss."

I suddenly remembered his dream. "Yes, we never did finish our conversation."

"Actually, there's someone at Dundeid who wants to speak to you, Lily. That's how we found out you'd gone. We thought you'd arrive for dinner and when you didn't, and you weren't in your room—"

"Who is it?" I interrupted. I wasn't going to feel guilty forever.

"Ian found a letter. After you spoke to him, he went through the family papers and he found it tucked into the family Bible. He wanted to show it to you."

"He's still at the castle?" I somehow couldn't imagine Ian staying inside the castle for any length of time. Too many people, too many walls.

"Well, no," Andrew admitted. "But the letter is there. He seemed quite anxious—anxious for Ian, that is—that you read it."

I glanced at Greg, who was doing a terrible job of hiding his irritation. "Can you call me later?"

He shook his head stubbornly. "It's not something I wish to talk about over the phone."

"Well, maybe tomorrow?"

He looked regretful. "I'm leaving to Edinburgh tomorrow. A business meeting. I won't be back until the Gala. But I will be back." He aimed that one at Andrew.

"Ah." I felt strangely disappointed. "Well, have a good trip, and thank you for lunch."

He nodded curtly. "You'd better go. Your caretaker looks afraid I might devour you at any moment." I laughed, then bit down on it seeing the look on Andrew's face. I thought maybe he'd be happy if Greg left and never came back. "Wait," he commanded. "Give me your phone." I frowned, but pulled it out and handed it to him.

"What are you up to, Huntington?" Andrew demanded.

After tapping it a few times, Greg handed my phone back. "Call me if you need me. Any time." I nodded and slipped it into my pocket.

"Shall we, Lily?" Andrew offered his arm. I disengaged from Greg, immediately missing the warmth of his body and hobbled over to Andrew. "What happened to your leg?" he exclaimed, aiming renewed venomous darts at Greg.

"I tripped." He met me halfway, took my arm proprietarily, then tried to pull me away as though the house was on fire. "Thank you for the tour…" I said over my shoulder as Andrew rushed me away. Greg only nodded. He stood next to the table, hands in his pockets, expression dark as a storm cloud ready to burst.

Andrew hurried me expertly through the hallways. Obviously he'd been here before, and more than once. "Sorry to intrude, Lily," he apologized, "but I thought you'd want to see that letter."

"Are you sure that was all?" I questioned him, a little breathless.

He glanced down and saw me grimacing. "Sorry." He slowed down. "I just…I just don't trust Greg Huntington."

"Why, Andrew?" I remembered that he'd told me to stay away from Greg, that I hadn't listened.

"There're a lot of reasons." He paused, then took a deep breath. "But a big one was that he convinced his sister not to marry me."

Chapter Fifteen

✦

I stared at Andrew, completely surprised by his accusation. "Why would Greg do that?"

He opened the door of the Jeep and helped me climb in, then went around to the driver's side. "We were young," he continued, as he started up the engine. "I was eighteen and she was sixteen, and we really liked each other."

"He mentioned something about you two."

"I'm sure he also mentioned that I was all wrong for her; that she wanted a career, that she didn't want to get stuck having bairns and living in a run-down heap like Dundeid Castle."

Actually, recalling what Greg had said, I thought *I* had been more skeptical about the relationship than Greg. "He actually said he thought you two might make a go of it."

"I don't believe that." Andrew pulled out of the driveway, driving too fast, making the Jeep protest with squeaks and groans at every pothole.

"He did," I retorted, buckling my seatbelt as quickly as I could and pinching my fingers twice before finally hearing the click. Stubborn sod.

"Well, I see he's got you under his thumb like everyone else round here."

"What are you talking about?"

"Phe likes him more than he deserves, and Viv finds him attractive."

"Ha! He says the same thing about you. That all the ladies flock around you, ready to do your bidding."

Andrew's smile escaped before he quickly terminated the traitorous movement of his lips. "He's just trying to win your sympathy. Greg Huntington is the big catch in our village. Always has been."

"And you're the poor, wee ugly duckling nobody loves?"

He laughed, his grip on the steering wheel loosening, his foot easing off the gas pedal a bit. "Okay, so I'm not going to win your sympathy with that. But Greg Huntington has always gotten whatever he wanted in life."

"Oh, really? I thought he had to get a job to save the estate after his father died and left behind a load of debts."

"He told you that, did he?"

"Greg never said anything. Ophelia told me."

"Oh. Well, that's true about the money, but Greg had the freedom to make his fortune elsewhere."

"Unlike you."

He smacked his hand against the steering wheel. "I have to do right by my family. They rely on me. But sometimes…"

"Sometimes…?" I prompted.

But he only stared straight ahead as we drove back to the castle. Realizing he wasn't going to elaborate, I looked around at the scenery, thinking about all the different stories I'd heard. Everyone seemed to have their own version. Maybe there was a snake in the grass here, planting bad ideas in everyone's heads. We'd gone through a situation like that at the newspaper. One of the interns, Jenny Buckle, loved drama and she would stir things up whenever she could. She'd say things like, "Britney told me she doesn't think you're qualified for the new position. I think she's crazy. You're perfect for it." Then she'd go tell Britney, "Lily told me she doesn't think you're qualified for the new position. I think she's crazy. You're perfect for it." And who came out smelling like roses? Jenny Buckle, that's who. She was caught in the end, but by then, she'd done a lot of damage to a lot of people, some irreparable.

So who was the snake in the grass around here? My search pretty quickly took me to either Vivian or Amria. I could imagine both relishing the role of villain. I made a mental note to ask Ophelia about Amria when I saw her again.

As we drove along the darkening road, it hit me that I recognized where we were. This road was the same one I'd biked down by accident while trying to reach Dundeid Castle. Seeing the trees and long stretch of road, I felt a strange sense of déjà vu—like I'd been at this particular spot before, long before, many times before.

My heart knocked against my chest like a drowning creature trapped beneath the ice. "Of course," I whispered through numb lips. I couldn't fathom how I hadn't made the connection before. This was the road in my dreams—the road where my unseen captor caught me. Worst of all, this road led to Greg Huntington's house. And I'd been with him—alone. I shivered, feeling as though the Grim Reaper had just tapped on my shoulder.

"What's wrong?" Andrew demanded, returning from his funk to notice my pale face and tightly crossed arms.

"I want to know what you dream about me," I said through clenched teeth. "Right now."

He tapped the steering wheel, his lips a grim line. "All right. If you insist. I dream of you and Dundeid and…"

"And…?" I pushed, my nails digging into my palm.

"I dream of pain and suffering, then someone disappears forever. Scenes flash in my mind, but hard as I try I can never follow them or remember the details. All of us here are a part of the dream. In them, I know Greg's my enemy, and you're meant to be my savior. That's what I dream. Over and over and over." He inhaled a lungful of air. His knuckles were white and his jaw hard as granite.

My pulse quickened. "If I'm your savior, then that shows everything works out. Right?"

"You're supposed to be…but something happens. And then it's too late."

The air left my lungs in a hurry. Exactly like my dream. Should I tell Andrew that I dreamed what he dreamed? Get everything out into the open? He was already certain I'd come to Scotland for other reasons. "Do *you* believe that it's too late?" My voice broke a bit, knowing I wasn't being forthright.

"I don't know what to believe. I didn't connect you to the woman in my dream until I heard your name that first night. And now, to think we might be related. It seems like too much to be a coincidence."

"My family did come from this area so it's certainly possible. But—" I stopped, chickening out. I wasn't ready to tell him everything. Not yet. "That reminds me…did you see the letter?"

"Ian didn't want anyone to read it, but you. And besides, it's sealed." He smiled at me.

I rubbed my hands together, letting my mind be distracted. "Sounds delicious!"

"You'll fill me in, won't you?"

"I might. You know, maybe your dreams are a case of sins of the father."

"You mean my ancestors did something bad and now I'm going to pay the price?"

"Something like that."

"If that's the case, then the real question is: How do I undo what they did? How do I make amends?"

"Do you think your mother would know something? She's punishing herself for some reason, maybe something to do with a crime?" I held up my hand to stop the expected protest. "I'm not saying she committed it, but she might have witnessed one and said nothing for fear of getting blamed or hurting someone she loved."

"Something's going on with her," he conceded, slowing the Jeep, then taking a left turn. "I'm not sure what, though. As you might have noticed, my relationship with her is a bit odd. I know she loves me, but she keeps her distance. Once in a while she acts almost normal and tells me things." He nodded, more and more emphatically. "When you first arrived, she came to your room and we spoke and I said things I'm not sure I even understand."

"I heard what you said," I admitted. "You sounded strange. You said, 'She has come at last…just like you said.'"

He snapped his fingers. "That's it! And I wondered how she knew about you. She told me she sees things, but not everything. Then—"

"You said we need her, meaning me, and this time we can't fail. She replied that you do, and you won't." My spine tingled. "This is kind of creeping me out, you know."

"Me, too," Andrew said vehemently, surprising me. "What's she up to? And why was I talking like that? Like I was channeling someone."

"We have to find out who that someone is."

"But how?"

"I can question your mom. I'm a reporter, after all. I'll ask what you won't want to."

"I can't let you do that."

"I'll be gentle, Andrew."

"I didn't mean that…" He glanced over at me and the Jeep slowed to a near stop, barely crawling along. "I don't want you to do my dirty work. That wouldn't be fair. I'll talk to her."

"And risk ruining your relationship with her? No way. Besides, she thinks you and I are getting married…" As I spoke, routes in my brain opened up, striving to make a connection. "Could her secret have something to do with a marriage? Was she happy with your father?"

"He died when I was young and she never talks about him."

"Well, that looks good for our theory, bad for your mom. Are you sure you want me to pursue this?"

He pulled in a deep breath. The Jeep was at a complete stop now and we sat in the gently vibrating machine, staring at each other. "I want to end this." He reached out and placed his hand over mine. I looked down at it and a warmth spread through my body.

"I'll be extra careful with her, okay?"

"Yes," he agreed, neither removing his hand nor his eyes from mine. "And watch yourself, Lily. Each moment we spend together I find myself liking you more and more."

Before I could ask why I should watch myself, he pulled his hand away and the Jeep moved forward once more. We didn't talk for the rest of the drive, which was only another mile. The outline of the castle against the gray sky came into view and I smiled to see it. I did so love a good castle.

"I'm going to park the motor," he told me when we pulled up to the front entry. "Why don't you put off your questioning until tomorrow? I want to warn Mother to expect a visit from you. She doesn't like surprises."

"That's fine. I'll spend the afternoon working on my article."

"Don't forget Ian's letter…"

"I won't." With a small smile, I hopped out of the car and headed indoors. I met no one on the way to my room, my bruised knee protesting each step. Once there I found that no one had disturbed my bed or bags, but Gertie had taken my ball gown for cleaning. Good. Tomorrow I would ask her a few questions about the household—before I tackled Mrs. Dering. The more ammunition I had before going to see Andrew's mother, the better.

Interesting how I made it sound like I was going into battle. But that's how I felt. Truth be told, she rather scared me.

Ian's letter sat on my desk and I picked it up, fingering the rough paper. There were two pieces: A small white note and a yellowed parchment. I opened the white note and read it. The handwriting was terrible, but legible enough to decipher.

I found this in the family Bible, along with a list of kin, which confirms that yer ancestor, Robert MacKenzie, is related to the Dundeid MacKenzies. Which makes us related, but we already knew that, didna we? The letter tells what happened between the brothers, why my kin damned yers, but leaves out a lot. Do with it what ye will. I'm done with it.

There was no salutation, no name. Feeling both anxious and excited, I picked up the aged paper and carefully unfolded it.

To my brother, Ian (oh, this already looked bad),

I'm not sorry for what I've done. Aye, I took yer love, but she never loved ye as she did me. She <u>never</u> really loved ye, actually, she just didna ken it until I returned home. When ye meet the one for ye, ye'll understand that I've done ye a service. Remember what Mother would tell us? "Good enough isn't ever good enough. It's just what we tell ourselves to get through life." Hate me if ye must, but also ken I saved ye from a life of 'good enough' so that ye can have better.

Robert

I stared at the words, going back over the lines three more times to be sure I understood what I was reading. There was no sugarcoating it—my ancestor was a cad, a certifiable jerk, and a full-blooded bull-shitter. Great. If the Ian of yesteryear was at all human, he certainly would have cursed his brother with all his might, very likely including subsequent generations. And that would mean me.

Setting the letter back down on the desk, I took a deep breath and wished I had some of Ian's mead right now. Surely after reading this letter he would want nothing more to do with me. He'd offered his help, but I couldn't imagine him meaning that now. My ancestor had royally screwed over his. And the Scottish had long memories. They were like American Southerners, the ones who still harbored grudges against the Yankees because of the Civil War. There was no way I could go to him for help now, not after reading the letter. Likely he'd given it to me as a way of letting me know he'd washed his hands of the whole deal. "I'm done with it," he'd written. No, I could not rely on Ian.

I sighed and rubbed my eyes tiredly. I hadn't imagined how personal this would get—how emotionally involved I would become. A reporter is supposed to maintain objectivity, but right now I felt about as objective as a lobbyist.

A knock sounded on the door and I started nervously. "Come in," I called.

Ophelia entered, gripping a Siamese tight to her chest. "Want to hold my cat?" She held the thin, delicate creature out to me, but I pulled back.

"No thanks. I'm allergic," I told her. I took in her demeanor. She acted as though nothing was wrong; that Vivian hadn't said what she had. Still, I remained wary. She had to feel *some* resentment toward me about Greg. "What's her name?"

"*His* name is Styx."

"As in sticks and stones?"

"As in the River Styx. I was hoping that if I named him this, it would serve as a sort of talisman to protect me against my dreams."

"What do you dream?" I asked breathlessly. If she'd named her cat after the river, which served as the boundary between the land of the living and the dead, her dreams couldn't be good.

She seated herself on my bed and while I took a seat at my desk she stared up at the canopy. "It's always the same thing," she recited tiredly, as though she'd told the story many times. "I'm in a boat, being ferried across a wide, dark river that scares me with its unending depth, but when the boat docks on the other side and I move to get off, a bony hand holds me down. I struggle, but it's no use. I'm not going anywhere. And then we return across the river, going back and forth again and again and again. I'd rather just die and have it done with."

"Someone needs to put gold coins on your eyes when you die," I told her, wondering why I was playing into her macabre fantasy. "To pay for the ferry."

"Would it work if I just did it when I went to sleep?"

"It might, but then you might not wake up."

"Well, I don't want that. As pathetic as my life is, I want to keep it. Speaking of my pathetic life, I heard you went over to Greg's house." She managed to sound both pouty and admiring. "I can't believe you went without me!"

"I'm a reporter here to do a job," I said steadfastly. "There are times that if we don't make things happen, we won't get the story."

"Well, did you get the story?"

"Not as much of it as I wanted. On my way to his house I fell and hurt my knee and he had to give me a ride on his horse up to the house. It was rather embarrassing." Worse, I just remembered I was still wearing his sister's clothes. How was I going to get mine back? He was leaving for Edinburgh tomorrow.

She pet her cat fiercely and it hissed. "Embarrassing? I dream about things like that happening to me!"

"I don't like relying on anyone."

"But he *rescued* you!" Her eyes narrowed. "He rescued *you*," she said again, less happily.

"I would've been fine on my own. He just happened across me while riding his horse."

"Still…"

"You could do what I just did, Ophelia. Go over to his house, talk to him."

She shook her head. "No, I never could. I just…well…"

"Fine. He's leaving for Edinburgh tomorrow and won't be back until the Gala anyway. But afterwards—"

"You know so much about him now," she interrupted, her voice distressed.

"You could easily know more about him than me, Ophelia." Her helpless routine was starting to wear on me. "Take the bull by the horns. Seize the day! Be all that you can be!"

Styx stared at me blandly with blue, almond-shaped eyes, as Ophelia stroked his cream-colored fur—more gently now—with trembling fingers. "Easy for you to say, Lily. You've traveled. You've been places."

"It's not like I had someone holding my hand when I did all that, Ophelia. If you want something, you have to be willing to do whatever it takes, illness or not, controlling aunts or not." I was being reckless with my advice giving, but I couldn't help myself. Life, with all its attendant risks, is meant to be lived, not dreamed away.

Ophelia looked at me for a good long moment. Her blue eyes were thoughtful and I wondered what she was thinking, but it turned out not to be much of anything. "I gave Gertie my dress. I can't wait to see it when it's cleaned!"

I gave a stiff smile, stifling my sigh of disappointment. "I did, too. I hope it's not too much for her."

Ophelia waved her hand. "Oh, she lives for that stuff. I'll bet she dreams about stains. I'll bet she gets all *orgasmic* about them."

A laugh escaped me. "Ophelia! I didn't know you had it in you."

She grinned mischievously. "Surprised you, didn't I? I bet I could surprise Greg, too."

I felt my hope for her returning. "That's the spirit!" I stood up and pushed my chair in. "I'm going to do some work now. See you at supper."

Ophelia frowned, opened her mouth to protest, but stood anyway, clutching her cat as I opened the door for her. "I guess I could work on my dance steps for the ball."

"Good idea," I agreed, using the door to herd her out. The latch clicked, silencing her last words about her dress.

For the next three hours, I worked on my genealogy article. I wrote about my adventure in the dungeon (making a mental note to snap a few more photos down there since my others had been deleted) and about tracking down a living relative (insert photos of the croft here), then I turned my attention toward Dundeid Castle itself and how well it served as a place to stay for those searching out their Scottish roots. By the time I shut down my computer I had a good rough draft and I figured I could turn it into at least four articles. Mr. Willeton would be pleased. I needed to include some website links, figure out what photos I wanted to use, and fill in three or four gaps, but I'd made good progress.

Feeling some of the stress lifted off me, I cleaned up for dinner, for once taking special care with my hair. My new outfit, courtesy of Greg's sister, was actually quite flattering and I decided to keep it on. Remembering my own clothes, I dug out my cell phone and called Greg at the number he had typed in for me when he'd 'borrowed' my phone, though he'd listed himself as Gregor. I listened to a brief message before speaking.

"Hi, Gregor, I mean, Greg. It's me, um, Lili…a. Um, I wanted to thank you for lunch and the house tour. I wish we'd had time to discuss your, um, dreams. Um, and I need my clothes back. Can I pick them up? I mean, I know you're busy, so I can come fetch them. Just put them in a bag, I guess, and leave them by the front door. Um, that's it. Oh, and have a nice trip." I quickly hit the button to hang up, cursing my idiocy and wishing I could undo my lame message.

Um, Lily? Um, learn how to speak!

Typically, I was quite crisp and professional on the phone. I'd been making phone calls since before my mother had gone away. One gets quite good at it after a while. But today my inner bonehead had come leaping and bounding out of me. This place was making me soft.

I swiped on some peach lip-gloss, with more vigor than was necessary, and had to use a tissue to wipe most of it off. With one last glance in the mirror, I headed down for dinner.

I found I was looking forward to it.

Chapter Sixteen

As it turned out, I was all dressed up with no place to go. The dining room, when I entered it, was empty. After ten minutes passed, it was still empty. My fingers started tapping. Another ten minutes passed and Gertie arrived to serve my meal and deliver a message. "His Lairdship apologizes, but he and Miss Ophelia and Miss Vivian have been detained. They're working on the Gala, he says to tell ye."

"Oh, well, thanks." I didn't want to see him anyway, I told myself. I downed nearly half my glass of wine in one gulp, then coughed and sputtered for the next thirty seconds. Wine really isn't meant to be gulped.

After I'd calmed down, Gertie looked about her, then leaned close to me. "I've been working on yer lovely dress, and it's cooming along right nice." She beamed.

I dredged up a smile. "That's great, Gertie. Thank you." She left me to eat with a broad smile.

When she brought out dessert, I asked, "Are you any relation to the Derings, Gertie?"

She clapped a hand to her ample chest. "Me? Lord, no! Me family has served them for a long time, though. That's aboot as close as we get tae being relations."

"Do you know anything about Mr. Dering? Senior?" I added.

She shook her head, her lips thinning tight to hold in secrets. "He died a long time ago."

"Oh?" I pretended ignorance. "How?"

She briskly cleared my dinner plate from the table and looked about ready to swipe my dessert. I grabbed the blue bowl and held on tight. "I dinna ken. I wasn't born then."

"You never heard anything? Rumors?"

The look she gave me was far from approving. "Why do ye want tae ken? What's past is past."

I lowered my voice. "I'm going to talk to the Laird's mother tomorrow, with Andrew's permission, of course. I just wanted to be prepared, so I wouldn't say something stupid." All true and yet, not the whole of it.

Gertie looked uncertain. I donned my sweet, innocent face—the one I used when interviewing old ladies and politicians. I placed my injured wrist on the table and rubbed it for good measure. Eyes on my wrap, she nodded. "Well, all right. But ye didna hear it from me." She bent toward my ear, her voice a whisper. I smelled her perfume—lemon detergent and cooking and sweat from her day's work. She smelled good and simple and I promised myself to be very careful with the information she was about to give me. "He killed himself, he did."

I gasped. I had not expected this. Illness, a ruined liver, even an accident from driving too fast. But this? Suicide? "How awful."

"Me mum said it were the worst thing ever tae happen tae this house. Mrs. Dering went downhill after that."

"How old was Andrew when it happened?"

"Oh, two or three. Young enough tae escape the worst of it."

Somehow I doubted that. "Why did Mr. Dering do it?"

"Something tae do wi' a family scandal and I dinna ken nothing aboot that."

"Thanks for telling me. I'll keep this to myself, Gertie." And I fully intended to. I really did.

She took a step back and bobbed a curtsy. "Just thought ye should ken. I dinna want the mistress getting hurt. She's been real good tae me and me mum."

"I understand." I pushed back my chair and stood up. "Do you need any help clearing up?"

She looked aghast. "I've got it, thank ye." Her face was stiff, her voice flat.

"Sorry, Gertie. It's just that where I come from, you make the offer. It's not an insult."

She thought this over. "Well, all right. I won't take it as one. But I will say this. Ye're a queer one, Miss Lily."

I grinned. "I shall take that as a compliment!"

She gaped at me, then laughed. "Oh, go on! Ye foreigners are a mad lot!"

"Oh, I'm not entirely a foreigner, Gertie. I just found out that my family comes from Dundeid. At one time we were probably neighbors."

She blushed, grabbing my dishes. "I best be getting back tae me work." She paused, glancing down at my wrist. "Ye'll be all right on yer own?"

"I've taken care of myself this long, Gertie. I should be fine for one night."

She looked doubtful as she left to take my dishes to the kitchen, and as I crossed the Great Hall, I reconsidered my proud words. The whole evening stretched ahead of me, leaving me alone with my thoughts. I walked over to a window and peeked outside. It was dark, but glimpses of little lights could be seen off in the distance and were likely outdoor lamps lighting the garden paths. The rain had stopped and I thought I might take a stroll in the flower garden. I'd taken a couple pain pills and my knee felt nearly back to normal, but I would take it slow to be on the safe side. Before heading out, I ran upstairs to fetch my MP3 player and a sweater, a distant part of my mind hoping I might see Andrew coming or going, but he remained elusive.

The dying garden looked both beautiful and eerie in the lamplight. I walked the stone paths, humming along to a song. Voice lessons at Mademoiselle Lefit's Charm School had made me a passable singer, plus I enjoyed my bellowing to no end. Singing soothed my savage inner beast, and most likely also kept other beasts at bay.

As I bent over to examine a strange plant, something grabbed hold of my arm and I automatically took a wild swing at my attacker. He smoothly caught my fist in his hand, as though expecting it, and pulled me against him, holding me close. My free hand whipped off my earbuds. "What are you doing sneaking up on me like that!" My heart threatened to jump out of my chest and for a moment I felt dizzy from a cascade of emotions.

Gregor…*Greg* smiled. "I didn't mean to frighten you. As to what I'm doing, I got your message." He held up a paper bag with the hand not binding me to him.

My breathing had yet to slow. For one thing, he really had startled me. For another, I could feel the warmth of his body all the way through my sweater and shirt. "Sorry." I pushed away from him and took the proffered bag.

"No need to be sorry."

I swallowed. "You still have my arm."

"Ah, so I do." He didn't let go.

"I'd like it back."

He grinned and gave my arm a squeeze, before gently letting it go. For a moment the traitorous limb hung suspended in mid-air before I let it drop. "Did you and the Laird have a pleasant afternoon?" From the way he said the word laird, I could easily imagine him substituting bampot in its place.

"Andrew had work to do and so did I."

"So you're continuing with your farce?"

"It's not a farce! I can't return home without a story. I'd lose my job." Mr. Willeton might favor me, but he was a ruthless businessman when he needed to be. Many people had lost their jobs because they'd made the mistake of underestimating him. "I like my job, and I want to keep it."

He nodded. "You're so practical, Lilia."

"You say that as though you really mean calculating."

His eyes darkened in the dim light. "Don't put words in my mouth."

"Then don't imbue the words you use with *other* meanings."

"I was trying to be polite."

"Try harder." He laughed and some of the tension building between us slipped away. "I didn't think I'd see you again before your trip."

"Are you pleasantly surprised?"

"If I say yes, will it give you a big head?"

"Absolutely not." He grinned.

"Hm. I don't believe you. I will admit that I am surprised."

"So do you want to know what I dream about?"

"I don't know. What I've heard so far hasn't been good."

"This part is new. Last night I dreamt of *being* with you. In the Biblical sense."

I felt like someone had lit a basket of fireworks in my stomach. "Ah."

"And it's amazing."

My cheeks fired up in indignation. "You're making this up!"

He shrugged. "I might be."

I felt like punching him, getting my hopes up like that. "But why?"

"Because I like to see you like this."

"Dare I ask like *what?*"

"All feisty."

I snorted contemptuously. It wasn't a sexy sound, but damn it, it's how I felt inside. "You want to see feisty, Gregor? Because you haven't really seen me in action."

"Dare I say yes?"

My eyes narrowed. "Are you through having fun at my expense?"

"You're having fun, too. Admit it."

I absolutely would not! "I want to know what you really dream about."

He shook his head, sobering. "No, you don't."

There was a sound behind him, running footsteps and a shout. Oh, for the love of Pete, was I ever going to find out what he dreamed?

"Huntington! What the hell are you doing here?" Andrew hurried toward us, his blond hair flowing behind him like an avenging Viking. My eyes automatically searched him for weapons.

"I was returning Lily's clothes to her." I noted Gregor didn't call me Lilia in front of Andrew. I wasn't sure I liked that. I had been on *his* road in my dream, and I'd been frightened out of my mind. Plus he was hiding the fact that he called me Lilia. I should not trust him with anything.

Andrew turned to look at me, stunned. "Lily?"

I nearly laughed, his overreaction was so absurd. But his expression warned me off. "I was soaked through so I borrowed some of Sophie's clothes."

"First you go to his house without telling me, or anyone. Then you—" He bit off the remaining words as though even he could tell his reaction was too much.

"Something wrong with visiting a friend, Dering?"

"You two are not friends. You barely know each other. Lily and I, on the other hand, are likely related. So I feel a certain responsibility for her welfare. Allowing her to be alone with you is not in her best interests."

I drew myself up. "I'm not sure what's going on here, but both of you are acting like…like *nyaffs*! I'll decide who's my friend. I'll decide where I go and when. Stop acting like my father, Andrew, and Greg, we're barely acquaintances and don't you forget it. So both of you can go jump in the loch. I'm going inside."

"Do you see what you've done?" Andrew shouted and Greg retorted, "I'm not the one who's acting like a Victorian father!"

They continued arguing as I stalked off, growing angrier with each stomp. How dare they? Both were taking liberties neither had the right to take. If I didn't need to solve my mystery, I'd pack my bags and leave.

I heard the nasty sound of flesh hitting flesh and spun around in time to see Gregor tackling Andrew. They began to roll around on the ground like schoolboys. I ran back to them.

"Stop it! You're acting like idiots!"

My words had no effect. The two idiots were determined to beat the crap out of each other. "I'll leave. I'll go back home and you won't ever see me again!" My voice grew higher and more frantic with each syllable.

Andrew shoved Gregor off and pushed himself to his feet. Gregor stood up quickly and they faced off like boxers, fists raised high. Not an even match, as Andrew was taller and broader. Still, Gregor had managed to hold his own on the ground, though he had a bloody lip for his efforts. Andrew shook out his sore hand. Punching someone never comes without a price.

"Take it back," Andrew growled.

"It's the truth and you know it," Gregor persisted. "So stop acting like an overgrown numpty and accept what I'm telling you. She's not *yours*."

"Andrew…" I warned, sensing he was about to spring forward. "Don't do it."

He glanced toward me, his face hard. "You don't understand, Lily. He'll hurt you."

"We're nothing to each other," I said ruthlessly. "He can't hurt me."

Gregor looked at me, wounded. "Nothing?" he repeated. "After what we shared this morning?" He lifted a suggestive eyebrow, which Andrew, of course, caught.

"Knock it off, Greg. You're only making things worse."

"What's he talking about, Lily?" Andrew demanded.

"Nothing. Nothing happened. He's just pushing your buttons. Besides, what business is it of yours? Both of you just stay away from me and each other. Got it? I have a job to do, and I'm going to do it. I don't know what's going on here, but I'm getting sick of it. As soon as I find what I came for, I'm leaving." Chest heaving, I made my exit.

At the house, I slammed the front door behind me and took the steps two at a time. By the twelfth step my knee began to protest and I slowed down, still fuming. But I didn't stop moving in case one of them happened to be chasing after me. I didn't want to be caught.

In my room, I plopped down on my bed and cursed the both of them. My pillow became an effective scapegoat and I slammed it against the bedpost several times, taking turns imagining those two in its place.

At last my fury faded to a dull roar and I fell back onto my bed. It was time to think. What was I angry about exactly? I had two men who seemed interested in me and both had taken a certain proprietary role with me. Was that really so bad? Most women would feel flattered.

Not me.

After mulling this over for a while, I finally realized I wasn't just angry, I was scared. Despite believing I was in charge of my own destiny, things were happening here that I had no control over. I felt like I was peering into a crystal ball, watching my life as it happened, but could do nothing to intervene or change things.

Even so, I was going to have to keep looking for answers. I needed to know what it was about the road leading to Gregor's house that frightened me so much. I also had to find out what Andrew's mother was up to. I couldn't believe she'd want her son to marry a stranger. My charming looks and sophistication certainly weren't the answer. Simply put, I wasn't laird's wife material.

And lastly, there was the elusive Lilia. Who was she, and why had my mother felt forced to name me after her? Did she even exist, or would I finally have to acknowledge that my mother was crazy?

This trip I'd made had been—still was—a last-ditch effort to save myself. Because if my mother was crazy, then maybe I was, too. I had her dreams now, and the only way to get rid of them would be to pass them along, as my mother had.

Or…die.

Chapter Seventeen

At breakfast the next morning, I thought I'd be spending my meal alone once more. Instead, I was joined by all three Derings. Andrew looked defiant, Vivian looked calculating and was directing that calculating look at me, and Ophelia appeared full of feverish anticipation.

"I can't wait until the auction," she confided, sliding into her seat.

"Good morning to you, too," I mumbled, sipping my creamy, Irish blend-flavored coffee, which Gertie had obliged me by making, though she made a sour face at the idea of a Scottish girl doing anything Irish. I hadn't slept well, my night full of dreams, but not my typical ones. This time I'd dreamed of Andrew and Gregor dueling at dawn. They both shot each other and I didn't know which one to run to first. As I dithered, sobbing and gasping, my mind jerked me awake. Then I fell back to sleep and relived the whole scenario all over again. By the time I woke up, I was ready to shoot them both myself, just to be done with it.

Perhaps an Irish coffee—the one laced with whisky—might have been a better choice.

"Good morning, Lily," Vivian greeted. Her calculating demeanor had changed to a superior smile, which made her blood-red lips curve ghoulishly upward. "You look like you had a bad night." My poor sleep seemed to please her, but I couldn't be sure about that. Her concerned expression seemed legitimate; still I couldn't quite believe it.

I nodded, taking another sip, hoping the combination of rich sugar and caffeine would penetrate my brain cells and knock some sense into them. I was having a hard time focusing, and I needed to stay sharp. I was mad at Andrew, and I had to remember that or I'd somehow lose ground. "Bad dreams," I replied, shooting a glance at Andrew. He met it with his blue-violet eyes, darkened by ill temper. I returned it with a nonverbal version of, "sod off," then downed more coffee.

"I can't believe you got Greg to agree, Auntie Viv."

"Agree to what?" Andrew and I asked at the same time. I didn't bother to look at him. I'm sure it wouldn't have been a pleasant experience for me.

"It's dead exciting." Ophelia looked about ready to burst and I sat up straighter. "He's letting himself be auctioned off. The highest bidder wins a date with him!"

"When did he decide this?" Andrew demanded.

"Last night," Vivian replied. "He actually called me and agreed to do it." She looked triumphant. There seemed no other way of describing the "I win" vibe that she was sending out. Fortunately, Ophelia was too high on her excitement to notice.

"I can't wait!" Ophelia went on, oblivious to the tension. "I've loads of cash. I'm going to win."

Vivian's face went still with displeasure, glimpsed briefly before a serene mask fell and covered it up. "Ophelia, darling. We cannot bid at the auction. We're the organizers. It would look bad."

"Look bad? Why would anyone care if I bid on Greg Huntington?"

"We have to maintain an image, Ophelia. Your cousin is the Laird, after all."

Once again I was surprised at what they talked about in front of me. Don't get me wrong, I liked it. It was like watching a favorite drama, but I shouldn't forget that these were real people with real feelings.

Ophelia stood up, throwing her linen napkin on the table. "Image? What image? The gentile lords and ladies of Dundeid? Or the broke, dysfunctional family in danger of losing their home?"

"Sit down, Ophelia," Andrew ordered, looking thunderous. "We have a guest."

"You told me to treat her like one of us, and that's what I'm doing."

"With disrespect?" Vivian put in, looking equally angry, calm mask now gone. "No. I cannot sanction it. You'll not be bidding on anything or *anyone* in the auction. It wouldn't do."

Ophelia bit her lower lip, her eyes darting about. She was angry, but I also sensed fear in her heaving breast. Over and over she beat her wings against the bars, and over and over, her every effort to gain her freedom was stymied. "You're such a hypocrite, Auntie Viv! And you, too, Andrew!" She clawed at the buttons of a gossamer-blue blouse, her long fingers curled and desperate. "You never let me do anything! How am I supposed to grow up if you don't let me make mistakes?"

"Because the mistakes you make could affect us all." Vivian had the final word.

Ophelia's wild eyes looked at each of us in turn, and though I met her gaze, I wished I could look away because she now seemed to include me with the others. Without another word, she fled from the room.

The moment the door closed behind her, the kitchen door swung open. Gertie silently filled each teacup, except mine, and placed glasses of orange juice at the top of each plate. After determining what we wanted to eat—haggis, porridge, back bacon, and toast were on offer (I agreed to everything but the haggis, Vivian took only porridge, Andrew didn't bother to answer, apparently assuming Gertie could read his mind)—she disappeared back into the safety of the kitchen. I envied her.

"So you both believe that the whole is greater than the sum of its parts?" I spoke into the silence that settled over us.

"Dundeid Castle is greater than all of us," Vivian answered, self-righteous as a Bible thumpin' zealot.

"No building should be more important than a human."

"We all know that Greg Huntington has no interest in Phe," Andrew said.

I turned on him. "Maybe because he's never had the chance to get to know her."

"He'd be bad for her. She needs a certain kind of man who can put up with her…illness." A man like Dr. Mills? I'd once thought Dr. Mills had been ruled out as a suitor for Ophelia. But maybe not. Maybe he was being pushed on Ophelia.

"Ophelia's not a normal girl," Vivian stated without batting an eyelash. "So encouraging her to live a normal life would only make her miserable." Her words were meant to put me in my place, but they only ignited a fire inside me. I clamped my lips down on my typical retort, "We shall see about that," and instead plotted in my head. I had a plan, and I wasn't about to give myself away to Vivian. She'd do everything in her power to block me—and all in the name of Dundeid.

I did have to say something, though. "I hope that your meddling doesn't backfire on you."

I was surprised to see Vivian's face blanch, as though she'd been tipped upside down. "Why would it backfire?" She turned to Andrew. "What does she know?"

"Know about *what?*" I asked.

"She doesn't know anything because there's nothing to know." He looked directly in my eyes. "My mother will see you this morning after breakfast," he said, changing the subject.

"Great," I replied, going along with him. "Thank you."

Vivian glanced back and forth between us. "You're going to talk to Mrs. Dering?" Her eyes settled on Andrew. "Do you think that's wise?"

"Wise or not, it needs to happen. Mother started this. I'm hoping she can clarify some things for all of us. Lily will, of course, fill me in, won't you, Lily?"

"I won't violate any confidentialities," I said, feeling contrary. There was no need for him to be so high-handed.

"I wouldn't ask you to do that. But I would hope you'd trust me."

"Trust you? I'm surprised you haven't insisted on being there. To protect helpless, little ol' me against—" I glanced at Vivian, who was watching with avid interest.

"I've only your best interests in mind, Lily. You know nothing about Greg Huntington. All my life I've known he'd be trouble, and he's proven me right."

"What are you two talking about?" Vivian demanded. "What happened?"

Andrew just shook his head, focusing on his teacup, which he spun around and around on its saucer. I smiled to myself. Baited and caught.

"Andrew?" she demanded again.

Gertie pushed against the door at that moment, bearing a silver tray laden with our steaming breakfasts. Feeling vindicated, I felt my appetite return. Funny how success can stimulate the desire to consume. As soon as Andrew and I received our food, we tucked in. Neither one of us wanted to say any more on the subject of last night—Andrew, undoubtedly because he knew he was in the wrong; me, because it was better to keep Vivian in her proper place, which was out of the loop.

She obviously wanted to ask more questions, but refrained from doing so. Andrew and I finished eating before she did, and we pushed back our chairs at the same time. As we headed toward the door, Vivian's voice grabbed our attention, catching us before we could escape. "You'll be coming back to work on the layout for the Gala, Andrew." It was not a question.

"Of course." I wished I could see his face, but his back was to me as he headed into the Great Hall. Without a word, he marched for the stairs. I hurried after him as he took them two at a time. His long legs were no match for mine and soon my bruised knee began to throb.

After a couple minutes of suffering, not quite in silence, I called out, "I'm not a mountain goat, you know!"

Andrew stopped altogether, halfway down a dark hallway, and his shoulders dropped low. "I wish we wouldn't fight."

"Are we fighting?" I wasn't being coy. Fighting was something two people did when both thought they were right. No way could Andrew think he was right.

He turned to face me, his hands held out in appeal. "I can't explain why I feel toward you the way I do, Lily. I want to protect you, but I feel that I can't. At the same time, I think you're the answer to all our problems here, though I couldn't tell you why." His last words came out weakly, as though he wasn't sure he believed them. I was touched. I didn't think Andrew was used to appealing to anyone.

"Fine. But it's got to stop. I know you think I need protecting, but I've been taking care of myself for a long time. My dad is overprotective, and he goes about it in all the wrong ways. The worst thing you could do is act like you own me, which is something he does on a daily basis. And when you confronted Gregor, *Greg*, I saw my dad in you."

He smiled grimly. "That's got to be the last thing any man wants to hear from a beautiful woman."

One of his words temporarily made me speechless. Did he really mean that, or was he laying it on thick? "It's…it's the truth. The truth is very important to me."

"If it were so important to you, I'd think you'd practice it more often."

"What are you talking about? I—" Oh, crap. He couldn't have hit the nail on the head any more accurately. I expected the truth from everyone else but myself. From the get-go, I had told a story—a lie—and expected everyone to think that was okay. Actually, I simply didn't think anyone would find me out. "Okay. You're right. I came here for other reasons, not just to do an article on genealogy. I came here to end my dreams. I have them, too, you see. This is where they take place. In Dundeid."

Andrew didn't look as surprised as I thought he would. "I wish you'd been honest from the start, Lily. I shared with you that I had dreams. You could've told me then."

My hands twisted together. "I know. But I…I…" How do you tell someone that you think someone living either in his house or close by is going to murder you?

His hands grasped my arms. "You have to tell me these things, Lily! If we can't trust each other we'll never figure this out."

He was close enough to kiss me, and my whole body trembled at the thought. "I suppose," I muttered noncommittally. He still hadn't shared the whole story of his father with me, so why should I share my whole story with him?

"Look at me, Lily," he commanded, and I did, briefly sensing his laird's blood coming out. "Viv's right when she says that Dundeid must be protected. You understand that, don't you? Of course humans are more important, and Phe, especially. But this building has been in my family's possession for centuries—my ancestors helped build it with their own hands. The walls are stained with our blood. My ancestors breathed the very air we breathe. We must protect this legacy."

I pulled away from his grasp and rubbed my arms where he'd held them so tightly. "I agree. I meant to tell you what was in my uncle's letter."

He leaned back. "I'd forgotten about that."

"Well, it might have something to do with our mystery. I'm not sure what, but perhaps you would know."

He nodded, warming to the idea. "You're right. It might explain how we're related."

I wasn't so sure about that, but I continued. "My ancestor, Robert MacKenzie—the one who left for America—wrote a letter to his brother, Ian, who's obviously our Ian's ancestor. It wasn't a nice letter…"

"Go on."

"What my uncle wrote was pretty heartless. Robert basically stole his brother's woman and told Ian that she'd never loved him anyway. She thought she did until she met Robert. Then Robert ends the letter telling Ian that he'll only understand true love when he finds the one for him. 'Good enough is never good enough,' their mother always used to tell them. He had the nerve to claim that he was saving Ian from a fate worse than death—*settling*."

"He didn't want his brother to settle for the wrong person?" He sounded thoughtful.

"Andrew, what is it?"

"Hm? Oh, I wonder if that's maybe what happened between my mother and father."

"How did your father die, Andrew?"

He shrugged. "Some kind of accident." He looked away. "I was pretty young."

Was he ashamed to admit the truth, or was he hiding something more about his father's suicide, something that might be linked to his mother? "Shall we go?" I said, not wanting to pursue the subject any longer, because if I got him to tell me the truth, I'd have to reciprocate, and I wasn't ready to do that. It was bad enough Gregor knew about my mother. I certainly didn't want to give that information to Andrew, too.

He nodded and turned, continuing down the hall. I followed after him, feeling shabby and ashamed. I wasn't any better than anybody else here, it seemed. My whole worldview had been built on discovering the truth, but when push came to shove, I hid my secrets right along with everyone else.

When we reached the tower door, Andrew knocked, then let himself in. He took several steps into the room before I went in after him. I wasn't sure if I was ready for this interview. But if I didn't do it now, I might never get another opportunity.

Mrs. Dering sat by the window, looking even worse, if possible, than at our first meeting. "Hello, Mother," Andrew greeted, bending down to peck her wrinkled cheek. "I brought you a visitor." He straightened up and indicated me with a swing of his hand.

She turned to look at me, and her face transformed into such a beaming countenance that I would have thought he'd told her I was Mary, Queen of Scots, come for tea. "You've brought your fiancée, Andrew!" She clapped her hands. "Sit down, dear," she urged. "I'd stand, but my hip has been bothering me lately. I think I must have twisted something when I was getting out of bed this morning." Since her bed looked more like a plank than a resting place, I thought sleeping on it was more likely the culprit behind her pain than the leaving of it.

I sat down on the chair she indicated and Andrew leaned against the wall by the window, staying close. The chair's brown and tan fabric was worn, overrun by thick threads peeking outward like curious inchworms. "Hello, Mrs. Dering. It's good to see you again."

"And you, too, dear. The wedding is to be very soon, I hear. You must be so excited!"

I glanced up at Andrew. Should I keep denying what she believed, or go along with her delusion? His expression was stony, offering no help at all. Then I remembered reading an article Jamie had written on working with people who have dementia. The overriding opinion was to go along with the delusion as long as it wasn't harmful to do so. Pretending to want to marry someone couldn't be too damaging, could it?

"I *am* terribly excited," I said, making my eyes shine as a bride to be's would. Andrew's eyes darted over to me, startled, then gave way to cautious optimism—whether that had to do with thinking I meant it, or thinking I was being kind, was up in the air. I shrugged as if to say, what else can I do? He nodded encouragingly. "We both are," I added for good measure.

Her eyes sparkled as her spotted hands gripped the wooden armrests. "I can't wait! This is the answer to all our hopes!"

"How's that?" I asked smoothly, a smile pasted on my face. Andrew swiftly left his post and stood behind me, placing his large hands on my shoulders. I felt their warmth and strength through my sweater and took solace in his presence.

Her ancient head swung from side to side. "I'm not sure I remember. Someone told me once."

"Who?" I pursued. Here was my chance to find out who Andrew might be channeling. The hands squeezed, lightly, but enough to send a clear message. *Back off.*

I glanced up at him, puzzled, then back at Mrs. Dering. Her joyous smile fled before my eyes, replaced by confusion, consternation. "I don't rightly know, dear. A little birdie, perhaps!" She brightened with a giggle. "And it was right!"

"You were married yourself once, weren't you?" The squeeze tightened, but I ignored it. Andrew had claimed to want answers about their marriage and I was going to get them. "Andrew's father?"

"Lovely man," she murmured, looking out the window. "But he was weak."

I gaped at her. I hadn't expected this. Neither had Andrew. "Mother!"

"Weak?" I echoed, not letting up. When Andrew's fingers started to hurt, I glared up at him. "You wanted this," I hissed. He removed his hands, but he didn't look the least contrite. "How was Mr. Dering weak?"

"He didn't like conflict. Couldn't see things through. It's best anyway. He wouldn't have been able to handle all this."

"Our getting married?"

"Oh no, dear! He would've loved that. He would've loved you. No, he wouldn't have been able to handle the reasons you and Andrew need to marry."

"Mother, you look tired," Andrew interrupted, moving to kneel by her. He took her wrinkled hand, giving me a look that told me this interview was over.

Over, my bippy! I wasn't leaving until I found out a few things. "Andrew, maybe you should leave your mother and I to discuss the wedding. You know, girl stuff."

"I don't mind staying."

"But don't you have Gala planning to do? Vivian said—"

"Andrew!" Mrs. Dering roared, and her voice boomed in the small space. "You're still having the Gala?" Gone was the sweet, little old lady, wandering in mind but essentially harmless. In her place crouched a demented wildcat. *This* was why she frightened me. "I told you to cancel that!"

"We can't cancel it, Mother. We need the money." Andrew's voice was tight with humiliation. "And I really don't think we should discuss this in front of Lily."

"Andrew, I know you're having money troubles," I said. "Of course you would with an ancient pile like this. I don't have a problem with that, just so you know."

"The Gala cannot happen, Andrew!" Mrs. Dering might be furious with her son, but she was staring at me in fear. I leaned back in my chair, my heart thumping wildly.

"It has to go on as planned, Mother, or we lose Dundeid." His hand gripped her arm, seeming to restrain her.

"But that's why we need Lil—"

"Enough of this!" Andrew cried. He lunged at me, grabbed my arm, and dragged me from my chair and out of the room. "She's sick," he hissed as I stumbled after him down the treacherous stairs. "I should've known this would happen. I should never have let you talk to her."

"What did she mean about the Gala? About needing *me?*"

Andrew didn't answer as he dragged me along after him. "Andrew, stop!" I cried, but he took no heed. Finally I had to resort to violence. It wasn't easy with his long strides, but when we were halfway down one of the halls, I managed to kick him in the back of the leg.

"Hey!" he shouted, dropping my arm and leaning down to rub his calf. "Why'd you do that?"

"Andrew! I've been asking you to stop for the last two minutes. You wouldn't listen to me, so I kicked you." I rubbed my sore arm, the opposite one that I'd injured, of course. "That really hurt."

His eyes widened and he hurried to my side. Pushing up my sleeve, he peered down at my exposed skin. "Oh, Lord," he gasped, gently rubbing the puffy white area surrounding the red fingerprints. "I've hurt you. I-I'm so sorry, Lily. My mother—she doesn't know what she's saying and I didn't want her to hurt your feelings. Sometimes she gets…mean."

"I can handle hurt feelings, Andrew. Besides, didn't you say she only wished to hurt herself?" I wasn't sure if I believed that, but I wanted to soothe him somehow.

"Ice!" he cried, his eyes frantic. "You need ice on that."

"Andrew! Are you listening to me? I, *we*, need answers. I know about your father—" The words once spoken couldn't be taken back.

He grew still, though his fingers continued stroking my skin. Back and forth, back and forth. We both watched the movement with avid interest. "Who told you?" he finally asked, his voice husky.

I bit my lip, working at it as furiously as my mind was spinning. I couldn't tell the truth even if I wanted to. I'd as good as promised Gertie I wouldn't give her up, and really, I shouldn't have said what I had. "I have to protect my sources."

"Then you're asking me to interrogate my staff?"

My mouth dried. "Who said it was one of your staff?"

"It's the logical place to start."

"It was Greg Huntington," I blurted out. "I mean, at his house."

"Ah."

One little syllable, yet imbued with so much meaning. "I don't want anyone getting in trouble because of me, Andrew. If you're to be mad at anyone, it's me. I'm the one snooping around." I jabbed at my chest with my free hand.

"My father wasn't weak," he said distantly, and I wondered if he'd heard me or was even talking to me as he stared at an old painting of Dundeid Castle. "From everything I've heard, he was a good, kind man. But not weak. He just couldn't stand it."

"Stand what?"

His fists clenched. "I don't know exactly. No one will ever tell me! Not Mother, even though I'm certain she knows what happened and why. I've tried to find out, Lily. But she won't talk. I can't stand not knowing!"

I laid my hand on his arm, surprised to find him trembling. "I'm sorry, Andrew." I was about to tell him my own sordid story about my mother and why I'd come here, to finally tell the truth about myself, when he turned away.

"Come on. Let's get some ice on that."

"It's fine, Andrew. The red's already fading. See?" I held out my arm for his inspection.

To my surprise, he gently took my offering in his hands, leaned down, and kissed the inflamed skin. His lips felt soft and electric as they touched each red spot. I just managed to stifle my gasp as I stared down at the top of his lowered head, his blond hair golden and sweetly soft. My eyes teared up at the gentleness of his gesture even as a wave of arousal swept through my body. I wanted more.

But I was not to get it. Without once looking at me, Andrew let go of my arm and walked away like a beaten man, his head hung low and his shoulders slumped with the weight of the world. I wanted to chase after him, make him press those lips to my own, but my feet were rooted to the ground. And then he was gone.

And I was left standing alone.

Chapter Eighteen

✤

My room was cold, I discovered, as I slammed the door behind me. I leaned against it, trying to keep the demons trapped outside, but they were inside me, and they wanted to be heard.

What just happened back there? Andrew's gesture had meant more to me than all his words about a connection between us, about getting married. He was a beautiful man, inside and out. But something was going on here that he had no control over, something that involved me. Or at least, that's what his mother thought.

Did I have feelings for him? Judging by my reaction to his kisses, the answer was a resounding *yes*. I could still feel the touch of his lips on my skin; my heart started pounding at the mere memory. I pushed my sleeve up and stared down at the place where his fingers had gripped my arm. The red was gone, leaving no evidence of our contact. There would be no bruising. I wondered if I would have felt differently about Andrew if there had been. I hoped so. Still, he hadn't meant to hurt me. He'd only wanted to keep me from hearing what his mother had to say.

Which could mean he was keeping secrets from me. Which could mean we were playing the same game.

A knock on the door startled me. "Who is it?"

"I've brought yer dress, Miss."

"Gertie!" I cried with more enthusiasm than the situation warranted. She seemed to take it in stride, however, as she marched into the room, holding the dress out proudly.

"I got all those stains oot," she told me as she pulled open the door of the wardrobe and hung the hanger on it. I stood next to her. The dress was spotless, seemingly brand new.

"It looks wonderful, Gertie. You did a great job."

She beamed. "Well, it weren't easy. Mud is one thing, but blood? That takes some doing."

"Blood?" I heard my voice echoing weakly. "Are you sure it was blood?"

"I ken me business, Miss."

"Of course you do, Gertie," I soothed. "It just seems strange to find it on a dress. Was there a lot?"

"It spotted the front of the dress along the hem and there were some smears farther up on the skirt. A few on the left sleeve cuff. No match for me, though!"

"You're a whiz," I said faintly. "Thank you for taking care of it."

"Is there anything else ye'd like done?"

"Um, could you wash these?" I scooped up my outfit from yesterday. "They're not mine. I borrowed them when I got wet."

She nodded, taking the pile from me. No doubt she'd already heard the story of my visit to Greg Huntington's house, along with several embellishments. "Just leave it tae me."

"What do you think of Mr. Huntington, Gertie?"

She looked away. "I really dinna think of him, one way or the other, Miss."

"What about the Laird?" Here, she blushed.

"What aboot him?" She began backing away from me, toward the door.

"I just wondered what you thought about him."

"He's a good boss, and a good laird." The blush deepened, and the speed with which she moved increased.

"Is he seeing anyone?" Might as well be hanged for a floozy as a lamb.

She drew herself up. "I wouldna ken." But she had her suspicions, I thought, watching the distaste spread across her face.

"Any guesses?"

But Gertie wasn't talking. "Anything else, Miss? I've work tae be doing."

"No. You can go. You're a loyal worker, Gertie."

She relaxed and gave me half a smile. "I do me best, Miss."

"Thanks again, Gertie."

She nodded and scurried out the door before I could ask her any more questions she didn't want to answer. I watched the door shut, then turned my attention to the dress. It really was very lovely and I felt a strange desire to try it on. I locked the door, then remembering its fault, shoved a chair under the knob. I had no wish to be caught trying on my costume. I wanted the dress to be a surprise, but I also didn't want people seeing me indulging in whimsical pursuits. Especially that gargoyle, Vivian.

Unable to tie the stays in the back, I ended up holding the gap closed with one hand. My reflection in the mottled mirror was startling. I looked like a different woman. Slowly I began to spin about, humming to myself a tune that reminded me of lazy summers and a million stars shining in the sky.

My cell phone rang, and I shook my head to clear it. I hurried over to dig my phone out of my pants pocket where I'd left it. "Hello?"

"I tried calling earlier."

"I thought you were in Edinburgh."

"I am. I'm between meetings at the moment and thought I'd call you."

"Why? What do you want?"

"I wanted to apologize to you about last night." There was silence.

"So what's stopping you?" I finally caved.

"Are you very angry with me?"

I sighed, blowing air through my teeth. "Not very. But I am mad. You purposely taunted Andrew and now he feels he has to... I don't know. Make things up to me."

"Don't you like that?" His voice was brittle.

"Why would I? I'd just as soon be left alone to do my job. I don't want anyone feeling like they owe me anything."

"Do you have anyone in your life you feel you can rely on?"

It was a very personal question—for me, anyway. "I don't know. Maybe."

"Name one person."

"Why do you care?"

His breath whooshed out. "I don't know."

Okay, harsh, but I'd asked. "Because of your dreams, maybe?"

"Maybe."

"Can you tell me what they're about? Finally?"

More silence, heavy as a death shroud. "There's not enough time. My client'll be here soon."

"Are they that bad?"

He coughed twice, as though choking. "I dream..." Long pause. "I dream that you hate me, Lilia. That you despise me and want to kill me."

"Gregor!" I gasped. "I don't hate you. You can be aggravating, but..." *I actually rather like it.* "But I *don't* hate you."

"In my dreams I do something to make you hate me."

"What?" I whispered. "What do you do?"

"I don't know. I don't *know!*" There was a muffled curse. "Listen, Lilia, I have to go. I shouldn't have called. Check your messages, and I'll talk to you at the Gala."

"I really don't hate you, Gregor."

"You will."

And then he hung up the phone.

Before I turned off mine, I clicked on my messages. Gregor's voice came on the line. "Lilia. I need to speak to you. Last night—things got out of hand and I'm sorry for that. This will sound like an excuse, but I wish only for it to serve as an explanation. Simply seeing Andrew provokes me in ways I don't understand. We're no longer friends, but I can't remember why. I'm sorry you got dragged into the middle of our battle. It isn't the first time we've clashed. But it is the first time there was so much…emotion…on both sides. Please say you'll forgive me and that you'll save me the first dance." The message ended and I set down my phone, my thoughts churning.

Say you'll forgive me.

Save me the first dance.

He sounded so sincere that I felt that forgiving him was the least I could do. Maybe in doing so, I could change his dreams. By absolving him, I wouldn't hate him, as he dreamed I did. Of course I didn't actually hate him. I was simply angry with him for provoking Andrew, and a bit scared of him, after learning my dreams took place so close to his home.

Maybe something was going to happen at the upcoming ball. Maybe if I was ready for whatever that was, then I could prevent it from happening. Or at the very least, keep myself from reacting so strongly. I would do everything in my power to keep from hating Gregor, I resolved, and instantly felt better.

Taking special care, I pulled off the gown and re-hung it, smoothing out the silky material. Then I dressed and settled down to work on my article until lunchtime, pushing everything out of my mind. I simply could not think about all of this another moment.

~

Everyone gathered at the table to eat our midday meal, even Ophelia, though she looked tired. I remembered my plan to help her and determined to find a nearby town where I could put the first half of it into play.

Andrew nodded at my arm, a question in his eyes. He didn't look quite so defeated and I felt better seeing him improved. I smiled to show I was okay and no hard feelings. Even though I'd been working on my article, a part of my mind had continued to process my earlier encounter with him. The idea occurred to me that he didn't want to lie to me, but felt he must protect his mother, or me from his mother. Something strange was going on with her and while he seemed to know something about it, I had a feeling he didn't know everything. Vivian, I sensed, was probably holding back information from him.

"I was hoping to go into town this afternoon," I announced after Gertie served us garden salads. "I have a few things I need."

"Oh?" Vivian replied, looking up from the cherry tomato speared on her fork. There was a strange animation to her features. I would have thought she'd look exhausted, like Andrew. "Perhaps we could provide it here?"

"I doubt it," I said cheerily. "It's quite a list. A girl can't pack everything."

"I'm afraid we can't spare any time to give you a ride and Brian left this morning for Edinburgh to pick up several items for the Gala. If I'd known you wanted to go, I would've told him to wait for you."

"Did he fix my bike, do you know? He told me to come back tomorrow, so it should be all set."

"He might have. But it's started raining. I doubt you'd want to bike in that." She indicated the windows. I saw spots hitting the glass and dark clouds gathering up over the loch, where whitecaps were forming.

"Is there a car I could drive?"

"Sorry," she shrugged. "One of the things Brian needed to fetch was a new battery for the Jeep."

Andrew glanced at her. "I didn't know there was anything wrong with the Jeep."

"Brian was going to take it this morning, but the engine wouldn't turn over. He thought maybe someone had accidentally switched the lights on and forgotten to turn them off."

They were looking at each other and so missed Ophelia ducking her head and launching into her salad with a gusto I had yet to see her apply to food.

"I always check the lights."

She smiled sideways at him. "I'm sure you do, Andrew. But with the Gala and our guest…" She gave him a meaningful look. "Well, you've been rather distracted lately."

"Well, as long as he gets it fixed," he said. "I'll need it for the Gala tomorrow."

She smiled and promptly changed the subject. "I hope we get good weather."

"The forecasts call for it. Another unseasonable warm front is coming in after this rain."

She nodded. "That's exactly what we need."

"Who cares what the weather's going to be if you can't have any fun?" Ophelia grumbled.

"You should," Vivian pointed out. "You do want to keep your home, don't you?"

Ophelia's lips pursed angrily. "With any luck this won't be my home much longer."

Andrew slammed his fist on the table and I jumped. "That's enough of that, Phe. You'll do as you're told tomorrow, and you'll do it with a smile on your face."

I realized that I was holding my breath and slowly released it. "So I guess I'll try to find another way into town," I said as brightly as I could. "Any ideas, Ophelia?"

She shook her head, not looking at me.

"Sorry, Lily," Vivian smiled. "Maybe after the Gala."

I nodded and focused on my salad. The rest of the meal passed without further drama, though I couldn't help wondering why it made Vivian happy that I couldn't go anywhere. Andrew and Vivian discussed the menu for the ball, Ophelia pushed her food around her plate, and I ate as quickly as I could. I had once offered Andrew my help and now I was afraid he'd take me up on it. I simply couldn't handle any more of Ophelia's sulks or Vivian's condescending arrogance right now. And I had work of my own to do.

As soon as I politely could, I dismissed myself from the table. Andrew watched me go and Vivian watched Andrew with a calculating look on her face. I didn't like that look and walked faster, escaping as quickly as my feet would take me. On my way down to the dining room, I'd left my camera and portrait kit propped by the door to the dungeon and headed toward it to re-take the photos I'd lost. As I was crossing the Great Hall, I heard a loud chime. Someone was here. Gertie appeared from a side room and swung open the main door. I didn't bother waiting to find out who it was, since it was probably someone involved in the Gala.

Once downstairs in the cold, damp space, the work progressed more slowly than I'd planned. The globe diffuser added some extra light to the glow from the lantern and my homemade softbox helped reduce shadows, but that all took time to set up and move around. My trembling fingers didn't help, either. The longer I stayed down here, the more my dungeon dream insisted on being heard.

I'm trapped. Behind bars. Screaming to be let out. Fingers bloodied. All hope lost.

I moved faster, finally finishing my work. My equipment swiftly gathered and packed, I headed past the cell where the ghost had appeared in my photo, my heart pounding uncomfortably in my chest. Something cold reached out and grabbed my arm. Stifling a scream, I raced up the stairs, even knowing that it must only be a draft of air. The door when I pushed it gave way and I realized I'd expected it to be locked.

I was free!

Unfortunately, at that moment, voices coming down the stairs halted my steps. It was Vivian and Ophelia, and I didn't want to see them. I slipped back behind the dungeon door, leaving it open a crack to watch their progress. I wanted to know as soon as they were out of sight. I hadn't expected to eavesdrop.

"You like Dr. Mills. He's such a nice young man."

"Oh, Auntie Viv, not now!" Despite Ophelia's protests, the feverish look in her eyes was at odds with her words. She looked excited to see Dr. Mills. Maybe she really did like him.

"He wants to check and see how the new medication is working for you. Humor me…and Andrew." A loud chiming filled the hall, echoing off the walls. "He's here now, so be on your best behavior with him, Ophelia. I'm warning you."

Ophelia curled her lip at her aunt, but didn't argue. Vivian, satisfied, clicked across the floor to open the door.

"Dr. Mills. Do come in. Thank you for coming on such short notice."

A thin man of average height passed by her and entered the hall, looking around for Ophelia. "It's my pleasure, Miss Dering." His hair, neither blond nor brown, was somewhere in between—a tepid cup of tea color. He was dressed in an ill-fitting dark suit, the pant legs a shade too short, revealing brown dress shoes, and the jacket a bit tight in the shoulders. He wouldn't pass for a fashion maestro, but his eyes, dark and piercing, blew all that away. He looked the sort of man who would get what he wanted through sheer force of will. I wondered if what he wanted was Ophelia.

Ophelia smiled weakly at him as he crossed the floor to take her hands. They lay limply in his as he examined her. "Tsk, tsk, Miss Ophelia. You're wasting away. You must not be eating properly," he scolded. His expression was professional, though I sensed an under-current of tension in the way he stood, one brown shoe tapping as he studied his patient.

"It's this damn medication," she muttered.

"It does suppress the appetite. Come, we'll go to the parlor and you'll tell me everything."

"Tea, Doctor?" Vivian inquired, glancing at her watch.

"Nothing for me, thank you, Miss Dering. Come along, Ophelia." He seemed anxious to get going, guiding Ophelia with authority toward an open door, his hands on her shoulders. She went along meekly enough, though a slight smile curved her lips.

Vivian watched them go, a speculative look on her face, then pivoted and returned back upstairs to do more Gala planning, no doubt. I was curious about Dr. Mills. Why wasn't Ophelia seeing Dr. Weatherby, the one who had attended me my first night here? Perhaps Dr. Mills was a specialist. If so, he looked awfully young to be putting so much faith in. Not that young doctors couldn't do a good job, but they lacked experience and could be more naïve about human behavior than older doctors. I couldn't imagine putting anything past Dr. Weatherby, but Dr. Mills might be more susceptible to manipulation.

Satisfied the coast was clear, I scurried up to my room, set up my computer in the window seat, and downloaded my photos. I viewed each one carefully, looking for ghosts. There were no spirits, which, on the one hand, was a disappointment, and on the other, a relief. But the photos looked great—spooky, eerie, and perfect for my project.

After that I spent a couple hours editing and rearranging and resizing photos (I also watched about fifteen different people coming and going from the castle). Ken, our grumpy editor, would likely change everything I'd written, but I was nothing if not optimistic. One of these days I'd get him to take my article as is. Okay, maybe idiotic would be a better term than optimistic, but I refused to give up hope.

I pressed save and closed the program, then transferred everything over to my USB-stick. I hid the stick in my wardrobe, then put my computer to sleep. One piece was still missing—the bit about Lilia. I'd written about Ian finding proof of our shared ancestry after consulting his family Bible—a big resource for learning family birthdates, deaths, and marriages. I left out the bit about the letter. No sense revealing too many family skeletons. Unfortunately, putting the story to paper had done little to help me figure out how any of this might relate to my dreams. I couldn't quite imagine Ian seeking revenge for his ancestor, other than not wanting to talk to me again. On the other hand, who knew what lurked beneath his Scottish breast? *Braveheart* was all about revenge. Perhaps I should learn something from it and watch out for Ian.

My watch told me it was a little after four. Maybe Brian had returned from town and I could convince him to take me in or give me my bike. My phone was where I left it on the bedside table, and I grabbed it and checked my messages. Gregor had called. Feeling disturbingly excited, I tapped his name and listened intently. "I've sent you something. He'll be arriving at 4:15. Meet him outside."

Intrigued, I grabbed my wallet and a jacket and hightailed it down-stairs. Just as I was shutting the door behind me, a small, dark car pulled up and the door swung open. "Get in!" a nasal voice called. "I'm running late."

Thinking I must be crazy, I dashed through the rain and hopped into the car, slamming the door shut. The back of the car was filled with newspapers and a pile took up space at my feet. My driver stepped on the gas and soon we were roaring off down the drive. I hastily donned my seatbelt, then looked over at my companion. Rusty-haired, freckled, and bony as a skinned cat, he looked almost too young to be driving.

"You must be Lily. Greg sent me to talk to you, but we had a parish emergency—we've run out of sacramental wine for services tonight—and so I'm off to fetch some. I've got the cold from hell and I'm run-ning behind on everything so we'll have to talk in the motor." He glanced over at me and sniffed thoroughly. "I'm Harry, by the way. Father Chisholm's assistant and Father-in-training." He grinned and scratched his narrow red nose with a skinny finger. He was the one Ophelia had mentioned. The one who'd carted all those parish records down to the dungeon.

"Nice to meet you, Harry. Did Greg happen to have any idea how you could help me?"

He shrugged. "Not a clue, but he thought it was worth a try. Who knows? Father Chisolm says my strength is in my way with people, not with learning." He barked a laugh, then went through a coughing, wheezing spell for several seconds. I was about to bang him on the back when he pulled out of it. "I guess that's a compliment."

"If I'd known it was you coming, I would've brought along the regis-ter to show you. You could've looked at it, maybe seen something in it that I didn't."

"If you don't mind me asking, what is it you're looking for?" I frowned, calculating just how much I could tell him. He saw my face. "Harry Ringwold is my name, and keeping confidences is my game."

I laughed. "All right. I'm looking for a person. Her name is Lilia and I was hoping to track her down."

"Lilia, almost the same as you."

"My full name is Lilia, so exactly the same as me. I did find her name, too, but it didn't match the date I was looking for. She became a "new life" in 1880, so she was only a baby then. I need her to be older." The wind buffeted the car and Harry jerked the steering wheel, nearly running us off the road. Instead of braking, he stepped on the gas and just barely pulled us out of near disaster.

"Ah, but that's where you've got it wrong." Harry looked very pleased with himself, his sunken cheeks filling out like a chipmunk with a mouthful of nuts.

"What do you mean?"

"At that time, when the priest wrote "new life" about a person, it meant they were getting a chance to start over. Oftentimes, just someone moving to our wonderful country was considered getting a new life."

"You're saying she moved here in 1880—that this date had nothing to do with her birth?" I felt almost breathless.

"That's what I'm saying." He leaned forward. The rain had picked up intensity, washing over the windshield like a bucket of water dashed against the glass.

"So Lilia could've been an adult at that time?"

"That's right."

Lilia. New Life. Could she be the woman my ancestor Robert had stolen from his brother? Could this be the connection I was looking for? I grinned. "Harry, you have lived up to your chosen profession today. Thank you."

"You can thank me by putting in a good word for me with your friend, Huntington. Father Chisolm rather likes him, as much as the old curmudgeon can like anyone, that is."

I grinned at him. "That, Harry, I can do."

Chapter Nineteen

Harry turned out to be a godsend—*ha*—in more ways than one. On the way to picking up the sacramental wine, he dropped me off at the bank. I finished my transaction and was in time to slip into the car moments after he pulled up to the curb.

We chatted about American celebrities the whole wild drive back to Dundeid. Being a *Star Trek* fan, he especially liked Spock. I promised to hook him up with some celebrity photos I'd taken while on assignment in New York City for a piece on Broadway. Harry was very impressed and I felt I'd gone a little way to repay him for his kindness.

By the time he dropped me off, the rain had let up and it was suppertime. "Cheers!" he called, then whizzed off, the little engine sounding more like a scooter than a car.

There was, of course, another uproar when I arrived. Andrew stormed into the dining room, saw me, and started yelling. "Where the hell have you been? You said you'd tell me if you were going to leave the house!" He looked tired, his hands working through his blond strands again and again.

"You're right. I did say that, but it was very last minute and I wasn't gone all that long—a couple hours at most."

His hands dropped. "A couple hours that seemed like a lifetime."

I stared at him, perplexed. Wasn't this overdoing things just a wee bit? "I'm an adult, Andrew. I don't need looking after 24/7. I had an errand to run and Harry Ringwold gave me a ride."

"Harry Ringwold? How did you meet *him?*"

"Gregor…y sent him. He thought I might need another source for my article. Harry gave me a ride into town since he was going in to fetch more sacramental wine. It all worked out quite well!" I said cheerfully, wanting the interrogation to be over and Andrew to stop glaring at me like an angry bulldog.

"Quite *well*! That's not the word I would've chosen. I was worried sick about you, Lily." He gripped the back of his chair, his knuckles whitening like popcorn.

"I'm sorry about that, Andrew, but you really do worry about me too much. I can take care of myself. Now, for heaven's sake, sit down."

He paused, looking for one moment like he wanted to defy me, but in the end, he pulled out the chair and sat down hard. "My dreams…" he said softly. "I worry about you so much because of my dreams…"

"And because you like me so much," I teased, wanting to coax a smile out of him. He always seemed to be carrying the world on his shoulders.

His smile, when it came, was grim. "I like you very much and if anyone ever hurt you I'd kill him."

My stomach lurched. "That's a bit extreme. Are you talking about Gregor?" There, I'd said it y-less.

Andrew immediately picked up on the change, his eyes darkening. "Gregor? When did you start calling him that?"

"I don't know." I tried to look unconcerned.

"And, yes, I'm talking about *Greg*. He's trouble, Lily."

"I wish you'd be more specific about how he's trouble, more than just that he was opposed to someone dating his sister."

"I wish I could be. All I know is that he's going to hurt you."

My mouth dried up suddenly. "Hurt me?" I tried to laugh, but it came out as a stuttering noise, like an engine trying to catch and not succeeding. "How?"

"My dreams don't tell me." He pounded the table, making the silverware jump. "If I could only know what he meant to do…"

I swallowed uncomfortably. "Maybe they really are just dreams, Andrew. Maybe we're all too sensitive and simply need to let them go."

"Do you truly believe that?" He actually looked hopeful.

"I don't know what I believe." Which was true, though not what he wanted to hear. The trouble was, I had found my Lilia, and if she had married Robert MacKenzie, she was my ancestor. Perhaps I was meant to pay for what they'd done—a sort of ancestral karma. But if that were true, then what did Gregor and Andrew have to do with it? Or Ophelia, for that matter, with her death dreams.

A horrid thought occurred to me. Maybe *I* was the problem, not someone from the past. Maybe I was the curse, and I hurt everyone in my path. My mother had tried to kill me—maybe she knew something, maybe she'd seen the future and what I meant to do.

The idea made me sick.

Vivian marched into the dining room and took her place next to Andrew. "You two are very serious." She didn't look happy about it. "Glad to see you're back, Lily." She didn't look happy about that, either.

I nodded at her, my mind still whirling with my theory. "How are the plans going for the Gala?" I asked her, though I couldn't care less.

"Fine. We're having a cold dinner tonight—I hope you don't mind. I have to eat and run. Ophelia isn't feeling well, and she's worried she won't be able to attend the ball."

"That's too bad," I replied. "She was really looking forward to going."

"Yes, well. There's always next year." I stared at her, wondering how she could be so unfeeling.

Gertie entered the room with a pitcher of milk. "The buffet's ready," she indicated the sideboard. I hadn't noticed it when I'd come in, but saw that there were silver trays of lunchmeat, cheeses, lettuce leaves, and sliced tomatoes, along with an array of breads and condiments. "Milk, anyone?"

"I'll have a glass," I said, standing up and following Vivian and Andrew to the sideboard. I only wanted to get my food and go to my room.

I prepared a thick sandwich, grabbed a couple pickles and a handful of chips, then picked up my glass from the table. "I'm sure you two have business to discuss. I'm going up to my room to eat, then an early bed for me."

"You don't have to go," Andrew protested.

"I'm quite tired—"

"Let the poor girl go," Vivian interrupted, looking pleased. "Tomorrow will be quite chaotic. The fair starts at eight in the morning, Lily, and goes until four. The ball begins at seven, leaving everyone plenty of time to change into their finery."

"You're sure there isn't anything I can do?"

"Perfectly sure," Vivian smirked. "We have everything under control."

I sneaked a peek at Andrew, who looked both annoyed and tired, then hurried up to my room. The sandwich was delicious and I was glad my appetite always remained healthy, even in times of great stress. No delicate stomach, mine.

After removing my Ace bandage for good and washing my face, I grabbed a mystery novel from my bag and for the next three hours tried to read about death and mayhem. It was a good book, but I kept thinking about Lilia—my namesake. Something about all this was bothering me. If Lilia were my ancestor, she would have been a great, great etc. grandmother. And while I'd found Robert's name and date of birth in our family records, I had not come across Lilia's name in my research. If they'd been married, her name should be on the list, but it wasn't. I hurried over to the window seat where I'd left my laptop. I was picking it up when a movement outside the window caught my eye. I peered down into the courtyard to see a figure, hunched over, leaving the castle.

Dr. Mills. What a long visit he'd had with Ophelia. Her case must be quite complex, or she really did like him and did everything in her power to keep him close for as long as possible. He did possess a certain air of authority about him that was appealing.

When he reached his car, he stopped for a moment and peered up at the castle with that intense gaze of his. It was quite dark outside, with only a yard light for illumination, still I could see enough of his face, which was softened by a yearning expression that surprised me. I wondered who he was directing that look toward? Was it really Ophelia? Or maybe it was Vivian. Andrew? I giggled at this last bit. If I told Gregor this, he could now claim that truly *everyone* fell for Andrew.

Sliding under the covers, I flipped open the laptop and searched for my Family Tree file. Opening it, I scanned the list of names. No Lilia. I did some searching on the Family Tree website until I found what I was looking for—Robert MacKenzie had married a Julia Ross. Not a Lilia. I chewed on my lip. I'd been so certain this Lilia was directly related to me! Well, not certain, but hopeful.

My cell phone rang and I picked it up, glancing at the number, which I recognized. My palms grew sweaty as I pressed the button to talk.

"Hello, Gregor."

"Did you figure it out?"

"Figure what out?"

"What I did to make you hate me."

"I don't hate you."

"I told you, you will."

"Well, then, maybe it's up to you to figure out what you did and not do it again."

"You think I'm not trying?" he rasped. "I think about my dreams all the time now—I watch my every step. But I can't figure out what I could possibly do to you that would make you hate me like you do in my dreams."

"Maybe it has to do with calling me at 11:30 at night."

He laughed, relaxing. "Sorry about that, but I couldn't sleep."

"Now you sound like Andrew—"

"How the hell would you know Andrew doesn't sleep well at night?" His anger could have fried the phone lines.

"Because he told me, idiot."

"You do like him, much as you deny it."

I thought about Andrew's lips on my skin, his violet-blue eyes. "His mother thinks we're getting married."

Silence. "You're having me on."

"I don't think Andrew is all that against it, either."

"You can't possibly be considering—"

"*No!* I barely know the guy."

"Good. Is he pressuring you?"

"Not really. It's a moot point anyway. I'm not getting married. Marriage isn't for me."

"Me, either," Gregor said, surprising me.

"Why not for you?"

"I don't really know. I could say it's because of all the divorces in the world, or that it's not necessary to get that little piece of paper if you love someone, but that's not it." He paused and I waited. I was getting used to his little silences. "I just have this feeling that it's not going to happen for me. I'm not sure why." He was quiet again, but I barely noticed. I was hugging myself, hearing him echo my own sentiments. "What about you?"

"You just put into words the vague reason I've always carried with me about why I wouldn't get married. Do we have self-esteem problems?"

He laughed. "I don't think that's a problem for either one of us."

I sighed. I wished I could tell him about my dreams and about what I'd realized while down in the dungeon—that it played a big role in all this. Then an idea occurred to me. "Does Mochrie Manor have a dungeon?"

"Nice change of subject! Of course we do. What self-respecting manor wouldn't? Why do you ask?"

"Oh, nothing. I've just had this feeling that a dungeon plays a role in all this."

"And you wanted to know if it might be my dungeon?"

"I guess that would give me a reason to hate you."

"Do you truly think I could ever do anything like that to you?"

"I don't know what to think, Gregor." Not when it was the road that led to *his* house in my dream. On the other hand, I'd found the 'ghost' in Andrew's dungeon, though it may have nothing to do with me.

Ghosts in a dungeon were likely as common as rats. "Say, listen. Thanks for sending Harry Ringwold my way—he was very helpful, so put in a good word for him with Father Chisolm, won't you? Meeting him I managed to kill two birds with one stone."

"Poor wee birds. I hope it was worth it."

A giggle popped out of my mouth. Appalled at myself for such girlish nonsense, I promptly stifled it. "Yes, it was. I discovered something interesting. Maybe I'll tell you about it at the Gala."

"I do get the first dance, right?"

"I suppose so, since no one else has asked me."

"Good. Now I wish you'd stop calling me, I have to get some sleep. Goodnight, Lilia."

I smiled. "Goodnight, Gregor."

Fingers tapping on the computer's lid, I wondered how I could possibly come to hate someone that I liked as well as I did Gregor.

It didn't seem possible.

Chapter Twenty

✷

The day of the Gala dawned bright and beautiful, and I rolled out of bed feeling fluttery. Events like this in my father's world were stiff and formal and extremely boring. Judging by all the activity going on down on the front lawn, this wasn't going to be one of those events.

One woman with long, dark braids directed a white van as it backed up. She held up her hand and the vehicle jerked to a stop. Workers in navy blue uniforms poured out and joined her as she opened the back of the van. They worked in unison, pulling out tables and boxes. Each appeared to have a job—two stocky men set up long, white tables in a square and laid them with red tablecloths. The third worker, a young, red-haired woman, unpacked boxes. An array of woven goods and jewelry began to appear on the tables as I watched.

More cars and vans arrived in a steady stream and I checked my watch. Six a.m. Early, but I knew from doing stories on a few local craft fairs that crafters needed the time to set everything up and to check to be sure everything looked nice and professional.

I spotted Vivian crossing the lawn, speaking to a tall, dark man dressed in Renaissance garb and carrying a violin case. She pointed him to a stage of sorts set up on blocks and he headed for it. A mud-spattered Range Rover pulled up and two lanky young men jumped out. Vivian spotted them and headed their way. After some chatter back and forth, she pointed to a spot close to the castle. They jumped back into the Rover and roared off. Vivian visibly winced, obviously concerned at the mess they would be making of the wet grass. At the designated spot, they jumped out, laughing, and began to set up. Squinting, I finally figured out they represented the local pub—The Black Ewe. Their gray jackets boasted a black sheep on the back.

I sat there for an hour watching all the activity, taking note of the stands I wanted to visit. A striking figure cloaked in a glittery sapphire cape directed two scruffy men as they erected what looked like a miniature circus tent. I thought of Amria and wondered if she'd be coming today. I hoped not. I didn't want anything to mar this event. It had been a long time since I'd done anything just for the fun of it and I was really looking forward to it. Mother had always been depressed or sick, and after she left, Father acted as though he didn't know how to have fun—and maybe he didn't. I'd spent so much time proving to him and to the world that I could take care of myself that I'd forgotten to have fun, too.

That changes today.

Feeling lighthearted, I headed to the bathroom to get ready. By the time I reached the grounds, people had started arriving for the event and the field to my left was filling with cars, Brian and another young man decked out in plaid kilts and white shirts directing them where to park. There were a total of about forty vendors selling everything from hand-blown glass and pottery to kilts and kilt accessories to local foods and books on local lore. Rubbing my hands together, I headed toward Ophelia sulkily handing out the events brochure. She looked all right to me and I wondered what had been wrong with her.

"Have you seen Greg?" she demanded when she saw me. Her disappointment at not being able to bid at the auction hadn't prevented her from dressing her best in a long, flowing pale purple skirt and a lavender, organza blouse with puffy sleeves and matching heels. A warm breeze ruffled the flimsy fabric.

"You look like a princess," I said. "And no, I haven't seen him. I just came down."

She frowned. "I thought you two were best mates now."

"Why would you think that?"

She shrugged, her chin stubborn. "I have eyes you know."

A family came along—a heavyset mother and father with their two heavyset sons. They took their brochure from Ophelia and headed straight for the food booths. Watching them, I realized I'd forgotten to eat. I patted my pants pocket. Good thing I had lots of cash. The air smelled delicious—a combination of cinnamon and coffee and fried dough.

"Well, I guess we are friends. But that doesn't mean anything, Ophelia. This isn't my home. I can't stay here forever."

"That's what you said before."

I glanced over at her. She handed a brochure to a couple. "Before?"

"I think you want to stay."

"No, I don't. I like it here, but when my job's finished, I'll be happy to go home." But as I spoke the words, I wondered if that was still the truth. What would I be heading back to? I liked my job, but covering local events was growing stale. Pretty much every story that could be covered, I'd covered. And then there was my dad. I'd told him not to call, and he hadn't, but he'd sent a lot of email messages, all of which I was trying to ignore. But I was finding it hard when his subject line contained headings like, "Not feeling well," and "My heart's acting screwy." I had read these, of course, only to discover he had heartburn from eating at Taco Joe's every day for the past three days.

Ophelia didn't respond, turning her attention toward the crowd coming toward us. With one last look at her rigid back, I spun about and faced the fair, wondering what to do first. I didn't like that Ophelia was upset with me and I didn't like how she'd picked up on my uncertainty about going back home. She'd known something about me that I didn't and I found that unnerving and annoying.

The breakfast booth, sponsored by Kit's Diner, lured me with its heavenly scents of greasy sausage, and I proceeded to do my part to support Dundeid by eating as much as I could. As I devoured my syrup laden pancakes with a plastic fork that threatened to snap in half at any moment, I scanned the crowd. It took a bit for me to realize that I was searching for Gregor. And just as I acknowledged this, he appeared, walking toward me through the crowd, his eyes focused on me as though he were on a mission.

My heart fluttered a little and the pancake in my mouth dried up. I quickly chewed and swallowed, hoping I wouldn't choke. I wiped my mouth with a napkin and when I looked up again, he was standing in front of me. An involuntary smile took over my face at the sight of him—a Scottish vision. He wore a white, winged dress shirt under a black jacket. Instead of pants, he had on the traditional plaid kilt fastened with a kilt pin and a belt with an embossed buckle. Looped through the belt was a Scottish pouch, called a sporran, decorated with metal plating. Thick woolen socks, folded just below the knee, sported garter flashes and a sgian dubh—a knife sheathed and worn in the top of the right hose. Black leather Ghillie brogues completed the outfit.

"You should document this moment," he said, glancing down at my camera case. "This is the only time I'll ever be, if not welcomed, then tolerated at Dundeid Castle."

My smile widened. I couldn't seem to turn it off. And, I found to my surprise and pleasure, I didn't want to. "You look dashing. A real Scottish gentleman."

His brows lifted. "You like it?"

I nodded. "Lincoln, New Hampshire—that's a town up north from where I live—holds the Scottish Highlands Games every year and those guys look like wannabes compared to you."

He laughed. "I'll take that as a compliment. They do the Games here, as well, in the fall, when the various clans rally."

"Do you participate in them?"

"I used to. It's been a long time."

"So what are your plans for today?"

"I'm looking for Vivian, actually." He watched me as he said this.

"Oh," I tried to reply as casually as I could. "I saw her earlier." I turned toward Ophelia. She was staring at us, automatically handing out brochures as the people passed by. She didn't look happy. "Ophelia might know."

He turned around and waved. Her face brightened and I felt my mood sour inexplicably. "I'll go ask her," he said. He turned to go, then turned back. "What are your plans?"

"I'm free the whole day."

He nodded. "Then perhaps I'll see you about."

"Perhaps." I tried to sound coy, but coy was not my thing. The word came out sounding miffed instead.

His expression amused, he sauntered off, toward Ophelia. I noticed he had very nice legs. My breakfast, which I'd been enjoying up until his arrival, suddenly lost its appeal. I frowned. How annoying, and how unlike me. I dumped the paper plate into a metal garbage can next to the booth, purchased a cup of coffee, and headed toward the booth on local lore. I bought a book on the history of the Highlands from a smiley, round woman with rosy cheeks and wildly curly red hair.

"Shall I sign it?"

"Please do."

I watched as she wrote, "May you find your way again, Lilia MacKenzie," then signed Audrey O'Keefe with a flourish beneath it.

"How did you know my name?"

She winked at me. "When you seize the reins, you go the way you need to go."

What?

"Lily!" a voice beckoned from behind me. I spun around to find Andrew stalking toward me. "I'm glad I found you." He took my arm and pulled me away from Audrey. I glanced back at her, but she was already chatting with a tall man in a flat cap.

"What is it?" I asked, letting myself get pulled along.

"It's Mother. She insists on attending the fair."

"But I thought she wanted you to cancel it."

"She did, but since we're going ahead with it, she demanded to be here, keeping an eye out."

"For what?"

He stopped behind the pub booth and let go of my arm to face me. He looked uncomfortable. "For you. She says you're in danger of doing something."

"Me?" I squeaked. "But what am I supposed to do?"

He shook his head, swiping a hand over his tired face. I finally took in that he, too, was wearing a similar outfit to Gregor's, only Andrew's kilt was green plaid and the jacket a different cut. He looked every part the dashing laird. "I wish I knew."

"What do you want me to do?"

"Humor her. Stay with her until she tires and then bring her to her room. I hate to ask this of you, but she's so insistent...and she's not well."

My hand touched his arm. "I'll do it, Andrew. Of course I will. No big deal."

His eyes lightened and his shoulders lifted. "Really? Oh, Lily! You're wonderful."

I laughed. "I know. So where is she?"

"Gertie has her in the kitchen."

"I'll go fetch her and you go do what you need to do."

His blue eyes fastened on mine. "You're a lifesaver, Lily. I won't forget this."

I shrugged. "That's what friends are for."

"Friends. I'll take that…for now." Leaving that charged phrase electrifying the air between us, he left me, disappearing into the crowd.

Giving myself a mental shake, I headed for the house. Before going to the kitchen, I ran upstairs and tossed my new book on the bed. *I'll read it tomorrow*, I promised myself. And as far as how that woman knew my name, I quickly figured it out. Of course everyone would know the name of the American woman staying at Dundeid Castle. Gossip is what makes the world go round. Feeling less anxious, at least about the author and her seeming clairvoyance, I went to fetch Mrs. Dering.

"I won't have it!" a frantic voice cried out from the dining room. Mrs. Dering was dressed in an old blue gown, her hair untidy and her eyes wild as she passed back and forth in front of the windows.

"Hello, Mrs. Dering," I called, catching her attention. "Andrew thought you and I should see the fair together."

"Oh, Miss MacKenzie!" Gertie's face was flushed. "How good of ye tae coom…"

"No problem, Gertie." I held out my arm as I approached Mrs. Dering. "We'll have fun, won't we?"

She eyed me suspiciously. "Who are *you*?"

My feet stuttered to a stop. "Why, I'm Lily, Mrs. Dering. Lily MacKenzie. Remember? Andrew sent me…"

"You must leave here now!"

I jerked back as though slapped. "But…"

"Get her out of this house!" she screamed to Gertie, her claw-like fingers beseeching the maid to do something.

Gertie threw me a panicked look. I took several steps back, holding up my hands. "I'll go, Mrs. Dering, I'll go!" I turned around.

"Go *now*!" she cried at my back. "Before it's too late…"

I spun back. "Before what's too late?" But she was crying and babbling through her tears and didn't hear me. Gertie tried to calm her. "Mrs. Dering?"

Gertie looked up at me. "Me and me mum'll take her upstairs and I'll stay and look after her."

"But what about the fair? You'll miss out."

"I ken me place and it's by Mrs. Dering." She was suddenly years older, and I looked at her with new respect.

"I'm sorry, Gertie. I'll let Andrew know what happened."

"Dinna say nothing that'll worry the Laird," she said fiercely.

I shook my head. "I won't."

"Make her go!" Mrs. Dering sobbed, pointing at me.

"I'm going now, Mrs. Dering. Everything's going to be all right."

Her shoulders slumped with relief. I turned to go, wondering with a sick stomach what had changed between us. First she thought I was her son's fiancée and now she only wanted me gone. Was she afraid she would hurt me to stop me from doing whatever it was she thought I was going to do?

"She'll ruin us all," she muttered as I shut the dining room door behind me with a click. Feeling horrible, I leaned against the door to catch my breath, then hurried on rubbery legs to find Andrew.

He was over on the activities field, preparing to announce a potato sack race for the kids. I beckoned to him. He looked at me for a second, then set the microphone down on a wooden box.

"Where's Mother?"

I had already decided on a story to tell him. "She wasn't feeling herself so Gertie's going to stay with her in her room."

"Not herself?"

"She's feeling a little off. Otherwise, she's fine."

His forehead crinkled up. "Are you sure that's all?"

I couldn't meet his eyes. "How's the fair going?"

He didn't say anything for a few seconds. "It's going well. A success, actually."

I smiled, daring now to look at him. "I'm glad. That must be a big relief for you."

He nodded, surveying the field. "A large marketing firm in Edinburgh sent a representative to check us out. If all goes well, they'll want to use Dundeid Castle for all sorts of business activities, ranging from team-building to a reward for good work."

"Andrew, that's great!"

He looked down at me and grinned. "I know. So wish us luck."

I pointed to the kids, who were getting restless. "If you don't want a rebellion on your hands, I think you'd better start the race."

His head swiveled toward them, then he laughed. "Good idea. I'll see you later."

I nodded, tossing him a little wave.

She'll ruin us all…

Perhaps it would be best for me to leave, after all. And the sooner, the better.

Chapter Twenty-One

❧

After watching the race, I headed back to the house. I was halfway there when I heard footsteps behind me. A hand grabbed my arm and spun me about. "Where are you going?"

Gregor.

"I was just going inside to do a little work."

"Work?"

"I'm feeling a bit tired. I thought I'd save my energy for the ball tonight."

His dark eyes scanned my face. "You aren't really feeling tired, are you?" I shook my head. "Something happened."

I nodded, then looked down at my feet. I didn't want to start crying. Not here, not now, not in front of Gregor. "Mrs. Dering said something about me... Well, I thought she liked me, but I guess not."

"What did she say?"

"It's not important. She's clearly not herself. I'm not sure what's wrong with her, but she's not happy with me right now and I don't want to make things worse for her."

"What did she say, Lilia?"

"Th-that I'd ruin them all."

His mouth dropped open. "She said that?"

"First she thinks I'm going to marry Andrew, now she thinks I'm the antichrist."

He glanced around, then leaned toward me. "I've heard rumors—I'm not one to spread them, but this one might help you feel a little better."

"Go on."

"Amria tells me things all the time. I don't like her spreading gossip, and have told her so, but she doesn't listen to me. Amria doesn't listen to anyone, I think." I was glad to see her behavior didn't particularly amuse him. "Anyway, she said that Mrs. Dering has had problems for a long time now, but they've gotten worse in the past few years. I've been in Edinburgh, so I wasn't here when her decline started. The rumor is that she's lost her mind."

"She does act a bit strangely," I said carefully, not wanting to betray Andrew's trust.

"I'm only telling you this so that you won't let what she says spoil your day."

"She hasn't spoiled it. I've really done everything I wanted to do."

"Everything?"

"Well," I admitted, "there are a few more things I wanted to see. I thought I might get my fortune told. I've never quite had the nerve to do anything like that before."

He held out his arm. "Why don't we do it together? We'll be each other's moral support."

I hesitated, then looped my arm through his. "All right, then."

His arm was warm and solid and it gave me a feeling of security. We approached the bright red tent. There was a line so we waited our turn.

"Did you find Vivian?" I asked as we moved a step forward. He nodded, his eyes scanning the crowd over my head, his lips curved into a tiny smile. A triumphant smile. "But you're not hanging out with her today?"

"Later on."

"Oh."

He laughed. "Come on, Lilia! I'm doing the auction, remember? I had to check in with the boss."

"Andrew's not the boss?"

He laughed again. "Why do you care that I talked to Vivian?"

"I don't." I tried very hard to sound nonchalant, but judging by his beaming eyes, I was failing miserably.

"You do care, and you don't know why?"

"Maybe." My eyes drifted toward the hand-lettered sign, black on white, "Palms Read. £ 5."

"Come now. The truth."

"The truth is that I don't understand any of this, or what I'm feeling, or why. I barely know anyone here and yet I feel like I do know all of you. Like it's been so much longer than it really has. None of it makes sense—nothing's logical."

"Have you ever felt really sure of something even when you don't have the slightest bit of proof to back it up?"

I lifted my eyes to meet his, my lips trembling with the effort to speak. "I-I can't say I have—" I frowned, my thoughts coalescing. "No, wait. That's not true. I traveled to Scotland because of such a feeling."

"So you can understand why I feel like I know you more intimately than what should be possible in such a short acquaintance."

"Intimately?" I echoed, breath short.

"Emotionally, mentally…physically. I feel like we knew each other in another life; that we're wasting time."

"That's a good line," I said, feeling winded.

"It's not a line."

The curtain parted and two teenage girls stumbled out, clutching each other's arms and giggling. "It's our turn." I pointed. He pulled back, regarded me silently, then swept his arm outward. "After you."

I pushed open the thick velvet curtain and entered the dark space, lit only by candles. The strong scent of patchouli made me feel light-headed as I blinked in the dim light. I felt Gregor behind me, close enough to experience his warmth. The desire to turn and run filled me.

"Sit down," a voice directed and my eyes found the woman I'd seen earlier, though her sparkly hood was thrown back revealing a face I didn't want to see. Amria.

"So this is why you wanted to go to the fair," Gregor said behind me as he directed me into a chair. He took the one next to me. "I thought you were going to have fun."

She shrugged, but her expression was defiant. "I'm not going to spend my whole life waiting on other people."

"Very commendable," he replied.

Her head tilted to the side as though she were assessing the sincerity of his statement. "I don't need your approval."

"Why should you?" he responded simply. "I don't own you. You're free to leave any time." There was a steely edge to his voice.

She threw back her head and laughed, her straight, white teeth catching the light. Her long throat revealed itself—a demonstration, I couldn't help thinking, of her lack of fear regarding the two of us. "All in good time, Mr. Huntington." She looked back and forth. "So who's first?"

Gregor pulled a wad of cash from his pocket and peeled off a twenty-pound note. My eyes flashed up to his face in surprise, but he was staring at Amria, his face hard. "I'll go first, then Lilia. Make it good."

She took the note and slipped it into her cleavage. The move was so clichéd that I relaxed. Amria wasn't a threat. She saw herself playing a role—the gypsy maid destined for better things. I could handle Amria.

She took Gregor's hand in her own and turned it over. Palm up, she traced the lines with the tip of her black fingernail. The seductive touch would have broken many men, but Gregor remained unperturbed, meeting her several upward glances with a bland stare.

Clearing her throat, she spoke. "I see— I see—" Suddenly she dropped his hand. "I can't see anything for you. I must be growing tired. I need a break." She went to stand up, but Gregor grabbed her arm, stopping her.

"Sit down. I want to hear it. All of it."

She looked at me and I saw a glimmer of uncertainty before her gypsy mask slipped back into place. She sat back down, taking his hand once more. "Something you do will be seen as very bad," she said in a hoarse voice.

Gregor's expression never changed. "What do I do?"

She shook her head. "I can't see. Darkness and desperation surround you." She dropped his hand. "No more."

He seemed about to push for more, but seeing her stubborn expression, decided not to. "Fine. You'll read Lilia's palm."

I held out my hand to her, willing my fingers to keep still. They did not obey. She took hold of my hand and I realized she was trembling, too. That scared me more than her reading. She looked down at my lines. "You are betrayed."

"By whom?"

"I cannot see. You're in pain. You suffer much. I feel, I feel—a murderous rage so hot, so consuming, like a fire." She leaned closer, gasped, "Oh, dear Lord!" then dropped my hand like a hot coal. "Go now!" she shouted. "Leave here!"

Gregor looked pale. He took my arm and pulled me to my feet and out of the tent. I stumbled after him, into the bright light, blinking, my mind whirling. "What did she mean?" I called to him. "What are you going to do?" *To me?* I might have added, but bit down on the words. Gregor heard them anyway.

"I don't know!" His expression was tortured as we reached the castle wall. He leaned against its rough wall, breathing hard. He didn't let me go. "I care about you, Lilia. You're a lovely, wonderful girl. I'd never hurt you. I *couldn't*!"

I wanted to believe him, but he wouldn't be the first person in my life who supposedly cared about me and had ended up hurting me. Hell, he wouldn't even be the second. "So what do we do, Gregor?"

"The only thing we can do. We must stay away from each other."

"No!" The word was involuntary, but I wouldn't take it back. Not when I saw the hopeful look in his eyes when he heard it. "I mean, there must be another way."

"I can't take that risk. Tonight at the ball…we'll call it our last dance." His smile was sad. "I won't hurt you, Lilia. I won't."

"There's got to be another way," I repeated, unable to make any other argument.

"Listen to me." He pulled me to him so that our faces were only inches away from each other. I felt his warm breath on my lips, saw the blackness of his pupils as his eyes bored into mine. "I'll see you tonight. We'll dance. And then I'm returning to Edinburgh. I think this is the only way to change our dreams. To make the hard choice now, not when it's too late."

"But—"

"I'll see you tonight." He leaned forward and kissed me on the forehead—a warm, soft touch of fevered skin on fevered skin.

Oh, Lord. What was going on? What was I going to do? Did he really care for me? If so, what should I make of Amria's fortune of doom? Andrew's words seared a path of suspicion through my mind. *Don't trust him.* I had to know the real reason he thought that.

I wanted to escape to my room, but belatedly remembered that I had a mission to complete, so I couldn't. I spent the next three hours exploring the booths—buying my own sgian dubh at the *Everything Scotland* booth, sampling various ales at The Black Ewe, and keeping an eye out for Andrew. Every time I spotted him, he was with Vivian and I couldn't muster up the courage to confront him with her there.

I ate shepherd's pie for lunch, which was delicious, or could have been, if I'd been able to focus on the taste for longer than a few bites. Gregor had disappeared—I couldn't find him anywhere. At last, over the loudspeakers, I heard the announcement I'd been waiting for—the auction. According to the schedule, several items were to be auctioned off, with Gregor listed as the last item on the bill of goods. I made my way, along with the crowd, to the stage.

Andrew stood in the center of the stage, microphone in hand, wide smile on his handsome, sun-colored face. I found myself responding to his charm and the stress and fear of the last few hours lessened to a dull ache in my chest, barely noticeable now. I found myself thinking he would make everything all right.

"Good afternoon, ladies and gentlemen! I hope you're enjoying our festivities on this miraculously warm day in November." There was a raucous cheer and I joined in, raising my mug of gooseberry ale into the air. "For our last big event—until the ball this evening—we're going to be auctioning off a slew of local treasures, ranging from a two-night stay at Dundeid Castle, to a cask of single malt whisky donated by our very own Black Ewe, to a date with our local heartthrob, Greg Huntington." There was thunderous applause, the women in the crowd particularly boisterous.

I had to give Andrew credit. He spoke of Gregor with as much enthusiasm as he did the other prizes, but knowing him as I did, I was able to detect the slight, fleeting grimace as he spoke Gregor's name. But say it, he did. He really would do anything for Dundeid Castle, and suddenly I felt quite proud of him. This life is not what he would have chosen, but he was making the best of it.

A short, balding gentleman took the mike from Andrew and began the bidding in auctioneer quick-speak. Getting into the spirit of the event, I bid on the whisky, a beautifully hand-woven blanket, a painting of Dundeid Castle by a young man with long blond hair, and a gift certificate for an upscale restaurant built in an old jail. I didn't win any of these prizes, but felt I'd helped Dundeid by raising the bids. Now it was Gregor's turn. He stepped up onto the stage and the crowd grew silent. Silhouetted against the blue sky, he looked wonderful in his Scottish kilt, its hem lifting slightly in the warm breeze. Many a woman—myself included—was hoping for a stronger wind to pick up and reveal a bit more of the merchandise.

No such luck.

I glanced over at Andrew, who was watching me, his expression hard to read. I smiled at him and gave a thumbs-up. He relaxed slightly. "Slainte and thank you, Dundeid," he called out. "This year you've topped yourselves. Your generosity has helped our local businesses, raised money for the school, and gave you all a good excuse to get sauced." The crowd cheered. "And now for our finale, and what I believe will be our biggest moneymaker of the day. All you ladies dig out your checkbooks and get ready to bid. Good luck and I'll see you tonight!"

He handed off the microphone again and the bidding began. I waited until the bidding, which was fast and furious, trickled down to one bidder. Ophelia was watching the proceedings, looking as though she would happily blow everyone up.

"250 pounds, going once, going twice…"

I raised my hand. "Three hundred pounds," I called out and there was a collective gasp as the crowd swiveled about to catch a glimpse of me.

"We've three hundred pounds from the beautiful young lady in red. Do I have three-ten?" He looked meaningfully at my competitor. She bit her lip, then shook her head. "Going once, going twice…" He scanned the crowd. "We have a winner!" Yes! Being an eBay aficionado had finally paid off.

I received several congratulatory slaps on the back as I made my way up to the stage, though a few maybe weren't as amiable as they could have been, and my skin stung as I climbed the steps. I passed by Andrew without looking at him—I already knew there'd be fire in his eyes. But I was surprised to see how unhappy Gregor looked as I went to stand by him.

"You don't need to look so grumpy," I leaned over to whisper. "Give me a minute and you'll understand."

I scanned the crowd, saw Ophelia, and waved. Her lower lip quivered. "No, Ophelia!" I called out, suddenly realizing how she saw this, but she didn't hear me over the noise of the crowd. "I did this for you!" But it was too late. She spun about and ran toward the castle.

Damnit!

"Thank you again, Dundeid!" Andrew boomed. "All you lucky winners come to the stage and collect your prizes. Don't forget to bring your money, though." Laughter. "I hope to see everyone at the Gala Ball tonight. Your ticket not only buys you a lovely meal prepared by MacDougal Catering, but a night of music and dancing you won't soon forget!" His eyes struggled to stay bright and enthusiastic. The crowd clapped, then began to disperse quickly as everyone seemed anxious to get home and prepare for the event of the season. Andrew, Vivian, and the auctioneer took over the prize distribution and money collection, with Brian helping carry the whisky cask for the winner, a little old lady who was beaming.

Gregor and I remained on the stage as I waited to pay. Andrew kept sneaking scowling glances at us. "Why did you bid on me?" he asked in a quiet voice.

"I did it for Ophelia. She has a major crush on you and I thought it would be nice to make her dream come true—if only for a little while."

"You shouldn't have interfered," he said coldly, and I winced.

"I was trying to do something nice for her."

"Are you sure you weren't trying to get back at Vivian? I'm certain you know her view on Ophelia having anything to do with me."

A valid point, maybe, but I hoped I wasn't that shallow. "Ophelia needs someone standing up for her. She tries to fight for herself, but

Vivian always overrules her, and Andrew goes along with it. I was trying to make things better for her, but now they're worse. I've got to find her and give her this certificate so she knows I was doing this for her."

"And here I thought you were doing it to be with me." Gregor's voice was dry and cool.

"You told me we needed to stay away from each other!"

"For your own good!" he hissed.

"Lily?" Andrew called, staring hard at us. "You're our last winner." I looked around. Only a few winners remained and were collecting their prizes from Vivian. Without looking at Gregor, I went over to Andrew, digging in my purse as I walked. Finding the bank envelope, I pulled it out. Standing in front of him, I counted out the three hundred pounds.

"There you go." I slapped the money down on the table in front of him. "I take it I get some sort of voucher or coupon?"

He handed me a white envelope. "I hope you two have fun." With that sour look on his face he might just as well have said, "I hope you two rot in hell."

"I did it for Ophelia," I told him. "Someone has to stand up for her."

He pulled back as though I had swung at him. "What? Wait, Lily—!"

But I was already leaving him, my chest heaving with indignation, with fury! I had done nothing wrong, yet I was being treated like a criminal. It was time to find Ophelia and straighten things out between us.

But Vivian found me first. "Lily!" I looked back to see her hurrying across the lawn. Beyond her, the last of the winners were heading for the makeshift parking lot. "Please wait!"

I slowed, but I didn't stop. She caught me at the door to the castle. "I have to find Ophelia," I told her.

"About that…" She paused, glancing around first, one hand smoothing back her hair as she worked to catch her breath. "Andrew told me what you'd done. Very commendable, but entirely impractical. You see—"

I narrowed my eyes. "I see things perfectly, Vivian. You're in love with Gregor…y, and want him for yourself. Well, too bad. Ophelia needs this! If you continue to treat her like a little girl, she's going to act out and make herself sicker. Give her a break, Vivian. It very likely won't work out between them, but at least let her try."

"You see nothing as it is!"

"I need to find Ophelia." I turned around and ran into the castle, leaving her staring after me.

I spent the next hour searching, even recruiting Gertie, who was leaving Mrs. Dering's room, putting a finger to her lips when she saw me. "She's finally asleep," she said, looking exhausted. "Ye didna coom tae see her, did ye?"

I shook my head. "I have to find Ophelia."

She didn't ask why, simply took in the frantic expression on my face and said, "I'll search her room and the west wing."

"If you find her, tell her she's got it all wrong and that I'm looking for her and will explain."

She nodded and left me at a trot, adopting my anxiety. She understood Ophelia's illness better than I did. A horrible thought occurred to me. What if Ophelia took it into her head to run off, onto the moors like a heroine in a romance novel? I had to search outside.

Most of the booths were gone now, with only two remaining. Brian and Andrew were disassembling the stage. Andrew's jacket had disappeared and his sleeves were rolled up past his elbows. He didn't see me and I did nothing to gain his attention. I had to fix this with Ophelia before it was too late. I didn't need his judgment and anger right now.

I searched the gardens, then ran along the path toward Mochrie Manor. Ophelia was nowhere to be found and I didn't dare go too far as night approached. Cold and exhausted, I returned to the castle. Standing in the Great Hall once more, I looked dazedly about me, wondering what to do next. Then I remembered the dungeon. The thought of going down there chilled me to the bone, but I hadn't yet searched it.

Garnering my courage, I headed toward it. "Miss MacKenzie!"

I swung about. "Gertie! Did you find her?"

She was smiling and I felt my spirits lift. "She returned tae her rooms just as I went tae knock on her door."

"She's all right? You told her what I said?"

"She looked all right tae me. I was going tae tell her what ye said, but Miss Dering came along and I didna have a chance."

"Oh, well. Vivian knows everything. She'll tell her." I breathed a sigh of relief. "I'd better go get ready. The ball starts soon, doesn't it?"

She nodded. "Do ye need help, Miss? The caterers have taken over the kitchen and I've little else tae do."

"Oh, I'm fine—" I stopped myself, seeing her face fall. "Actually, if you don't mind, I would love some help. There's no way I'll get those stays tied myself."

She beamed. "I've always wanted tae be a lady's maid!"

I shook my head. "Seriously, Gertie. You need to set your sights a little higher. You're smart and capable. You could have a great career."

She gave me a look that once again spoke of a maturity beyond her years. "I'm happy wi' me life, Miss. Sometimes a person just needs tae accept what they've got and make the best of it. I love what I do. How many folks can say the same?"

I laughed. "All right, Gertie. You've got me there. I just don't like people waiting on me."

"Consider it a favor tae me, then, Miss."

I groaned. "You've just made it worse."

She pushed me toward the stairs. "All right, then. Consider it a favor tae yersel. Ye look a right mess!"

Full of laughter, we hurried up the steps to my room. By the time I was dressed, with makeup applied and hair arranged, I had to admit that Gertie would make a great lady's maid. "You did an amazing job," I breathed, staring at myself. "Thank you."

She smiled at me over my shoulder. "It were me pleasure, Miss."

I turned around and faced her, feeling suddenly emotional as I peered into her bland blue eyes. "I feel like we just did something sisters would do…" Or a mother and daughter. "That means a lot to me, Gertie." A tear slipped down my cheek.

She clapped me on the back. "Oh, Miss. Stop that right noo or ye'll ruin all me hard work!"

I sniffed and laughed. "Okay, fine. But I appreciate what you did, and I had fun."

Her eyes gleamed. "Me, too, Miss." She straightened up. "I best be off noo tae clean me own self up. I'm tae be serving drinks." She looked excited.

"I'll see you there."

She nodded, gave me one last approving glance, then left the room, humming a little tune. I turned to the mirror. Mother and daughter time. I'd never experienced that with my mother. She'd never had it in her to reach out to me like that. I understood why she was the way she was, with having those dreams for years and years, and in far greater detail than I had them. What I didn't understand is why she tried to kill me based on a dream. My eyes flitted over to where my cell phone sat

on the nightstand next to my bed. It was time to find out. Unbeknownst to my father, I had tracked my mother down a few months
ago. I knew her Paris address. I even had her phone number in my cell
phone. Hands trembling, I crossed the floor. Not letting myself think
any more on it, I found her number and pressed dial.

She answered on the first ring. "Oui, allô?" Her voice was eager, as
though she didn't receive many calls.

"Mom?" I cleared my throat. "Mom, is that you?"

"Lily?" Her voice was as breathless as mine. "This isn't a joke, is it?
This is really you?"

"No joke, Mom. I wouldn't have bothered you, but I— Well, I need
to ask you something." There would be no tearful reunion for us, no
cries or grateful sighs. There wasn't time.

"What is it? Are you all right?" Her time in France had lent a slight
French lilt to her words.

"I'm fine, Mom," I said, feeling strange that she should care. "I'm in
Scotland, actually. Right across the pond, as they say."

"What?" She sounded sick.

"I'm in Scotland, doing research for the newspaper."

"Scotland? No, Lily! You can't stay there. Leave now! I beg you!"

"I can't leave, Mom. I have to follow this through. It's my job."

"Oh, Lily!" She sounded frantic. "I thought what I did would be
enough. Tell me it was enough!"

"You thought *what* would be enough? Mom, what are you talking
about?"

"I wasn't trying to kill you, you know. You have to believe me, Lily. I
was trying to...to change things."

"If you weren't trying to kill me then what was it you were trying to
do? I still have scars."

"I only tried to stop the dreams."

"You didn't stop them, Mother. Not for me. *I* have your dreams
now."

"Oh, no!" Her words came out hoarse and raw. "Lily, *no!*"

"Isn't that what you wanted? To get rid of your dreams? To get rid of
me?"

"Oh, Lily! I never wanted that. I was trying to protect you. I thought
that if I took your blood I could change things. It's a ritual—a cleansing. I read about it in a book. I had to let your blood, and I also had to
make a sacrifice. So I tried to do that. My sacrifice was to give my life
for you, the most precious thing in the world to me. But then I failed.

Still, when the dreams stopped, I thought I'd done it. I thought I'd made the change and everything would be all right. I'd lost you when your father made me leave, but you got to keep your life."

The shock of what she was telling me made me dizzy and my mind buzzed with questions. "You weren't trying to kill me? Does Dad know?"

"He doesn't know anything. He never understood. Those dreams—are you sure you have them?"

"Oh, I'm sure. That's why I came to Scotland, where the dreams take place. I dream that I'm going to die. At least, I think that's what's going to happen. And I just couldn't stand it anymore. I had to find out what they meant."

"No, no, no, Lily!" Her voice was horrified. "You don't die, dear ..." *Crackle.*

Our connection was growing bad. I slapped the phone against my hand, then lifted it to my ear. "What happens to me, Mother?"

"You're *crackle* and...*crackle*—" her voice wavered, then the phone went out. My battery was dead. I slapped it against my palm. "Mom!"

Nothing.

Chapter Twenty-Two

✿

The halls leading up to the ballroom were packed with people wearing gorgeous gowns and sophisticated tuxedos. The simple townsfolk of Dundeid knew how to have a party. I pushed my way through the throng to a glowing ballroom, where couples waltzed and one little girl danced a Highland jig. The setting reminded me of a simpler time, back when people had to make their own entertainment.

I spotted Gregor right away, likely because he was making his way toward me. He had traded his kilt for a formal suit with long tails. He looked very handsome and I wasn't the only one to think so, judging by the longing eyes following him and heads turning with his every step. When he reached me, he held out his arm and I took it. I'd gotten over my anger with him, mostly.

"You look stunning," he said, his eyes taking in my gown. "Where did you find that dress?"

"Ophelia found it for me. She says it's very old."

"Looks brand new," he mused, his eyes speculative. "Are you ready for our dance?"

"You still want to dance with me after what I so cruelly and thoughtlessly did at the auction?"

He sighed. "I might have overreacted a wee bit."

"A wee bit?"

"A wee lot. I'm sorry, Lilia. I wish I'd handled things differently."

I smiled. "Personally, I'd like to use the voucher myself, but Ophelia needs this. She needs to feel like someone believes in her."

"And that's you?"

"It isn't Vivian."

He shook his head. "I'm a right dobber, aren't I?"

"If that means idiot, then yes."

"I deserved that. The question is, will you dance with this dobber?"

I laughed. "In a moment. I have something to tell you. I called my mother."

His dark eyebrows flew up in surprise. "That couldn't have been easy."

"I had to know…about why she—" I stopped. I hadn't told him about her murder attempt—that according to her it wasn't an attempt, but a form of purging. "I mean, I wanted to know about the dreams. I thought I died in them, but she told me that I don't."

His gaze sharpened. "So what does happen?"

"I don't know. We got cut off. But it sounds hopeful, doesn't it?"

"Perhaps." He looked skeptical. "But I still do something that hurts you."

"But now that we know it isn't the "biggie," we can still hang out together."

His smile was lopsided. "I'm not the optimist you are, Lilia."

"Work at it, then. I want us to be friends."

"But what if that's the key to all this? What if the choice we should be making to end these nightmares is to end our friendship?"

"I can't believe our doing something hurtful to each other is going to right a wrong. You know what they say…"

"Yes, yes. Two wrongs don't make a right."

"Exactly. So, shall we dance?"

"Did you ever find Ophelia?" he asked as he led me out onto the floor. The music had just ended and we were in time for a new dance to begin. Gregor placed one hand on my waist and another on my shoulder. His touch was warm, even through the fabric, and I couldn't suppress a delighted shiver.

"I didn't, but Gertie told me Vivian found her. And since she knows what I did for Ophelia, I'm sure she'll tell her."

Gregor nodded. "You've a good heart, Lilia."

"Not really. I just don't like it when people don't like me."

"You don't like seeing people unhappy," he corrected. "I've learned that about you today."

The music began, cutting off any protest I might have wanted to make. Instead, I was forced to accept his words without argument and I found them rather to my liking. Who doesn't want to think well of themselves? I was glad to know that when push came to shove, I was willing to help out someone in need.

The music was a waltz—a rather dark version, but I enjoyed its sultry, intense rhythm. As the musicians wove their magic, Gregor spun me around the floor, in and out amongst the other couples, dresses swishing, coattails flying. Hothouse flowers and perfume and cologne scented the warm air like exotic spices. We were flying birds, all of us, and I felt completely safe, and at the same time, exhilarated in Gregor's strong, capable arms. We whirled until everything blended together—

music, scents, breaths, heartbeats, and through it all, we didn't once take our eyes off each other.

We danced with equal intensity for the next three songs, until, breathless, we left the floor. I felt quite unlike myself, laughing and hanging on Gregor's arm, not wanting to let go. Everything felt so wonderful and heady.

Until I saw Andrew. He stood across the room from us, his eyes like blue fire as he made his way to our side. "I see you're enjoying yourself, Lily." He didn't look at Gregor.

"I am, Andrew. Thank you. How about yourself?"

"I was hoping to dance with you."

"The night's still young," I replied, full of mischief. Who can resist the intoxication that comes from the attention of two gorgeous men focused on one's self? Not me.

"Go ahead and dance, Lilia," Gregor offered, his tone suggesting that he was granting permission. "I'll get us something to drink."

Andrew opened his mouth, but the scathing words he obviously meant to speak went unheard, as Gregor had already turned and was making his way through the crowd. "He acts like you're his property, Lily. I don't like it. I wish you'd stay away from him. I've told you he's going to hurt you, and I'm not saying that out of jealousy." He spoke this last part in a rush before I could make the accusation myself. "I wish you'd believe me."

The trouble was, I did believe him. Gregor, himself, had dreamed of hurting me, and my dreams put me near him when something bad happened to me. But I didn't want to believe Andrew or my own dreams or any other truth that might be staring me in the face. Not tonight. Not ever.

"How's your mother doing?" I asked instead.

"Gertie told me what happened," he said, diverted. "I'm sorry, Lily. Why didn't you tell me?"

"You carry enough worries on your big, broad shoulders, Andrew."

He gave me a small smile. "You're so good to me, Lily." His hand passed over his tired face. "Even when I set you up to be insulted, and by my own mother. I can't think why she'd act so strangely to you when only a short time before she wanted your company."

"She had a bad episode," I replied, knowing what those were like, having lived with my mother's episodes for years. "I'm sure she'll recover and remember nothing."

"I hope so, but I'm worried she's getting worse. Viv wants to put her in Havensrest."

"Havensrest?"

"A home for the mentally ill."

"Oh." I didn't like the sound of that. "She'd hate being away from you."

"I know. That's what makes it so hard. I'm all that remains of her old life, I think. She hangs onto me with both hands, even though she doesn't seem to like me very much."

"Oh, Andrew. I'm sure she loves you in her own way." As my mother loved me in her own weird, warped way. Which made me wonder what I should do about her, now that I knew the truth. *Go see her, of course*, I answered myself. What else could I do? At the thought, I felt a rush of excitement, followed quickly by a torrent of nerves. What would it be like to have a mother again? Not perfect, not healthy, but a mother all the same? I could travel to Paris after my stay in Scotland was over and we could start again. The idea intrigued me.

"Love can be a burden, Lily," Andrew sighed, interrupting my thoughts.

"Hm? Oh, yes. And a blessing."

He laughed and held out his arm. "You *must* marry me, Lily. You're the only one who makes me feel like I can live this life."

"Maybe I will." I smiled back at him as he led me out onto the dance floor. Where Gregor was intense in his every movement, Andrew was light, swinging me around as though I were a feather boa. We laughed quite often, and Andrew's eyes were bright and mischievous, like the young boy he'd once been. I was glad to see the weight lifted off him, even if for just this short time. The joy ended when Vivian tapped me on the shoulder after the third dance, her eyes amused. She wore a simple white gown, diamond earrings, and her dark hair was tied back in a loose chignon. She looked stunning. Pasting a polite smile on my face, I gestured to her to take my place, leaving Andrew with a wink. He gave me an apologetic smile, then the next song began and he danced away with Vivian.

Gregor was waiting with my drink—bubbly pink champagne that tickled my nose. "Are you trying to get me drunk?" I said, taking a sip.

"Can't blame a chap for trying."

I lifted an eyebrow. "Actually, I'm more hungry than thirsty."

"Then let us see what repast is on offer," he said in a posh accent.

We made our way to the buffet, which was resplendent with an array of meats and breads and hors d'oeuvres. Gertie passed by with a tray of drinks. Her full cheeks were pink and her eyes sparkled. "Isn't this grand?" she asked as she passed by.

"Absolutely!" I called back.

Then she saw Gregor behind me and her expression darkened. "Mr. Huntington," she greeted coolly, giving a slight bob.

"Hello, Gertie. Ever the faithful servant, I see."

Her forehead puckered up. "I ken me place," she replied simply. "Unlike some folks." With this, she sauntered off, thick white fingers gripping her tray with purpose.

I watched her go. "What was that about?"

"You don't know?"

"Should I?"

"Gertie's devoted to her employer, who wants you. I stand in the way of that, which means I don't have a chance with her."

"Andrew doesn't want me. He's just playing at it."

"But do you want him?"

I turned to look at Gregor. "Is it any of your business?" I was being purposely evasive. I didn't know what I wanted. I also wasn't sure if Andrew was teasing me, or if he actually wanted to marry me. The idea of a man like him wanting me all seemed so fantastic, like a dream.

"You know I like you, Lilia," Gregor persisted. "You know we have a connection."

"I enjoy your company, too, Gregor. We get along quite well."

His lips tightened into white lines. "You're being purposely obtuse."

I turned away from him. "Maybe I am." Picking up a delicate plate, I slid a seasoned chicken breast onto it and deftly buttered a thick hunk of bread, moving quickly down the table. When I turned back, Gregor was still looking at me. "Eat something. You're going to need your energy."

"For what?"

"For dancing, of course."

A small smile lifted the corner of his mouth. "With you?"

"If you behave."

The smile broadened and he began to fill his plate. We found a quiet corner and ate our meal together, occasionally looking up at each other and smiling. I liked Gregor's smile. I found that I wanted to make it appear as often as I could. When we finished our lovely meal, he reached out and placed his hand on mine. "How was it talking to your mother?"

My heart jumped at his touch and I wiped my mouth with a napkin to hide my pleased smile. "I was nervous. I mean…" I leaned forward. "Well, I didn't tell you this part—you see, I thought—father thought, that she was trying to kill me."

Gregor's eyes grew angry. "What?"

I pulled back, but he didn't let go of my hand. "I was too ashamed to tell you—"

"I'm not mad at you, Lilia. Your mother…why would she do such a thing?"

"She told me on the phone that she wasn't trying to kill me. I think she was desperate. She has the dreams. *Had* them. And she saw everything that was going to happen to me and she thought if she…" I stopped. It sounded so ludicrous, so crazy, but I had to say it. "She cut me, as a sort of cleansing ritual. She only meant to kill herself—make the ultimate sacrifice. She was messed up, I suppose."

"Living with those dreams could do that to a person."

I thought about that. "Yes, I suppose they could."

"Are you angry with her?"

"I should be—I was at one point. But she's always been so fragile, so pathetic, that I can't keep being angry with her."

"You're more forgiving than I'd be."

"I don't know about that. I'm just tired of being mad all the time. I want the truth so I can stop feeling this way."

"So do I know the whole truth about you now?"

"I think so. It doesn't paint a pretty picture, does it?"

"I think it paints a gorgeous picture." He eyed me up and down and wriggled his eyebrows lasciviously.

"That was really bad."

He laughed. "Would you like to dance now?"

"Yes, I would."

He picked up our plates. "I'll be right back."

When he was gone, I pulled out the little pocket mirror I kept tucked away in my reticule. No food stuck in my teeth. Hurrah! Finishing the last of my champagne, I stood and brushed off my skirt. Not being the neatest of eaters, there was more than a fair share of crumbs clinging to the luxurious fabric. Luckily no stains, though a splash here and there would have made Gertie quite happy.

Mud is one thing, but blood?

Are you sure?
I ken me stains.

I closed my eyes as a rush of heat flooded my body. Why did I have to think of that now? I was going to spoil the whole evening with my imaginings.

"Lilia!" My eyes flew open. "Are you all right?" Gregor took my arm, his expression concerned as he looked me over. "You look like you've seen a ghost. Come, we'll get you outside."

"I'm all right," I tried to protest, but he was steering me through the crowd and out a verandah door, into the gardens. Drafts of warm air winged past us as he pulled me toward a stone bench tucked beneath an archway covered in dead leaves and thorny, brown vines.

"Better?"

"There was nothing wrong in the first place. I was just—" *thinking about blood and how it got on my dress.*

"How could you!" a voice cried out. I looked up, startled. Ophelia stood facing us, her body shaking with fury and hurt, her delicate lace shawl wrapped tightly as a cocoon about her thin shoulders. I tried to pull away from Gregor but his grip was too tight, defiant even. "You know that I—"

"Can you leave us for a moment, Gregor?" I quickly interrupted, wanting to save her from making a fool of herself.

His grip tightened. "I don't think that's a good idea."

Ophelia's entire body seemed to wilt. "What did you tell him about me?" she whispered.

I stared at her. "What? Nothing! Didn't Vivian explain things to you?"

"Explain what?" Her lower lip trembled.

I stood up, pulling my arm from Gregor's grasp. Ophelia shrunk back as I moved toward her, arms open. "Ophelia! I was trying to help you!"

She glanced over at Gregor, then quickly away. "By making me look bad? By spending your day with—" She cut herself off once more, on the verge of bursting into tears.

"No, Ophelia. You've got it all wrong." I clasped my hands together, almost begging her to understand.

"That's enough." The voice came from a distance and I looked up to see Vivian striding toward us on the flagstone path, with Andrew close behind. "Ophelia, I think you'd best retire to your room for the night. You're overwrought."

"She's perfectly fine," I argued, though my eyes told me a different story. Ophelia's slender frame shivered despite the warm air. Her cheeks were hollow and her lips dry and cracked.

Vivian turned her professional eyes on me. "Please stay out of this, Lily."

The attack put me on the defensive. "How can I? You argue in front of me. You talk as though I'm a part of your family. You got me involved. So I was trying to help!"

Vivian's lips pursed. "I think you've done enough for today with your *help*. First, Andrew's mother. Now Ophelia." She waved her hand toward Ophelia's shaking figure.

Gregor stood up, taking my arm. Ophelia saw the move and blanched. "What's going on here?" he demanded. "What're you saying, Vivian?"

"Ophelia isn't well, as you know, Greg. And Mrs. Dering…well, Lily does insist on questioning her."

"But I didn't do any—"

Andrew stepped forward, eyes wary. "Is this true, Lily? Did you say something to my mother to set her off?"

"No! Ask Gertie. She was there. I didn't say anything offensive."

"Then why did she change toward you?" Vivian asked coolly. "So abruptly? First she wants to spend the day with you, then suddenly she wants you gone?"

I threw up my hands. "I don't know! I don't understand it, either."

"And you know Ophelia's fragile," she continued her attack. "You know she's ill. Why would you encourage her to do something that would make things worse? Did you want her to be rejected?"

"I told you I was trying to help her—"

"By dancing with Mr. Huntington?"

"You danced with him?" Ophelia gasped, and I wondered how she could have missed seeing us.

"But I did the auction— I wanted to help—" I needed to get the right words out, but they wouldn't come. "Your aunt knows, Ophelia—"

"Why did you dance with Greg?" Andrew interrupted, purposely putting me on the spot. He knew I'd danced with Greg.

"Because he asked me to!" This was going from bad to worse.

"You could've said no," Vivian asserted.

"Yes, but—"

"I'm disappointed in you, Lily," Andrew said quietly. "I thought I could trust you with my family. Now I don't know what to think."

"I trusted you, too!" Ophelia bit down on her lip, about to cry. "I shared my secret with you and you used it to hurt me."

"That's not true!" I cried, feeling more and more trapped by their unfair accusations. "Tell her Andrew!" I pleaded with him. "What I said about the auction…"

"Take Phe inside," he told Vivian. With a condemnatory look at me, she took the sobbing girl by the arm and drew her around the side of the building to another, less visible door leading into the house. When they were gone, Andrew stared at the ground for several seconds as though thinking on something long and hard, then finally he looked at me. My stomach sank at the disgust darkening his eyes. "You're not what I thought you were, Lily MacKenzie. I'd thought you were pure and good and kind, but it appears that I was terribly wrong about you. I think you'd better leave Dundeid."

At that moment, anything I might have felt for Andrew Dering was gone, disappearing like a candle snuffed out. My heart contracted at the loss. I had liked Andrew; he'd been like the sun to me. And now he despised me, when I had done nothing wrong. The unfairness of his reaction made me want to cry and sob like Ophelia. It also made me want to punch him in the face.

"Now see here!" Gregor shouted. "I've had just about enough of this witch hunt. Lilia was trying to help Ophelia, not hurt her. Vivian's making Lilia out to be the bad guy, though I'm not sure why. But both of you should look in the mirror first. You've sheltered that girl to the point of criminality. You're turning her into your mother, Andrew. You feel guilty about what you're doing and decided to take it out on a stranger. You know your mother's out of her mind, yet you blame Lilia."

Andrew's eyes narrowed and his cheeks sucked inward. "Her name is Lily."

Gregor tightened his grip. "Come on, *Lilia*. You don't need this." He pulled me along the path after him. I glanced over my shoulder at Andrew as I stumbled forward in my long dress. There was no kindness in his eyes, only a seething fury. "Remember what I told you about him, Lily!" he called after me. "You're making a big mistake!"

I quickly looked away. "Where are we going?" I breathed, running to keep up with Gregor.

"I'm taking you where it's safe. To Mochrie Manor."

Chapter Twenty-Three

❦

Up in my room I hurriedly packed my clothes and stashed my computer in my bag. As I was rushing around, a vision flashed through my mind and I had to stop. Dizzy, I grabbed hold of the bedpost and closed my eyes. Darkness momentarily soothed me until it lifted like a curtain and I saw myself running down the road to Gregor's house. I was wearing the ball gown, the one I had on right now.

"Are you all right?" Gregor, who was keeping watch at the door, asked worriedly.

My eyes opened and I knew what I had to do. "I have to change out of this dress."

He nodded, still looking concerned. "All right."

"I'll need your help. I can't untie the stays."

He stepped away from the door and bowed low. "At your service, Miss." He straightened up, a devilish grin lighting his face.

I quickly turned about so he couldn't see my blush. I felt like a girl of sixteen again—a Victorian maiden, gauche and inexperienced in the ways of the world. "Please hurry."

I felt him approach, his steps silent and slow. When he touched me a thrilled jolt ran through my body and my breath sped up. His fingers found the tie and he slowly, slowly released the knot, each passing second increasing the sensation of pleasure I felt at his nearness. When the knot was undone, he leaned close and I could feel his breath as it warmed the back of my neck, for ages, until I thought my skin might burn. After what seemed like centuries, his fingers loosened the stays with a delicacy that belied his quickened breathing.

"You're free," he said after several moments, shaking me from my mesmerized state.

I turned around, pulling away from him. "Thank you," I said with as much dignity as I could muster when my heart was thumping away in my chest like a wild horse.

"You're most welcome." He didn't move.

"Could you turn around?" I made a circle with my finger.

"Do you want me to?"

My breath jerked inward. "I have to change now."

"You didn't answer my question."

"Please turn around." He was making this very hard.

His smile was triumphant. "As you wish."

With quick backward glances, I pulled off the dress, slipped the hanger into the neckline, and hung it on the door of the wardrobe. There. I had done something different. I'd changed the dream. Would it be enough? After swiftly dressing in jeans and a sweater, I pulled on my shoes. "I'm ready to go."

Gregor lazily turned toward me, one eyebrow raised. "I know."

I swear he had eyes in the back of his head, or had he peeked? The possibility warmed me, like a steaming cup of hot chocolate on a cold winter day... Better yet, a shot of whiskey burning down my throat and spreading through my chest.

I shook my head. I had to knock it off. Even my thoughts were starting to sound like a cheesy romance novel. Besides, someone I liked had just given me the shove-off. I should at least mourn that a little. But Gregor was making it hard for me to think about anything but him.

He took my bags and we headed down the stairs. No one demanded to know what we were doing; no one attempted to stop us, and we made it to Gregor's car without incident. No doubt everyone was still busy with the ball. He pushed my bags into the back seat, then opened the passenger door for me.

We drove in silence to Mochrie Manor. I didn't know what was on Gregor's mind, but I knew what was on mine. I was wondering if I'd made the right decision. One wrong choice and my dream could come true. One right one and all my nightmares would be gone forever.

"Are you scared?" he asked when we pulled up in front of the manor.

I peered out the window, looking up at the imposing building. "Only a few hours ago you wanted us to stay away from each other."

He reached over and placed his hand on mine. The heat of his skin went straight to my brain, along with various other body parts. "We did the right thing. I can feel it."

All I could feel were hormones surging through me, making me dizzy. "I hope so."

"Let's go in. You can unpack, take a shower."

I nodded. Together we carried my bags up to a beautiful room decorated in Regency style and fit for royalty—elegant and ornate with lots of mahogany and stripes. It was a loving tribute to Jane Austen's time. A fire crackled in the fireplace and I felt a little like a queen as I stroked the plush bedspread. Gregor set my bags on the bed next to me. "Will this suit?"

"Perfectly."

He nodded. "Good. Are you hungry?"

"No. Though I could use a drink."

He smiled. "You take your shower, and after getting out of this monkey suit, I'll see what the wine cellar has to offer."

He left me and I hurried into the adjoining bathroom. The room was modern and fresh and I enjoyed the hot water shooting at me through the huge showerhead. I was glad to get away from Dundeid's tub. Even after knowing the truth about that day, the image of my mother beckoning me to her, of the blood on the floor and swirling in the water—that did not simply go away. Twenty minutes later I was dressed in my white nightgown and a sapphire robe and sitting by the fire, feet tucked up under me.

A light knock sounded on the door, but before I could say come in, it swung open. "Damn!" Gregor cursed as he entered, a dusty bottle of red wine in one hand, two crystal glasses in the other.

"What's wrong?"

"You're already dressed."

I laughed and blushed at the same time. "You're incorrigible, Mr. Huntington."

He grinned. "But you like that in me."

"Maybe."

He sat down across from me. He'd changed into dark slacks and a white oxford, open at the throat. The white made his dark hair and dark eyes even darker. "Still thirsty?" he asked as he screwed in the corkscrew he'd pulled from his pocket with slow, deliberate twists. He watched me while he worked.

"Very." I swallowed.

He eased out the cork, eyes still on mine, then focused on pouring. When the glass was half full, he raised it to face the fire and peered at the dark liquid. "Looks like a good year."

I took the glass from him and waited while he poured his. "Slainte," he said.

"Slainte." We clinked glasses. I took a sip and tasted black cherries and roses, anchored by a hint of oak. I took another sip, then another, and felt myself finally beginning to relax. "This is lovely," I murmured, gazing at the flames.

"Yes, you are."

My head swung toward him. "I said—oh."

Gregor shook his head. "Don't you ever receive compliments? Because you're horrible at accepting them."

"Not many, I suppose. And when I do, I don't really believe them."

"You think we're all lying to you?"

I took another sip. "It's not that. I just—" I paused, took a deep breath. "I just don't believe what anybody says. Past experience has taught me that people are either lying or telling me something I want to hear to get their way." I thought about this. Was this really true, or was I being dramatic? My friend, Jamie, back at the newspaper, had never let me down.

"You have to believe someone some time."

"And get burned? Again?"

"I'm sorry that happened to you, but I'll tell you this, Lilia. I won't lie to you. Ever." Feeling almost panicky, I drained the rest of my wine. Looking grim, he took my glass and filled it. I took another drink. "You don't believe me."

"I want to," I whispered, drank another mouthful.

"You came here with me. That must mean something."

"It means I had nowhere else to go."

He scowled. "What did they do to you?"

"Andrew and Vivian?"

"Your parents."

"You know what they did. I told you all that. I had to get away."

I had to get away. The voice sounded as though it had slipped its way through fog and time. "They wanted to own me because of what I had."

"What did you have, Lilia?" he asked, his voice distant and full of echoes.

"Money. They wanted my money." My wine glass was already empty again and my mind spun. I held out the glass.

"No more. I need you to focus." He set down his glass and moved over to me. With very little effort, he relieved me of mine. "Who wanted your money?" he asked, peering into my eyes.

I stared at him blankly. "What are you talking about?"

"You just said 'they wanted my money.' Who did?"

"I never said that."

He blinked. "I think you've had too much to drink, Lilia. Why don't I put you to bed?"

"All right," I said meekly, like a child. He pulled me out of my chair and over to my bed. I stumbled, fell against him. He steadied me as he pulled back the covers, then lifted me onto the bed.

"Get some sleep. We'll talk in the morning."

He smoothed my hair off my forehead, then turned to go. I grabbed his arm. "Stay," I entreated. "Please don't go."

He gritted his teeth, then nodded. "I'll sit in the chair." He indicated the one by the fire.

"No. Lie by me," I begged, my pride be damned. "If I dream again, I don't want to be alone. I don't think I can take that. Not tonight."

"Oh, Lilia. Don't tempt me."

"I need you, Gregor."

"This could all go very wrong, you know."

"We're just sleeping by each other. I think we can handle that."

"I'm not sure I can," he said, then sighed and lay down next to me. I snuggled into the covers and was asleep before I could remember to say goodnight.

~

I awoke the next morning, with a mouth lined in cotton and a throbbing head, to find Gregor gone. An indent on the pillow remained and I thought he must not have left all that long ago. The bed was still neat; my nightgown was still on—nothing had happened. I felt keenly disappointed, much more than I should have. Would I have him take me while I was drunk? Or would I rather he'd been a gentleman?

Damned if I didn't know what I wanted.

After another long, blessedly hot shower and two ibuprofen later, I felt quite a bit better, surprisingly so. Two glasses of wine weren't enough to devastate me, it seemed. Lovely. I was turning into a lush. I gave myself a lopsided grin in the mirror before clipping my barrette. My watch as I headed down to the dining room told me it wasn't yet eight o'clock. I always awoke surprisingly early when I had too much to drink. I would pay for it later, I knew.

Gregor was drinking tea and reading the paper. He put it down when he saw me and stood up. The chair next to him was pulled out and I was ushered into it. "Tea?"

"Coffee, if you've got it."

"And breakfast?" he asked hopefully.

"Yes, I'm starving."

He breathed a sigh of relief. "You're okay, then?"

"I'm fine," I replied, spreading the white linen napkin over my lap.

He rang a bell and Amria flounced through the door in near-record time. She must have been listening at the door. "Yes, Mr. Huntington?"

"We'll have a full breakfast for Ms. Mackenzie. Eggs, toast, coffee."

She gave me a long look. "And will *Ms.* MacKenzie be staying long?"

"I don't see how that's any business of yours, Amria."

Her eyes narrowed. "I need to know if I should tend to her room."

"I'll let you know when things change. Until then, just do your job."

I thought he must be angry to deliberately prod her like that. Her expression was defiant, almost seething. "Oh, I'll do my job, Mr. Huntington. A poor, simple servant girl like myself must do as she's told."

He waved his hand at her. "Enough with the dramatics, Amria. Fetch Ms. MacKenzie's breakfast and be quick about it."

"Yes, Master." And before he could respond, she was gone.

"You were a little hard on her, don't you think?"

"Last night, before I came to you, I found her in my room."

"I take it she wasn't cleaning it."

"She was lying on my bed wearing only a smile."

"Ah."

"When I asked her to leave, she got mad. Threatened to tell you she and I were sleeping together." He was very carefully avoiding looking at me.

"But you're not…"

His head swung up. "No! Amria's trouble. I've always sensed that in her. If I didn't love my sister so much I'd curse her for sending that girl my way."

"Can't you ask her to leave?" I spoke this quietly. No way was I going to get on Amria's bad side. Well, not any more than I already was. She wanted Gregor and I was staying in his house at his invitation.

"I plan to, after the holidays. We can't go on like this, especially not after she tried to seduce me."

"Does she have somewhere to go?"

"I'll leave that up to my sister. I'll give her a good reference. She'll do all right."

"I agree." I smoothed the napkin over my thighs. "So I was wondering if we could visit your waterfall today."

He brightened. "So you don't hold this against me?"

"Why should I?"

"I don't know. I know I'm going to do something wrong, but I don't know what or when. This was a big one. You could've chosen not to believe me."

"It would've been worse if you'd chosen not to tell me and I found out later on…from Amria herself."

The door banged open, followed by Amria storming across the floor toward me. She stopped, stared at me until I looked up at her, then gave me a wicked smile. "Breakfast, your Highness!" She banged the plate on the table in front of me. "Enjoy!"

"Amria!" Gregor began, but she pivoted on her heel and marched off, ignoring him.

I laughed. "I've always wanted to be royalty."

"I should let her go now." His face was pale, his eyes livid.

"She's just paying you back. It'll blow over."

He didn't look so sure of that. "I hope so."

I dug into my breakfast, hoping she hadn't spit in it, or worse, and Gregor eventually calmed and returned to his paper. The pleasant feeling of being an old married couple filtered through me as I finished my coffee and wiped my mouth. "Much better," I sighed.

Gregor folded his paper and set it on the table. "Ready to go?"

"Let me get my camera."

"I'll wait for you at the door."

In my room, I checked my teeth for food, chewed on an Altoid to cover the six spicy sausage links I'd eaten, and grabbed my camera case. Gregor was standing in the doorway with the door open, an old-fashioned wicker picnic basket in one hand, a red plaid blanket over his arm. "I ordered us lunch," he announced, lifting the basket. "It should be warm enough to picnic."

I smiled, pleased. "Such strange weather for November," I commented as we walked outside. "It must be seventy degrees! It's not always like this, is it?"

He shut the door and transferred the wool blanket to sit atop the basket. "I wish. I've never witnessed anything like it in my lifetime. November is typically raw and cold here in the Highlands."

"Well, I guess we should enjoy it while it lasts."

"That should be my motto for life," Gregor mused.

I glanced over at him. "You don't enjoy your life?"

He shrugged. "I'm beginning to think that all this time I was just getting by. I have great wealth, a beautiful home, my health…and have I been truly appreciative?" He shook his head, as though disgusted with himself. "I'm finally seeing how lucky I have it."

I nodded, slowly. "You're right, you know. I've had some problems, but all in all, I have a good life. And yet…" And yet, *what?*

"And yet something has been missing."

"That's it. It's like there's something I need to do and until I do it, I won't be able to relax. This anxiety—it's always there, like a perpetual storm cloud over my head."

"Then I guess we both need a change." He looped his arm through mine and we circled around to the back of the castle, moving toward a wide river flowing in the distance.

Gregor pointed. "The waterfall is about a mile up the river."

"I can't wait to see it." I grinned at him. He smiled back and tightened his grip, his expression as pleased as I've ever seen it. Perhaps this was how things were supposed to go. I had liked Andrew, but what he'd done had forced me into Gregor's arms, so to speak. The choice had been made for me.

The way grew rocky and I took the blanket from Gregor after it had fallen to the ground twice. The warm air and the walking were making me sweat and I briefly considered jumping into the river, but it soon transformed into rapids, ruining that idea. Rocks jutted up with increasing frequency, like soldiers being called to battle, and white water brightened the dark expanse. Cliffs rose up on either side of the river until at last I saw the waterfall. It wasn't very high, but magnificent and full as it fell into a wide pool.

"Shall we stop here?" Gregor indicated a rock jutting out over the pool. "You'll have to climb. Can your knee take it?"

"I can climb," I said, pushing past him. My knee was fine now, and even if it weren't, I'd find a way. In moments I was at the top of the rock, fingertips smarting from tiny scrapes. "This spot is gorgeous," I declared as I helped Gregor with the picnic basket. "Can we explore?"

"We can do anything you'd like." His voice was so serious and earnest that I had to smile.

We scrambled back down and spent the next two hours climbing rocks and getting wet shoes and taking photographs. Gregor captured me standing in front of the waterfall, then I set the timer and caught both of us, smiling, cheeks flushed, eyes bright. By the time we returned to our picnic basket, I was starving and brimming with happiness. I didn't think I'd ever felt this carefree in my life.

"This is my favorite place to come when I need to think," Gregor told me as I spread out the blanket and he unpacked our lunch.

"I can see why. Thanks for sharing it with me."

His brown eyes sparkled. "I can't imagine anyone else here but you."

I touched his arm. "Me, neither."

As we ate thick meat and cheese sandwiches and drank cold lemonade, Gregor told me of the times he and his sister would skinny-dip on the rare hot days of summer. "One time she was mad at me and stole my clothes. I had to dash home naked as the day I was born. I had scratches everywhere."

"What did you do to deserve such wickedness?" I asked, giggling helplessly at the thought of serious, dignified Gregor dashing naked across the castle lawn.

"Practically nothing, I tell you. I only put toads in her knickers drawer."

I hit him on the arm. "You cad!"

"In my defense, I was trying to find her a prince. She was going through a princess phase that summer."

"Ah. Good excuse."

"You don't have any siblings, do you?" He already knew the answer, but I went along with his attempt to pretend he didn't.

"Just me."

"No one to share your mother's illness."

"And no one to take some of my father's attention off me." I bit into a crisp apple and juice spurted onto my one somewhat dry shoe. I lazily wiped it away with my sleeve.

"So how was your mother doing when you called her?"

I picked at the rock. "She sounded lonely and sort of empty, like a part of her had gone away."

"We could try to call her again, you know. You said she remembered all of her dream."

I smacked the hard stone. "My phone! I never plugged it in. I meant to…and her number's in my phone."

"I could probably track it down."

"You could?" I felt suddenly hopeful. "Let's call when we get back."

We finished our dessert—feather-light pastries—in companionable silence. I took more photos of the landscape, of Gregor lying back with his hands tucked under his head, his eyes closed, his dark lashes shadowing his pale skin. The desire to reach out and touch him made me dizzy. I held back, but I did lie down beside him, taking in the warm sun. He didn't say a word, only reached out and took my hand in his. We lay like this for a long time. Clouds occasionally blotted out the sun, but then it would come back, soft and warm and full of promise.

When it went behind the clouds for longer than usual, I opened my eyes with a shiver. "It's getting cold."

We both sat up at the same time, blinking and slightly dizzy. Gregor looked around. "The clouds are building up. I think our little respite from winter is coming to an end." I shivered, feeling suddenly as though his words were a foreshadowing of things to come.

We quickly packed and headed back to the manor. "Do you really think my mother can tell us what's going to happen?" I asked as we walked along.

"No harm in finding out."

"But what if she says you and I have to part ways? Forever," I added quietly.

"She won't," he said firmly.

"She might."

"She won't," he repeated. "And if she does, I won't listen." He stopped suddenly and turned to face me. "I'm not losing you. Not now. I'll find a way for us to be together, Lilia. Trust me." He was so intense that I felt a little strange. We'd known each other for so little time. It just didn't seem normal or typical. But nothing about this was normal or typical.

"I'll try, Gregor."

"Don't try. Just do it."

The rain started and we dashed back. By the time we got inside, we were both soaked. Gregor dropped the picnic basket on the floor and I threw the blanket on top of it. "We need to get you out of those wet clothes." He grabbed my hand and pulled me up the stairway.

"You, too," I panted as we raced down the hallway.

"I was hoping you'd say that," he said and I laughed. He opened my door and flung it wide. "I'm going to help you." He ushered me into the room and shut the door behind him.

I started to laugh, then saw he was serious. "I'm all right, you know. I can do it."

"I can do it better."

I shivered as he approached me. He reached out and unbuttoned my cardigan, one button after the other. His eyes never left my face as he worked. When the cardigan was unfastened, he pulled it off my shoulders, leaning close to me. I stayed still as a rabbit, scarcely breathing.

"I should do the rest," I managed to say.

"No. I want to help you."

I took a quick breath, then dove. "Then I want to help you, too." I reached out and unbuttoned his shirt, but more quickly than he did mine. I was feeling rather in a hurry now, my breath had found itself again and was coming faster and faster. I pulled his shirt open and gasped. A 'T' of black hair covered his hard stomach and chest.

"Do I pass muster?" he murmured.

"Definitely. But I'll need to see it all before making a final judgment." And then he was kissing me. Fiercely. Hands cupping my face, lips desperate and full and hot. Oh, dear Lord, this was amazing.

Before I knew it we were on my bed. "I've wanted this for so long, Lilia," he breathed in my ear. "A century and more… Forever… Far too long."

And then he was kissing me and nothing else mattered but him.

Chapter Twenty-Four

&

I awoke the next morning, hungry and thoroughly in love as I snuggled under the warm, soft covers. Turning over I saw Gregor was gone, replaced by a folded piece of paper on the pillow next to mine.

To protect your reputation, I slipped away in the night. Some day soon I hope to prevent my ever having to do that again. Do not leave your bed. Mrs. Lennox will bring you breakfast and then I'll come to you again.

I shivered with delight, recalling the night before. I was not a virgin, not in the technical sense, but in terms of knowing what making love could really be like I was a complete rookie. I hadn't expected to feel such overwhelming passion, such dizzy desire. Now I understood romance novels. There really *were* such feelings to be felt. What a lucky girl I was!

My cell phone rang, and I stared dumbly at it, wondering how that was possible. Sitting up, I saw that it was plugged into the wall. Gregor must have plugged it in for me. We hadn't called my mother, of course, after returning from our picnic, being otherwise occupied, but now I could. I picked it up and answered.

"Hello?"

"Lily?" Andrew. My elated mood deflated slightly, and I wondered how he'd gotten my cell phone number. Then I remembered I'd given it while making my reservation. Dang. "Are you there?"

"Yes, I am," I replied coolly, pulling the blanket up to my chest and thinking I really should put something on before Mrs. Lennox came. There was my reputation to think of. I smiled, then sobered. "What do you want?"

"I want you to return to Dundeid Castle."

"What? But you told me to leave—"

"I didn't truly want that. I was angry and feeling protective, but I'm over that now. I realize that you were only trying to help Phe."

I sighed. "That's what I told you, but you wouldn't believe me."

Silence, then, "I'm sorry about that. I, well, I have trouble trusting people." We had that in common. Used to, anyway. I had Gregor to trust now. "After you left, Mother made a scene…at the ball. She ranted and screamed at me, then threw things at the other guests. The sponsors saw everything. This morning I received a polite phone call letting me know they've decided to go with a hotel closer to the city."

"Oh, Andrew! I'm sorry."

"I need you here, Lily. Mother wants to talk to you."

This was not expected. "The last time I talked to your mother, Andrew, she went berserk. I'm not sure I'm up to that again."

"I understand, Lily. I do. But *I'd* still like to see you. I miss you."

"Yes, well—"

"I only want to talk. I've been such an idiot. You're so sensible. Promise me you'll think about it."

I didn't want to promise him any such thing, but he sounded so bereft. "All right, I'll think about it."

"Call me and let me know what you decide." His voice was quiet and contrite. "You have our number?"

"Yes. Goodbye, Andrew."

"Goodbye, Lily."

I hung up the phone to find my hands shaking. What did Andrew *really* want with me? And why did I feel like I would do whatever it was he asked? *Because he reminds you of yourself, complete with crazy mother and a needy cousin who acts exactly like Father. He's struggling like you've done for so long and you want to help him.* That might be true, but it didn't excuse his behavior toward me. He'd taken Vivian's side over mine, and I wasn't sure I was big enough to forgive his defection. *Some might call what he did loyalty,* the little voice insisted. *He's loyal to his family.*

Yes, and they would always come first, I answered back. *Them, and Dundeid.*

I sighed and slid out of bed to take a shower. At first I was reluctant to wash away Gregor's smell—his sweat, his spicy cologne, his essence—but the hot water was too seductive and I began to sing as I soaped up my hair. When I returned to my room, a breakfast tray sat on the dresser. I peeked at the contents, thrilled to see eggs and bacon, pancakes and maple syrup, orange juice and coffee. I was starving after missing supper, and from all that cardiovascular activity I'd recently enjoyed, including our hike to the waterfall.

I was nearly finished eating when a knock sounded at the door. "Come in!" I called merrily. The door swung open and Gregor entered. My smile died when I saw his face. "What's wrong?" I pushed my tray aside and rushed to him.

He took me in his arms. "I have to leave. Today. *Now,*" he forced out, his voice ragged.

I pushed away to look at his face. "What happened? Are you sick?"

"It's Sophie. She was in an accident. The hospital just called."

"Is she all right? What happened?"

"I don't know exactly. They wouldn't give me any details, said I had to speak to the doctor. She's in surgery as we speak."

"Oh, Gregor. I'll come with you. We can go right now."

He shook his head. "The weather's turned. We're in for a blizzard." My eyes took in what in my blissful state they had missed before—it was snowing outside. "I can't risk you getting hurt, too. Stay here and I'll be back as soon as I can."

"I can't let you go alone! We'll be fine, I'm sure."

He gripped my arms. "You're too damn important to me. I've lost too many people in my life, I won't lose you. Hell, I didn't have a life before you. Please..." There were tears in his eyes. "And maybe my mistake—what I do wrong—is to bring you with me and you get hurt. Much as I want you to be with me, I just can't take that risk."

I nodded, feeling suddenly emotional myself. "All right, Gregor. But know that I'd rather come with you. Call me as soon as you get there."

He leaned forward and kissed me on the forehead, his lips lingering as though absorbing every last bit of me he could. I leaned back, break-ing the connection for just a second, before pulling his lips to mine. Our kiss was soft, yet filled with longing and desperation.

"I'll call you, Lilia."

"Be safe, Gregor. Come back to me when you can."

"I will, Lilia. I promise you, I shall return."

And then he was gone. But he would be back. He'd promised.

I shall return.

Appetite gone, I sat on the bed and stared at the falling snow. I heard a door slam and ran to the window in time to watch Gregor pull away. I watched him go until he was out of sight, too late remembering the superstition that doing so was bad luck. I firmly pushed that thought out of my mind and with a heavy heart cleaned up my room, folding my clothes and making the bed. After getting dressed, I downloaded and viewed the photos I'd taken yesterday, when all was well and won-derful. I hoped Sophie was okay, wondering with a chill what could've happened to her and why the hospital wouldn't say.

When there was no more left to do, I carried the breakfast tray down to the kitchen. No one was there so I set the tray on the counter and washed my dishes, then dried them and put them away. On my way back upstairs I heard running feet. I stopped and a moment later Amria rounded the corner. She saw me and drew back, stopping two steps above me. In seconds a triumphant look replaced her anxious one.

"Good luck with your new man," she said, her voice high and bright.

It was then that I noticed she was carrying two suitcases. "You're leaving?"

"I've a friend who's taking me to London. I've had it here. Nothing to do, cold all the time. I'm better off far away from Scotland, I can tell you that."

"Oh, well. Go slowly, then. The roads are sure to be slippery."

Her eyes narrowed, and for a moment she looked uncharacteristically uncertain. "That's all you've got to say?"

"I guess so. I mean, I wish you a safe trip. We didn't get along, and I'm sorry for that, but I wish you well, Amria."

The uncertainty disappeared. "You're already sounding the lady of the manor, aren't you? Well, you can have Mr. High and Mighty all to yourself. But you'll pay a price for it."

My body went cold. "What do you mean?"

"There's her at the castle who wants him, too. And when she wants something, woe be to those who get in her way." Vivian. Amria paused for a moment, studying me. "I don't know what he sees in you, pale and bland as vanilla ice cream."

"Love is strange that way."

Her full lips pursed in annoyance that her insult hadn't succeeded in making its mark, then she barked in laughter. "Love is strange, all right. Funny how Mr. Huntington left you here alone to go see his sister."

"She was in an accident, Amria!"

She smirked. "Oh, was she now? Really, that girl only has to call and he goes running." I could only stare at her. "Now step aside. My ride's here."

I moved out of her way. "What do you mean, Amria?" I called after her. "Are you saying he lied to me about the accident?"

Her only response was to move faster down the steps, her heels clacking on the stone. *She's just jealous*, I told myself. *Jealous of Gregor and me.* Of course she'd want to put doubts in my mind.

Back in my room, I called my mother. There was no answer and I left a message telling her I wanted to speak to her. After that, I wandered around the small space, touching objects, straightening a landscape painting. After a while, I plopped down on the bed and my phone rang, startling me.

"Mom?"

"Not even close."

"Ophelia?"

She sighed. "Yes, it's me."

"How…how are you?"

"I'm not feeling too great, but Andrew asked me to give you the rest of your money since you didn't stay the full time. Can you come by?"

"I can't imagine why you'd want to see me."

"Oh, that. Andrew told me what you did at the auction. I didn't realize what you were trying to do. When I found out Auntie Viv knew all about it and didn't tell me, we had a fight. And now, well, I feel horrid."

I glanced out the window. The snow was coming down harder, but if I hurried I could get to the castle and back before too much accumulated. "I guess I can come now. I'll bring you the ticket from the auction." And fetch my bike.

"You might as well keep it. You and Greg are together now, aren't you?"

I coughed. "I don't know about that," I replied, speaking the truth. I certainly hoped so, though. "Your brother kicked me out so I came here. Are you okay with that?"

"Oh, I'm more mad at Auntie Viv than anything. If she'd told me what you'd done, this wouldn't have happened. I blame her, really."

"Again, I'm sorry, Ophelia. Nothing has turned out the way I expected it to."

She sighed again. "Either way, you'd better come now. It's snowing pretty hard."

"I'll be there in twenty minutes."

"Fine." She hung up. I pocketed my phone and went over to my pack. Pulling out a notepad I wrote two notes—one for Gregor, on the off chance he'd come back early, having turned around because of the weather. One for his housekeeper, Mrs. Lennox. I left the note for Gregor on my bedside table.

After changing into my leather boots, a heavy jacket and hat, and grabbing my camera case to catch a few pictures of the castle in snow, I headed down to the kitchen. Mrs. Lennox was nowhere to be found. I searched the dining room and all the other rooms Gregor had shown me, ending at the family parlor room. There I found her slumped in a chair, snoring. Beside her was a glass bottle labeled Mrs. Rumple's Nerve Tonic for the Sensitive Lady, cap removed. Did they still make such stuff? I picked up the bottle and sniffed it, nearly gagging on the strong odor. Pure, unadulterated whisky. Mrs. Lennox was drunk. It seemed much too early for that, but who was I to judge? Okay, I did judge, but even so, I grabbed a soft, woven throw from the other chair and covered her with it. Then I tucked the note back in my pocket and left the room, pulling the door shut behind me.

Giant snowflakes the size of goose feathers pelted me in the face as I trudged across the moor, taking the shortcut to the castle. An inch of white stuff had covered the ground already and I determined to get Mr. Willeton's money and leave immediately. I didn't want it, but I hoped to see Ophelia and be sure things were all right between us. I felt awful about Gregor, about blighting all of her hopes. I'd wanted her to live life, to learn from it, but not from me, not that way.

Approaching the castle, I took a few photos, taking care not to let the lens get wet. Before entering, I hurried over to Brian's little building. The door when I tried it was unlocked. Inside the dark, cramped building, stuffed with flat car tires, springs, and rusted tools, was my bike looking nearly brand new.

"Hello?" I called. No answer. I shrugged. I might as well just take it. Wheeling the bike outside, I turned and shut the door behind me. The sensation of eyes watching me made me shudder and I glanced around, seeing no one. I parked the bike just outside the castle door, behind a small shrub in the hopes of keeping it somewhat dry, and went inside.

"There you are!" Ophelia cried, rushing toward me. "Here's your money." She waved an envelope at me. I took it without looking at it and shoved it into my camera case.

"Oh, you brought your camera! You remembered!"

"Remembered?"

"So you can take pictures of me in my ball gown?"

"I don't know," I hedged. "I'm not sure I should stay here, Ophelia. There's a blizzard coming, and Vivian isn't happy with me, nor is your grandmother."

"Vivian isn't here. She and Andrew had a meeting in Edinburgh—to try and change that company's mind about backing out. They won't be back until late this afternoon, if not tomorrow. We can take the pictures in the dungeon, just like before. And Grandmother never leaves that depressing tower. She'll never even know you're here."

"The dungeon?" I felt suddenly lightheaded.

She nodded excitedly. "I'll go change!" She ran off, then stopped and turned back. "You change into your gown, too. I want a picture of us together to remind me of all that you've done for me. You'll do that for me, won't you?"

I stared at her, feeling nauseous. "You want me to put on my ball gown?"

"Yes. Oh, please! It'll be brilliant!"

She seemed so excited that I couldn't find a nice way to say no. "All right," I replied sickly. "But I can't stay long. Not with the snow. We'll have to hurry."

"Then let's go!" She grabbed my arm and dragged me up the stairs. After depositing me at my old room, she rushed off to hers. Slowly, reluctantly, I stripped down and climbed into the ball gown. Where before I had felt sumptuous and romantic in it, I now felt only horror at the touch of silk on my cold skin. I pulled the slippers on and headed back down to the Great Hall. Ophelia joined me a few minutes later.

"Down we go!" she cried as we headed down the stairs.

When we arrived in the open area, Ophelia lit the lantern and I immediately went to work. I only had my camera, so I hoped something would turn out. "Together now!" Ophelia demanded, after posing by a cell door. "Let's do it inside a cell—it'll be like a magazine. Decadent fashion in the midst of misery and despair." She laughed delightedly. "I really ought to look into this as a career."

"You should," I encouraged her. "You have a flair for it."

"I think I will." She headed for a cell, and too late I remembered it was the one where I'd seen the ghostly face. "Now in you go!" I entered very reluctantly and she had to push me forward to get me through the doorway. She followed behind me and seeing her with me, I relaxed as I set up the camera and flash. It was very dark in the dank room, so I turned on the low light setting and hoped for the best.

After taking eight or nine photos, Ophelia ran toward the cell door. "I'm getting claustrophobic. Hurry up!" she urged nervously as I struggled to get my camera into my bag. I was done taking pictures. She scuttled out of the cell and beckoned frantically for me to come. In her haste, her hand knocked against the door and it swung shut with a click. "Oh, no," she moaned, clasping her hand and inspecting it for wounds.

"What's wrong?" I demanded. "Did you hurt your hand?"

"Yes, I did. Stupid door." She yanked on the door, but it didn't budge. "Bollocks! I just locked you in." She went to grab the key from her pocket, then froze. "The key! I can't believe it. I never leave it upstairs!" She giggled a little hysterically. "But where would I have put it? There are no pockets in this thing."

"Go get the key, Ophelia," I said in a low, urgent voice. "I need to get out of here."

She stared at me, her blue eyes round. "I'll run," she promised. "I'll run fast."

"Very fast. Now go!"

She spun around and dashed down the hall. I heard her footsteps bouncing about in my cell until finally I heard no more. I waited to hear them return. And I waited. And waited. How long had it been? I started counting to sixty—five times, ten. Had she lost the key? Was it in her room? Or still in a pants pocket?

When I had counted to sixty a hundred times I gave up and panic started to set in. I was locked in a cell in a dungeon, just like I'd dreamed. And I had only myself to blame. I'd been warned, and I'd failed to heed that warning.

Ophelia wasn't coming back.

Chapter Twenty-Five

It did not take me long to lose it. I started screaming and banging my fists against the bars, and when that produced no effect, I tried working on the lock. After a few minutes of poking and prodding, a rough piece of metal sliced my index finger. I held it up, surprised at how much blood was spurting out. I sat on the cold, hard floor and used the hem of my dress to stem the blood. When I pulled the material away to examine the wound, blood dripped onto the fabric. I could only stare at the blood as it welled up again and again and fell like rain onto my skirt.

The stains. They were blood. I was doing it again.

Wait a minute, *I*? I hadn't bled on this dress before, at least not in this life.

Not in this life.

I shuddered. I was scaring myself. Finger still wrapped up in my dress, I blinked back tears as I looked out the bars at the empty dungeon, lit only by the flickering lantern. What was going on? What had happened to Ophelia? Had Vivian and Andrew returned early? Did Ophelia tell Vivian I was down here and Vivian promised to release me, but didn't? She might have forgotten. There might have been a crisis. Or maybe Vivian meant to keep me down here. To punish me. Frighten me.

Andrew had said she liked to lock people up, but that she always released them. Tomorrow she'd let me go, all apologies, but her message would be delivered. *Don't ever mess with me. Andrew is mine. Ophelia is mine. Gregor is mine.* She wanted them all.

Gregor is mine! I screamed at her in my head. "He loves *me*," I sobbed.

Really, that girl only has to call and he goes running, Amria's smug voice echoed in my mind.

"Oh, shut up!" I moaned. "Just shut up!"

I eventually fell asleep, my throbbing head heavy against the cold bars, my cut pulsing. It had finally stopped bleeding, but not before leaving a noticeable amount of blood on my dress. *Here we go again,* I mused dazedly.

A noise woke me. Someone was coming. Vivian had finally come to her senses.

"Lily!" *Ophelia?* She dropped to her knees to face me. She had changed out of her gown and was now dressed in sensible pants and a sweater. She almost didn't look like herself. "Sorry it took me so long to come back. Vivian and Andrew returned home earlier than I thought. Because of the storm. The roads are really bad."

"Do they know I'm down here?"

"Of course not, Lilia."

"Did you just call me Lilia?"

She looked bewildered. "Why would I do that? Your name is Lily."

I shook my head as though trying to dislodge something in my ears. "I could've sworn... Well, whatever. Can you let me out now, please?"

Instead of moving to unlock the cell, she cocked her head to the side, her expression thoughtful. "First I have a question for you and this way you'll answer me truthfully. Why don't you want to marry Andrew? Your marriage would've solved all our problems."

I coughed, surprised. "Marry Andrew?"

"Why not? I know he asked you."

"Did he tell you that?"

"No, I happened to overhear him telling Auntie Viv he asked you at the ball. You said, 'Maybe I will.' But now you're with Greg, so you must not have meant it. I don't mean to eavesdrop, you know," she confided, "but I find myself doing it quite often. I get bored."

"Ah. Well, we were just playing around. Besides, I'm not sure if he really loves me."

"He doesn't. He's in love with Auntie Viv and she with him."

"He is?" I wasn't sure I believed that.

"Didn't you know?"

A dizzy wave swept through my mind. "But he's never shown any feelings toward her. Why don't they get married, then?"

"Auntie Viv has no money. He's to marry me, and she'll marry Gregor. That way she can stay close to Andrew. His mother's against it, of course."

"How...how long have you known about this?"

She shrugged. "All my life...and before that, too."

"Before that?"

She gave me an exasperated look. "We've been through this before, Lilia. Lots of times. Don't you remember?" I shook my head. *Lilia.* This time I was sure of what I'd heard. "Your dreams! You do have them, don't you?"

"I do. But they're only bits and pieces—"

"Are you sure, Lilia?" she persisted, grabbing hold of the bars and leaning forward so two rusted rods framed her face.

I nodded. "They're only dreams, Ophelia. They aren't real..." *Please, don't let them be real.*

"Oh, Lilia! Don't be such a dobber." I looked at her startled. "We both know what needs to happen next."

"What needs to happen next?"

"You need to disappear." Her voice, usually so light and sweet, was suddenly dull and forlorn.

"You aren't going to kill me, are you?" My voice was a mere squeak.

"I might be crazy, but I wouldn't stoop to that."

"Crazy?"

"Certifiable. Didn't you know that?" She gazed at me earnestly.

"I knew you were sick. I thought—"

"That I had a physical disease." She laughed, bitterly. "I wish that were all that was wrong with me." She sighed. "I really shouldn't marry Andrew."

"Because of your illness?"

"Oh, no. That's not the problem. The problem—and it's a big one— is that I'm his half-sister."

I gasped. That was a big one. "What? How?"

She smirked. "How do you think?" When I didn't return her smile, she groaned. "Fine, I'll tell you. Andrew's mother—and mine, too, of course—hides herself away for a reason." She leaned closer to the bars and whispered, "She cheated on her husband with my father. Mr. Dering found out and killed himself. He loved her so much. And so she's punished herself all these years. My mother already punished my father for his part. She agreed to take me and pretend I was hers, though she didn't really want me. Not long after I was born, she started drinking heavily. When I was six, she insisted on driving them home and she hit a tree and killed them both. A good punishment, don't you think?" She pulled back again, smiling brightly.

It was a horrible story, but I couldn't dwell on it. I had to work this out, and quickly. "That's why she wanted me to marry Andrew," I said aloud. "Because she knew about you, but she couldn't tell anyone." So Mrs. Dering wasn't the one who was going to hurt me, it was her daughter. And I hadn't seen it coming. Why, after all those horrid dreams, hadn't I seen it coming?

"Very good, Lilia. Now you know all our dirty little secrets." Which wasn't good.

"But Andrew doesn't really need to marry, does he?"

"Oh, yes. How do you think he's going to get the money to run this dump?" She pointed to herself and gave me a sour look.

"You have money?"

"Loads of it. When my parents died, they left me everything, but tied up in a trust fund. I get an allowance, but I don't come into my full inheritance until I either marry or turn twenty-six. Auntie Viv was counting on my money to save Dundeid Castle. I overheard her arguing with Andrew about it."

"Does Vivian know that you're Andrew's half-sister?"

"I saw no reason to tell her. Not yet. I wanted to be sure I had Gregor first." There it was again...*Gregor*, not Greg, like she usually called him.

"But...but what if Gregor doesn't love you?"

She dismissed this. "He doesn't love Auntie Viv, either. She's been working on him, but to no avail. I still have a chance."

"Of course you do," I soothed. "Why don't you let me out of here and we can talk about it?"

She smiled. "Oh, Lilia. I wasn't born yesterday. More like centuries ago." Her eyes lost their focus for a moment. "I know he likes you."

"How do you know that?"

"Amria's quite a gossip. I pay her for it. That's how I found out about my father's shenanigans."

Amria? I shuddered. What did she know? What had she heard? The thought of her listening outside our door made me sick.

"This happened last time, too. He fell in love with you and I lost him. I'm determined to make sure it doesn't happen again and again." *Last time...again and again?* Had this really happened before, or was this just the workings of a sick mind?

"Why do you think things will be different now? Do you know what happened before?"

She frowned. "I'm not sure exactly what went wrong; I've yet to figure it out. But I'm nothing if not persistent. That's why I thought we should talk before—"

"Before what?"

She sighed. "Before I do something desperate."

I shivered. "Why don't you just let me go back to America? Then Gregor will be yours."

"Do you really think that'll stop Gregor?" she sneered. "Once he gets it in his mind to do something, nothing can stop him. He'll go after you."

Despite the danger of my situation, I couldn't help feeling a little tingle of pleasure. "What else can I do, then?"

"I've been thinking on that. What could change things? I asked myself. And just now the answer came to me. You can write him a letter. Tell him things won't work out between you, that you can't stay here. Whatever." She waved her hand. "Lie through your teeth if you have to, just convince him you want nothing to do with him. I'm pretty sure you didn't do that last time."

"I'm not sure he'll believe me."

"You're a writer. You'll figure out what to say to convince him. Now don't go anywhere, I'll be right back."

I laughed a little hysterically.

She returned a few minutes later with paper and pen, shoving them through the bars. "Make it good."

"And then what?"

"Hm?"

"Once I give him the letter what will you do with me?"

"I'll let you go, of course!"

I frowned, not believing her... *of course.* "He's not home, you know."

"Oh, I know. I paid Amria to pretend she was calling from hospital about his sister. Nothing happened to Sophie. I just needed him out of the way for the moment. So you'll write the letter, collect your things, and I'll drive you to the airport."

"Just like that?"

She snapped her fingers. "Just like that!"

"The roads are pretty bad, you said. Andrew and Vivian had to return."

"Oh, I'm sure Brian is taking care of the roads as we speak. We'll be fine."

I didn't know what else to do other than go along with her mad scheme. It might be my only chance to get away. I shrugged casually. "All right, I'll do it. I was never sure about Gregor, anyway. He's a nice guy, but I had this feeling there was someone else."

She brightened. "Really?"

I nodded. "I know you think he loves me, but I think he's just using me to get to you. When he saw I won the bid, he was mad. Didn't you see his face? But when I told him I'd won it for you, he got all excited."

Her eyes narrowed. "Nice try, Lilia, but I don't believe you. Amria said you two spent the night in your bedroom."

"What? She's lying! Amria's in love with Gregor herself. I'll bet she didn't tell you that. The first time I visited him to get the parish records, she was flirting with him like crazy. He didn't like it and made it clear he had no interest in her. She must have figured out he liked you and did this to get revenge."

The skeptical look eased a little. "I still want you to write the letter."

"Sure. I think of us as friends, Ophelia. I'll do whatever I can to help you. Didn't I win that auction for you? I even brought the ticket because I knew. It's in my pocket upstairs."

"Well, I'm glad you see the truth—that Gregor loves *me*. I always thought so, but Auntie Viv never let me act on anything. She's probably kept him from me, too. She always was a conniving bitch." There was such venom in her voice, such hatred. I saw now that Vivian's actions towards me regarding Gregor were due to typical jealousy, nothing more. That's why she didn't want me going anywhere, because she knew I'd go to him. And when she was trying to keep Ophelia away from me it was because she knew Ophelia was mentally ill. But she hadn't succeeded in either case, though she should have tried harder when it came to Ophelia, I thought bitterly.

"I'll write the letter now."

"Good." She pushed the light close to the bars so I could see. I thought she might leave, but she sat down on the floor and watched me write.

Dear Gregor,

I'm leaving Scotland and returning home. We will always remain friends, I'm sure, but my father is ill, as I've told you, and he, who is typically so self-reliant, needs me with him. I had to get away from this place anyways. I love Andrew, but as his heart is elsewhere, I can't bear to be around him. I know you truly love Ophelia. Go after her. Don't listen to Vivian—she's a liar. I wish you the best and want you to be happy. Go to Ophelia.

Lilia

The letter was filled with lies so that if things went wrong, Gregor would know I hadn't willingly written it. I shoved the paper through the bars and waited to hear what Ophelia had to say. She read the note quickly, her pale brow furrowed, her eyes darting back and forth across the page.

"Perfect!" she declared at last, no doubt re-reading it to be sure she hadn't missed any tricks. Of course she knew nothing about my family and wouldn't know my father was the least self-reliant person I knew, or that he wasn't the parent who was ill. "Now I'm going to let you out." She stood up. "But don't try anything stupid, Lilia. I know you love Andrew, but he doesn't want you. So let's just stick with the plan and get you back home. I didn't know your dad was sick. He'll be happy to see you, I'm sure."

"I'm sure," I muttered.

As I left the cell, I couldn't fail to see the dagger in Ophelia's hand. She saw me looking at it and laughed. "I thought you'd be more trouble about Gregor. I had it all wrong, though. I'm glad we talked. I bet last time we didn't talk it out. I'm sure that's where it all went wrong."

"Communication is key," I said dryly as I climbed the stone steps. When we reached the top, Ophelia turned and locked the door behind us. "Can I change before we go?" I asked. I wanted to get to my phone.

She giggled. "You'd look pretty crazy wearing that to the airport. Wouldn't that be fun?" I raised an eyebrow at her. "Oh, all right. But hurry." I started crossing the floor, with her right behind me, when we heard voices coming down the stairs. "Someone's coming!" she hissed. "Go to the front door, and not a peep out of you, or I'll kill you and I won't care who sees it. I'll get off on an insanity plea." She shoved me toward the main entryway. Knowing she had the dagger, I moved quickly, though that was the last thing I wanted. I tried tripping, but she grabbed my arm and dragged me to my feet with a strength she should not have possessed.

She pushed me out into a white world and pulled the door shut behind her. Snow blew hard, pelting my face and bare arms. My feet in the kid slippers grew cold almost immediately. A dark car was parked in the drive, which had been plowed, but was already coated with an inch of wet, slushy snow.

As we neared the vehicle, the engine roared to life and the lights flicked on. Ophelia yanked open the back door and pushed me in. Despite my grim situation, I felt grateful for the warm interior. "This is Dr. Mills," Ophelia introduced the driver. He turned around and I recognized the man who had visited her the other day.

"I look forward to working with you," he said.

What?

"Let's go," Ophelia snapped. "To the manor first."

"As you wish." He gunned the gas and the car skidded as he turned it about. We quickly straightened out and I snapped on my seatbelt. We drove in silence, soon turning onto Gregor's driveway, which remained unplowed. The wet, heavy snow made driving difficult and several times Dr. Mills had to gun the gas to keep moving forward.

"Are we going to my place after this?" Dr. Mills asked Ophelia quietly as he pulled up in front of the house. I barely caught the words over the hard beating of the windshield wipers.

"The airport?" she said loudly. "Yes, we're taking Lilia to the airport."

"Of course," he replied heartily, confirming my suspicions. We weren't going to the airport. Ophelia had other plans for me.

She climbed out of the car. "I'll fetch your bags, Lilia!" Dr. Mills said nothing during our wait, and feeling stunned, I had no energy to start a conversation. Not even to dig for information.

Ten minutes later Ophelia returned, empty-handed. "All set!" she said cheerily as she climbed in, bringing a shower of snow and cold air with her. "That's done! Now we're off!" They gave each other a significant glance and I suppressed a shudder; she hadn't retrieved my luggage, but I was pretty sure she'd hid it somewhere after she'd left the note for Gregor. And when she got back to the castle, she'd hide my clothes, too. She wasn't leaving anything to chance.

We were halfway down the drive when I made my move. With one hand positioned on my seatbelt button I reached over and yanked hard on Dr. Mills' seatbelt. "What the hell!" he yelled, jerking the steering wheel to the right. The tires lost their grip and slid on the slippery snow. Ophelia cried out just before we slid into a giant yew tree.

My seatbelt kept me fairly secure, though I hit my head on the seat in front of me. Dizzy, I struggled to push the button. "Idiot!" Ophelia screamed. "Get us out of here!"

Dr. Mills gunned the gas, but the car didn't move. My fingers, numb with cold, wouldn't work. He gunned the gas again and the tires caught. *Damnit, fingers! Work, work!* My thumb jammed down on the gray button just as the car raced backwards. "Turn us about!" Ophelia shouted and I realized we'd spun around and were now facing toward the mansion. Finally the button gave way and the seatbelt released me. I pushed down the car handle. As the doctor shifted into drive, I opened the door and let myself fall out as the car roared straight ahead.

I hit the ground hard, winding myself. *Damn dress!* I cursed as I struggled to stand in the wet snow. Grabbing up the skirt in one hand, I raced toward Gregor's house, and my breath came in harsh, ragged gasps.

Run! Don't look back, just run!

Must get away.

Oh, dear Lord. My dream. I was living my dream!

"Please don't!" I shouted aloud. "I didn't mean for it to happen this way!" Words I hadn't meant to speak came flying out of my mouth.

There was no response, only the sound of thudding footsteps catching up to me. In this stupid dress and awful slippers, I was nearly helpless. Still, I kept running, all along knowing there was nothing I could do to escape, nothing I could do to stop her from catching me. Finally, unable to help myself, I glanced back and saw them. Then I stumbled and fell and they were on me like starving wolves. As soon as their hands encircled my arms I knew I wouldn't get away. I wouldn't ever escape. I fought and kicked, but sweet, slight Ophelia and her accomplice hung on tight. I let myself drop and they had to drag me through the snow, shoving me into the car with all the delicacy of a linebacker. Once inside, Ophelia pulled a snub-nosed pistol and pointed it at me.

"Please, Ophelia!" I sobbed, shivering with cold. "Just let me go home."

"What do you think I'm doing—" she began, then laughed. "Oh, who am I kidding? You already know I didn't mean to bring you to the airport. That wouldn't be very prudent, would it? Oh, Lilia," she sighed. "Why did you have to come to Scotland? Couldn't you have just stayed in Ireland?"

"I had to get away…" I began, then stopped. *Ireland?*

"Yes, yes, I know all about your sob story. How your parents were so overprotective because you stood to inherit from a trust fund given to you by a doting uncle. And the moment a less than stellar prospect, a Mr. O'Reilly, I believe you said, showed just the slightest bit of interest in courting you, they sent you off to Scotland to stay with cousins—*family*." She snorted. "Who then proceeded to woo you for your money."

"So we really are related?" The idea was more than distasteful, it was repugnant.

"Oh, yes. Sort of. Very distant, mind you."

"And Ian MacKenzie?"

"Who?"

"The man who lives up on the hill. He herds sheep."

"Oh, that old geezer. He's your family, too, but it was just him, so they couldn't send you there. But there were happy to place you with relations they hardly knew, because we lived in a castle. Ironic, hm?"

She was utterly mad. "What year is it, Ophelia?"

She laughed, glancing over at Dr. Mills. He was still trying to start the engine and didn't return the look. "And they think *I'm* crazy! Why, it's 1880, of course!"

Considering she was a century and a third off the mark, I figured I wasn't the crazy one. How could she reconcile the fact that we were driving a car and she was dressed in pants and holding a gun that hadn't even been invented yet?

"Why aren't we moving?" she demanded. "Are the horses stuck?"

Question thoroughly answered now, I grew really frightened. "What do you plan on doing to me?"

She turned to look at me, her beautiful eyes narrowed coldly. "Why, I think you need a good long rest. Dr. Mills knows just the place, don't you, dear?"

He nodded, giving the key another wrench. This time the car roared to life and he gunned the gas. The car shot forward and he spun the wheel, expertly turning the car around. Then he stopped, put the car into park, and opened his door. I looked back and forth between them. "What's he doing?"

She didn't answer. Dr. Mills opened my door. "I need you to stay still." He held up a hypodermic needle, pushing the plunger so that a little droplet of liquid sat on the tip of the needle. I stared at it for too long.

"You don't need to do that!" I cried, pushing away from him.

"Stay still, Lilia," Ophelia warned, "or I'm going to have to shoot you. I really don't want to do that—I'm not a killer—but I'll overcome my qualms if I have to."

"No, Ophelia! Please, I promise I won't try to escape again."

Dr. Mills grabbed my arm. "Too late." He shoved the needle deep into the muscle and pushed home the plunger. I stared at him in horror. Within seconds, my mind grew hazy and my body weak. The urge to fight drained out of me. Darkness flooded my mind and my head tilted back against the seat.

"Let's go," I heard Ophelia order. "I'm sick of looking at her."

The car rolled forward and after that, nothing.

Chapter Twenty-Six

❧

I woke, but did not open my eyes. I sensed someone in the room with me.

"She still won't eat, Doctor. And she keeps screaming in her sleep. She's frightening the other patients."

He tsked, tsked. "I hate to do it, Nurse Cooper, but solitary confinement might be our only option."

"*No...*" I pushed through chapped lips.

"She's waking up!" the nurse exclaimed.

The doctor came over to my side and took my wrist, strapped firmly to the bed, in his cold fingers. His fingers were always cold. "Why don't you leave us a moment, Nurse? I'd like to have a talk with Miss Jacobson here."

Miss Jacobson was my name now. An alias to hide my identity, I could only assume. Every time Dr. Mills spoke it, he laced the words with a self-congratulatory tone that pricked every time I heard it.

"Of course, Dr. Mills. I'll come back when you're done and check her vitals."

"Excellent." He waited a few moments, then spoke again, a chill replacing his gentle tone. "He's not coming, you know. You might as well accept that now."

"Why hasn't he come?" After the first day I'd stopped asking Dr. Mills why he was keeping me here and when he was going to let me go. He never answered. And when he didn't even bother to make up a lie, I knew it was hopeless to keep asking.

"Ask Ophelia," he said bitterly, pressing hard on the soft skin. "She'll tell you."

I felt a trickle of hope through the bruising pain. "You don't sound too happy with her."

He let go of my wrist and leaned close to my ear. "I've half a mind to section her here to Havensrest," he whispered. "Vivian would support me on it. Then Ophelia could never leave me." I had heard the nurses talking about sectioning; how doctors could issue orders to confine a person up to six months if they were a threat to themselves or others. "Or I could take her just like we took you. I'm almost stunned by how easy it was."

"My father will come looking for me."

He pulled back and looked me in the eye, his own eyes fierce. He had a fresh pimple, pink as a rose petal, blossoming over one thin eyebrow. "Oh, Lily," he said coolly, controlling his anger. "You're terribly naïve, aren't you? Your father thinks you're traveling Europe. Ophelia wrote the email on your computer when she was at the manor—did I tell you computers were my hobby? Your password was atrociously easy to crack. But I didn't need to have it that first time, since you so stupidly left your computer on." He shook his head disapprovingly. "I was able to tell Ophelia over the phone how to delete the photos after she called me about the picture she spotted of you in the cell. You saw it, didn't you? But you didn't know it was you. Ophelia thought our little scheme would drive you away, but it didn't. So then she made Brian lie to you about your bike, anything to keep you from seeing Greg Huntington," he added angrily. "But she failed, didn't she?" He looked happier about that. "Andrew and Vivian believe you've gone back to the States, so you've no help there, I'm afraid."

But my mother thought I was still here. She could tell someone that I'd called her, that I needed help. But who would believe her? According to my father, she was insane.

Sensing my despondency, the doctor's eyes calmed a bit. "Talk to Ophelia. She's coming in for a session today. She'll tell you the news."

He straightened, tugging his white coat back into place. "You'd best start eating, Miss Jacobson. Otherwise I'll be forced to stick an IV in your arm and hide you in a dark room all by yourself until you cooperate." With a sinister smile, he turned and left me.

I lay there, cold and frightened, turning his threat over and over in my mind. Where was Gregor? Why hadn't he come? Dr. Mills wouldn't tell me and I had yet to see Ophelia since I'd arrived three horrible days ago, groggy and disoriented. The first time I awoke, I was in bed. Remembering who had put me there, I lurched out into the hall where an orderly caught me and dragged me back. I put up a fight and two of the nurses who'd come to help still sported raised scratch marks on their cheeks and one of the doctors had a black eye. In the end, I'd only made my situation worse, proving to everyone that I was indeed a danger and deserved to be in a hospital. They put me in restraints, and after that, no one would listen to my claims that I'd been kidnapped, that I wasn't Miss Jacobson. Yesterday, though, I did overhear one of the nicer nurses tell another nurse that I was very believable. "The believable ones are always the sickest, luv," her co-worker replied in a matter-of-fact voice. "You'll learn that in time."

As bad as all this was, the dreams were worse. Now that I knew what they were warning me about, they came in full force every time I fell asleep, which was often, as Dr. Mills liked to keep me drugged. I tried hiding the capsules under my tongue, but the nurses were too wily for that, and had their methods for making sure I swallowed if I became obstinate, which was as much as possible, early on anyway. I've since given that up, though my jaw still hurts.

In my dreams, I was the Lilia of long ago—the one who'd been sent away from Ireland to escape a suitor. The one who the vicar had mistakenly thought had come to start a new life. Instead, once she had angered Ophelia, she'd been kidnapped and put here in this old hospital with the torn scratchy sheets that smelled of despair and misery and urine.

And her Gregor hadn't come, either.

But this time, he would. I just knew it. I'd left him a note. And the note I'd written for Ophelia, with all the clues, was also in his house. Hopefully the Lilia of before hadn't done that.

But whatever had happened before, I knew this time he would come. He'd promised.

I shall return.

I was trying to reach an itch on my nose when Ophelia sashayed into the room. She didn't look happy.

"You can't keep me here," I croaked. My throat, sore from swallowing pill after pill and from screaming, made me sound like a grumpy bullfrog.

"And who's going to rescue you, hm?"

"Gregor."

She eyed me. "I thought you didn't love him."

"I lied." My chin rose defiantly.

Her left eye twitched three times in rapid succession. "Well, it doesn't matter anyway. I'm going to marry Andrew. He's a fool, with that alchemy business and thinking he can turn metal into gold—he's stuck in his past life the worst of all of us, I think." She snorted contemptuously, though she didn't realize Andrew's ancestors had also done experiments to prolong life. Maybe, in this, they'd succeeded. "But he's all I've got. No one else will marry a psychotic. Except Dr. Mills, and he's creepy." She shuddered delicately, wrapping her thin arms around her slender frame.

"*You're* marrying Andrew?" When I had figured out that Ophelia had a secret concerning Andrew, the idea of her being his sister had never entered my mind, and probably never would have. "How? Where's Gregor?"

She stared at me for several long moments. "He decided to stay in Edinburgh," she said at last.

"What? Why? What happened to him?"

She shrugged and looked away. "Who knows?" Her voice cracked as she said this. "But I know I'll never see him again—it's what happened before."

I was having trouble breathing. "He said… He said…" I couldn't get the words out.

She spun to face me. "What? That he'd come back for you? Well, he's not ever coming back, Lilia MacKenzie. You'd better get used to it."

I bit hard on my lip, clamping down on the scream rising up like boiling bile. "Let me go, then. I'll look for him. Ask him."

"It's no use. He won't listen to you. He won't listen to anyone." She gave a wry laugh. "Besides, I can't let you go. You'll head straight for the police. Besides, why should I be the only one who suffers? I'm marrying a man who's in love with another woman, and who asked yet another one to marry him. Aren't I the lucky girl?"

"You don't have to marry anyone, Ophelia."

"Oh yes, I do." Her fingers curled into fists. "He ruined my chances with Gregor and now it's too late. So I think he deserves to suffer a little, don't you?"

"But you're his sister…"

She smiled. "Half-sister. And I'm saving that little tidbit for after we have our first child."

I tried to hide my disgust, but failed. "Why would he marry you if he loves Vivian?"

"The same reason he wanted to marry you—for money."

"And…and Vivian?"

"She has nowhere else to go—she'll stay with us and suffer. If only she'd let me have Gregor we wouldn't be having this conversation."

"He doesn't want you!" I cried. "He wants me! He loves *me*!" I struggled to sit up, fighting against the coarse leather straps that bit into my skin like teeth.

She pushed me back against the bed. "You're pathetic, you know that, Lilia? A spoiled brat who always gets everything she wants. The perfect job, the perfect man… Well, not this time." She turned to walk away, then suddenly spun back. "You're going to rot in here, Lilia. I've just made that my life's mission. To see you suffer." She shook her head. "Why didn't you just keep your mouth shut about Gregor?"

"Because I'm tired of all the lies." She gave me a sharp look. "And," I forged on, finally truly acknowledging that this had happened before...in another life, maybe more than that, maybe a dozen. "And because I know that if something doesn't change this time we're going to end up going through all this again."

Her lips thinned. "I'm beginning to believe I'm not the crazy one, after all. I've always thought the trouble was with everyone else. Now I'm sure I'm right, no matter what Auntie Viv and Dr. Mills try to tell me. It was my best decision ever to go off my meds...finally cleared my head. Goodbye, Lilia. Enjoy your hell."

"Don't, Ophelia! We have to end this!"

"Oh, I think it ends here, don't you?" She pulled open the door and left me alone, my nose still itching.

"Oh, Gregor," I moaned. "You have to come. Soon. Please come!"

When Nurse Cooper returned to take my pulse and blood pressure I told her I would eat something later. She was a kind soul—the one who had called me believable—and she nodded.

"If you promise you'll eat later..."

"I promise. I only want to sleep now."

She pulled the blanket up to my chin and smoothed back my hair. "You remind me of my sister."

"Your sister's crazy?"

She laughed. "No, but she's feisty. The nurses say you're a real fighter. I wasn't working that night, but I heard what you did." She sounded almost impressed.

I didn't want to correct her, tell her I'd given up the fight, so I only smiled. "Perhaps I'm fighting the wrong battle."

"Aren't we all?" she chuckled. "Now get some sleep, dear. I'll check on you later."

~

She did check on me, and I did eat a little bit, and then I slept some more. Three weeks passed this way—eating, sleeping, dreaming dreams. Every night in my dreams I begged for Gregor to come to me. Only now, I vacillated back and forth between the Lilia of 1880 and the Lilia of today, and sometimes I thought there were other Lilias— vague shadows, lurking and watching, waiting and hoping. But all our prayers went unanswered. Gregor never came.

He has to be looking for me, I told myself over and over. But Dr. Mills had checked me in under a false name—I would be hard to track. And, really, why would Gregor look for me here? If he did come, surely Dr. Mills would have instituted some sort of system, something like, "Let me know immediately if someone comes asking for a girl fitting Miss Jacobson's description. He could be her attacker." Or whatever story he'd told them to account for my current state.

And then, at the end of the third week, an unrelenting nausea hit me like a wall and I could think of little else. The flu sweeping through the institution had caught me. At that time, Dr. Mills had begun to allow me to take short walks around the snowy yard, but only in the company of a male nurse. I had grown docile and he had come to treat me more kindly. I think he liked victims. Being around them made him feel his most superior, and that, in turn, improved his mood.

"Must have caught the bug going round," he told me when the nurse reported my bouts of nausea. "Fresh air and exercise is just what the doctor orders." He chuckled and I gave a sickly smile. Life was easier when you went along with Dr. Mills. When you didn't, he made you regret it.

I shall return.

But when, Gregor? I was losing hope, and the will to keep going. I felt tired and sick all the time even though I was no longer taking medication. My docility had been rewarded, thank goodness. I hated those pills. They made me feel flat and empty inside. Might just as well be dead as be on those soul killers. So I stopped fighting and ate whenever I could keep something down.

And I started plotting ways to escape.

The male nurse, Jason—"but you can call me Jay"—was a surprisingly nice guy. At six foot five and well over three hundred pounds, he made me look positively diminutive, but he had a gentleness to him that I fully intended to exploit.

"That fence is so scary," I said on our fourth walk. On our first three walks I'd said nothing, but he'd talked enough for both of us. I think my silence made him nervous. "Doesn't it make you claustrophobic?"

"What? That thing? Naw. I suppose it's cause I can come and go." He gave me an apologetic glance. "I mean, well, let's go take a look at it. Then you'll see it's nothing but iron. Nothing to scare you."

We trudged through the snow to meet the black rods rising out of the ground. I hesitantly reached out and touched one with my bare hand. The metal was cold and my fingers didn't want to linger, but I forced them to as I scanned the area looking for weaknesses, rusted bars, indents in the ground. There was nothing that I could see, and the snow didn't help any. "Do you think I'm crazy, Jay?"

He was standing next to me, hands in his jacket pockets, little clouds of breath floating above his head like word balloons. "I'm no doctor," he replied without looking at me.

"But you have a brain—I can see that."

He laughed a little nervously. "I'm not supposed to talk about any of that. Dr. Mills said."

Of course he did. The little Hitler. "Well, I'm not crazy, just so you know. I'm sure patients tell you that all the time, but I mean it. I was staying at Dundeid Castle doing a job. I write for a newspaper…"

"You don't say!"

I glanced up at him. "You like newspapers?"

"Well, my brother does. He's always reading them."

"That's nice. I was doing an article on genealogy. In fact, I was tracing my own roots, starting with the records from the parish church."

"You don't say!" he exclaimed again.

"I do say."

He chuckled. "You're a funny lass. But I mean that I have a brother who works for the parish."

I felt my heart pick up pace. "The same brother who reads newspapers." I remembered Harry's car—how the back of it was jammed full of papers. I'd thought he was on recycling duty, but apparently not.

"Exactly!"

"I met your brother," I said slowly. "I met him, Jay, and he gave me a ride to the bank."

Jay turned to look at me, his heavy lids blinking slowly. "You know Harry?"

"Talk to him, Jay. Next time you see him, ask him about me."

"Well, I don't know… I need this job, see, and I don't want to lose it."

"No one will know you asked him about me. Harry has to keep whatever you say confidential. Like you have to keep things here confidential. Right?"

The broad brow wrinkled. "I guess so."

"Just ask him about a girl named Lily MacKenzie, who he gave a lift into town."

"You ain't Lily MacKenzie."

"I am. Trust me."

"But why do they call you Miss Jacobson?"

"Listen, Jay. I don't want you to get into trouble. So the less you know, the better. In fact, we should be heading back now. I don't want anyone getting suspicious." We turned around and made our way back by stepping in our footprints.

"It's that Dr. Mills, isn't it?" Jay asked from behind me.

I looked back at him, surprised. Then I quickly turned around. "Why do you say that?"

"I don't like him." There was a pause. "But I do like you."

"Well, I like you, too, Jay. You seem like a good person to me."

"I'll do as you ask, Miss— Heck, I don't even know what to call you."

"You'd better stick to Miss Jacobson."

"Right."

We reached the building and Jay escorted me to my room. Before leaving, he gave me a knowing nod, and I felt my spirits rise.

Finally I had someone who could help me.

Chapter Twenty-Seven

※

A nasty snowstorm delayed any outdoor walks for the next week. During that time my nausea continued to rage and I put it down to the awful food and nerves. I was not yet allowed to mingle with the other patients in the public area, which was just as well.

Without my walks, I didn't see Jay. But on the eighth day after our talk, when I thought I really might go mad, Jay came to my room after lunch—pale chicken, hard biscuit, and applesauce—to take me for an outing. It was the first nice day since the blizzard, with bright blue skies and plenty of sunshine. Once outside, we hurried over to the gate, making new tracks in the snow and soaking the bottom half of my institute pants. "Did you talk to your brother?" I asked once we were standing in front of the gate.

"Did I!"

"Shhh, Jay! Someone's going to hear." The warm day had encouraged other inmates to venture outside. I was the only one who had to be escorted, it seemed, but I did spot a couple nurses huddling outside the door, surreptitiously smoking cigarettes and scanning the yard to make sure no one escaped or skewered someone with one of the nasty icicles dangling from the roof's edge.

He nodded sheepishly. "Sorry. I talked to him yesterday and I've been waiting to tell you about it ever since. He said you were telling the truth about knowing him. I couldn't say where I met you, cause I can't, but now he's going to Dundeid Castle to ask some questions about you."

"What? No, Jay!" This time I was the one who had to keep my voice down. "Tell him not to do that."

He looked stricken. "Too late. He's heading there today."

"Can you stop him? Call him on your cell phone?"

He shook his head. "He meant to go this mornin'."

The urge to vomit nearly made me fall over. "Take me back to my room, Jay. I can't let them see me with you."

"Did I do wrong?"

"Not if we're lucky." I trudged through the snow, head down, watching my boots. "Not if your brother knows how to ask questions without making people suspicious."

There was a nervous cough behind me. "Well…"

That one word said it all. "You'd better stay away from me, okay? Just in case…"

"But what's going to happen to you?" His deep voice trembled a little.

"I don't know," I whispered. "I'll be all right," I answered more loudly. "Don't worry about me, Jay. Just worry about yourself."

His expression when he left me in my room was almost pensive and I worried he meant to do something. For the rest of the day I sat by the barred window and fretted, my hands resting on my queasy stomach.

The sound of the door when it banged against the wall was almost welcome. "You little bitch!"

I didn't bother to turn around. "Hello, Ophelia."

"Sent your spies to do your dirty work," she hissed. "Got Auntie Viv looking at me funny now." She came to stand over me, her whole body tense, her knuckles white. "You're not ruining things for me now."

"What do you plan to do?"

"Get that idiot fired, for one."

"Whatever," I sighed.

"Nice try, Lilia. I know you care what happens to him. And I know it'll hurt you that you're the one who lost him his job. Who's going to hire the moron now?"

I looked up at her. "Please don't get him fired, Ophelia. He's a good guy. It's not his fault I tricked him into helping me."

Her eyes narrowed. "You destroy people wherever you go, don't you?"

I blinked. "What are you talking about? Who have I destroyed?"

Anger darkened her eyes. "How dare you pretend you've done nothing wrong! You've ruined *my* life, of course!" Her pale fist beat against her chest like a wild dove. "Did you never once stop to think about me?"

"I did think about you, Ophelia."

"Yes, you thought about ways to destroy my life. I told you you'd sacrifice me for the greater good, didn't I? *Your* good, maybe, but not greater!"

I shook my head, feeling immensely weary. "I only wanted to help you."

"You did a bang-up job of it." She regarded me with a sour smile on her face. "It's your own fault you're in here, you know. You put the idea in my head. Remember? 'If you want something,'" she mimicked my voice, though I didn't think I sounded that whiny, "'you have to be willing to do whatever it takes.' So I did whatever it took to get Gregor and look where that's got both of us? Way to go, Lilia."

"You have to let me out of here, Ophelia. Harry knows about me."

"Harry has no idea you're here. In fact, he thinks you scurried back home to the States to mend a broken heart. I convinced him of that."

"He still might be suspicious. He might make some calls. You have to fix this."

"I have to do nothing you say. In fact, I'm thinking that if you were to disappear, I'd feel a whole lot better."

"I'm pregnant," I told her, giving voice to the niggling, prickly notion I'd been nurturing for the past few days. The nausea, the period that never came, the endless lethargy that not even depression over my situation could explain.

"What?" Her cheeks flared red.

"I'm going to have Gregor's child."

Her hands smacked together and I imagine she wished my head had been between them. "You're lying."

"Have Dr. Mills run a test."

"I will."

"And if I'm pregnant, what will you do?"

She stared at me as though I were a poisonous toad. "I don't know yet. I'm not a monster."

"I know that, Ophelia."

"But *you're* a monster," she said in a low voice. "You've ruined all my dreams—devoured them with your greed. Devil's spawn!" she hissed.

"It would be Gregor's baby," I persisted, ignoring her growing madness.

"What if it isn't?"

"Do you want to take that risk? It would be like killing Gregor."

"I'm firing that dotey bampot," she threw back at me. I didn't respond. Nothing I could say would make things better for poor Jay. "Did you hear me?"

"Have Dr. Mills order that test, all right? Or maybe I'll tell him myself."

"Oh, I'll tell him. If it's Gregor's…" Her voice faded away.

A knock sounded on the door and she pulled a shawl over her head. "Goodbye, dear. Get some sleep."

A nurse came in holding a tray—someone I didn't know. An hour later the same nurse returned and handed me a small paper bag. When I opened it I found a pregnancy test. Apparently Dr. Mills didn't want

anyone to know I was pregnant. The results a few minutes later, a +
sign, confirmed what I already knew. I was pregnant.

Dr. Mills visited me that evening. He looked both angry and wary.
"So you think I'm a fool?" I didn't bother to answer. "I hope you're
happy. I had to fire Jay, threatening him with a lawsuit if he said anything about you. I couldn't give him a recommendation, either. He
went against my orders. How can I pass him along to some other un-
suspecting professional like myself?"

"You fired him because you know that when I get out of here, and I
will, you'll not only be out of a job, you'll end up in jail."

His sallow face paled. "Just for that, I'm going to have to put you in
solitary confinement. You're a threat to yourself and others, and I can't
have you wandering about stirring up trouble."

I held up the stick. "But I'm pregnant!"

He looked disgusted. "I guessed as much. How stupid of you."

"Gregor will find me. He'll save me."

His upper lip curled. "We'll see about that." *He didn't last time...*

He stormed out, his back rigid and his shoulders hunched. He looked
like the mad doctor frustrated that his experiment kept going wrong. I
shuddered, realizing suddenly that *I* was his experiment. My suspicions
were confirmed when he and a new male nurse—big and leering, complete with a heavy jaw and scars on his face—escorted me to solitary.

"I wonder what she did to end up in the Cave?" one of the patients
whispered to another as we walked by. We passed through an empty
hallway, our footsteps echoing, or shushing, as in my case since I wore
only slippers. At the end of a short hallway I spotted a thick metal door
the color of tarnished silver and my mind went fuzzy. My feet stopped
moving, but the nurse and Dr. Mills grabbed my arms and dragged me
forward.

"No!" I screamed, jerking backward, suddenly remembering. "Not in
there! I'll do whatever you say, just don't put me in there!" I began to
cry, wretched, painful sobs that I couldn't control. "*Please!*" I begged,
feeling truly frightened for my baby and myself.

The hired thug opened the door with one hand, his other gripping
my arm tightly. My kicks didn't seem to affect him in the least. He and
the doctor maneuvered me around the door and into the dark room.
There were no windows, no chairs, and no bed, only a mattress on the
floor and a thin blanket.

"N-n-*no*." My chattering teeth bit the word into pieces and I felt
them clatter around in my mouth like rocks. I turned to race out,

blindly, wildly, desperate to escape, but the thug caught me without a word and pushed me back inside. The door slammed shut and the blackness was complete.

"Open this door!" I screamed, kicking it and hurting my toe. The pain made me double over and I nearly threw up, just barely swallowing the bile in time. The smell of vomit would have made this place unbearable. As it was, the sharp ammonia of urine, the dank smell of sweat and desperation, and the metallic odor of blood and darkness were enough to drive me crazy. "Let me out of here!"

Fàilte ...

He's mine!

I cannot believe he could ever love another.

Let me out of this hellhole!

Help me...

Oh, dear Lord...

I must have screamed for an hour before dropping to the floor and sobbing long and hard. Claustrophobia kicked in and I felt the walls closing in on me. My lungs tightened as though grasping hands were squeezing the air right out of them. My mind grew dizzy, my heart pounded too hard, too fast.

"Oh, Gregor," I gasped before passing out from hunger and exhaustion. "Why won't you come for me?"

~

I received my answer the next day.

"Are you in there, Miss Jacobson?"

I awoke and blinked swollen, crusted eyes that felt full of sand. "Please let me out, Dr. Mills," I croaked.

"I talked to Ophelia and she asked me to pass along a message."

Despite my situation, despite knowing Ophelia, I felt a small surge of hope. "Has she changed her mind?"

He laughed. "She wanted you to know she found Greg Huntington and asked him why he hasn't returned to Mochrie Manor. She loves him, you know." He stopped a moment, obviously struggling to maintain his calm. "He told her he'd met someone—a woman his sister knows. They hit it off." Now he sounded almost happy. "He's not coming back. Not to Mochrie Manor, not to Ophelia, and certainly not to you."

I couldn't believe him. I wouldn't. "Why are you telling me this?"

"Because Ophelia asked me to. Even though she loves someone else and plans to marry that ass, Dering, I still love her and will do what I can for her."

"You're lying. She would've told me this herself. Ophelia would never miss a chance to rub it in."

"She's preparing for her wedding, and besides, I forbid her coming, though she wanted to. You're in solitary confinement. No visitors!" He sounded so pleased with himself, that's when I really began to hate him. My stomach ached with the ferocity of it.

"He's coming…" I whispered, half to myself.

He didn't hear me, nor would he have made the attempt. He heard only his half of the script. "I'll have to put the baby up for adoption. You can't keep it here, of course."

My arms wrapped around my torso. "No!"

"I already have some prospective parents in mind. Americans. That should please you."

"You can't have her," I growled, a tiny part of my shocked brain wondering how I knew what sex my child would be. "She's mine!"

"Don't fight me on this, Miss MacKenzie. You'll lose." He paused and I heard fingers tapping on the door. "We'll talk in a week. For now I want you to think about your long, long stay here and how you want to spend it. Miserable and always fighting me, or giving in and accepting the inevitable?"

"I'll never give up." But even as I spoke the words, I didn't believe them. Already I felt my will to fight slipping away. If what Dr. Mills had said about Gregor was true then I had nothing to live for.

"One week…" Dr. Mills called out and then there was silence. He had gone.

Crying, I fell asleep and dreamed out the rest of my life. I bore my child—a beautiful little girl with dark hair and dark eyes and the spitting image of Gregor. Dr. Mills took her away from me with a triumphant smile, and I wanted to die. Depressed and lethargic, they released me from solitary confinement and I spent my days sitting in front of a window staring out at nothing.

The clock measuring the years of my life began to spin like a top…season after season passing by. "Drink this now," I heard one of the kinder nurses say. "It'll make you forget." I remember crying out, "I don't want to forget!" And then one day, I did. And I drank from the cup. One month, two months, a year, ten years passed. Thirty years. Gray and bitter and worn out, I made up my mind to die. After decades of complacency the staff no longer watched me. As far as they were concerned, I was not a threat, not even human. One early, gray morning when the new staff was coming in—typically a time of distraction—I sneaked into the kitchen, found a bottle of rat poison, and drank it. And then I watched myself die a horrible, agonizing death.

That's when I woke up and knew what my mother had seen in her dreams. She had watched her daughter suffer decade after decade, growing less human with each passing day. How painful that must have been for her. I think my hatred for Gregor began with that knowledge.

Oh, Lilia. My darling love. I will return for you. I shall return. It is only a quick trip and then we shall be together. I promise.

Not only had he not returned for me, he had found another woman to replace me. He'd betrayed me and I was going to die in this hellhole just like that other time. The Lilia of yesteryear likely had it worse than me, though, hard as it was to fathom that. Asylums of the past were not known for their hospitality or good treatment of the mentally ill. Reform in 1880 was underway, but I sensed from my dreams that Lilia—me—had never seen it.

"You killed her, Gregor," I ground out in a low guttural rasp, "just as surely as plunging a knife into her heart. And you're killing me."

The idea of seeking revenge sprouted like black mold in my feverish mind. I had to get out of here, if only to end this. I knew now what I had to do differently. I had to see that Gregor paid for what he'd done to Lilia. And then I would tell Andrew he'd married his sister. And I would think of something to do to Vivian, too. Something nasty.

But first I had to get out.

Unlike the Lilia of the past, I had my modern sensibilities to guide me. I was an independent woman used to figuring out difficult problems. I didn't need a man to save me. I would save myself. Poor Lilia, a casualty of the Victorian age, would not have known how to play any other role but victim. Would subterfuge even have occurred to her? I, on the other hand, would do what I had to do to get myself and my baby out of this nightmare. Truth, I was beginning to see, was—ironically—a fallacy, and not to be trusted or worshipped as I once had. The moment I got away, I would track down Gregor and see that justice was done.

And then? Who knew?

Chapter Twenty-Eight

❦

The spirit was strong, the body, despite its growing bulk, was willing. Opportunity, however, remained elusive. One week after my resolution to escape, Dr. Mills came to release me from solitary confinement. When I'd failed to respond to him during two visits in a row, he entered the cell with the male nurse right behind him.

I was prepared.

"You'd better not be trying to trick me. Sven has quite a temper. He's been known to take it out on a patient or two. That's why no other hospital will hire him."

My breath wheezed in and out of me.

"What's wrong with you? Why won't you answer?" He shone a flashlight in my face. "You're sweating!"

"Don't feel well," I gasped.

"Get her out of here," he snapped at Sven and the nurse complied, lifting me into the air and out of the room. "Take her to the infirmary."

The walk was long, but I kept my bleary eyes open, scanning every hallway and every door as best I could as my eyes adjusted to the light. Whenever we neared someone, I let my eyes fall shut. When the footsteps were past, I continued my scan. The infirmary when we entered it was bright and airy and warm, an unexpected contrast to my previous abode. My eyes closed again as Sven set me down on a bed and soon my head rested on a delightfully soft pillow.

"What's wrong with her?" a peremptory voice demanded.

"She, um, well, she's ill, I believe, Nurse Craig. With child, as well."

"Don't tell me this is the lass you had in solitary? Why she's no more than a child herself."

"She tried to escape." I was thrilled and heartened to hear uncertainty in Dr. Mills' voice.

"And what harm would she have done? She's skinnier than a post. Now get out and leave her to me."

He got out.

Nurse Craig cleaned me up, tsking at the bruises on my hips and shoulders where the thin mattress could not protect me from the stone floor's stubborn hardness. She changed me into a light, soft gown and I let myself drift away, feeling safe for the first time in weeks.

When I awoke, the room was dark. I nearly panicked, thinking I was back in solitary, before spotting a lone lamp shining from the nearby office, which was encased mostly in glass, except the back wall where a white nurse's uniform hung. Inside it, a young nurse chatted on her cell phone and laughed loudly before clapping a hand over her mouth and scanning the dark room. No one moved and she eventually relaxed and sat back down to continue her conversation.

As I lay there on the soft bed, I thought about my plan to escape. Was I really doing something differently this time around? Had I missed seeing in my dreams a similar effort on Lilia's part? I couldn't be sure, though if she'd tried to get away and failed yet again, I could see why she'd given up after that.

The next morning I awoke to a nurse taking my blood pressure. I didn't open my eyes. "Did I do it right?" she asked.

"Right enough, Nurse Gilford," Nurse Craig responded.

"Oh, I meant to tell you. We're nearly out of towels."

"Delivery's tomorrow…in the morning, eight sharp. You'll be in charge of it as I'm off on weekends. They're never early and never late, so be sure to meet them right on time. Mr. Bonner don't like waiting and he'll as like to drive off in a huff if you're not there."

"I'll write it down. There's so much to learn," the young nurse sighed. "I feel like I'll never remember it all."

"Aye, it's a lot. But you're doing all right for yourself. In time you'll be able to do this job in your sleep."

They moved onto another bed, about five down from me. I cracked an eye. Both of their backs faced my way as they bent over their next patient. Quickly I scanned the room, taking note of how many beds were occupied—five—and what the occupants seemed to be doing—sleeping. Except one. I recognized her. Loony Laura, the other residents called her, because she was known to start screeching without apparent cause and the only way to stop her was to stick a needle in her arm. I'd seen it happen while on my second walk with Jay.

"How are you feeling today?" Startled, I jumped, my arms immediately circling my stomach. I looked up to see Nurse Craig. A white, starched uniform did little to improve her square figure. "Now, now. Take it easy. I'm not the enemy." My eyes betrayed my skepticism. "Did somebody hurt you here? You can tell me, you know." Bent low over my bed, her large blue eyes looked a little too determined to worm the truth out of me, so I silently shook my head. I didn't want that kind of attention on me right now. Obviously disappointed, she straightened up.

"Bad dreams," I answered haltingly.

She gave a grunting laugh. "Oh, well, that's perfectly normal. Worried about the baby, I suppose."

I nodded, grateful she'd given me a believable excuse. "Is she going to be okay?"

"Ha! Listen to you already knowing what your baby's going to be! I checked you over while you were sleeping, and everything seems to be all right. And we can do an ultrasound later, just to be on the safe side."

My eyes teared up. "Thank you. That's good news."

"I read your charts, you know, and I'm not exactly sure why you're here, Miss Jacobson."

"Me, either."

"I don't care for Dr. Mills, but he knows what he's about. At least when it comes to the mind, mind you." Her nose twitched, the only indication that she found herself amusing.

I wanted to shout out the truth so badly that I made my lip bleed biting down on it. "So I'm guessing it's nerves for you." I gave a small nod and she patted my arm. "Well, not to worry. We'll fix you right up so that when you leave here you can be the best mummy you can be."

I was thankful when she turned and left, marching to the office to do paperwork, no doubt. Thankful, because the hysterical giggle bubbling up inside me was struggling to get out. *Mummy*, indeed.

~

That afternoon Nurse Gilford helped me get up and move around. Using the toilet was a treat—solitary confinement involved a bucket and stiff, rough toilet paper, though I was thankful even for that. Still, the humiliation I'd gone through added to my anger. Gregor had abandoned me. He'd left me to die in this nightmare of a place!

He doesn't know you're here, a little voice attempted to remind me.

What do you know? I snapped at it and it retreated.

I spent the rest of the day alternating between stretching my muscles and resting. Tomorrow I needed to be ready to move fast. I ate all my meals with relish, earning the approbation of the nurses that came and went. Each time I had any contact with them, I was quiet and polite and very cooperative. And each time, they relaxed their vigil over me just a little more.

For her part, Loony Laura stayed blissfully quiet, which I already knew boded ill for the nurses. Loony Laura reminded me of a storm— still and calm for a while, but building destructive energy with every passing moment. I watched her, as did the nurses, with increasing frequency as the day wore on. She twitched and moaned in her sleep, but she did not wake.

The night passed in a fit of dreams and anxieties as I tried to rest. Whenever I woke with a jerk, I rehearsed my plan in my head, going over each step again and again. I'd written an article once where psychologists had discovered that visualizing an action in your mind can be just as powerful as physically enacting it. Sports players often use the method, especially for shooting free throws, when a person has more time to overthink and screw up. I wanted to run on automatic and not have to think at all if I could help it. Thinking had a way of messing things up.

Morning arrived, and the clock with the metal cage over it told me it was four minutes after seven. Soon. Nurse Gilford was on duty as expected and I felt a twinge of remorse knowing that what I was about to do was going to get her into trouble. I pushed the feeling aside. Pity wouldn't help me any, and she could always find another job.

Like Jay?

She delivered meds at seven thirty on the dot, looking a little flustered by the time she reached the patient next to me. Loony Laura was beginning to rouse herself and hadn't wanted to take her meds, so Nurse Gilford gave up for the moment. Later I knew she would fetch another nurse to help her—that's what they had to do with me in the early days.

Watching Laura, I could see the tempest brewing. Poor thing. But if I didn't want to end up a 'poor thing' like her, I must not let myself get distracted by sympathies.

"You're looking better today, Miss Jacobson," Nurse Gilford said to me, pushing back a clump of hair. She was sweating a little, her struggles with Loony Laura taxing her.

"Thank you. I feel better," I said quietly.

She gave me a tired smile. "Keep eating all your meals and you'll feel even better."

"I will."

She turned to leave. The clock read 7:50. She saw it and frowned. "The towels! But how am I going to fetch them?" She glanced worriedly at Loony Laura, who was babbling. "I can't leave her," she said half to herself, "and Nurse Lane is taking care of the meals."

She wasn't looking at me, but at Loony Laura. Loony Laura *was* looking at me, though. I made a face at her and her eyes widened. I stuck out my tongue. She screeched. The nurse hurried over to her side. "Now, now, Miss MacTavish. Just calm yourself. Everything'll be all right." Loony Laura head-butted Nurse Gilford and she reared back, stunned. But not for long. She went at Laura and pushed her back onto the bed. The wrestling match began in earnest and I crawled out of bed and slipped over to the office. The other patients started yelling encouragements to Loony Laura, not noticing me at all.

When I reached the door, I turned the knob. It was locked. Damnit! Why hadn't I thought about this part? How was I going to get in? I quietly wriggled the knob. It didn't budge.

"Nurse Lane!" screeched Nurse Gilford and I yanked on the door-knob several times, my heart in my throat, my sweaty hands growing slippery. Nothing happened.

Then I noticed something. The door was a Dutch one, split into two halves that opened independently of one another, allowing the nurse to see out while staying safe behind half the door. Even better, one of the nurses hadn't latched it correctly. My trembling fingers pried at the crack.

"Help!" came another muffled screech. I whipped around. The tide had turned. Loony Laura was now sitting on Nurse Gilford and hitting her with a pillow. My conscience relaxed. The nurse would be all right, physically anyway. Luckily the other patients were too sick or too doped to join in.

The top door opened and I reached in and unlatched the bottom door. Moving fast, I closed both behind me. Then I dashed over to the nurse's uniform I'd seen earlier and pulled it down. Two minutes later, I was dressed, thankful I hadn't gained too much weight from my pregnancy. Unfortunately, I had no shoes. Crap. Well, I would just have to wear my slippers and hope no one noticed. There was a pass card on the desk and I snatched it up.

I peered through the window, then jerked backward. Nurse Lane was rushing through the door. A quick glance at the clock showed 7:59. I had to get moving. But how was I going to get out? I peeked again. Nurse Lane was wrestling with Laura, trying to pry her off Nurse Gilford. Taking a deep breath, I slipped out the door, quietly shutting it behind me.

The fighting continued. I crept toward the door when Nurse Lane, while whipping Laura around, spotted me. "Get over here and help us, Nurse!" she cried.

"I'll go for help!" I yelled back in the best Scottish accent I could muster. I sprinted for the door, waved my pass card over the scanner, and yanked it open.

The hall was empty as I ran, my slippers quiet on the shiny surface. My eyes searched frantically for the gray metal door I thought I'd seen on the way to the infirmary yesterday. And then I spotted it. About fifteen feet away, an exit sign stuck out from the wall. I was rushing toward it when a male nurse rounded the corner. My heart skipped a beat.

"What's going on?"

"Loony Laura is losing it in the infirmary." I pointed down the hall.

He gave me a suspicious look. "Why aren't you helping?"

I pointed to my stomach. "I'm pregnant. They told me to run for help."

"Sorry. Didn't see that. Go fetch Tony. He loves this stuff."

"I will."

I waited for him to disappear into the infirmary, then tried to open the door. Locked. That had to violate a few safety rules. I quickly scanned my card and pushed opened the exit door. A set of stairs led down to the outside door. I clattered down them, hanging onto the railing to keep from falling. With one last scan, I opened the door just in time to see a white van backing up, its exhaust pipe burping smoke like a factory. After propping open the door with a brick likely used for just this reason, I headed down a small set of steps to meet the driver.

An incredibly tall, homely young man, back bent like a willow tree to decrease the distance between himself and the rest of the world, left the van still running as he jumped out of the driver's side and scurried around to the back. He wore ear buds and reached down to pause his music player. "Sorry I'm late…accident on the bridge." He gave me a quick grin that brightened his face as he opened both doors. "I'm filling in for Mr. Bonner and he runs a tight ship. You won't tell him, will you?"

"Of course not," I said, suddenly feeling the cold through my slippers. "I'm new so I'm not even sure what you do with them."

"Since I'm running behind, do you mind if I just set them inside the door?"

"No problem." He grabbed two large bags and hauled them inside. "I'm going to go fetch another nurse to help me carry the bags upstairs," I told him. "I'm not supposed to lift anything." I indicated my stomach, though nothing really showed yet.

He blushed. "Oh, congratulations! Sure, go on. Wait!" he cried. "I need you to sign off." He ran to the front of the van and fetched a machine.

I signed Nurse Gilford's name on it very sloppily. "I hate these things. Always looks like I'm drunk when I'm signing them."

He laughed. "You're not alone, luv. Go fetch your help, then." He went to return the machine to the front of the van, and as soon as his back was turned, I climbed inside. It was dark and smelled of chlorine and linen. I found a spot behind a stack of bags and wiggled into a corner. Seconds later, he grabbed two more bags close to the opening, then slammed the doors shut. After counting to twenty-three, the van tilted a little as he climbed in. I crossed my fingers and was pleased when I heard the van start up.

We hadn't been driving very long when the van slowed. My heart started to race. Had I been found out already? I pushed myself farther back behind a bag and tried to hold my breath.

"Thanks, buddy!" the driver called after a few moments and we jerked forward. It must have been the gate, and now we were going through it.

The ride was bumpy and wild and I felt sick enough to throw up, but managed, through sheer determination, to keep it down. My stay in solitary confinement had served some purpose, I reasoned to myself.

My emotions were all over the place…elated at escaping, fearful of being caught, scared that this boy would end up taking me somewhere useless. I wasn't dressed for running around—not in snow and this cold. No shoes, no jacket, and pregnant.

Already I was cold, as heat didn't seem to reach the back of the van. I found a few empty laundry bags and covered my bare legs, then wrapped one around my shoulders. The extra layers helped but still my teeth chattered from the cold, from the worry. Each time the boy stopped I waited for him to take his load, then scanned the area through the open doors. Nothing looked familiar to me, especially covered in snow. I could only hope we were heading in the right direction. My goal was Mochrie Manor. Gregor would have to return some time and when he did I would confront him. In the meantime, I could hide out in the sprawling mansion. The alcoholic Mrs. Lennox would have no idea I was there.

When there were only two bags and the one I was hiding behind left, I knew I was in trouble. I thought about jumping out and taking my chances when the boy driver returned. Instead of shutting the doors, he climbed into the back of the van and grabbed the bag I was hiding behind. Even so, he nearly missed seeing me. "What the—?" he yelped, his startled eyes meeting mine. He yanked out an ear bud. "What're you doing in here?"

I put up my hands. "I'm sorry! This was the only way. I won't cause you any trouble." This time I didn't bother with an accent.

"You're American? And not a nurse, either? The towels!" He smacked his forehead with the palm of his hand. "I'll lose my job. Mr. Bonner don't like it when a person screws up."

"No, you won't. You delivered the towels. The nurse who was supposed to meet you is new and she was a bit occupied at the time and couldn't come. She won't say anything about you. And neither will I. Please!"

He frowned. "Why were you in there? Did you kill somebody?"

"I didn't do anything wrong, but you probably won't believe me. So please just take me to Mochrie Manor. Do you know where it is?"

"I should take you back to Havensrest."

"Please don't! I can't go back there."

His face softened. "I hate that place, too. Gives me the willies, it does."

"If it makes a difference, you'll be helping an innocent person."

"And you won't say a word about me?"

"I'm hoping to disappear without a trace. I won't be saying a word about anyone."

"Even if you're caught?"

"I won't get caught." He looked skeptical. "And even if I do, I wouldn't rat you out."

He sighed. "All right, I'll do it." He went to shut the doors. "You might as well come around to the front. It's freezing back here. But wait until I drive a little ways."

A couple minutes later, he pulled over to the side of the road. He helped me out of the van and into the cab. As far as I could tell, we were in the middle of nowhere. "Thank you. I won't ask your name…just in case."

The boy laughed. "You don't seem crazy. Are you really pregnant?"

"That part was true. I don't really like to lie, but lately it seems the only way to save myself."

"The truth is overrated." He started up the van. "Now be sure to duck if anyone comes along. We're actually not that far from Mochrie Manor. I only know it because my first time working the routes I accidentally drove down their drive."

"Where were you headed?"

"Dundeid Castle. It's my last stop today."

"Ah."

He reached down and turned up the heat. "You're shivering. I hope you don't get sick."

"I usually don't. But I'll be sure to take a hot bath when I get to the manor."

"Is that your home?"

"A friend of mine lives there. He'll help me."

He nodded. "You looked fagged. I'll stop asking you questions now. I guess the less I know, the better." He flashed a smile at me and I returned it.

It was only midday when we arrived at Mochrie Manor. I was happy to see the place plowed out. I'd been worried that Gregor had shut down the house entirely. "Just drop me off here," I told the boy.

"You'll be all right? I can drive farther in."

"I don't want anyone to see your van. You've risked enough for me. Thank you so much. You've saved my life, you know."

He ducked his head. "Actually, I think you saved mine."

I paused, my hand on the door handle. "What do you mean?"

"I was beginning to think life was a load of crap and it wasn't going to get any better. I mean, I deliver towels for a living, for pity's sake."

"And then you met someone more pathetic than you?"

He grinned. "Well, I was trying not to say it like that."

I gave him a wry smile. "I appreciate your tact. Good luck to you…"

"It's Fergal," he said.

"Goodbye, Fergal. Take care of yourself." I left him with a wave. When he was gone and the last of the exhaust faded away, I confronted the house.

My destiny was at hand.

Chapter Twenty-Nine

❀

The door when I tried twisting the knob was unlocked. I pushed against it and peeked inside. I saw no one, and heard nothing. Holding my breath, I stepped inside and closed the door softly behind me. A click echoed in the cavernous foyer and I froze.

No one came running to catch me and drag me back to that horrid place. No one screamed *stop*! Though why I thought they should…I'd done nothing wrong. There was no evidence against me of any kind of insane behavior. I was innocent. Other people were not. Other people should be taken there. Gregor and Ophelia, for obvious reasons. Andrew for telling me lies. Vivian for her manipulations.

I stifled the laughter, slightly hysterical, bubbling up inside me and quietly made my way up the stairs to my room, hoping against hopes that all my stuff would still be there. Getting out of this tight nurse's uniform was my first priority, followed by a hot shower and a change of clothes.

Oddly, nothing in the room had been touched. Granted I'd cleaned up before leaving, but still I thought someone would eventually have found my luggage, which Ophelia had shoved under the bed. Seeing it there, you'd think someone might have wondered why I hadn't taken it with me. Of course, Amria had quit, and Mrs. Lennox was a drunk. But still, Gregor hadn't even bothered to check my room or look around long enough to find my note. It was where I'd left it, obviously untouched.

Damn him.

Shaking and cold, I hobbled to the bathroom and took a long shower. The hot water was therapeutic, but once I stepped out, its positive effects wore off. I was angry, and I couldn't seem to shake it off. Didn't want to.

He left me to die. To rot in that hellhole. Thirty long years! Our child was taken from me!

The voice was hers, and also my own. We were one now and I felt I must do her bidding. It seemed the only way to end this.

I shall return.

You lied to me!

You are my life.

You are my *death!*

Joints swollen and aching I pulled on a sweater and the loosest pants I owned. They were tight, but still fit. My shoes felt delicious on my feet, safe and comfortable and familiar. My toes wiggled about for several seconds, happy to be home.

How to do it was the question. How does one seek revenge?

First I had to track him down, maybe lure him here. Then what? Yell at him? Hurt him? Find the other woman and tell her what he'd done to me? Frighten him? Kill him? All these ideas were tempting. All were possible, with the exception of killing him. I couldn't do that.

I will kill him.

Lilia.

Just stand aside and I will do it. I simply need you to find him.

I could do that.

~

I discovered Mrs. Lennox fast asleep in the parlor. The cook was gone, as was Amria, of course. She'd done her dirty work and then fled weeks ago. Had she known the full extent of her actions? In telling our fortunes had she seen what her role would be? Should I go after her, too?

Destroy them all and this will never happen again. You'll be free, Lily, as will I.

She was right. They all had to go.

When you seize the reins, you go the way you need to go. That's what that woman at the fair—the author—had said to me. Now I knew what she meant.

While in the kitchen, I found a butcher knife. There was evidence of residence—dirty dishes in the sink—plates, teacups, crumbs on the counter. Mrs. Lennox was failing in her duties; she couldn't even clean up after herself. Something would have to be done about her.

Knife clutched firmly in hand, I set about ensuring that no one else was in the house. Now was not the time to make mistakes. If I wanted to succeed, I could not be caught. All the lower rooms were empty, lifeless without people to give them purpose. I left them quickly, not wanting to remember my time here with Gregor. So brief, but so meaningful.

I loved you so much, Gregor!

"And now we hate you," I whispered to the walls, to the portraits of ancestors in the long hall, to the air, to whoever or whatever might be listening.

Upstairs I found room after empty room, until at last I came to a room with the door shut tight. I paused. Odd. All the doors up to this point were open. Quietly, I turned the doorknob and pushed open the door. The room was dark, the heavy curtains pulled tight, the air thick and silent. My breathing sounded loud in my ears as I slowly entered.

Carefully, I closed the door behind me and waited for my eyes to adjust. After a few seconds, I could make out a bed against the opposite wall. I nearly cried out when I saw someone lying on it. I waited for them to call, "Who's there?" But nobody spoke.

With light steps, I made my way to the bed where the dark form lay still and quiet, covered by blankets like a mummy. When I was within two feet of the bed, I stopped. Gregor? He was here. Sleeping in bed without a care in the world. I longed to shake him, wake him, scream at him with everything in me. Amria had been right about sensing a murderous rage when she'd done my reading. Only it wasn't directed at me, it was coming *from* me.

"You lied to me." The words were dull and flat. I said them again, with more emotion this time. "You lied to me!"

He didn't stir.

"Wake up, damnit! You *will* listen to me!" I slapped my chest with my open palm, hard and stinging. "You left me to die, you son of a bitch! I rotted inside that filthy place for thirty years! My child was stolen from me!" I was screaming now, spilling all my secrets. "I did as Ian told me, I followed my heart and it led me to ruin. I hate you! I hate you so much!" I began to sob. "Answer me! Why won't you answer me?"

The figure stirred. "Lilia?" His voice was hoarse and weak from sleep.

"Surprised?" I snarled. "Hoping it was someone else?"

"What are you doing here?"

I gave a harsh laugh. "I suppose you thought you'd gotten rid of me. How stupid I was to give in to you. How naïve!" I became aware of the knife in my hand.

Step aside, Lily. The voice was insistent. *It is time to end this.*

I raised my arm into the air.

"Lilia! Good God, no!" Gregor cried.

At that moment, the door opened behind me and the light switched on. "Greg?" A strange woman entered the room. "Are you all right?" She saw me, and her eyes widened in fright. "Who are you?"

I blinked in the sudden brightness, then looked at my raised hand, the gleaming knife. I quickly lowered it. "I suppose you're the one."

"I'm Sophie, yes. And you are?"

"Sophie?"

"Yes. I'm Greg's sister."

"Lilia..." Gregor breathed behind me.

Sophie's eyes changed. "You're Lily? Greg mentioned you, but why are you here? We thought you'd gone back to the States."

She's lying. Buying time so that she can trick you. End this. End it now!

I tightened my grip on the knife again. "He didn't come back. He said he'd come back."

Sophie frowned, her pretty brown eyes concerned. "Come back from where, Lily?"

"There was a storm. He went to see if you were okay, but it was a trick to lure him away. Then he decided to stay in Edinburgh and now he's seeing someone else, isn't he?"

"Lilia..." Gregor gasped behind me. "Not true."

I spun around. "You left me to die, Gregor. They took me and put me in that place and while I was there, you forgot all about me! Did that night mean nothing to you? Don't you realize I'm ruined now?"

"Greg has been in a coma for weeks now," Sophie said gently from behind me and I turned sideways so that I could watch both of them. "He came out of it two weeks ago, but hasn't been able to communicate much of anything. From what I can get out of him, he was coming to see me and some fool ran him off the road. The police said his motor was nearly wrapped completely around a tree. He should be dead. A century ago, he would be."

A century ago.

"He's been unconscious all this time?"

"Most of it. He's been saying your name in his sleep. Calling out for you. *I shall return*...he kept saying that over and over."

Something broke inside me—a dam of hatred and pain and suffering. The knife fell to the floor and I kneeled down at the side of the bed, taking Gregor's cold hand in mine. "You were coming back for me?"

"Always," he breathed.

"But I thought...Lilia thought..."

And then I understood everything. Lilia—trapped in that hellish place for decades, her child taken from her, thinking her lover had abandoned her, slowly, slowly the hatred grew into a poisoned entity that never died, not even when her body did. And now, here I was, reliving her life, giving her the opportunity to seek revenge. Revenge for a crime that had never been committed.

Pulling in a deep breath, I felt infinitely lighter. "It's over," I said to Gregor, reaching to push back a shock of hair on his forehead to reveal a long scar the color of angry storm skies. "I wanted to kill you," I pushed out. "Just like you dreamed. We, Lilia, wanted revenge. I was going to *kill* you."

"I understand," he rasped. "I've been having the dreams. I know everything now. Ophelia did this to you, didn't she?" His voice grew stronger with each furious word.

"She's crazy. She got Amria to make the phone call to lure you away, then that Dr. Mills kidnapped me and held me at Havensrest. She made me write a note—it must be somewhere around here. She's going to marry Andrew, even though she knows she's his half-sister."

Sophie made a choking noise behind me. "She's his *what?*"

I told her and Gregor everything. Sophie looked sicker with each passing second; Gregor grew more agitated. Finally, I stopped speaking, my story complete.

"We can't let her do this." Sophie sounded old, weary, and scared.

"You have my blessing, Sophie. If he's the one…"

"He is. He always has been."

"Ophelia said that Vivian and Andrew were in love," I said to her. "Are you sure he wants you?"

"I'm sure Vivian made Ophelia believe that. Vivian wants Andrew, but she knows she can't have him. Saving Dundeid is too important."

I thought about Andrew speaking of marriage to me, then decided not to say anything about that to Sophie. In all likelihood, he was merely hoping for a way to get himself out of the situation he was in—having a mad cousin, well, two of them, counting Vivian, a sick mother, a legacy falling apart.

"I'll come with you," I told Sophie. But as I stood up, my mind whirled and I sank to my knees. "Maybe not," I managed to whisper before blacking out.

Chapter Thirty

❧

I awoke, feeling warm and safe, until I remembered everything that had happened. I sat up. "Gregor!" I called, staring around me. It was dark, but a lamp by my bed cast a reassuring glow over the room. I was in my guest room at Gregor's home, and I was safe.

I flopped back on my pillows and sighed with growing contentment. Despite nearly killing the love of my life, I felt pretty good. My hand ran over the smooth mound of my tummy. Had Sophie guessed my secret? Did Gregor know?

The door swung open and a head peered around it. "You're awake!"

"Sophie!" I greeted happily.

She came over to my bedside. "You've been asleep for two days. Greg's been asking for you."

I sat up. "Is he all right?"

"He's fine. In fact, he's getting better every day. He thought he lost you. If only I'd known you'd been staying here. At the very least I would've checked your room. We've only been here for a few days. Mrs. Lennox has been taking turns with me for the night shift, and Dr. Weatherby has been kind enough to check up on me, provide a few pointers."

Dr. Weatherby. I felt good about that, and glad to know that Mrs. Lennox wasn't a complete lush. "Is Gregor going to get better?"

She nodded happily. "He sat up today. And he was talking. Like mad. He told me the minute you wake up he wants to know. I should go fetch him."

"No, wait." I stayed her with my hand on her arm. "What happened to Ophelia? Did she and Andrew…?"

She smiled. "I got there in time. He didn't want to marry her, but Vivian was pushing him and then they lost a big client. He was trying everything he could not to have to marry anyone, including trying to make that daft alchemy scheme work. He loved me all along. He told me so last night." Sophie glowed with happiness, her eyes far away as she relived that moment.

"I'm so glad, Sophie. Ophelia told me Andrew and Vivian were in love, but he never seemed to be. I'm not sure he even saw her that way. He thought she was a great businessman, so to speak…"

"Well, he doesn't need her anymore. In fact, she left."

"Really?" That surprised me.

"After Ophelia was taken away and Dr. Mills arrested—"

"Taken away? Dr. Mills arrested?"

"She's staying in the same facility where she put you—Havensrest. And Dr. Mills, after it was discovered that he helped to kidnap you, was brought up on several charges. We think he might have been the one to run Greg off the road—there was another set of tracks, but no other car. The police advised us to keep Greg's situation quiet, see if we could get someone to make a mistake. No one knew he'd been hurt—I told Mrs. Lennox to let on that he was staying in Edinburgh, that he'd met someone. It was the best I could come up with on short notice since I didn't know he had you. Anyway, when I told the authorities what happened to you and gave them the note I found in Greg's office that Ophelia made you write, they went to question her. At first, she refused to even speak. Then she tried to blame Amria, but when I told her you were at our house, that Jay could prove you were in Havensrest, she told us everything, then she attempted to jump out the window. I feel rather sorry for her, actually."

"I do too." I truly did. The thought had occurred to me that maybe Ophelia's change in medication had set her off down this road to destruction. Or maybe she'd gone off it altogether. I remember how awful medication had made me feel. But no medication meant no control and no control meant bad things for Ophelia...and anyone in her path. "Now, anyway. Before, I wanted to kill her. Make her suffer like I did."

"Lily..."

"Yes, Sophie?"

"Do you really believe that all this happened long ago? That we were destined to repeat our fate until someone changed it?"

"I can't see any other way to explain it. There was a Lilia from 1880, maybe others before her, maybe after, I don't know. She had a baby— I mean—"

"I know you're pregnant," Sophie said softly. "You keep touching your stomach. A friend of mine is pregnant and she does that. Just so you know, I'm very happy for you and Greg." She stopped. "It *is* Greg's, right?" Before I could be insulted, she added, "Someone didn't do something to you in that horrid place?"

"It's his," I confirmed, glad she thought the best of me. "And no one touched me that way in there. Poor Lilia. What an awful life she had. Imprisoned, thinking her lover had abandoned her, losing her child, then finally killing herself. No wonder she was so angry. No wonder she wanted revenge." I shuddered, thinking how close she'd been to getting it.

"The truth shall set you free."

"Yes, I guess so. But sometimes, what we think is the truth is far from it."

She smiled grimly. "If you can walk, I'll bring you to Greg now."

"I can walk. Slowly," I added as I slid out of bed and found myself feeling weak. "I think I need to eat."

"I'll bring something to you in Greg's room. Now come," she held out her arm and I took it.

Together we shuffled down the hall. Fortunately Gregor's room wasn't all that far from mine. I liked that—knowing he'd chosen one close to him. Sophie didn't knock and we walked in on Gregor trying to get out bed. He looked so pale and drawn. I hurried to his side. "You're sitting up."

"I was coming to get you."

"I've been sleeping."

"For two days?" he groused and I sat down next to him on the bed.

"I have something I need to tell you."

He turned to face me, his eyes full of anguish. "I'm so sorry I failed you, Lilia. This time, and last time. Please don't leave me."

"I'm not leaving you. You told me you'd never lie to me, and I didn't believe you. Besides, you didn't fail me. Last time you were dead and this time around you were in a coma. You must have changed things by refusing to die, you stubborn goon!"

He grinned, looking more like his old self. "Modern medicine helped with that, I think."

"And your willpower."

"And my love for you. I couldn't leave you again. I've missed you so much."

I leaned against his thin shoulder, thinking I couldn't wait to feed him and nurture him and take him for long walks to build up his strength. "I hated you, you know. She did, anyway. She thought you'd left her."

"I'd never have done that on purpose. She must have suffered so much. You too, Lilia! You were in that place."

"I'm okay now. I got away."

"Then you're part of the change, too. I can't imagine she got away last time."

"I'm stronger this time."

"I wonder why she chose you to relive her life."

"She didn't choose me, I was chosen. My guess is that you're Gregor's ancestor, either through reincarnation or through Sophie's line. And I'm Lilia's."

"What?"

"She was with child. She had the baby and they took it away from her. Gave it to a couple from the U.S. That's how I ended up as an American. Lilia's ancestor, my mother, married my father, a MacKenzie. It's really only a coincidence that I'm related to Ian. If there's such a thing as coincidences."

"That poor woman," Ian sighed and rubbed at his scar. "I guess that was something different for us. We didn't have a baby to lose."

I hesitated. "Um, not quite. I think we're following their path the way it was meant to go. I'm going to have a baby."

His whole body tensed. "You mean…"

"I mean," I watched him carefully, "you're going to be a father." I waited for his reaction, but when he looked at me in fury, I was stunned. "It h-happened," I stuttered. "That night we were together."

"Oh, Lilia!" He pulled me to him and squeezed tight. "I'm thrilled about the baby. But you were there, in that awful place, and you were pregnant and all alone. I'll kill him! I'll kill *her!*"

I pulled back and took his face in my hands. "It's all right, Gregor," I soothed. "We're alive, we're having a baby. Our life is good. We have the power to let this go. To begin again."

He looked defiant. "I guess I can try."

"No," I said sternly. "You will do it. And I will, too."

He pulled me back to him and I nestled my face into the hollow of his shoulder. "I love you, Lilia," he breathed. "For so long and so hard. When I saw you again I thought my heart would break with joy, and with this strange sort of sorrow. I was afraid to love you, but I couldn't help myself."

"I'm glad you couldn't help yourself," I murmured. "But perhaps we should go back to our old names…Lily and Greg…so we can separate ourselves from the past once and for all."

He nodded. "I can do that."

"Good. Now, Mr. Greg Huntington, I think you should get some sleep."

"Don't go."

"I won't. I have to eat something, then I'll lie next to you."

He turned and kissed me with trembling lips. "The next time I do that to you," he said when he pulled away, "I'll take your breath away."

"You just did," I whispered.

~

We married four months later, on a glorious April day. It was a double wedding. Sophie and Andrew, Greg and myself. Andrew and Greg, after a long talk, patched things up between them. Greg offered to help Andrew put his business ideas into effect, and Sophie, having her own money, would help finance these new ventures. She planned on taking a sabbatical for a year to help out, and maybe write a book, too. After that, she'd play it by ear about what she wanted to do career-wise. During a dress fitting, she'd confided that there was no way she was chucking it all to become the dutiful laird's wife. She thought she could do both, and I agreed.

Andrew apologized to me, as well. "My mother's doing much better," he told me after saying how sorry he was and that he was so thankful I'd saved him from making a huge mistake. "She's torn up about Ophelia, of course. How could she not be? But she goes to visit her several times a week and is even volunteering at the local old folk's home every Tuesday. Once a week she takes tea with Ian MacKenzie. She once had a crush on him, I've learned, and he with her. Until Father came along. They seem quite happy now. And Ian and I are actually getting along, now that he knows I wasn't behind her living in that tower."

"I'm so glad, Andrew," I said, and I meant it.

"And I'm glad to finally know about my father, about why he… well, you know."

"How do you feel about Ophelia?" I asked hesitantly. "That she's your half-sister?"

He shrugged and looked away. "I'm not sure. I tried to visit her with Mother, but she doesn't want to see me. She hates me."

"That's not your fault, you know. This happened way back and nothing you could've done would've stopped it."

He sighed. "Thanks, but I still feel awful about it all. I know she wanted to punish me by marrying me, but she's still my half-sister. I feel I owe her something."

Maybe he was right. "Are you mad that your mom cheated on your dad?" It was an uncomfortable question to ask, but I had a strong feeling we had to clear this up now, hash it all out so it wouldn't fester and maybe manifest itself somewhere down the line.

"Not really. She punished herself long enough for what she did." He looked me in the eye. "So we're okay?"

"We're okay. As long as you understand I can't marry you."

He laughed. "Got it."

I gave him a hug and he took a while to let go. "I did love you, you know," he whispered in my ear. "I still do."

I pulled away and gazed up into his forlorn eyes. "But you're better with Sophie."

"Yes. You're right. She and I have loved each other for a long time. I told you I didn't always make good choices." He smiled without humor. "Ah, well. Here's to second chances."

"To second chances." We parted with one last hug, and I hoped that was the end of it.

Even Gertie had thawed toward Greg, but that may have had to do with my suggestion that she come and be my 'sort of' lady's maid, and he not only wholeheartedly agreed, but practically begged her to do it. Not that she had to be begged, but she did seem to enjoy having Greg Huntington on his knees. In time, I would convert her to my way of thinking, slowly, but surely. I thought that she could eventually open her own laundry service. It wasn't a huge dream, but it was something. In the meantime, I planned on tracking down my savior, Fergal, deliverer of towels, and do some matchmaking between the two. Or at the very least, find him a better job.

Greg was nearly recovered now, though he sometimes had nightmares about the accident, which he can't remember, but imagines again and again. I thought that maybe if he could remember what happened, he wouldn't make up the gruesome details. But I said nothing. I had my own dreams. Only time would heal us.

My father and mother came to the wedding, along with Dr. Weatherby and his wife (who was a real spitfire, even in her sixties), and Ian MacKenzie and Andrew's mother. Greg's mother sent an apology— she and her new husband had been building a school in Africa and she'd become quite ill, strangely enough, at the same time Greg had been in his accident. She was doing better now, but couldn't yet travel. I wouldn't have minded putting off the wedding, but Greg wanted us to be married before the baby came. Once she heard about her impending grandchild, Cecily promised to be home in time for the birth, and to throw a grand party, to boot. I found myself quite looking forward to meeting her.

Surprisingly, Ian and my father got along quite well. Even more shocking, Father forgave Mother, and although they weren't reconciling, it seemed that both had found a way to live again. I wondered if the parents of the first Lilia ever had that chance. I would never know, though my guess was that they hadn't. Father also seemed to accept Greg with no qualms. Had he always known I was meant to be with Greg and was keeping me, albeit clumsily, from being with anyone else? It was something I'd rather believe than the alternative—that he was a spoiled brat who liked having control over me.

Jay also attended the wedding. He had a new job in Edinburgh that he loved. Sophie had found him a great position as a guard at the art museum and there he met his current girlfriend, Carina, who's an artist and a lover of Picasso. I warned him he better watch out for his ear and he gave me a funny look. Harry, his brother, officiated the wedding, and was quite good at it. During our first meeting to plan the ceremony, he shamefacedly admitted that he'd been a numpty to fall for Ophelia's lie. "I should've known you weren't the type to cut and run." To show him there were no hard feelings, I made sure to print out several of the celebrity photos I'd promised him, including one of Leonard Nimoy doing his famous Vulcan salute.

Terri and Jamie, along with Mr. Willeton, represented the newspaper and arrived bearing good news on all fronts. Terri and Jamie had gotten engaged, and Mr. Willeton was thinking of buying a newspaper in Inverkinn, which would give me a job if I wanted one after the baby was born. He still made me finish my article—the little dictator, which I did, and I made sure to give Dundeid Castle a glowing review.

Sophie and I worked well together, organizing the wedding in record time. It helped that we had similar tastes and that we liked each other. Everything looked beautiful, with lots of flowers everywhere. I've always loved lots of flowers everywhere. We all wore period outfits, as homage to our past lives. During the ceremony, I avoided Andrew's eyes until we had all said our vows. Afterward, during the reception I caught him looking at me, his eyes a little sad. I raised my champagne glass to him, nodded at Sophie, then took a sip, my first and last for the day. He did the same, then turned to talk to her, his back to me. Hopefully forever. I wanted him to be happy with her, with his life.

"They make a good couple, don't they?" Greg asked, seeing where my eyes rested.

"Not as good as us." I smiled, gazing into his brown eyes.

He discreetly rubbed my belly. "Of course not. That would be impossible."

Someone dinged a crystal glass with their fork and we leaned forward to kiss one another, our lips warm and open and our bodies yearning to be alone. Soon we would be. I couldn't wait.

~

We spent our honeymoon in Paris—not too original an idea, but lovely all the same. Neither of us could travel very far at the moment. Being pregnant isn't the most romantic of situations, but Greg was so thrilled to be a father that I couldn't help but feel excited, too. We daydreamed about our child to be, picking names for a girl or boy, even though I knew it would be a girl. We were quite aware that we were being silly and idealistic, imagining blissful feedings and playing in the park, but sitting outside at a café in the warm spring sun, we didn't care.

The other wonderful part of our trip was getting to know my mother again. She was a little rusty at mothering, so she rather overdid it, fussing and hovering over me, but I didn't mind. She was trying, and that's all that mattered.

"It's such a short trip these days, crossing the channel," she often said during our days together. "Then I can hop on a train and—*voila!*— I'm in Scotland to see my babies!" I sometimes thought she was more excited about her impending grandchild than I was. Perhaps she saw it as a second chance—a way to make things up to me.

"We'd love to have you any time, Mother," I told her over lunch at her apartment, as I did every time.

She reached across the small, round table, setting her hand on top of mine. I studied the blue veins pushing up against her pale skin. "You truly forgive me?"

"Truly," I told her, honestly, placing my other hand on top of hers.

"Your father has forgiven me, too," she said, wonderingly. "He really has. I'm not sure I deserve that." Her eyes darkened as she said this.

I snorted, pulling my hands away and grabbing my sandwich. These days I just couldn't get enough food in me. "Oh please, Mother. Drop the martyr act." Her eyes brightened and she gave a girlish laugh. I smiled to hear it. "It was the best thing for him," I told her. "And for me. Now he can move on and stop hanging on me."

She laughed again. "I suppose so. He always was a bit of a clinger."

"Besides, none of this nightmare was of our making. We all tried to stop it from happening—in our own way. We all tried to do something different. None of it worked, really. The passage of time is what saved us."

"Nonsense," my mother said. "I think that what all of us did together made the difference. We all contributed."

"Except Ophelia."

"Yes, poor Ophelia. With a name like that she was destined to failure."

We both suppressed smiles. Ophelia's fate wasn't funny, of course. But mother's comment was. A little.

"Life will be different from here on out," she declared after eating a bite of her salad.

"Yes," I agreed. "It will be."

"Perhaps not always better, but on the right track."

"You're very wise." I toasted her with my Perrier bottle.

She smiled. "I had over a century to get there."

~

In a few months, I would be a mother myself. I wondered what I would do for my child, what sacrifices I would make. Knowing that I might get a second chance, that maybe this one life wasn't all there would be was heartening.

Greg had said to me, "I shall return." And he had. Not even death had stopped him from getting to me. Now it was up to me to hang onto him.

We wouldn't want Lilia getting mad again, now would we?

About the Author

When author, Kristina Schram, was growing up she wanted to be a star. When that didn't turn out quite like she expected, she turned her mind to achieving other goals: Earning her Ph.D. in Counseling Psychology, working as an Artist-in-Residence at local schools, being a free-lance editor and reader, coaching parks & rec basketball, and publishing her first novel, a YA fantasy called The Chronicles of Anaedor: The Prophecies.

Knowing what it's like to struggle with self-doubt and lack of confidence, her biggest dream (in addition to owning a castle) is to stamp out low self-esteem for everyone, especially young people. "Feeling bad about yourself is the number one deterrent to achieving happiness," she says. "So for the sake of a better world, it's got to go." She lives in New Hampshire with her husband, three boys, and various pets, and can also throw a tomahawk, if need be. For more information, visit her website: www.kristinaschram.com. She's also on Facebook and Twitter.

Other Books by Kristina Schram

The Wrath: A Paranormal Gothic Romance

When a cryptic letter arrives from Evalina Filmore's two aunts, she travels to England to find out what they want, figuring this will be the chance to experience the romantic adventure she has so often read about in her beloved gothic novels. When she arrives, she finds the eerie mansion, the strange atmosphere, and the adventure, as hoped. But there are troubles. On the train, she meets a man who, upon learning her name, walks away without a word of explanation. Not long after, she passes unharmed through a wood called the Wrath, even though, as she later learns, no one ever has. While in the Wrath, she meets a tantalizing and seductive stranger, one who just might be her gothic hero. But he has a secret. It seems everyone in the village does, including her aunts, and it's up to Evie to figure out what is going on before the Wrath lures her in and never lets her go.

Mayhem at Nepenthe Manor: A Pandora Belfry Adventure (Book One)

Precocious and morbidly obsessed with death, Pandora Belfry has spent her entire life at Nepenthe Manor, a dark, Gothic mansion also known as the local loony bin. Recently turned fourteen and growing exasperated with her stifling life, Pandora wants two things more than anything else in the world—to make her escape from the asylum, and to get her mom to finally act like a real mom. Until these wishes are granted, she acts as self-imposed ringleader to a wayward posse of inmates. Known amongst themselves as the Secret Six, Pandora and her friends spend their time at Nepenthe Manor stirring up trouble—holding weekly Midnight Meetings to concoct schemes, sneaking into places like the Nepenthe family cemetery and the forbidden attic, and generally doing everything they can to avoid the curse of living a mundane life. But when a mysterious new inmate arrives at the manor, things change for Pandora, and not for the better. In retaliation for a trick she plays on him, the charming and handsome Xavier connives to take over the posse, threatens to divulge one of Pandora's biggest secrets, and refuses to tell her what he did to get himself locked up. This boy is obviously hiding something, and it's up to Pandora to use whatever nefarious means necessary to find out what it is, before he destroys the only world she's ever known.

The Labyrinth of Lunacy: A Pandora Belfry Adventure (Book Two)

Pandora Belfry, along with the eccentric members of her posse, is back, and looking for trouble. The posse's first order of business is to break into the off-limits labyrinth, even though they can't find its door. Against her mother's wishes, Pandora also works to solve the mystery of her father's identity. Perhaps he's a staff member, or maybe he's the stranger haunting the beach late at night. Topping the list of possible dad candidates is the new therapist, Dr. Steele, who keeps popping up in Pandora's life like an annoying, but handsome, nanny. To add to her problems, Pandora's date with the slimy, but oddly fascinating, Dougie Daft, is fast approaching. She isn't sure how to get out of it, or even if she dares to. Her new acquaintance, Giganticus, certainly doesn't want her to go, but if she doesn't, she'll be obligated to Dougie Daft, and that's the last thing any sane person would want... Come join the posse on their latest, a-maze-ing adventure. Just one warning: Watch out for snakes!

The Chronicles of Anaedor: The Prophecies (Book One)

Strange things happen to fifteen-year-old Lavida Mors. Maybe that's why her father sends her to Portal Manor, a mysterious family estate she never knew existed. Lavida quickly discovers that not everything at Portal Manor is as it seems when she stumbles across a secret passage to a hidden world—Anaedor. Long ago, humans drove the Anaedorians, a civilization of magical and strange beings, into the dark world of huge caverns, frigid rivers, and bottomless pits deep within the earth. Malevolent forces, led by the evil Malvado, seek to control all of Anaedor, but an ancient prophecy tells of a hero who will save them from destruction. While trying to escape the dark realm, Lavida must battle overgrown leeches, survive a poisoned arrow, and outwit a giant, all while trying to convince the hopeful populace of Anaedor that she is not the savior they believe her to be.

The Chronicles of Anaedor: The Return to Anaedor (Book Two)

After escaping from Anaedor, fifteen-year-old Lavida Mors starts a training course with her guardian, Mrs. Keeper, in hopes of improving her magic skills before the dreaded Malvado returns. But while trying out a new spell, something awful happens, and she vows never to do magic again. When an unexpected discovery forces her to return to Anaedor, she is faced with her most terrifying challenges yet. Strife reigns in the hidden underground world as lootings and burnings break out, and numerous enemies conspire to capture Lavida, fight her, even kill her. Without magic, how can she possibly flee from dragons, escape the Goblins, outwit the ruthless Frio, and fight a duel with a young rebel intent on proving she's not the One? Time is running out. If Lavida doesn't learn to trust herself and her skills, a series of catastrophic events will ensure that she and her friends never make it out of Anaedor again.

The Chronicles of Anaedor: The Lost Ones (Book Three)

Sixteen-year-old Lavida Mors is in for a long, hot summer. With no way into Anaedor, the Lost Ones seeking refuge at Portal Manor are taking over the house, creating havoc and misery. Lavida is overwhelmed trying to keep up with her chores, learning magic, and fighting off the Pixies— tiny creatures who have made it their mission to harass Lavida at every turn. Meanwhile, unbeknownst to the residents of Portal Manor, the AAK is hard at work opening a Portal to the Upland. They are successful at last, and the twins, Loria and Darian, on the run from Malvado, and the AAK leader, Trey, manage to make it through the opening only to have it collapse behind them. With no way back into Anaedor, they are forced to take refuge at Portal Manor. As they try to settle into this strange new life, tensions between the humans and the Anaedorians grow, creating rifts between Lavida and her friends. To make matters worse, Frio, Amoral Hunter Leader, is hiding out in the Upland, and when he goes after Lavida, he starts in motion a series of events that could end up costing Lavida her life.

The Chronicles of Anaedor: The Uprising (Book Four)

In this final book of the Anaedor series, sixteen-year-old Lavida Mors is placed in grave danger when a group of young Anaedorians infiltrates the Upland. Their orders are to eliminate the evil one, whom they believe is Lavida, and then launch an Uprising to take over the Upland. Disguising themselves as humans, they befriend the unwitting Lavida and her friends, allowing them easy access to Portal Manor. Darian and Loria, Blendar twins and Lavida's friends, and Trey, ex-AAK rebel leader, have come to the Upland to warn Lavida about the intruders. But before they can, Darian learns something about Lavida's past that turns him against her. Surrounded by betrayal and danger, and faced with an astonishing revelation that makes her question everything about her existence, Lavida feels increasingly alone and afraid. If she cannot convince Darian and the others that she is not the evil being they think she is, she will lose everything to the Uprising.

The Battle to Become an Author:
When Great Expectations Go Awry

Are you looking to find an agent and/or get published? Are you a published author frustrated with the whole process? Or have you simply heard the horror stories and are looking for a ray of light before plunging into the fray? In this short booklet, author Kristina Schram discusses how one's unrealistic expectations about becoming an author can contribute to feelings of negativity and isolation. Dr. Schram offers a real-world discussion of this growing issue, humorously incorporating her own experiences throughout. She also offers insights and ways to cope with the increasingly difficult battle to become a published author. Come prepared to challenge your own expectations, to laugh and to cry, and to battle against the forces conspiring to keep you from reaching your writing potential!